ULTIMA THULE

NIKLAUS RICHENBACHER-DAWES

COUNTRY BOOKS

Published by Country Books/Ashridge Press
in association with Spiral Publishing Ltd

Country Books Courtyard Cottage, Little Longstone,
Bakewell, Derbyshire DE45 1NN

Tel: 01629 640670
email: dickrichardson@countrybooks.biz

www.countrybooks.biz

ISBN 978-1-910489-87-1

© 2021 Niklaus Richenbacher-Dawes

The rights of Niklaus Richenbacher-Dawes as author of
this work have been asserted by him in accordance with the
Copyright, Designs and Patents Act 1993.

All rights reserved. No part of this publication may be
reproduced, stored in a retrieval system, or transmitted, in
any way or form, or by any means, electronic, mechanical,
photocopying, or otherwise, without the prior permission of the
author and publisher.

British Library Cataloguing in Publication Data.
A catalogue record for this book is available from the
British Library.

Printed and bound in England by 4edge Limited,
22 Eldon Way Industrial Estate, Hockley, Essex SS5 4AD

*This book is dedicated to my wife.
May god rest her soul.*

– ABOUT THE AUTHOR –

Niklaus Richenbacher-Dawes.

Niklaus is descended from white Russians who escaped from Russia after the fall of the Tsar. They travelled to India where His mother was born. Niklaus was born on a tramp steamer out of Bombay heading for Moz ambique. His mother married a white hunter from England and Niklaus was born in 1950 in Zimbabwe. His mother was killed by a white rhino when he was six and his father then left east Africa to come to the UK. They spent two years in north Germany where Niklaus attended a local school. Niklaus then led a very normal life working in a government department before becoming an architect a husband and father. He has a daughter who lives near Bristol. Niklaus lives in Oxfordshire.

. . . .

Thanks:

I would like to thank everyone who gave me encouragement to continue writing this book, my daughter for getting me to resurrect it from the ashes of the past, my family and friends for believing in me and especially Isaac Asimov whose own story of searching for our home planet inspired me to write my own version; however, my story is very different from his. I would also like to thank Jonathan Taylor from Spiral Publishing for his professional assistance in bringing this book to publication.

The author

– PREFACE –

In the space between galaxies there is nothing except ionized helium and vast clouds of unseen hydrogen, in all directions. Unseen because the atoms are transparent after having been split apart by energetic quasar radiation. Anything solid that had been there had been sucked into the gravitational maw of the nearest galaxy, leaving the space in between swept mind numbingly clean of anything tangible to the human senses.

A vast, uncomprehendingly vast volume of nothing that the mind can see!

From ND-space into this cold void of vacuum between the galaxies a vessel suddenly appeared. It happens sometimes, so they say, that a vessel goes astray like this and is never heard from again. With all the best safety checks and balances there is always one that will get away. It is an unfortunate thing with chance. There is always the chance that something will go wrong. In space travel any accident is likely to be tragic. No help will be able to be given as the distress signal, without the portals, could take thousands of years to reach the rescuers. Even if they could find the distance and direction of the distress call it would still then be too late.

Into this deadly vastness this poor vessel is suddenly plunged without warning. An infinitesimally small fragile bubble of life in a place that has no meaningful dimensions, no up nor down, no here or there, no major light source, no plane of reference, no coordinates, no help. Without a nearby sun to activate the hull's solar panels, the life support system will shortly begin to fail. In terms of galactic evolution this will happen in such a small space of time. Long before the food and water runs out, the tiny bubble of breathable atmosphere will have been exhausted. Long before the tiny bubble of breathable atmosphere has been exhausted the human mind would have been overawed by the predicament and probably shut down. A blessing.

From outside, this tiny piece of human ingenuity, a tiny speck of glittering solar panels (had there been a light source close enough to cause a glitter), appears calm and serene. Like a tiny speck of dust caught in the early morning sun glancing through a gap in the curtains.

If not struck by pieces of space debris it would be possible for this vessel to remain unchanged on the outside for thousands of years (this is very likely considering that there is nothing of any size at all in this world between galaxies).

Not so on the inside!

– CHAPTER 1 –

PLANETS ARE BIG.

Enceladus 421. Evening.

'You are going to do what?' I could not help the embarrassing squeak in my voice or stop myself from standing up and putting my hands on the old xyloid desk. The seat I was sitting on fell backwards with a thump onto the floor. The big man sitting opposite me, who had a shock of white hair and a neat close-trimmed beard smiled and waved me to sit back down. I did so after picking up the seat and righting it again. His beard helped cover a ruddy round face and his hands were large and rough skinned from many years work.

It had started as any normal ordinary workday but then had come the call from Djon, which was unusual to say the least. He had been a family friend for as long as I could remember but since I had grown up we had seen him less and less. I could not remember the last time I had visited his office; so, it must have been when I was very young. As a rule, I did not come to this part of town either and as a consequence had to type in the coordinates to be able to find my way here. Not only did Djon have his office here but he also lived in this lonely part of the town. He was not completely alone though as a few other oddballs also lived around here. They all said they preferred the quiet and freedom. Most people, myself included, thought they were mad, as the planet had not long been inhabited and most of it still had not even been visited. Who knows what was lurking beyond the relative civility and safety of the town and the mining works? Not that the mining works could be considered 'civil'. It was a vast sprawling deep scar in the surface of the planet. Any beauty there was long ago ripped away by deep nucleonic blasts. Gigantic machines, like alien monsters, scrape up the ensuing pulverised crust and tip it into equally gigantic sieves and other crushing machines which in turn fed the kilometre long extraction plants that extracted the valuable ores, diamonds and anything else they found. Anything of no value was then dumped into huge mountainous heaps of spoil and left. There was no incentive to attempt any rehabilitation of the planet. The process stirred up massive clouds of choking dust that rose high into the atmosphere and slowly circled the planet mingling with the natural clouds of dust from the still active volcanoes.

The town, the only settlement on the planet sat in a large natural bowl which had high hills on three sides and sloped down gently on the fourth. In that direction was the large lake. There was very little of the primitive natural vegetation in this bowl, the forests began on the other side of the hills. Only the very tops of the tallest 'trees' could be seen over the tops of these hills. Djon's office was located well up the side of these hills which framed the town, the ground was sloping and undulating so the units were scattered randomly on the flattest pieces of ground. It was uncomfortably close to the top of the hill as if something could sneak up unseen beyond the horizon and jump out without warning. But that fear was now left outside.

The town itself was also an apparently random collection of buildings but at least it was more landscaped than the mining works. But even calling it landscaping was a grand word for the half hearted attempt at making it home. I longed for the time when this place became permanent enough to have a proper settlement and facilities. I longed for a sense of permanence and beauty although not really able to define what either should be. No one else seemed to notice or care. No one except Djon that is. Perhaps that is another reason for liking the man.

'I am going to find the original planet from which mankind came all those years ago.' He replied calmly as the patient parent speaks to the tiny child, but the words hit me like a lightning strike. I sat shocked into inaction. As he spoke, he pulled open a drawer on his side of the old desk. It did not open smoothly or silently. I always wondered why he kept this ancient piece of furniture. Modern stuff was so much better and worked properly too. He took out a small flat metal object, about the size of a good thick sandwich, and placed it carefully on the desk. I thought I recognised it immediately. At least I recognised it as part of something all too familiar, but certainly not in this context and never on a desk.

'That makes you an ....' I managed at last. But why was I still sitting here like a dummy? Why did I not leave?

'An originst. Yes. Surprised? Yes of course you are, because originists are all mad aren't they! And someone who was a good friend of your father could not possibly be so mad could they?'

The mention of my father sent a shiver down my spine. I had not seen him for over twenty standard galactic years; ever since he had vanished while on a routine space flight. He was a quiet man, not one to express his emotions, but kind and generous. He had dark hair, short I remember, like all pilots, and a lined face from the cares of life in space I had assumed. As he was not normally one to express his feelings, fears or worries, it was a surprise then that last day anyone saw him. I clearly remember him taking me aside the day just before he disappeared for good and saying, "trust no one."

It was a funny thing to say and being so young at the time I had not understood what he meant or made any connection before. He had not explained his statement any further. There had been other more pressing things to worry about such as my mother's well being. I was only ten standard galactic years old at the time, so my sister and brother would help out as well as Djon. He had been a good friend to my father for years before he disappeared and continued to look out for my mother ever since. She has never remarried as she continually hopes that my father will one day come walking back through the door. I felt the same way. I longed to see my father again.

It was Djon who had helped me through the hard times

at rudimentary school and pilot college. He appeared to have no family of his own or at least he never spoke of any and I had never seen or heard of any others except his wife. She had disappeared or had died; we never knew which and Djon would not say. We thought this was because he had been hurt too much by her loss. Still, I was grateful for his thoughtful and consistent help in looking after me and my family. He did it without complaint. I had never expected Djon to turn out to be one of these originists. Still, it was a worryingly growing phenomenon these originists, and no one can work out why.

Everyone knows there was no original planet.

Djon looked round the room as though he was searching for something. It was a small room, typical of the offices on the planet. Plain, simple and modern. But somehow Djon managed to make it look unique. A worn carpet of some drugget fibre went from wall to wall; at least I assumed it did as the room was full of odd objects which Djon had collected over the years. I had never known him to leave the planet though so many of the objects must have been given him from my father. I had no idea what most of them were or what they were for. The walls were full of doors, presumably for storage or leading to a toilet or kitchen as well as supporting pictures which gradually faded from one image to another. Family members morphed into images of the planet into evening views of the planet and so on in an endless cycle unless the process was stopped, and one picture chosen. For some reason I had never liked those things. My father had once shown me an old picture that he had found somewhere. It was on a piece of what he had called paper and was hand drawn using some carbon-based implement. I had been captivated by it and held a secret desire ever since to find more of such evocative pictures. So far, I had had no luck in finding any. All we had were these digitalised mechanical pictures. Highly accurate but lacking some indefinable quality that I could not quite place. That picture my father had once shown me did have that quality. I expected Djon to have similar paper pictures.

Only the desk struck a discordant note, being of some unknown xyloid material and an old style not familiar to me. This was not surprising as Djon was an enigmatic character with odd ideas and tastes. He had also been a friend of my father who also occasionally appeared with strange objects, like that picture. I was still not sure what Djon did for a living.

He had never explained what the desk was made from, why he had it or where it came from and I had dared not ask. He had always seemed such a large powerful and somewhat frightening character who did not like anyone prying into his private life. He was not so frightening of course as I discovered later in my life. He was certainly big and strong and had a large voice that carried well over a distance. My father had always jokingly said that Djon could stop a hovercar in mid air with a shout. It had always made me laugh when I was little. Djon's laugh was also larger than life and when did laugh buildings shook to their foundations.

"And of course," He continued "If I am an originist then probably your father was too and no doubt you will find that unacceptable." He looked deep into my eyes. I still sat shocked to the core unable to utter a word. I nodded slowly and looked down at my now shaking hands.

He picked up a remote and pressed a button. The window blind snapped shut and the hidden lighting flicked on instantaneously, making the whole ceiling glow. It made his white hair on top of his head shine. He then pressed a button on the object on the desk and immediately a halo of light sprang up between us and developed like a globoid soap bubble, which then snapped firmly into shape. Within the ethereal sphere there then appeared a million tiny points of sparkling lights.

Immediately the 'galaxy' appeared the room lights dimmed so the sphere of light could shine even brighter and the 'stars' appear clearer. At the same time there was one of the minor earth tremors that plagued the planet.

An omen perhaps?

Now I was getting silly, the real crackpots were the ones who watched every tiny event and tried to make out it portended something bad, or occasionally good. Of course, we all knew that most of the inhabited planets were young in geological terms and therefore were still subject to tectonic shifts which caused the earthquakes and the volcanic activity. This contributed to the dust in the atmosphere. The other main contributor to the dust was the mining for valuable metals and minerals; the prime reason that planets were colonised in the first place. The mining was not done very carefully as there was no intention to remain on the planet for ever. The soil and rock were blasted away to reach the valuable seams. This procedure caused an awful lot of dust which entered the atmosphere and was spread around the planet by the constant high-level winds. It meant that the clouds took on the colour of the rock or ground being excavated.

The town was located well away from the mining operations to keep it free from most of the dangerous dust and particles and also allowed the freedom to rip up the planet's surface without much care. The town was also located in the most stable weather pattern area that could be found as well as on the most stable ground, well away from the earthquake zones. It was temperate and out of the zone of dust bearing clouds. These could be seen most days on the southern horizon forming what appeared to be a belt of gloom below which the sun never seemed to shine. At night the electric storms, created by the atmospheric chemicals and the constant dust, could also be easily seen flashing along the horizon. If the local wind were in the right direction the sound would roll ominously around like angry gods fighting and shouting in the darkness which was punctuated by brief but brilliantly dangerous flashes of lightning. It became so constant that no one took any notice anymore.

We only took notice when the storms came much closer or even rolled noisily overhead. At such times we were told to stay indoors until they passed. No one knew just yet how dangerous the storms were. Sometimes there was rain and sometimes not. Even when there was rain, we were warned to stay indoors as the rain was considered dangerously acidic.

Enceladus 421 was no exception to the other planets so far

inhabited in the galaxy I was told. They were all picked for their mineral and other rich contents and I suspected that Djon was something to do with this mining. My job was to ferry the valuable products up to the portal for onward delivery to the refining planets and return with food and water and other products that Enceladus 421 required. It was not an exciting job, but it kept me and my mother supplied with food and a home. I did not want to risk a more dangerous job in case she lost a son as well as a husband.

'You are of course familiar with this.' He said, staring at me through a tiny glittering illusion of the galaxy. The bright bluish light made his face appear purple as he looked at me with that expression that gave me the idea that I should be impressed.

'Of course, I am.' I replied, concerned that he even had to ask. I was a pilot and used these things every day of my working life, although not usually showing the whole galaxy. I most often used it for local space, so it did make a change to see the whole of the galaxy, and I never ceased to be amazed at the sight. I did not think all of these devices had the entire galaxy in them, so it was probably an expensive one.

'I am a pilot.' I nearly added "first class" but decided against it. He was obviously working towards something, and as a lifelong friend of my father I owed him some respect. He moved again and a red dot appeared in the shimmering galaxy between us. Hovering near the dot was a small list of details and numbers. I knew that he could see the same details. Some very clever technology allowed the viewer to see those details no matter where they were standing.

'Our dear planet, Enceladus 421.' He said. He moved again and thousands more coloured dots appeared with similar details all hovering and moving to give the best view of the details. 'The inhabited planets of the galaxy.' He added, unnecessarily. 'Now we know that the galaxy is thousands of light years across, and we are approximately twenty-eight thousand light years from our furthest neighbour.' All this I knew. We were one of the latest planets to be colonised and there was still a frontier feel to the place. We were also at the far end of the galaxy. It felt as though we were at the far end of the galaxy, mainly because this planet was the last to be colonised, or so we were told. I sometimes wished I could visit the centre of the civilised galaxy, but I had no free time or authority to visit as travel was severely restricted.

There were no more inhabited planets or human habitation between us and the end of the galaxy. It was not something I normally thought of or particularly wanted to think of. It made me feel very remote and vulnerable.

'This precisely explains why we cannot have originated from one single planet. Even if we could identify one!' I felt I had to butt in here at least to put the side of common sense.

'Exactly.' He was standing now, making the room seem suddenly smaller. He was tall and had broad shoulders. He was wearing the standard one-piece suit which fitted him surprisingly well. The suits were a necessity to help keep out the dust from the volcanic and mining activity which hung in the air constantly. We also wore goggles with a face mask whenever we went outside for the same reason. And if for any reason you found yourself outside without either of these then very soon the dust particles would work their way into every tiny crevice in your body and cause a really bad irritation. Possibly worse. His goggle mask lay crumpled on his desk. I had mine pushed up on the top of my head as I had only just come in from the outside and had not thought I would be staying long. He continued.

'You know and I know that long distance space travel is only possible because of the portals, which allow us to traverse the vast distances of space by reducing it to a few metres. The technology of these portals I do not profess to understand.'

'Nor do I.'

'But the portals must be set up before that is possible, which would mean that assuming the original planet is central would require fourteen thousand years of travel at the speed of light to get here. We all know of course that the colonisation is only two hundred years old!' He paused. 'Hence no original planet was possible, and that is the myth which is perpetuated.'

'So, you are saying that faster than light travel was possible more than two hundred years ago, before the portals were set up, and is now forgotten? It is not possible to traverse the vast distances of space without the start and end portals to skip from and to. They could not have done it.'

'But they did. In some form or another.'

'Only if we….they came from one planet. We know that is not true.'

'I am saying that they did manage to travel the distances in a very short space of time and now it is not forgotten but, hidden!' He turned and stared at me intently, his grey eyes flashing.

I couldn't think of anything to say to that, it was just too absurd. My gaze fell again on the galaxolabe shimmering over the table. It was the development of this machine along with the portals that had made travel across the vast distances of space possible. The galaxolabe allowed you not only to find out where the other planets were but also where you were in relation to everything else. Not only that but they could undertake the vast calculations required to get you from one place in the galaxy to another. This was essential in any form of long-distance space flight. Therefore, they were in short supply and not normally seen as separate pieces of equipment. They were almost always fixed in spacecraft and I really did not think they could be separated. They also contained a beacon that alerted space flight control of their operation, for safety reasons. They were also usually called a 'V20' as the word galaxolabe was such a mouthful and V20 was easier to remember. The name came from the layout of the twenty buttons used to control it. Also, the cost of a V20 was astronomical – because of the immense power the machine possessed – and commonly was about half the cost of a spaceship!

'How did you get that?' I asked, looking at him again. 'You know they are restricted. Not only that, but when you fire one up it sends out a signal. That is one way of knowing where other vessels are in space.' I was concerned that it would attract attention by not being where a vessel would normally be found. Djon was taking some risk in operating it as it could easily alert someone who may come asking questions. Not necessarily in a hostile manner, but merely out of curiosity, to check there was not a spacecraft crashed on the ground or something. Being an originist was one thing but also having a V20 operating on his desk as well made me nervous.

'I got it from your father. He gave it to me just before he disappeared. He gave me other things as well and told me to trust no one. Not even you. But do not worry, he has disabled the beacon, or rather he has made it possible to turn it off!'

Hearing those words "trust no one" again out loud gave me another chill down my spine. It was even more so hearing it come from someone else. And why did my father not give it to me? Did he not trust me? Djon had suggested as much. Why did my father not trust me? And what was he doing tampering with a V20? That was a dangerous thing to do, who knows what other affects it may have had? I was brought back to hear Djon continuing. '…..and another reason. Standard Galactic English.' He paused, as though this should mean something to me as well. As I did not respond he continued. 'It is spoken throughout the galaxy we hear, hence its name. Had we originated from many planets then there would have been many languages. Already on this planet there are variants creeping in and odd words that set us apart.' Djon was standing now and staring out of the window after having opened the blind manually. I could only see the sky, which was reddening in the evening sun, as it does on many planets with breathable atmospheres. Two of the moons were coming into view.

Fortunately Erebus 421 was not one of them.

This was due to the fact that it had a geostationary orbit on the other side of the planet so it could be ignored. It was a dark black moon that not only did not reflect light, it had an albedo of nought, and generated a depressing feeling. It usually featured if someone wanted to convey a dark or sad message. I had never been there and hoped I never would. Another effect of its geostationary orbit was the shadow that it created on the planet's surface. Nothing could grow properly; it was always cold and dark even on a sunny day, so they say. I had never been to that side of the planet to find out and was not keen to either. The odd climatic effects meant that no one would go to that part of the planet and the winds were whipped up into a spiral frenzy caused by the difference in temperature between the air under the moon and the hot air outside it.

The two moons now showing were called 'Mother' and 'Daughter' but for the love of life I had no idea why, and no one I knew could tell me either. They were bright and shining as moons should be, but again I had no idea why moons should be bright and shining. They also strangely, orbited in opposite directions and appearing to be the same size always looked as though they were going to crash into each other as they passed. They were not of course. Mother was much further away and bigger so appearing to be the same size from the surface of the planet.

Evening could be a magical time on Enceladus as the dust that hung in the air was primarily composed of a shiny, mica like material which sparkled in the low sun. Strangely though, no one had bothered to name this material which again lent this place as impermanence that occasionally troubled me.

Some of the brighter stars were already blinking into view.

A brilliant dot of light arced slowly upwards to disappear above the top of the window. A rocket rising up to the satellite which was almost a continuous operation ferrying raw materials for transportation to the refining and manufacturing planets and bringing goods and drinking water back. I could almost work out who was piloting that vessel and what they were dragging up there.

As a result of the continuous flights, city life was a twenty-four-hour activity; even though there were not twenty four hours in our day here. The twenty four hour standard galactic day was another anomaly here. Perhaps Djon will bring that up too, I thought. Another anomaly was the seasons as we did not really have seasons here. Because the planet did not tilt on its axis in relation to our sun the weather remained fairly constant. One heard that it was spring now but this bore no relation to any change in climate here.

It was handy though, the constant activity, as it meant there was always something open if you needed it. The town never slept. He turned round, the two moons now forming a pair of glowing 'ears' on either side of his white hair, or so it appeared.

'OK.' I said. 'So, you want to go and find this planet of yours. Why don't you just go and find it then? Why drag me over here to tell me? I have a job and family to look after. I do not have time to go skip through the universe for your whim! And what's more, What on Erebus do you mean about hiding?'

'You mean about hiding the ability to traverse space at speeds apparently faster than the speed of light?'

'Yes.'

'How on Erebus would it be forgotten? We have had a continuous history of development. There has been nothing to disrupt or destroy the evolution of the galaxy colonisation! That sort of information would not be forgotten. It must therefore be hidden. By whom or why we do not know. But I certainly want to find out.'

'Then go and find out and come back and tell me. I am no sleuth.'

He came away from the window and smiled kindly at me. The window blind gradually closed behind him so the V20 shone out again. 'I know, I know, it's just that.....well..., there is no one else!'

'No one else to what?'

'To pilot us around the galaxy of course!' There was a moments silence while my shocked thinking tried to come to terms with what he had just said.

'Of course there is. I finally managed to say, 'There are plenty of good pilots who would fly you for a few Galactic Dollars in the pocket.'

'Don't forget what your father told you. There are plenty of pilots yes, but we can only trust you. I have been watching your progress since your father disappeared, at his request of course. There is nothing sinister in that at all, I assure you. He recognised certain abilities and trustworthiness in you. He had to be sure though and you were too young at the time to be sure.'

'Are you saying then that my father was an originist?' Then what he had said stunned me. 'He asked you to look after me? Did he know then that he would not return?' I could not believe I was saying this or even thinking it.

'Yes, he was one of us. We think that was partly the reason your father disappeared or at least a contributory factor, but we cannot be sure now. He was a pilot who spent a lot of time travelling throughout the galaxy and picked up much news and information as he went. He was instrumental in setting up this plan to find Ultima Thule.'

I was horrified to hear that my father was one of these daft originists. I was also horrified to think that he knew he might not return, as if.....his disappearance was not an accident!

It was unthinkable.

'Was his disappearance not an accident then?' I asked with a small voice.

'We really don't know Djim, but we think so. The coincidence is just too worrying not to be. But we cannot be sure.' The information entered my consciousness like a bombshell. Djon looked really downcast as he spoke. This was also hard for him too, being a good friend of my father's.

I had looked up to them both and respected them both for all those years only to find he was…was…what? He….they are still the same men now as when I looked up to them from the viewpoint of youth. They have not changed it seems. My mind skipped back to the original topic. 'What made him think there was an original planet?' Djon looked relieved to have a different subject to talk on.

'At this stage, Djim, it would be unwise of me to give out such information. You need to be on board and committed before we put you fully in the picture.'

'You keep saying 'we', Djon, who is this 'we'?'

'Unfortunately I cannot divulge that information either. I cannot put other people's lives at risk.'

'Oh, for goodness sake Djon, do you really expect me to believe that lives are at risk just for looking for some old planet? What do you take me for? That is the most ludicrous suggestion I have heard for ages. Now I know you are off your rocker. I am not getting sucked into some little harebrained scheme with that sort of idea going round. You cannot tell me that my father was involved in daft schemes like this. You cannot trick me with ideas like that. I respect you for what you have done but I will not follow blindly.' Years of indoctrination would not leave me at an instant. 'I am going!' I got up from my chair and turned to go. The whole thing was just too farfetched to be true.

'Djim!' His voice was firm and strong. It made me turn back 'I know this sounds crazy. There is very little crime here and no murders that I know of. It does sound like something from ... from another galaxy even, but listen, your father disappeared, and it may not have been an accident.'

The thought that it was not an accident was just too fanciful to be true. Djon was right; there was little crime so how could it be anything other than an accident? But there was something in his manner that made me stop and think. But I could not let myself believe it. It was just too frightening so to do.

'Will you come with us?' He asked.

'I'm sorry but that is impossible, didn't you just hear what I said? I have a good job and a family and friends. I am not going to throw all that away on some harebrained scheme. If my father's disappearance was not an accident, then I do not want to end up the same way. That would be too unfair on my mother for a start. Besides, what do you want to go and search for this planet anyway? If you want to do something useful then try and find out if my father's accident was an accident. So far you have not provided any proof.'

'You do not have a good job.' He replied calmly. 'You have a job ferrying goods to and from the satellite. You have a lovely family but.' He let the 'but' hang in the air. 'Because of your father you are a marked man. You have not been allowed better pilot's jobs or jobs that take you away from here.'

'Marked by whom? And why? He vanished while on a routine space flight. Why would anyone do that to him?'

'We are not sure why, we can't think it's because we are originists, that would be too absurd. We hope to find out by finding Ultima Thule. It somehow seems to be the key. We think so anyway.' Djon suddenly looked half the size he had before, a shrunken old man huddled in his seat. I did not like to see him that way.

'Surely the governing body here is not going to be concerned over me.' I said, but not now really believing my own question anymore.

'Oh, are they not? No you are right, they are not, but it doesn't mean that nobody does.' There was that cold shiver down my spine again. That same feeling I used to get when my father came home later on in his life with a haggard look on his face. The same feeling I got when the authorities came and told my mother of his disappearance. I managed to put it behind me then and I could do it now. This was getting too fanciful and dangerous; I could not listen anymore.

'Look, Djon, I respect you greatly but this is just too much. My mother has lost her husband and if what you say is true then if anyone finds out what you are saying then we all may 'disappear' and that is not fair on her.' I got up, hot and shaking and left his office, the door seals hissing gently as the door opened and closed. He called after me again, but I did not stop.

Outside, the evening air was beginning to have a cold edge and the light was fading fast. I leapt easily into my hover car. Although they were called cars, they were in fact move like boats. They had curved sides like inflated tubes and rocked like boats when moving around in them and generally were open topped. I put my hand onto the fingerprint recognition pad which then allowed me to start the anti gravity gyros. With a flick of my hand I brought the goggles and face mask down. With another flick I brought down the vision enhancer which allowed me to see the flight paths, invisible to the naked eye.

With a puff of dust I rose up into the evening sky and headed for home, my mind in a whirl.

I found myself riding home slowly going over in my thought what Djon had been saying. How could he do that to us? How could he spread such unfounded stupid ideas? Why had he picked on me? Lots of people disappear in space, even after all these years of space travel. I automatically put myself in the correct hover car flight path for home. The flight screen glowed brightly in the evening gloom, showing the route and other airborne vehicles' trajectories. Mostly these would be other hover cars taking their passengers home or off to a new shift at the ground station or the mining operations centres out of town. I switched my gaze from looking where I was going to the screen and back again, to check on my progress and other craft. The dust in the air made it almost impossible to see ahead at night. Any lights on the hovercar just got reflected straight back to the driver. The vision enhancer was vital in these conditions. Even though the machine had an anti-collision system and other safety devices it was still advisable though to keep a visual check as best one could.

This time something made the hairs stand up on the back of my neck. It could only have been after Djon's revelations. Normally it would not have bothered me.

I was being followed!

No! I thought. I must not let Djon's paranoia get under my skin. I looked back to the speeding view in front of me, the tops of the warehouse units and offices in this part of town. Every colonised planet was the same. Well, they were the same in the way they have been set up. After it has been determined that there were sufficient resources to make colonisation worthwhile a cargo vessel is dispatched completely full of the basic building units. These in turn were completely full of machinery, food and all the necessities of life. The cargo vessel is landed on a suitable site and all the building units are removed and placed in a random fashion on the best plots of ground around the stranded vessel. So, although the system is the same the lie of the land and the random nature makes for unique towns.

The stranded cargo vessel is then turned into the ground station. Roads are not a priority because of the hover cars, so most areas between buildings are of compacted earth and left as such for many years. The dust would cover them in months anyway and the ground level is continually rising as volcanic ash settles everywhere. As streets are not important the buildings are placed almost completely randomly giving a very unstructured appearance from up here in the hover car. Each one has an identity mark on its flat roof as well as a transponder so helping guide people to the right one. As most travel was by hover cars they did not need numbers on their sides. I checked the usual landmarks to gauge my progress home, the communication mast on the hill, the essential supplies centre. I raised my gaze and could see in the distance the inland sea – also unnamed as yet – it stretched almost to the horizon, if at ground level that is, and was not a pretty sight. The surface was covered with a volcanic ash and dust and together with the oily skin gave it an unpleasant greyish sheen in daylight. At nighttime it became even worse and no one ever went there after dark. The mines were on the far shore. To the north the cleared ground gradually became scrubbier beyond the extremities of the town as the ground gradually rose up to a series of small hills. Most of the tree cover began beyond the hill tops. But however much I tried I could not stop myself looking back at the screen glowing in the fascia. There was still a trace showing up behind me and it had a colour that indicated it had been on the same flight path for more than a minute. It was unusual for this to happen, especially in this part of town. I thought I would try and see if it was following by making some direction changes. If the trace of the other craft followed my route then I would know it was no fluke. I took manual control and carefully checking the locations of other craft I made a series of direction changes which would eventually make a complete circle. It didn't follow. Stupid idiot I thought to myself. Fancy getting flustered by Djon's ideas.

But then I noticed the same trace taking up position behind me again!

Every hover had a distinct blip on the screen so I knew it was not another one. I put the craft back into auto again and after flipping up the vision enhancer I looked back into the now dark sky receding behind me. I could see nothing that appeared to be following me. It must be running without lights. I could not tell how far behind it was. The system on these things was concerned with things in front not behind! Could I spin the hover round and use the front sensor? It was a bit dangerous to do as well as being illegal so I decided to head down to somewhere busy. There was a hoverpark for the essential supplies centre below so I headed for that. I took manual control again as there was not time to reset the auto and in my haste to look back landed badly. A couple nearby jumped as I hit the ground, or rather as the field buffer, which protected the craft by keeping at least a fifty millimetre cushion, hit the ground.

Once stationary I stood up and scanned the sky. The sky seemed suddenly full of hovers all criss-crossing above on their own private journeys. I could not identify any one that could have been following me and all had their lights on. I stood in the hover car for some time scanning the sky but could not identify any other hover car that appeared to be the one following me.

I decided to head on home. The couple nearby gave me a funny look as I set off again, so I gave them a big smile as I rose up into the air. I could not spot anything following for the rest of the journey. Had I imagined it? Perhaps.

Home was one of the standard prefabricated housing units set on its own plot. It had a small garden front and rear and a hoverport. The front garden was a small decked area that had a metal screen fence surrounding it. The back garden was similar. As the planets are all very young geologically the surfaces are still moving and therefore the buildings needed to be able to accommodate this movement. Hence the self contained house and decking to maintain a self levelling unit keeping the house and its garden at a reasonable relationship. All the houses were the same although everyone managed to make them look surprisingly different. The housing units were also two storey being made up of two single storey units locked one on top of the other. This was one instance of people power making a difference, and perhaps the only instance that I could think of. On newly inhabited planets the residents felt very wary of sleeping at ground level in the basic unit and complained bitterly. It was then that the two storey units were developed. Perhaps Djon will make this desire to sleep on the upper floor a reason for an original planet too.

The planet had not long been inhabited and still had a frontier feel about it, and still gave the feeling of not being established or with any intention of root being put down. It was as though any moment the minerals would run out and the whole lot would be packed up and shipped to another planet. It had happened to one planet that I knew of but I could not remember its name. The inhabitants that did not want to go were left to their own devices. Even the portal was packed up and shipped off to another planet so the remaining inhabitants would have to be very self sufficient indeed as with no portal they would be completely cut off from the rest of the galaxy. Without the portal there would be no communication with the rest of the galaxy and therefore no chance of any rescue should anything go wrong. It suited some people but not me. I preferred to be in the company of others and linked to the rest of the galactic family, besides, I would hate to be separated from my family. The mere thought of being stuck on this planet made me shiver. Boy was I glad of the portal and the link it gave us to the rest of humanity. It was then the thought struck me that I had never been to another planet. Still, I did not want to be cut off, that was for sure.

I shared my house with my mother. My brother and sister lived not far away. I decided not to tell my mother of Djon's revelations, or of my journey home. As I reached our front door I looked back up into the now darkening sky.

There, in the distance, was a hover car motionless in the sky!

A silhouette only and too far away to identify. I just felt it was not right. There was nothing to set it apart from other hover cars in the sky; as occasionally one or two did stop, although usually not for long, especially in a flight path. This one however seemed to reach into my inner soul somehow. I quickly grabbed for my vision enhancer and pulled them down over my eyes to see if it was in a flight path or if I could call up some identification details. I was not hopeful as it was so far away. As I did so it dropped rapidly down and out of sight behind the buildings up on the hill on the horizon. I did not feel any better, in fact it made me even more suspicious, as if they had been watching me and saw me put on my vision enhancer.

I stayed a while just standing and looking but it never reappeared. Or rather the hover cars that did appear did not give me the same feeling. Eventually I got cold and tired so I turned and decided to go in. I put my hand on the fingerprint lock and the doors seals hissed open and the door gapped. I pushed it open quickly and shut it again behind me, the seals hissed shut again. I pulled off the mask and goggles and dropped them on the small shelf by the front door and called to my mother as I ran upstairs to my room manually turning off the room light as it automatically came on and shut the door behind me. I went to the window and looked out in the direction the hover car had disappeared. Still nothing, but I kept looking just the same, not really expecting it to appear but not wanting to stop looking either. I could not explain why, there was no logical reason to stand there. I could see the neighbours returning from work and wished that I could come home without a care like they did. Even though I always did and it was only today that I had this paranoia ever since Djon's revelations. Except that….my reverie was broken by my mother calling me down to dinner. I had to go or she would start worrying and wanting to know what was going on. Now was not the time to worry her unnecessarily.

Food was on the table as I came down. My mother was fussing in the kitchen as was her wont. She was a small woman but neat and pretty still. She kept a neat house too. It made life very easy having her look after me. It was also good for her I thought, since my father's disappearance it gave her something to keep her mind off him. Her greying hair was tied up neatly in a bun at the back of her head pierced through with the coloured sticks, which was the fashion. The sticks changed colour randomly. It was her one concession to the youthful fashion on planet. She smiled as I came in.

'How's Djon?' She asked. 'I haven't seen him for a while. He always seems so busy these days and never comes over for a chat like he used to.'

'Oh, he's fine. He is very busy. He said he was sorry he had not been over to see you lately as a matter of fact.' I hoped she would not see through my little white lie.

'OK Come on then let's have dinner.' We sat down in the kitchen and ate quietly for a while. The kitchen was small and compact and doubled as a dining room having space for a table at one end. It was a standard kitchen unit in a standard housing unit. My mother had personalised it though with pictures of my father and us children along with little things we had made as children. The window looked out onto the small rear garden; it did not open as all ventilation here was via the conditioning units that filtered the dusty air. Young children usually had the job of emptying the dust collection boxes periodically.

We had glasses of cold water with our meal. Lovely cold refreshing water. I may have brought it down from the portal on one of my trips. We talked about the usual things and a warm glow began to course through me making me forget all about Djon and his daft scheme. She told me that my sister had called and gave me an accurate account of all they said. I began to get sleepy, We all had early nights here as work was all important and there was no time for slacking or slackers. Even my mother worked in the local crèche looking after the young children while parents worked. No one had the luxury of not working. My brother and sister both worked at the mines so had a very long journey into work. Consequently I did not see them much as they were far too tired after working to go out. Like most people here.

Then my mother said. 'Oh, I nearly forgot. A man came asking for you today. He was big and had short hair. He wouldn't give his name or his reason for calling I sent him over to the ground station. I didn't like him much either, also he was not from this planet, his clothes were wrong. What did he want? Did you see him? You haven't done something wrong have you?' I very nearly dropped my fork as she was speaking as the warm glow suddenly vanished. Fortunately she was talking absently and not looking at me at the time. A cold shiver ran down my spine. Again. Was Djon right after all? No, he couldn't be it must just be a strange coincidence and nothing more. Fortunately she usually asked many questions at once and often didn't really expect a reply!

'I have done nothing wrong, mother.' I had to stop myself from shouting. I hoped she didn't notice the tremor in my voice. I tried to cover up my hasty answer by continuing quickly. 'No. I didn't see anyone I didn't know today. No one came to the ground station asking for me either.' I had to take control of myself. Just because Djon saw danger in every dark corner there was no reason I should. It was unusual for off-worlders to be on planet but not totally unheard of. There must be a normal explanation. That's it; there must be a normal explanation. I felt calmer and took another drink of water and felt calmer still. That was better.

'Something wrong dear?' She asked suddenly shaking me out of my calmness.

'Er, no. Just thinking.' Would she spot my concern? Fortunately not.

Nothing more happened that evening and I went to bed early. Except that I did not go to bed. I stood in the dark room staring out of the window at the night sky for a long time before turning in. I did not sleep well; in fact I tossed and turned for what seemed like hours before falling into a fitful sleep. I had a strange dream that hordes of faceless people were outside and coming in the house through every tiny crack and squeezing up the stairs and into my room. I woke up sweating. I felt the minor earth tremors and saw the reflections of the distant lightning flashes during the night which I normally slept through. I heard the house groaning in the minor earth tremor which normally I no longer took notice of. I even heard the house's self levelling system make a small adjustment causing yet more minor groaning.

In the morning, as I was leaving for work I noticed some footprints on the decking left from the soil around. Were they there yesterday? My mother was usually most fastidious in keeping the garden perfect. Unlike myself I had to admit. Were they some from the neighbours? It was usual to cut corners, no one minded. I did not know, but I had to keep looking over my shoulder to stop myself feeling I was being watched. Except it did not work.

I never saw anything out of the ordinary. As I was flying to work though I could not stop myself thinking again about what Djon had been saying. My job indeed was not brilliant. In fact as a pilot I should be doing more. Why had I not been given more deep space flights? Then again, I thought that it was better to be close to home for my mother's sake. It would not be very good if I too vanished in an accident. It happened occasionally. Sometimes people did not reappear from ND-space at the reception portal. I had to put this stupidity out of thought. I watched instead the tiny brilliant dot of light rising up into the morning sky indicating another flight up to the portal satellite.

The ground station came into view. It was the huge shell of the original vessel that brought everything to set up here and it still dominated the even larger complex of additional buildings. The surroundings were full of large open landing areas for the space vessels and storage of standard pods for goods deliveries. Everything in space flight was interchangeable and standardised, the cargo pods were no exception. It was often just a case of fitting a space drive unit to the pod and shuttling it up to the portal. Before going through the portal the drive unit would be disconnected and the unmanned pod would go through. The drive unit then collects an incoming pod from the reception portal and returns to planet. This was my working life. Boring but necessary.

I finally landed at the hoverpark and walked to the nearest

building. It was covered with the fine dust, as were most immoveable objects on planet. I put my hand on the fingerprint lock and the door seals hissed open. I went into the briefing quarters. I was fortunate in working the day shift and not the night shift, which I put down to a deep seated desire of humankind to be in bed at nighttime. I met my night shift colleagues leaving and laughed and joked with them as we swapped over. I then went to flight control for the usual briefing. Big Djac was on briefing today. He was a large man, not particularly tall but big round the belly hence his name. His skin was darkish browny red and his hair was space black. He stood in front of us with his duty roster. He had a large strong voice not unlike Djon's to go with his big frame. When he laughed (which was not often) he flashed big perfect brilliant white teeth.

My fellow pilots today were the normal crew comprising; Yasher, who was a small slim young woman also with an olive coloured skin and black wiry hair; Kriss-UB who was a tall fair haired pilot who was very quiet and did not normally join in the banter; and finally, Erith, another female pilot, a bit on the chubby side and large on the humour and charm. Her hair was always on the wild side as though she had just been in a gale. I liked her enormously. As far as I knew we were all from Enceladus.

The briefing was quick and I was soon through togging up, which was the technical term for getting into the space flight suits. Although the vessels were complete with artificial atmospheres it was still a safety measure to wear a space flight suit – just in case. Accidents had been known when detaching from pods or more commonly when picking up a pod from the reception portal. The pods never emerged from ND space at the same speed, no matter how carefully they entered at the other end. It was an art to pick up and lock on smoothly and I took great pride in being one of the safest and smoothest at detaching and collecting pods. Get it wrong and the jolt as one thousand tonnes of pod collided with the drive unit could rip it in half.

It was then a short trip to the drive units' hanger. This was a huge, cavernous hall building containing the four drive units, which were big enough in themselves to be interplanetary space craft. Most of the size was required to lift the huge cargo pods up to the portal. Even with the anti-gravity gyros the inertia of the huge cargo pods still required enormous energy to control and the gyros still could not produce enough lift to raise the very heavy pods from the surface. This was something else that defied explanation. Elsewhere on the planet were the huge quarries where the raw products were extracted from the planet and brought here for transportation to the refining planets. We did not ask why we could not do the refining here. It was the way things were.

Then I noticed him.

A large man, not fat, just big, and something about him made me think of my mother's description last night. He was standing at the far end of the drive unit hall building where the light was diffused by the ever-present fine dust in the air. It meant that I could not see him clearly enough. He was not alone. There were the usual mechanics and ground crew staff but they were mostly moving around. Only one or two were just standing. But this man stood out, mainly because of his style of dress. He was not wearing the normal one-piece suit that was prevalent here. Then my platform hoist began to rise up into the air carrying me up to the drive unit's entrance hatch. As soon as I spotted him he moved off and disappeared behind the legs of one of the other drive units. That would be the one Kriss-UB would be driving. There was something about him that left an afterimage in my thought.

As soon as I was in the control room of the drive unit I called up Djac in space flight control. 'Hi Djac. It's Djim I've just seen a guy in the drive unit hall who did not seem to fit in. He was not one of the mechanics. He was just standing there. Do you know who he was?

'Of course Djim. The management said something about him being here. He's from...' There was a pause from the communicator as Djac thought. The walls shook when Djac thought. 'He's here to check up on the efficiency of our systems here. Productivity is the key. Is there something wrong?'

'No.' But I felt there was even though I had no reason to think so. I was getting as bad as Djon, seeing danger where there was none. I decided to go and ask this guy what he was up to, and see if he was the one who came to my house last night. I leapt out of the pilot's seat and ran to the airlock. As quick as I could I left the drive unit and jumped into the hoist to get me down to ground level. Then I ran to the far end of the drive unit hall.

'What's up?' Called one of the mechanics as I brushed past him.

'Hey, what's going on? Called another, I ran on without answering.

When I reached the place I saw him last I asked the nearest mechanic where the guy went. I followed where he pointed and the same with the next mechanic.

I finally found him.

He was in a hover car outside the drive unit hall, but there were others with him. I recognised them as the senior members of the board that ran the whole mining organisation. The car was just rising slowly into the air. I could hear the hum of the anti-gravity gyros and saw the faint glow from the underside as the energy was turned into heat. Dust swirled gently around the car, the distinct colours of the underside swirled around as the clique computers diverted energy to keep the hover car level and trim. The air crackled with the latent energy dissipation. He looked down at me as the car continued to rise and I could have sworn he sneered. But afterwards I could not think it was. Then the tannoy rang out. 'Djim Stone! Return to your drive unit and commence flight procedures. We have a programme to keep to.'

'Ghas!' I thought and at the same time felt the sting of Djon's words – 'you do not have a good job. You have a job.' I returned to the drive unit none the wiser as regards the visitor but humbled because I had been caught out holding up the programme. The others would chastise me later if we did not manage the full quota.

I went through the start up procedures in a dream. It was

only the jolt of the anti earth-tremor clamps releasing the legs of the drive unit ready for take off that woke me out of my reverie. The tugs towed my drive unit out of the hall building. I was the last one and it was a bit embarrassing, I had never been last before. Certainly, no one had been this far behind before. I spent the rest of my shift on automatic pilot, there in body but not in mind. Clamping onto cargo pods and dragging them up to the portal and then waiting for a return load. I was only waiting for my chance to get off work and find out who that guy was and then go and see Djon and give him a piece of mind. My opportunity came all too soon as I did not have to go to either of the moons today and that would have meant a longer shift.

Once out of debriefing I went to the manager's office and asked to see him. He would not see me so I asked his secretary to ask him who the guy was I had seen. She came back with a curt reply that it was none of my business. It was unusual and felt wrong. None of the others knew of whom I was asking about and only got annoyed that our shift might get a bad report. I decided to go straight to see Djon. I called him to make sure he was in.

When I arrived he let me in and waved me to a seat. 'Have you thought about our little talk yesterday?' He asked, without ceremony.

'Yes, I have you old dog.' I started. 'What have you done to me? I see strange men everywhere.'

'I know.' He replied. 'We are concerned about them. There have been a few unknown men on planet recently. We cannot find out why, which is even more surprising.'

'Look, someone followed me home last .....'

'I know, Djim. It was me.'

'You what!' I stuttered. 'Why?'

'I told you before; your father had asked me to look out for you. We suspect that the presence of these strangers is something to do with you. So I followed to see if I could see anything.'

'Me! Why?'

'Your father, we suspect as well as your naïve questioning. But we cannot be sure. We don't know why but it may be there was something he knew that should not be known and they are here to check up if that information is known. Sorry if that is a bit garbled.'

'The hover car that was near my home was not yours though. I know that much.'

'Really.' He seemed worried by this. 'I must admit I did not follow you all the way home. You were going in a very strange roundabout route. I wish I had now though, maybe I could have spotted the hover car too and got a reference number.'

'Not only that, but my mother said someone had been round to our house and had been asking to see me. She sent him to the ground station. I think he may have turned up today. There was this guy there whom I did not like. He seemed to be in with the senior board though.'

'Yes, the strangers do see to be very well connected with the upper echelons of our society. That is even more worrying, this seems to be a high-level problem. We must keep a low profile before we leave. We must also listen to your father's advice and trust no one. Under no circumstances ask any awkward questions or ask about these people.'

'Too late.' I said. 'I have already been in to ask about that man I saw.'

'Oh dear.' He replied. 'That is not good, do not do it again.'

'Look!' I yelled again getting up out of my seat. 'I am not leaving. It may be more dangerous to leave, and what is more I am not leaving my mother. She has already lost one member of her family; I don't want her to lose another. Besides, you have not produced any proof of anything.'

'If I had proof I may well have disappeared as well. I certainly couldn't stay here.'

'What do you mean by that?'

'I mean, Djim, that if I had evidence then I would be too much of a threat and would have been made to disappear.'

'This gets more and more ridiculous. I think it may be better if we do not see each other for a while. Not until this silliness has blown over. Do not try and come round and worry my mother either. I cannot stand this cloak and dagger stuff, it does not agree with me. I am beginning to feel unwell with it all and I could not bear my mother to see me like this. What is more if this planet of yours has been hidden, then someone wants it hidden and they will not want the likes of you and me trying to find it. It will be too dangerous. It is also pointless. There is no point in trying to find it. What good will it do? One planet more or less in the galaxy makes no difference.'

'Does it not concern you that your father's disappearance may not have been an accident?'

'Of course it does! What a thing to say. But if someone can organise that what chance do I have to do anything about it? Even if I can do anything, it wouldn't bring him back.' I did have at the back of my thought though a concern over what on Erebus my father had done to have such a drastic solution imposed upon him. Then common sense reasserted itself – it was just too ridiculous to be true. Djon got out the V20 again and placed it carefully on the desk and started it up. The shimmering miniature galaxy sprang into being above the table top. He typed something on the keyboard and a series of lines appeared.

'These are the last flights of your father.'

'What is the point of that?' I was beginning to get annoyed with Djon for the first time in my life. Why was he insisting on going on about this silly thing.

'It is this one in particular.' He used a pointer to indicate one of the flight paths. 'It goes somewhere where there are no planets. Why? What could have been there?'

'I don't know. Maybe it was something he was asked to do.'

'It did not appear in any of his flight logs!' replied Djon. I felt a cold feeling run down my spine again. It was a criminal offence to falsify a space flight log. I could not believe my father had committed a criminal act. It seemed so out of character. He had been one of the most honest and conscientious men on the pilot register, so his records had shown and my brief experience of his life also bore this out. There must be another explanation. Perhaps someone else had falsified his log. Then I pulled myself together again. He had no proof that there was anything wrong with this flight. I was concerned that he was using a restricted device again though, even if it had the beacon disabled.

'Maybe he had been asked to go there by these mysterious people who are here now. Maybe they are assessing if I could also do something for them.' I did not really believe myself even though I heard myself saying it. I wondered what my father had been doing and if it was irregular.

'Ever wondered what your father had done?' Asked Djon, as if reading my thought.

'No one ever told me anything. Why should they? He disappeared accidentally on a routine flight.'

'Ever wondered why you do not get to fly vessels further away in space?'

'I've told you I do not want to go further away. It would be unfair on my mother.'

'Do you think you have total control over your life?'

'Of course I ...' Something at the very back of my thought made me stop. Why does that question give me an uneasy feeling. I pushed that thought out of my consciousness. 'Of course I have.' I squared up to him even though he was much bigger and older than me. He stood impassively but not with any anger in his stare. 'But what did you mean about my naïve questioning?'

'Yes, I thought you would eventually come back to that.' He relaxed a little, his shoulders dropped slightly. 'You ask questions like "Where do all these substances go? What happens to the gold and silver etc?"'

'Well, where does it all go? Very little seems to end up here! Who benefits from it all?'

'Exactly. That is part of the search for Ultima Thule. It must end up there. I think your father also asked the same questions and also looked to find where it all went. I think that was his final mistake.'

'Mistake?'

'I know.' He said finally, putting his hand gently on my

shoulder. 'Your father made the one other mistake of calling me after that mysterious flight.' He pointed again to the odd little flight path to nowhere. 'And saying he had something he must show me when he got back. I never saw him again.' He gently pushed me back down into my seat and walked back round to his side of the desk.

'Do you still not want to come with us?'

'No. I've told you I cannot. Besides it is obvious we came from more than one planet, I mean look at the different skin colours and types people have. You and I are light coloured, Yasher has a darker skin, Djac is much darker and on the red side. Even your wife Tcho was different and had those beautiful eyes unlike yours or mine. So no.'

'That is your choice of course. If it is your choice.' He looked down at the floor between himself and the desk for a long time before looking up again. I think perhaps the mention of his wife still had a deep affect on him. He had loved her dearly (which was uncommon here) or so my father had said. I stayed rooted in my seat for some reason. Then I slowly got up. It was then that I noticed his office was different. The picture was off; his things that usually lay about were not there; the office looked bare. He was planning on going. He looked up at me as I stood.

'I really must be going Djon.' I said as I picked up my goggle headgear from off the desk. As I did so the door entry sounder chimed. I immediately sat down again, more in surprise than anything.

'Now, who is that?' He muttered, more to himself than me. He picked up the galaxolabe and put it back in the drawer – the miniature galaxy vanishing as he did so – and noisily pushed the drawer shut. He then pressed a button on his suit and the fabric began to stiffen visibly as he walked to the door. I turned in my seat to bring the door into my view. The fact that he had activated his suit defence mechanism surprisingly did not alert me at the time. The fact that crime on our planet was almost unheard of should have made me think why he had to be concerned when answering the door. The fact that we had been talking about searching for an original planet and the fact that he had been operating a restricted piece of equipment had made me think that someone had noticed and was coming to ask questions. It did not seem to register with me who that person might be, considering the abundant freedoms we had on this planet. I hoped it would not be the man I saw in the drive unit hall at the ground station.

The seals hissed as he opened the door.

There was a flash of brilliant sparkling light!

– CHAPTER 2 –

MOONS ARE NOT VERY FAR.

I became aware of waking up. It was dark and I could not quite work out who I was or where I was or why. But gradually in the quiet as my eyes became accustomed to the darkness and my thought began to clear I remembered.

The flash of light.

Who or what was it? I had no answer to that one as the light had obscured anyone or anything behind it. I had a dim memory though of a shadowy human figure outlined in the doorway.

So where was I now? I had no answer to that one either.

I tried to stand up but found my legs not doing quite what I wanted them to. I fell to my knees feeling nauseous. My mouth felt dry and I needed a drink. I felt the bristly feel of the standard drugget fibre carpet on my hands. In the dark I unsteadily stayed down on my hands and knees as my head swam disconcertingly. I could see nothing, which did not help my equilibrium, but gradually I could begin to think more clearly. Every now and again I tried to stand up until I finally managed to make my legs hold my weight and I stood up, shakily at first but then more steadily. What in galaxy's name had been used to put me out so effectively? I had no idea.

As I struggled round the room I bumped into something that was about knee height and sat down heavily onto it. Fortunately it had a soft finish. After a while I made myself get up again and I walked unsteadily round the edge of the room holding myself upright by leaning on the walls. They felt normal, so I was probably still on Enceladus. The room was about four metres square I assessed by counting my steps. The effort of so much thinking made me feel very tired.

Metres? The word came back at me.

The talk with Djon swam back into consciousness. What had that man done? Now I was beginning to find....find, what? So where did the word 'metres' come from and why did the galaxy use one system of measurement? It just makes sense that's all; it would not be possible to maintain a cohesive trading system without a single unit of measurement and a single monetary system either.

I must get myself back to reality and stop this silly dream, stop listening to Djon's daft ideas. All I need to do is wake up. I must be asleep and this is a dream. But I felt awake, at least I did now. I felt all the walls and anything I could reach. It was a standard room. There was one door and no window. There appeared to be something resembling a bed covered in fabric which was what I had bumped into and had sat on for a while. There was nothing to identify where I was or why. I stopped and listened as hard as I could, standing still if a little unsteadily, but could hear nothing. I kept listening for as long as I could but could still hear nothing. There was not even light showing round the door, probably because of the seals. When I began to feel stronger I called out at as loudly as I could a couple of times but heard no reply. I had to stop as my mouth still felt very dry, I needed a drink of water.

What had happened to Djon, was he alright? I hoped he was.

I found my way to the bed and sat on it again and began to consider what was going on. I felt all around it and then I found it. A bottle of cold water near the head of the bed against the wall. They were decent people after all in some respects. I managed to open the bottle and drank down the contents in one go. It felt good. In fact water had never tasted so good. It gave me the pleasant relaxed feeling and immediately I felt better and began to think more clearly.

Our planet was in a quiet corner of the galaxy; we mined for useful metals, minerals and other natural substances. I transported the materials up to the portal and I returned with products and materials we needed, including water, which we could not make or find here. It was difficult to find fresh water here, suitable to drink anyway. This was one reason why this planet had not grown in the way others had, or so they said. It was the standard way man had traded and lived for years. I made a good living and life was uneventful apart from the odd problem with drives, meteors, cosmic showers or earth tremors or volcanic activity. Most habitations though were kept well away from the trouble spots. Some people thought it was boring here and left for other parts. It had indeed been quiet and I wished it had remained that way. It had been until Djon started off with his silly ideas. But he had not just started off with his ideas. He and my father had been hiding these ideas for at least the last twenty years! I had had no inkling of this. Now look what had happened, this had got far too close for comfort and now I was imprisoned by person or persons unknown. Was it the police who had captured me? It did not seem quite like the way the police would go about it. I was not aware that they held people in darkened rooms all alone.

I thought back; man first arrived on Enceladus 421 some fifty odd years ago it was recorded, and life had been fairly hard then while the town was set up and the soil prepared for planting. But because of the acidic water here and the poor salty soil nothing would grow. Everything had to be brought in – which was what I did. I collected the pods and brought them down to the surface.

Specialists went around the galaxy preparing planets for the inhabitants and looking for animals that might be a problem and then moving on to the next. No other animals had been found and certainly no aliens had ever been found in the entire galaxy! There were some small annoying insect type things that flew around at sunset or crawled around in the short undergrowth and plant life. There was no diversity here and certainly there was no trouble here either. So who or what had imprisoned me? Why had they imprisoned me? I had done nothing wrong! And why keep me in a darkened room? We were more civilised than that! Surely? Was Djon right after all? Was I a marked man? Had they come for me?

But who were they?

Suddenly the door seals hissed and a thin line of light appeared around the door. Then the door opened and I had to squint against the bright light. I could just make out a shape silhouetted in the doorway. The door shut again before I could move, and as it shut I could make out that the shape was a toroid about half a meter in length hanging about a metre above the floor. The toroid now hung in the redarkened room, but this time lit gently by a glow from the underside of the machine itself. It was not anything I had ever seen before. It was not anything the authorities had on this planet that I was aware of.

The machine spoke. 'Name!' It was a harsh metallic tinny sound as though from cheap speakers.

'Djim Stone.' I replied, surprised at the strange scenario. Imprisoned in a dark room talking to some floating toroid, this surely must be a dream.

'Full name!'

'Djim Stone – N four two one. What....' The machine continued as if not hearing me.

'What were you doing in the office of Djon-20-N421?' The machine moved slightly, shimmering gently; the light now emanating from a haze around it like a tiny atmosphere. Should I try and take it down? Would someone then come and rescue it? Was it watching me? It! Machines don't watch; people do! So who was watching me or could they see me?

'Answer now!'

'Djon is a family friend, I was visiting him.'

'Are you the son of Rojer Stone-N421?'

'Yes.' I was acutely aware now of the conversation I had been having with Djon. Was he right after all?

'Are you an originist?'

'No.' At least I did not have to lie about that one. I wondered though if this machine was capable of detecting a lie.

'Is Djon-20-N421 an originist?' Here was my chance to see if this machine was capable of detecting a lie.

'No.' I said as clearly and levelly as possible.

'Is your mother an originist?'

'No!' I shouted back but suddenly at the back of my mind an awful nagging fear began to emerge at that question. Was she? Surely my tiny, slim gentle mother who had raised me all these years was not one of those daft people as well. It just did not make sense. But she had been married to my father all those years – had he ever talked to her about this? I put my head in my hands as I sat dejectedly on the edge of the bed. Except now by the glow of the machine I could see it was not a bed but a pseudo-wood box with a thick padded blanket draped over it. I did not dare move, now this machine was here, to look inside.

'What is Ultima Thule?'

'I have no idea.' I kept my head in my hands hoping the machine would not be able to tell if I was lying.

'Do you believe there is an original planet?'

'Of course not! Only those stupid originists believe that.'

'Why was a restricted device being used?' This was a bit more tricky. I did not know how to answer. If the beacon had been turned off how did anyone else know it was being used. Perhaps there was another way of knowing, the V20 was so complex it was not possible to understand all its workings or procedures. I decided to try a question to put it off.

'Why have you imprisoned me?' There was a slight pause.

'Answer the question.'

'I was not using a restricted device.' That was true at any rate. I hoped it would satisfy the question.

'A restricted device was being used.'

'Good.' I did not know if my sudden boldness would bring down some retribution or not, but I was getting very annoyed by this machine and my situation.

'Why was a restricted device being used?'

'I've told you I was not using a restricted device.'

'Why was Djon 20 using a restricted device?'

'I have no idea. I was not aware he was. Why not ask him that? Now why am I being held here? What have I done?' There was a long pause as if the machine was trying to make

sense of what I had just said. As nothing happened I got bolder.
'Well?' I said.

'Sit down!' Said the machine sharply. I did so, not realising that I had even stood up in the first place. It was the natural thing to do to be obedient to authority on Enceladus 421 although not normally a faceless machine. Perhaps that was why there was so little crime – in fact I could not remember the last time any crime of any sort took place here. Other random things entered my thought – we had good weather here as a general rule and rain was rare – that was due to the dust we were told – but that was a good thing too as it was so acidic. If you got caught out in a shower you had to come home or to work and shower immediately. That was the law here. With such a relatively small population it was essential that everyone was ready and healthy for work. Everyone worked too, even mothers. Children were looked after in large crèches. We were also told to have as many children as possible but for some reason births were too low. I was not allowed to marry and have children as I did not yet have enough credits. I hoped to one day.

'You will .....' As it spoke there was a noise in the room outside which drowned out what it was about to say. Light flickered under the door and the toroid suddenly dimmed, the haze vanished and it crashed to the floor and bounced away into a corner of the now darkened room. More noises outside, a crackle followed by a sickening smack, which sounded like a frisson bolt gun! But they were not supposed to be used against people! The light under the door went out and then it opened.

'Djim!' It was Djon's voice.

'You there?' A hand held light flashed on and waved around erratically I was caught in the beam of light. I put up my hands to shield my eyes.

'Yes, I'm here.'

'Come on then we must get out of here!' He ran in and grabbed my arm and pulled me up and dragged me out of the room. I was too disorientated to take in much. There was a lot of smoke and lights flashing, furniture in disarray. Something familiar caught my eye but vanished again in the gloom and smoke as Djon hustled me through the room. Then a door shaped hole in the wall loomed up through the smoky gloom illuminated by Djon's hand held light. He walked straight to the hole without stopping, but all I could see outside was dark. No ground! I struggled to stop, there was no ground outside only dark night air and Djon was walking straight out!

'Come on.' He muttered. It was then as we went through the hole that I saw something just below the floor level outside. He pushed me and I fell into something soft and cold.

I found myself in the familiar comfort of a hover car, often jokingly called a sick boat or sickie because of the sensation some passengers feel when first using them or if caught in a good wind! I used one every day to get to work and back, in fact this one might even be mine! They used the principle of counteracting the effect of gravity with anti-gravity gyros, much like making an object float at a certain level in water by adjusting the flotation. It was all possible after the secrets of gravity were unlocked in the distant past.

Djon jumped into the front seat and someone else jumped in with him. The hover car rocked wildly until the stabilising gyros could dampen the effect. I could imagine the underside a swirling mass of pulsating, swirling light as the heat generated was dispersed to the atmosphere as the gyros desperately tried to stabilise the rocking craft. It happened very quickly and very soon we were back at equilibrium. Lying in the back I certainly felt queasy, but before I could gather myself the hovercar surged upwards with such speed that it took my breath away. I was not often a passenger and being laid down and unable to see out made the sensation worse. And it was dark so I had nothing to focus on. Then I began to get my senses back – this was not what happened here and should not be happening to me! Even if it was Djon.

'What ...?' I began.

'Keep down!' Snapped Djon. 'We need to get away from here!' My stomach dropped into my boots as we rose abruptly again and then turned and dropped. All the while rushing forward at what seemed like full speed, but I was sure could not have been. As I began to regain my equilibrium so I gained a sense of outrage.

'For the love of mother Djon, what the Erebus is going on?' I yelled.

'Keep your voice down Djim.' Snarled Djon back over his broad shoulder. 'This sickie is an open top and anyone can hear. We are leaving. There are people here we have never seen before. We need to get you and us away from this planet! Hang on!' We took a sudden dive and I became momentarily weightless and grabbed desperately onto the slippery seating. As I settled I was able to reach for the grab handle and hang on tight. The wind whistled around the craft and tugged at my clothes. I could see the night sky above me full of stars ablaze above the clouds. The tiny specks of dust stinging my face and hands, I had to squint to keep it out of my eyes. My eyes were watering from the cold night air buffeting me. Djon then reached down and handed me silently a dust helmet and goggles. I took them and put them on with difficulty having only had one hand to work with as I did not want to let go of the grab handle. I finally managed to get them on reasonably well and could relax. That was another law I remembered that applied here – you had to give someone a dust helmet if you had a spare and they had none. I could look up easily now. I noticed that Djon had not put his dust helmet on properly and the ends of his white hair were being whipped into frenzy by the speeding air. Next to him it looked as though it was a woman driving. From under her anti dust helmet her long dark hair was streaming out behind her head like the strand waterweed in a violent storm. I did not recognise her.

'Who is your friend, Djon?'

'Just wait until we're safe Djim.' We banked sharply again and I could see the native trees and no buildings. We were not in town then, but I could not identify where we were. Away from town there was almost continuous tree cover with no distinguishing features. We turned again. The night air was beginning to get through my clothes. I tried to pull them closer but to no avail. I just kept on getting colder. Fortunately it was not too cold at this time of year.

The journey went on for what seemed like hours but probably was only a few miinutes. However it was a long journey and we must be well away from the town by now and into the jungle that covered most of the planet on this hemisphere. It was too dark to see any landmarks to identify where we were or where we were heading. I felt physically unwell lying uncomfortably in the back and getting cold. It was also travelling very fast and particularly far for one of these things. This far out in the galaxy we did not have the latest nuclear powered craft. The hover cars here were electrically powered and had to be recharged every few hours and had a limited range as a result. Djon seemed to have a long range version.

Then after a while I saw in the sky just above the horizon the awful disc of Erebus. It was not like a moon but more like someone had removed a disc of the night sky stars and left an empty black void. It made my skin crawl, but I had no idea why. We then turned and began to rapidly drop and kept on dropping into the darkness below, I hoped they knew what they were doing. Flying without lights and dropping so quickly into an unlit area was the most dangerous thing to do. Distances could be deceptive. In the gloom a building came into view in front of us in a clearing in the native trees. The trees were a strange native plant that looked more like giant ferns with short rugged stems. There was no diversity. All the trees were the same species. We pulled up and settled gently on the ground. It was very dark. A million living things crowded together and reaching out to touch the building as if feeling what had invaded their virgin territory. It sounded as though they were whispering in a million rustling leaf tongues. It was eerie beyond anything I hade ever encountered. I felt as though I was being watched. Can trees watch? Absurd, of course not.. yet. Yet. The feeling sunk deeper into my soul. I became transfixed with a fear I had never known. No one had ever found any other form of animal life on the planet but yet...was there something out there with malevolent intent? The only light came from the the doorway but even that seemed to struggle against the darkness of the forest.

I was awoken from my stupor by Djon.

'Quick, get out.' Djon leapt out of the hover car, his female friend leapt out of the other side and disappeared. I was too cold to move quickly so Djon lent over me and with his big hands grabbed my suit and heaved me upright. He was looking up at the sky the whole time.

'Come on quick, into the building.' He grabbed a big bag from the front seat and ran towards the building. It was a large cube, dark and menacing in the night, and loomed high above me. The clearing in which it sat was not much bigger than the building leaving only a small space for the sickie and room to just about get around the sides. The upper leaves of the trees brushed the sides of the building making a sweeping sound in the dark.

I swung my legs over the side and slid down onto the spongy ground. It was not grass but a short dense plant that was ubiquitous here. It was then that I noticed the sickie had been towing an additional microbial fuel cell pod. I did not know they could do that either! I turned and stumbled towards the light now spilling from the small door in the side of the building. I was glad to reach the safety of the interior. Nothing came following me inside. Almost filling the interior was what looked like a spacecraft. There was very little room around it and I could not make out what it was exactly. The open hatch faced me from directly in front of the doorway. Djon came down the steps.

'Get in.' he said unceremoniously and pushed me up the steps. I stepped into a familiar interior as all spacecraft were built on identical lines. This one however was very small and appeared to be very old too. I could not place it's make at first but it smelt just like any other spacecraft which was reassuring. The cabin I entered was small with three seats set in front of the control panels. All the surfaces were covered with dials, buttons and switches. It all looked so familiar. The lights were on, controls were alive and it was nearly ready to go. Someone must have used a remote to start up the pre-flight systems?

There was someone else in one of the seats, perhaps he had commenced the pre-flight start up?

'Who …?' But before I could finish Djon squeezed himself through the hatch and suddenly seemed to fill the control room. The woman followed him in. It began to get a tight fit.

'Into the pilot seat Djim, quick! I think we are not so far ahead as I thought!' He pushed me gently towards the middle seat. I sat down and automatically put on the restraint straps. My hands went to the switches, lights dimmed and the hum of the drives began to rise. I went into pre-flight mode. I then realised that this was a poor model of a mark one moon hopper, a short range craft. So we weren't going far. I noticed that the panels did not fit together too well, it looked home made. Most space vessels were designed along identical lines so that as many parts were interchangeable as possible. It made repairs simpler and also meant that stricken craft could easily be helped by other rescue vessels. This also reduced the number of parts that repair craft had to carry. It also made it cheaper and meant that any pilot could fly any vessel, which was also another safety feature. Besides, on remote planets like ours minimising duplication was essential.

However this one seemed particularly badly made, even for this outpost. I heard the hatch shut with a 'phut' and felt the pressurisation activate. At least it seemed to be working properly. I instantly fell into pilot mode, feeling every part of the vessel gradually reaching take-off readiness through my seat, the soles of my feet and my hands on the control panel. Even though I had never flown one of these before it was just so familiar and just like the simulations, I had no trouble getting orientated. One up for the standardisation.

'How do we get out of this building?' I asked. So much was I in pilot mode that all the rest of what had happened became secondary for the moment. I could not believe it.

'Don't worry Djim, the roof has already gone. Just go straight up. Carefully. There is very little room to play with.'

'You're not kidding there. Now Djon, while I take this up

you start talking.' As I spoke, I rubbed my hands together to get them warm again and restore the feeling before switching on the V20. The familiar bluish orb sprang into being and again the lights automatically dimmed further in response.

'Will this alert anyone by switching it on or has it also been tampered with?' I asked.

'It's the same one Djim.' This time it did not show the whole galaxy but the more familiar relevant part around Enceladus 421; as someone had instructed it. In fact in the bottom of the glowing orb, slicing a skullcap out of the light, was the surface of the planet with a red dot in the centre. That was us. Hanging within the glowing orb was not the stars this time but a dark sphere much smaller than the planet; the moon Erebus 421, so named for its dark surface. I did not know why that name meant a dark surface. Springing out of the moon was a dotted yellow line depicting the course of the moon's geostationary orbit. During all this time the drives were powering up and instruments were counting down to take-off time. Unlike a modern vessel the instruments were all illuminated equally instead of only when there was something to take notice of. Hence instead of the very familiar blinking on of instrument dials there was just a stationary illumination level. It was an old outdated craft to take so long to power up to take-off too.

'We are not going to Erebus, are we?' I asked nervously.

'Yes, we have already pre-programmed the V20.' Erebus was the last place I ever thought I would have to go. All my years on the planet and I had managed to avoid going anywhere near it. I had even avoided looking at it. There were some of course who thought it had magical powers and almost worshipped it. Personally I could not see it.

Djon began. 'Ok, Djim I'll fill you in but we must get off the ground now! I don't know how far these people are behind us.'

'This is a mark one moon hopper Djon.' I countered. 'It is counting down to take-off and we should be able to leave in two minutes.' As I spoke I got another cold shiver down my spine. Where did minutes come from? Our planet did not have a standard galactic day. It was about one and a half standard days with 36 hours to the day. Somewhere was a standard day planet? I shouted inwardly to myself to stop listening to this stupid originist rubbish and get a grip of myself. As soon as I could I would leave them and return. For the moment I would go along with them, just in case there was someone chasing us!

'Go on Djon. No. First, tell me who these people are.'

'OK. Right, the man in the seat beside you is called Terens.' As Djon spoke the man turned to me with a smile and held out his hand. We shook; his hand was firm, dry and rough. He had that rugged weather-beaten look to his face, consistent with a man who spends his days outdoors in all weathers and not in space. His straw coloured hair was pulled back into a ponytail. This strangely made me think of what straw was not having seen any and once before coming across the word no one I knew could explain either. He wore a small neat goatee beard too. High pronounced cheekbones made his narrow face look thinner than it really was. His smile vanished as soon as it had come and he turned away immediately after greeting. It was disconcerting. 'He is an adventurer, an explorer of worlds and has been trying to push into the vast jungles on this planet. He also knows his weapons. He needs them for dealing with any wild animals or other dangers.' The mention of weapons made me shiver. No one had weapons normally. I realised then that this man spent a lot of his time alone and this probably explained his disconcerting behaviour. Djon continued. 'The girl in the dicky seat is called Ruuth. She is another originist like me and has been very helpful to me. She worked in Enceladus Governing body. That's how I knew you were a marked man.'

'And the people following us?'

'We don't know them.' Said Djon flatly.

'How do you know they are going to do us harm then?'

'They imprisoned you didn't they. Besides.' He added quickly. 'It is too dangerous to find out. To wait for them would be too late.' As Djon spoke there was a buzzing, indicating take-off was possible.

'Hold on a second Djon, this may be a bit bumpy.' The

cabin began to hum and vibrate like a silent alarm clock. I took control with the take-off joystick and made delicate adjustments to keep us away from the walls. I had never taken off in such tight circumstances before. It was a tense few moments. As we left the ground we could see the walls of the building in front of the vision screen start moving. That was only an optical allusion of course as it was us that was moving. I had no space flight control to guide me or keep the vessel away from anything else. The anti-gravity gyros whirred into life making us rise away from the grip of the planet. But as we left the ground the vessel began to sway slowly without friction keeping us steady. I had to constantly adjust the controls to keep us away from the walls. Then the wall in front of us began to slide downwards, and then there were trees moving downwards and then the starry night sky. We felt the sudden surge as our upward movement increased like a super fast lift as I opened up the main drives.

'Keep low to start with.' Said Djon. So I did not take us up any higher but put power into forward movement. The dark trees below us began to pass under us and clouds above us at increasing speed until they were just a blur. Shortly a faint lighter glow appeared on the horizon.

'OK.' Said Djon finally. 'Now take her up and plot in the course to Erebus.' Words I did not really want to hear, but I followed his direction and punched in the course and pulled the moon hopper up into a steep climb. The rumble of the drives increased as they pushed us up into space. A green line appeared from the red dot which had now moved from off the surface of the planet. The line intersected with the moon's orbit. Once it had stabilised and the numbers and vectors appeared by our red dot and the moon's orbit line I set the automatic pilot to follow the line. There was a slight jolt as the V20 took control away from me.

'Sorry, Djon I was not really listening. Do continue I can listen now. That went rather well actually.' I didn't let on that I had never done that before.

'Thank you, Djim. I knew you were the man for the job.

We need you on board.' He paused. 'Looking for the original planet is not entirely the reason for our quest. The other reason is that someone or someones do not want us to try and find the original planet! There appears to be an active conspiracy ...'

'Conspiracy!' I turned to look at Djon for the first time in a while. 'Conspiracy theories have abounded for years and have been shown to be mostly figments of the imagination. You don't seriously think there is a conspiracy to stop you looking for some old planet!' I looked back at the controls, shaking, listening to the subtle roar of the drives behind us, feeling the well being of the craft's performance through the seat of my pants, looking at the proximity gauge, looking at the ... there was no proximity gauge or sensor detector! Of course, this was an early model, a very early model. 'How can we know if we are being searched for or followed?' I asked. 'This old thing has no detectors. If your pursuers decide to send some missile after us we will never know until it is too late and we are vapourised!' I was especially aware of the bright light our drives would be making against the night sky behind us. We could be seen by anyone.

'This is the best we could afford. I do not think anyone will waste a missile on us. Even if there is one on this planet.'

'At least you didn't steal it then. And how can you know these 'people' have not got some weapons, you keep saying they want to kill us?'

'No, we didn't steal it and I'm surprised you would even think we would. And as for these 'people' they will not kill us by firing weapons at us, that would not only be too obvious but would also attract too much unwanted attention. It will be much more subtle than that. It is more likely an accident would happen to us.' He paused, obviously thinking about what he had just said. He then continued absently. 'This was delivered to us in bits, mainly through your father originally. Ruuth and I have spent many hours putting the kit together in that building. You will have to rely on the V20 for sensors.' No wonder the panels did not fit well! This was home made!

'Ghas! You are right.' In our haste I had forgotten to switch on the 'all craft' programme which would show all other craft nearby, particularly those with trajectories heading for us. This prevented near misses and collisions. I switched it on. Nothing happened. 'Is this working properly, this V20 of yours?'

'Yes, Djim it works perfectly.'

'We are fortunate then. There is nothing within range on this side of the planet.' I touched the controls and the view in the V20 began to change. The 'skull cap' of the planet began to shrink as we saw more and more of the space around us. Soon our planet was 'seen' as a whole. On the other side, away from us there then appeared several other brown dots with numbers and trajectories shown. Then the satellite appeared in the bluish haze of the ethereal sphere. I stopped zooming out. The trajectories all converged on the satellite, all except our of course which was rigidly fixed on Erebus 421 unfortunately. There was nothing heading our way or even anywhere near us. Nothing big enough for the V20 to pick up anyway. Our red dot slowly crawled up our green line.

'No one seems to have seen us Djon. Why is that? Space traffic control should have seen us by now.'

'We won't register. We have deactivated the beacon. It will be ages before we are spotted.'

'Now we have broken a prime space flight rule. It is illegal to fly without location control. It is also very unsafe. It is dangerous too as no one can find you if there is trouble.'

'If we are found there is trouble.' Said Djon quietly.

'OK, so who is after us then?' I turned to Djon again. He smoothed down his ruffled white hair.

'I don't know Djim, I really don't know. Even Ruuth did not know who they are. But at least one person here was neither part of the community nor part of the governing body. We could not find out how many or who they were or even why they were here. But we are sure they are here to make sure we did not get anywhere looking for Ultima Thule. And to stop you too.'

'Ultima Thule, what is that? And how do you know they would stop you?'

'Ultima Thule means a distant place. We think that is what the original planet was called and searching the interstellar net was what brought these people here we think. Fortunately, as Ruuth worked in high places we heard they were asking questions about us, and you. It was too much of a coincidence to ignore.'

'Why would people call their planet a far away place? That doesn't make sense.'

'We think it meant they were far away from anything else, not that it was far away. They felt lost and alone in a vast universe.' There was a pause. We all fell silent. I became aware that Terens had not said a word and neither had Ruuth. She must be able to hear us even in the dicky seat. I turned round to face Terens. He was staring intently out of the forward vision screen at the blaze of stars that always filled the cloudless night sky of the galaxy.

'How did you get mixed up in this then, Terens?' I asked. He slowly took his eyes off the now pitch black, star filled sky and looked at me with intense dark brown eyes that made it difficult to distinguish his pupils. He spoke with a similarly weather-beaten voice.

'I have spent many years on planets exploring for many governing bodies. I have spent the last two years on your home planet.'

'What do you do?'

'It is my job to go through the most recently inhabited planets and check to see if there are any animals or aliens likely to cause problems. Hence the need for weapons. The only way to do it is by getting out into the terrain and search thoroughly. It cannot be done by overflying.'

'Have you ever found anything?'

'Strangely no. There appears to be no major life forms other than us in the universe.' He stopped again. It was like trying to push a heavy cart uphill to keep him talking.

'So how did you get mixed up in this?'

'It all begins to sound the same after a while.' He said, slowly and deliberately in the quiet way people do when they spend lots of time by themselves. Djon butted in, obviously impatient.

'Terens is a valuable asset to us, but he is taking a big risk. He has a licence to go to any inhabited planet or any potentially inhabited planet and go anywhere on that planet. But if he is ever found to be an originist then he will lose that freedom. That freedom is so valuable to us we cannot let him be found out.'

'Thank you Djon, but what do you mean by that?' I said to Terens, 'about it sounding the same.'

'I mean that everywhere you go you get the same answer to questions. There is the same feeling that.' He paused. 'That something is missing, like a piece of a jigsaw not in it's right place or is not even the right piece of the jigsaw at all. Do you follow me?' He looked directly into my eyes, not something he was used to I felt.

'No I don't.' I replied. I turned to Djon again. 'And Ruuth. Can she hear us or have you not fitted internal comms either?'

'Oh, I can hear you.' Crackled a young woman's voice from a hidden speaker.

'So what do you do and how did you get into this?' I asked the control panel.

'I worked for the governing body of the planet.' She replied levelly. 'I worked in the 'atmosphere' affairs but gradually became aware of being thwarted at every turn.'

'What do you mean?'

'People were not helpful when they should have been, there was no cooperation, no desire to notice anything wrong. It is difficult to put into words – it is more of a feeling.' I sighed, yet again, just like Djon.

'Did you know what happened to my father?'

'Sorry.' She sounded genuine, even through the speaker. 'I did not work there then, but I did hear of it.'

'So what happened then?'

'What I heard was that he was asking too many awkward questions.' There was a strained silence while I stared at the control panel, watching the red dot still climb slowly up the green line towards Erebus 421. Slowly but too fast for my liking, I did not want to get any closer to that moon. Djon put his hand on my shoulder.

'We don't think his was an accident. That's partly the reason why we are all here.'

'Are you suggesting there has been a travesty of justice here?' I could not believe such a thing could happen. We prided ourselves that true justice was what set us apart from beasts. 'If we cannot expect justice then what hope is there?'

'Exactly Djim. That's why we are going on this journey. To see if we can find out why.'

'There is something else Djon. Why are we going to Erebus 421? There is nothing there. It is a dead moon and no one even likes it.' I just had to change the subject. It was just too painful to consider that my father had somehow been murdered. No one had ever found his vessel or his remains. He may still be alive somewhere, in fact if Djon takes us on this journey and we can find my father it would make his allegations look rather silly.

'Exactly why. We have something waiting for us. How long is it going to be before we get there?'

'At this speed it will be over fourteen hours.' Fourteen hours crammed into this old tin can! I think I may have cramp by the time we get there.

'OK then let us get something to eat.' Before Djon spoke I had not realised just how hungry and thirsty I was. Terens reached down and opened a pouch under the console and pulled out some typical bags of emergency rations.

'It's the best we could do in the circumstances.' Apologised Terens, as he handed out the packets. It was the first time that I had ever been pleased to see these things and I ripped one open with relish.

'At least we'll survive.' Quipped Djon lightly. 'Give me some for Ruuth.' He took some packets and pulled himself out of his seat and more or less fell back to the rear wall of the control room. He pulled open the door to the rear compartment and handed the packets to Ruuth. 'You OK girl?' He asked with genuine concern. It made me remember the times he came to help my mother in the early days soon after my father vanished. He also made time to be a father figure to me too.

It was all the more of a shock to think of him being one of these originists. Everyone laughed at anyone who even suggested the idea of an original planet.

He came back and sat heavily in his seat. I did not catch her reply but it must have been in the affirmative as Djon also ripped open his ration packet with a degree of pleasure. We sat and ate in silence for a while. I spent time looking out of the forward vision enhancer at the familiar star patterns or looking deeply into the galaxolabe's bluish light. It was a well-known phenomenon for people to see their future or long lost friends in the galaxolabe's spherical glow. It certainly was almost mesmeric, and some had been known to crash because they were unable to tear their gaze away even though the machine was warning them of impending danger and the ship's own warning sounders and lights would be vainly trying to prevent the impending catastrophe.

I was watching for any sign that the planet had noticed our flight – but none of the other dots in the miniature galaxy deviated from their normal run of flights – as our little red dot still climbed slowly along its little green line, which still arced up towards the moon's orbit. How come no one had noticed our flight? We did not have any military defence mechanisms or sophisticated searching devices but there was a very good space traffic control system that knows the location of every object in the sky and the local space around the planet.

'Why has no one called us to find out what is going on?'

'I've turned off the communications system.' Replied Djon flatly.

'You what!' I spluttered. 'What if something goes wrong? We are completely helpless out here!'

'As I said before Djim, we are finished if we stay down there and we are finished if we have to call for help.'

'How do you know you would be finished down there? Not everyone is a psychopathic killer, there are many good people down there. You don't even know your visitors are killers!'

'I know that Djim, but anyone who met them always gave the same answer. They had a funny feeling about them, an unpleasant feeling. I know we would 'disappear' and the good people would not know what happened and no one would dare to find out.' He let the word 'dare' hang longer on his lips.

'That's another thing.' Said Terens suddenly but quietly. 'You keep meeting the same type of people throughout the galaxy. Like the ones that have appeared here recently.'

'You don't mean large well-built men with muscles and short hair or hair like sculpture?'

'Yes, seen any?'

'Yes.' I said. 'That is the description of the man I saw at work.' We again lapsed into silence and let the muffled growl of the drives lull us into a melancholic period of reflection. We all had a feeling that there was now no turning back. It came over me that I would not be able to set foot on my home planet ever again. I could not find any rational reason why I should feel that way. Only yesterday, was it yesterday? I realised I had no idea what day it was. Only yesterday in my mind I was living a normal life and doing a good job and now my whole world seemed to have been ripped apart and nothing made sense anymore. Ruuth's mechanical tinny voice erupted out of the console and made us all jump back into the present.

'We're effectively outlaws guys!'

I wished that Ruuth had not sounded so pleased about us being outlaws. I certainly did not feel pleased to be called an outlaw!

*

We were now in the shadow of the moon. In a shadow of a shadow. The surface was black and smooth. There seemed to be no evidence of impacts at all. The rock apparently was geologically 'soft' like melted chocolate so impacts eventually just vanished like ripples on a pond. That was the theory at any rate as no one had yet been out here to study the geology and no one had any desire to either.

We were in a dark void behind a dark, brooding, forbidding sphere of soft rock that was slipping silently past the viewing screen, if it was possible to see a black non reflective surface moving in a black airless shadow. By eye it was impossible but with the vision enhancer operating on the viewing screen we could 'see' the curve of the moon sliding past but only just as even the technology had difficulty with it! It was a black sphere about two thousand five hundred kilometres in diameter and apparently had a mass of about nought point nought five of a standard planet – whatever that was. It orbited at about two hundred and eighty thousand kilometres from our planet.

'I have never seen anything like this before' Said Terens grimly as he stared at the enhancer before getting back to his work.

I checked the V20 again. The little red dot and the two lines and the moon were now all in the same place and the planet was on the other side of the moon. As soon as the moon blocked out the planet below we all relaxed, quite independently of each other, but it was a tense relaxation as we were well aware of the black rock hanging in space beneath our craft. Its presence reached out through the shadow and penetrated the hull to inflict a terrible grip upon our thinking. How could a dead lifeless lump of rock exert any sort of emotion upon a living thing?

It became hard to think.

'Now Djim.' It seemed unnatural to hear a normal human voice. 'When we disembark we need to set this thing to self destruct. Can you set it up so we delay as little as possible?' I could not believe what I was hearing!

'You can't do that'. I said. 'Anyone finding it will know immediately that we were not on board. Not only that, how can you afford to destroy a vessel let alone a V20?'

'Oh my goodness, I am not going to destroy a good V20, I can remove the controls like I did in my office. The main part is in the Jergan, we only have a remote here. So we can destroy this vessel.'

'How can you afford to do that? Even a kit craft must have cost a shed load of money.'

'I know what you mean Djim, but we cannot let anyone find this. If they do they will know we have left and come after us.'

'It just goes against everything I have learnt. My whole life has been to try and preserve a vessel at all costs.'

'Well, now it's your chance to wreck one, in a good cause.'

'I'm not sure I can do that.' Djon seemed far too flippant over the destruction of a valuable – if rather old fashioned – vessel.

'How do we stop them finding this? What do we do with it? If we leave it they will follow.'

'Can you not give it to one of your originist friends, or bring it with us?'

'No. It is not possible believe me. We have thought this through. I do not like this any more than you do but I cannot see any alternative.'

'I cannot think just destroying this vessel will put 'them' of the scent.'

'Do you have a better idea then?'

'Give me a while Djon.' I said not knowing if I could come up with a better idea.

'We haven't long Djim.'

'I know, just give me a while.' I hoped he would keep quiet for a short time to give me space to think. There had to be a better way. I racked my thought for an alternative but reluctantly came to the same conclusion as Djon. It seemed an awful thing to do to destroy a space vessel. But there had to be another way. I went quiet as I tried to think through any other solutions, but the approaching moon made it difficult to think straight. We had plenty of time and I was in no hurry to get to Erebus. I put my head in my hands and shut my eyes to see if that helped. It did. Later I looked across to Djon and he looked to be asleep. I sat back and just went through the options. Two hours later I sat up. Djon snorted awake too.

Then something came to me. 'I think I may have a slightly better idea Djon.'

'Such as?' Asked Djon, his white bushy eyebrows raised below a wrinkled brow.

'I think I can set the automatic pilot to take it out from behind this moon and let it crash into the planet somewhere safe.'

'How is that better Djim?' His eyebrows now furrowed as he fought to think how this would work. I hoped he would agree with me.

'If anyone is watching us they will see this craft go behind the moon and then come out again. If it stays behind the moon then they will send someone out here to come and look. That means we have to get out of here quick whereas the other way we can stay here and hide for a bit to let the heat go down. They will go look for the wreckage but will not be able to determine if anyone was aboard. Even if they do bother. I am hoping they will not even bother to go look, they will just accept it. The forests here are very thick in places, it's not easy to get to.'

'Sounds good to me. I like the idea of being able to hide for a while. You don't think they will come up here anyway, just to see if we are up here?'

'No. They would not dream that anyone could have a vessel hiding here. I am sure of that. Knowing how the space travel works around this planet I was very surprised myself that you had a vessel here.'

'OK. What about you guys.' Called Djon over his shoulder.

'How can you be sure it won't land anywhere inhabited?' Asked Terens.

'Easy. A few calculations on the planets rotation and the moon's orbit and fortunately there is very little populated areas on this planet and the orbit is geostationary.'

'Sounds good to me too then.' Came Ruuth's disembodied voice from out of the control panel.

'OK, Djim do it now. How long will it take? Speed is of the essence to make it look realistic.'

'It should only take a few minutes. Give me some room.' I set about getting the system ready for automatic launch. It was not easy with such an old craft but my reputation was now on the line, so I had to do it. But it was better to be doing this than being drawn into the mesmerism of the dark forbidding moon. 'I still need some more room though Terens. Can you move into the back?' Terens looked at Djon and then slowly got up out of his seat so I assumed Djon must have nodded assent. I immediately reached down in front of his now empty seat and spun the toggles which held the front under-panel in place. I then ripped it off. These things were designed for this, as often running repairs were necessary. I bent down and peered into what should have been a mass of circuitry lit gently from some hidden light to assist repairs. There was not much in there.

'Djon.' I said, looking up from where I lay on the floor. 'There is very little in here.'

'I know.' He said with a wry smile. 'We didn't exactly have a complete vessel here. It only contains the very basics to get us into space for this journey.'

'Is there anti-crash circuitry in here?'

'I doubt it. Ruuth?' He said looking forward but thinking towards the rear where Ruuth was sitting quietly.

'No.' Came her disembodied reply again.

'What about the magnetic shield, I cannot see any controls for that either?'

'No.' Came her voice again. 'We will not be in the line of fire for solar winds or flares for more than a few minutes I estimate.'

'Good Ghas! I wish you had told me before. I would not have dared take this tin box up if I had known just how dangerous it was. What if you are wrong?'

'That's why we didn't tell you.' He said with that wry smile still on his face. I could have punched his lights out there and then but thought better of it. No anti-crash circuitry, how could they be so daft? I did not profess to understand the inner workings of the anti-crash programme, but one pilot had explained it like two similar magnetic poles, which repel each other. This would effectively prevent the craft from falling into a planet, or another craft if at all possible. It was not infallible. Still, it was one less thing to do.

'Is there an automatic pilot?'

'No.' Came Ruuth's voice.

'How did it work then?'

'It didn't. It was the V20 which was guiding us.'

'I don't believe this, someone pinch me and wake me up, please. If there is no automatic pilot I cannot set it to crash into the planet.'

'No.' Said Ruuth's voice. There was an awkward silence while I glowered at Djon. Then Ruuth's voice again. 'But you can calculate a drive burn and duration to let the moon's and the planet's gravity pull it around and into the surface.' What a woman. A great idea.

'That is one mighty calculation.'

'I'll help you.' Came her helpful voice again. 'Patch in the secondary panel for me back here. There is a calculator in it.' I searched round for the patch panel but was interrupted by Djon.

'Don't bother looking for it, it isn't there. I'll swap with Ruuth.' He got up out of his seat as he spoke. I let myself just sink down onto the floor, my head in my hands. I could have screamed but that would have been unprofessional. I picked myself up again and set to with the calculations using the V20 to plot the orbits of the planet and the moon and the vessel. Ruuth joined me and the numbers began to fly. We needed a small-time delay before operation. Ruuth then wired in a simple digital clock from the control panel to the drive control so all I had to do then was push the right button when we left the ship. It took longer than I had hoped. I was very concerned that we were spending longer here than would be good for my plan; it would not look as though we flew straight round the moon and back out to crash into the planet. I began to get testy. Finally we got finished to everyone's relief.

'Done Djon. So, what about this vessel you have waiting for us?'

'Exactly.' He said from the doorway. 'If I now just get this remote I can turn on the transponder so we can find it.' As he spoke he dug into his pockets and pulled out a small silver box a few millimetres thick and the size of his palm. He tapped the surface of the box. 'OK, now she should be visible.' Again as he spoke another purple dot appeared in the galaxolabe not far from our red dot. 'There she is Djim, now get us there and we can get out of this and into some decent accommodation. I hope your plan will work.' He added.

'So do I, so do I.' I turned us towards the purple dot and in no time at all a shape appeared on the vision enhancer in front of us. As we rapidly approached it grew larger and more distinct. I thought it had the outline of a Jergan interstellar cruiser!

How could they afford one of those? Well, we would find out soon enough if it was. Now it was a question of getting us safely docked with the Jergan, if that was what it was. There was no assisted procedure here so it was down to me and my training. I fell silent with the concentration as the bulk of the other vessel grew larger and larger. The others fell silent too, realising the concentration required, after all they had built it with no assistance programmes! Some rudimentary array appeared in the vision enhancer so we had a limited docking system in this thing. That was good; it would have been very tricky without that. The docking system was also switched on in the other craft too, it would have been impossible had Djon not switched that on remotely. I set about aligning the two sets of coloured lines, which meant we would be aligned for docking. This was awkward with no countdown numbers to aid me. It was all done by sight! And I had no idea how big the other vessel was! The solar panels! They are a standard size I recalled so all I had to do was concentrate on one of them for a while to gauge the size. It was bigger than I thought; it must be a Jergan then! It began to get fun, hand guiding us; it was like being in the simulator at pilot college when systems are down.

Then we were docked. I could feel the connection tremble through the fabric of our moon hopper and also feel the bolts closing. It was always a satisfying feeling. It meant safety, usually. I am not sure that was the case here though.

'Does this Jergan have all its components?' I asked

'Don't worry Djim.' Replied Ruuth. 'The Jergan is complete, it isn't a hand-built job like this was. We would not dare to build something as big and complex as that.'

No more words were necessary now, everyone had felt the connection and we all began to get our things together to disembark. I set the controls and set the delay programme in operation. I just hoped it all worked properly.

'OK, guys we have 30 minutes.' Even this was unnecessary, we had agreed the time while we were setting up the programme. For people who had not worked together before we managed to smoothly get ourselves out of the moon hopper and into the Jergan, this was testament to the basic training everyone receives.

We had barely got ourselves aboard our new home and sealed ourselves in when we all felt the moon hopper disengage. We all automatically made our way to the control room. This was a much grander room than the previous one. I was familiar with the room and the layout from simulations in training and the standard layout of all craft, but it was better in the flesh. Because of this standardisation it had the same look as the moon hoppers control room even down to the location of the controls; they were all in the same place. There were just a few more, that was all. This was supposed to improve safety in space. I just stood and looked round, running my hand over the fine fabric of the seats. I had never been in a control room that had been so beautiful before. I had seen the simulations of all control rooms, but the pictures had not conveyed the quality. Djon pushed me out of the way.

'Come on Djim, we haven't time to stand around.' Embarrassed I realised he was right and slipped back into pilot mode. The floor had a soft finish like velvet. There were enough seats for all of us and more. The controls were already operational as Djon had started them up remotely before we disembarked. The vision enhancer was a far superior model and the detail of the old moon hopper was better by far than we saw of the Jergan. A bright point of light appeared at the back of the moon hopper and it began to slowly move away from us.

At last we were safe and could get away from this dreadful moon.

Then suddenly from outside there was an even brighter searing glare!

– CHAPTER 3 –

STARS ARE MUCH FURTHER

The vision enhancer closed down protectively and alarms shrieked out warnings!

All the dials on the control panel suddenly flashed up in red instead of the gentle greyed out light level of normal flight. This was something I had never seen before. I was only used to the odd dial blinking into yellow or occasionally red for danger.

The drive engines of the moon hopper had obviously fired prematurely!

The shock waves sent us sprawling across the room. My foot caught on something and I went down hard to the floor hitting my head on something hard. There was the sound of crashing and falling objects. Djon fell across my legs but as my head was still smarting from the blow I did not feel a thing. He let out a horrible groan as he rolled off my legs. I felt some warm blood trickle down the side of my face. There was no time to stop and look at it though, we had to act.

As I recovered from the initial shock and fall I began to become aware of the vessels responses to the tragedy. I could feel the power of the drive flares of the moon hopper melting the polymetals and metaplastics, I could imagine the globules of molten materials spinning wildly off into space and the edges of the rapidly enlarging holes running with glassious material. I could almost see the vulnerable interior elements being exposed and vapourised, the self healing properties of the fabric desperately trying to close the wounds. Ghas, the training videos of such a disaster clearly running through my thought! I tried not to think of the vital fluids being discharged uselessly into the void as I crawled to the controls as quickly as I could.

With another groan Djon hauled himself into another of the seats, his training also kicking in. I must get us away from the drive flare as soon as I could or we would all be fried by the blast as the moon hopper accelerated past us!

Warning buzzers joined the shriek of the other alarms as I hauled myself into the pilot's seat. I could hear the safety hatches snapping shut in response to the distress signals the vessel was sending around its internal systems. I could hear the others behind me shouting. 'What have you done Djim, I thought you knew what you were doing?!' and 'What the ghas is going on here?' But I was too busy to answer.

I had to get this beautiful craft out of danger.

The emergency lessons from the simulations came flooding back into thought. Fortunately, Djon had woken up the controls remotely and we therefore needed very little time to get moving. There was no time to plan a trajectory or set up the flight controls.

As the drives powered up and the vibrations rippled through the craft, I set us moving away as quickly as the Jergan would go. It seemed impossibly slow, but I made myself think that in reality we were actually beginning to move at a colossal speed. I heard the nictitating shutters slam shut to protect the windows and vulnerable equipment on the exterior of the hull. The artificial dimness of the vision enhancer, which had now begun to operate again, gave a false sense of the danger we were in by not showing the true level of illumination outside, even though it had a warning signal flashing in the corner indicating such. But gradually I could feel the fearful vibration from the moon hopper's drives blasting the hull begin to fade. I began to relax but then the collision sensor buzzed into life. The Jergan was warning us that we were heading at great speed towards the moon below us! The damage warning screen flashed into life. I switched it off. I did not want even more graphical images of the damage inflicted on our vessel, save that for later.

'What the ghas are you trying to do Djim? Kill us all?'

'Not likely Djon. I am trying to get us away from the flare

of the moon hopper's drives. They fired too early! Are you sure you put it together correctly?'

The collision sensor still buzzed annoyingly. I finally fired the anti-gravity gyros and the de-acceleration thrusters. I hoped the anti-crash system was working. Thank goodness we were in the Jergan and not the hand-built moon hopper with half the bits missing.

'We are going to have to land on Erebus 421 I am afraid.' I said as I set up the landing programme. I manually reset the vision enhancer to normal and immediately a bright searing spot of light appeared. The drive of the moon hopper, fortunately now rapidly receding from us.

'I just hope the rest of it works.'

'What are you implying.' Said Ruuth. 'We built that properly'.

'Yes, but Djon turned off some valuable systems there, or didn't install them at all. What was turned off or not installed? It is very dangerous to fiddle with any of the systems, they all interlink. It may be that was what caused the premature firing of the drives. Now we have a more pressing problem, we need to check the hull of this craft. Do you know what to do?' There were some grudging grunts of assent.

I continued to lower the craft gently onto the moon's surface. Something I never thought I would ever do. Ever since I was a young lad I had had a morbid dislike of this black moon. In fact, I would always avoid looking at it if at all possible, and now here we were landing on the infernal place! I had no idea how quickly our vessel would take to start sinking into the soft crust of the moon. I hoped it was a reasonable time as we might not be able to take-off again if our landing gear had been swallowed. Best not to think about it.

A Jergan was not normally intended to land, but like all space craft it had a rudimentary landing gear just in case a landing was necessary – just like it was now! I had to think for a while before I remembered where the controls were located. I hoped I would find them in time. A crash landing would damage even more of our precious hull. Fortunately, I found the control in time and heard and felt the landing gear folding out into operational mode through the fabric of the hull.

Only moments later a bump signified that we had landed. I looked round. The others had gone. No one noticed the rather poor landing hopefully.

More alarms began to sound: hull integrity alarm, pressure alarms, fire alarm. The damage seemed extensive. I went to join the others. The smell of burnt plastics, metaplastics and hot metals filled my nostrils as I walked warily down the corridor. Fire extinguisher dry vapours punched the air with staccato bursts somewhere ahead. Groans and moans confirmed that the self healing apparatus was working and remoulding the vessel's fabric as best it could.

I investigated the first room and found Ruuth at a panel. I could hear the other two calling instructions to each other and then Djon's voice leapt out at us from the wall speaker. 'There's a lot of damage down here, we're going to have to seal off some rooms to prevent any further loss of environment. Can you isolate rooms five to seven?'

'OK, Djon.' Replied Ruuth. 'I am going to seal off some space up here too.' She continued to tap onto the keyboard on the wall. The door into the room behind hissed as the seal activated. Immediately the atmosphere improved, or was that my imagination? 'That will give us some time to sort out the problems anyway.'

Ruuth had finished and stood beside me. She was almost as tall as me and had piercing blue eyes I noticed for the first time. We stood looking at each other for a moment. I had never seen a woman like her before on Enceladus and it made me feel funny inside, but I had no idea why. 'We had better get back to the control room and assess the damage.' I said, not knowing what else to say. We walked back to the control room. The alarms had stopped their ear-splitting shrieking, but the warning lights still flashed. A series of warnings and damage alerts scrolled down the vision enhancer.

'I'll send out the drone.' I said and sat back down in the pilot's seat. Ruuth sat down in the co-pilot's seat beside me, the stress of the last few moments showing on her face and in her eyes. She smoothed back her dark hair away from her face.

'What do you want me to do now?' She asked. I had to think back through the training courses and simulations. Then the solutions came flooding back and I automatically began to snap out some quick commands while I got the drone sent out. The drone was a particularly useful remote-controlled craft for working outside the vessel without sending anyone into space. It was equipped with high resolution cameras, grabbing arms, etc. Other tools could be attached as necessary. It was primarily used for initial inspections or intercraft package delivery or any number of other useful jobs.

The images sent back by the drone flickered into life on the small screen on the control panel. I pressed a button and the images flashed up into a part of the vision enhancer and suddenly we were looking at a large picture of the hull of the Jergan. At first it was the normal shiny black finish showing the untouched solar collector surface but then as the drone moved down along the hull it began to get greyer and blacker and then space black before the shattered holes appeared in the outer skin. There were globules of fused and melted polymetals and metaplastics that had dripped and solidified in long rivulets. Tubes and pipes were exposed or hung smashed and broken, exposed to the vacuum of space, our protection to the harsh environment outside stripped back to a frighteningly thin veneer in places. It is a terrifying sight for any astronaut, especially if you are a pilot and not a mechanic. Your home damaged and at the mercy of the vacuum of space and exposing the delicate interior to the cosmic rays and other harmful radiations that pervade the galaxy.

I recorded the images for study later so we could decide on a course of action. Ruuth was busy with the actions I had demanded of her. She seemed very efficient and knowledgeable and was not requiring further explanations. I became glad that these were the people I was trapped in space with. I just hoped our ruse would work and that the moon hopper had drawn away attention and not landed anywhere inhabited. I went through the calculations in my head as I worked just to make sure it would fall to planet. Our ruse must work as we would need time to make good the repairs before going anywhere, and we could do without any unpleasant visits.

'How is the magnetic shield?' Asked Ruuth.

'It is fine.' I replied gratefully. The vessel produced a magnetic shield that replicates the magnetosphere of habitable planets which protect life from the solar winds and other dangerous particles that speed through space.

Djon and Terens returned and slumped into two of the empty seats. 'Table up' Said Djon as he came in. From the ceiling behind the control panel a table slowly and silently began to drop. The seats in the control room were set in a crescent shape and for flight controls faced outwards but could be spun round to face inwards and were then arranged around the table, which had now dropped to operational height. Set in the surface was a control panel. Djon tapped onto the keypad and an image of the Jergan sprang into life above the table's surface. It showed the damage that the clique computer knew of from the internal sensors and also as relayed from the drone. The clique computer was a contraction of the proper full name of the computer family known as the chrystal light quantum computers, which used slow light or dark state technology. Yet more technology that I did not profess to understand.

Down one side was a large chunk of the vessel highlighted in red – like a big bite had been taken out of the hull – showing the damaged parts. The flashing red sections showed the real danger areas requiring immediate repair. It looked bad, but then it always did (so the training simulations said). The same simulations helped me to control the rising panic. Here, this was not a training exercise and if we did not get it right we would be subject to a rather slow and painful death. Still, it gave me the knowledge to know how to get things under control.

'The good thing.' Said Djon. 'Is that it hit the right side of the vessel. The essential stuff is mostly on the undamaged side, so we still have food and materials for repairs.'

'That is good news. Do we have enough for the hull repairs?' Asked Ruuth.

'That I cannot tell yet. Hold on.' Djon tapped out on the keypad again. Gradually figures and numbers appeared in the ovoid shape containing the image of the vessel. Lines connected the information to various parts of the damaged areas. It was a list of the damage with part numbers for replacements. It was a worryingly long list. 'Terens, would you mind going to find out what we have in the way of materials? I'll patch this information through to the stores.'

'Sure thing Djon.' He got up and left the room. Ruuth continued to work at the control panel after having a short look at the miniature Jergan hovering over the table. Out in the remote parts of the galaxy colonisation everyone is well trained in all aspects of spacecraft repair. It is a safety measure and formed a big part of schooling. So even though Terens and Ruuth were not directly involved in space flight normally, they knew the basics. The standardisation of spacecraft suddenly made a lot of sense rather than a useful theory. We might get through this in one piece after all.

'OK, guys let's get busy.' I said.

*

Two days later we had made big strides in the repairs. The self healing parts of the interior had helped reduce the loss of fluids and gases, but there were still a lot of damaged parts that would have to stay damaged for some time. There were still repairs to be made as we go. We sat down around the table to discuss the plan of action. The V20 had been set up and was shimmering over the table. It showed the galaxy. It showed our location. Djon called up the inhabited planets.

'Are any of these planets called Ulma thingy?' I asked.

'It's Ultima Thule, Djim.' Replied Djon levelly. 'And no. None of the inhabited planets that we know are called that. But it doesn't mean to say that maybe one has changed its name in the last few hundred years.'

'We keep coming back to why? Why would anyone want to hide an original planet? Why not celebrate it? It's always more questions than answers.'

'Exactly.' Said Djon. 'We want answers.'

'And that is what I have not found in the galaxy.' Added Terens laconically.

'So, what do we do now?' asked Ruuth.

'More importantly.' I said. 'Is how the ghas do we leave here and go anywhere without drawing attention to ourselves or your quest?'

'Good questions. The second first. Once we can leave the local space of our planet then we should be relatively safe. As far as I know there is no integrated system for tracking us across the galaxy or any form of integrated intelligence apparatus to check up on us. You have been across a lot of the galaxy Terens what is your assessment of this?'

Terens thought for a moment before answering. 'In my experience you are right. There is no central control of the galaxy that I know of.'

'The colonisation seems to be a loose association of planets with no one particularly concerned over the whole.' Added Ruuth. 'There is no reason to be. This will be most helpful to us as there is no effective control over who comes and goes. Even though there are many people who travel between planets there is no perceived risk. And this should be useful to us as well.'

'So, we won't be obvious then?' I asked.

'No.' Replied Terens. I was expecting more from him but it never came.

'There must be some form of central control.' I said. 'Who controls all the huge amounts of trade and organises all the collections and deliveries? After all, our raw materials go somewhere and products come back.'

'That is a business enterprise. There is no form of central checking on who is where or why. It would be an almost impossible task considering the size of the galaxy.' Replied Ruuth. 'People are different to products.'

'How many inhabited planets are there Djon?' Asked Terens.

'I think there are about four thousand that are really well

populated. There are some others that have a few miners or small societies or even recluse societies on local moons or other planets within the same solar systems as the major inhabited planets. Only the major ones have a portal. You have to travel through normal space to, if I can call it that, to reach the minor settled planets or moons.' The four thousand or so well populated planets are these.' Djon tapped on the keypad on the table and a myriad of small yellow dots appeared in the miniature galaxy. 'The major inhabited planets.'

We looked at the dots hanging in the mass of stars strung out throughout the galaxy. The enormity of the task seemed to suddenly dawn on Djon as he looked at the dots. What had seemed like an easy little jaunt while on the surface of a planet took on another dimension out here in the vastness of space.

'How are we going to check all those planets?' He asked almost to himself rather than us. No one spoke. We all had the same question and did not have an answer.

'All we need to do.' I finally suggested. 'Is to find the oldest inhabited planet. That should be the one. So, does anyone know which is the oldest inhabited planet then?' This was not a simple question we knew. There was extraordinarily little history of the galaxy available. Considering the length of time that we have lived in the universe we know truly little about the past or even how the colonisation of the galaxy took place or who was involved. History was not a subject taught in school but had never been missed and had certainly not bothered me, until now. It then became strange that that we knew so little about our past, but that was just the way things had always been. We must look forward not back my old teacher had said. That made me think that perhaps I may have asked the question when I was younger.

'The most populated planet that I know of....' He stopped as he tapped again on the keypad and some figures and numbers appeared by one of the yellow dots. '...is Fyrest Prime D20...'

'Isn't that where your family originated?' Interrupted Ruuth.

'A long time ago, yes, hence my name is Djon-20-N421.

The '20' referring to my family origins.'

'Yes, but is it the oldest inhabited planet?' Asked Terens.

'I don't know.' Said Djon. 'But we could start there. Maybe they have some more information.'

'Isn't Fyrest Prime a bit close to the Arachnid Looped nebula?' I queried.

'Not in galactic terms no. It is perfectly safe otherwise it would not have survived all these years. That myth seems to have been around for years, but it is not true. Look at me, I am fine and so has been my family.'

'It seems a good place to start then.' Said Terens. 'But how do we get there?'

'Our first problem is to get to the portal here and to the next without being spotted. How do you intend to do that?' I asked.

'I think we can disguise ourselves as a dumb freighter.'

'What!' I spluttered. 'We are a fraction of the size of a freighter and we do not have the right transponders or ...'

'Hold on Djim.' Ruuth put her hand on my arm as she interrupted. 'I have worked for the governing body and have had a trip to the satellite and seen the control of traffic.'

'You must be in with the upper echelons then.' I said huffily. 'No one normally is allowed in such august places.'

'I know. I do not know how it happened. I must have been nice to someone. However, what I noticed was that no one bothers looking out of the windows. It is all done by instruments and ticking freight through. It is the most boring job, and no one is too fussed over checking too deeply. There is nothing to look for after all. There is very little crime here if you remember and nothing to smuggle. Everyone has a good life and all their needs are catered for. I do not think it will be any trouble at all. All we need to do is get ourselves from here to the portal unseen. That will be the more difficult part. I do not know how to do that. I can fabricate a transponder signal to fool the space traffic control at the portal but that is it.'

'Right then, we need a plan to get us there.' Djon looked round at us all but spent most time looking directly at me! No one spoke for a long time.

'I still have some issues though.' I began. 'Firstly, we can't just go without trying to get a message to my family, my mother in particular. It is not fair that we just go. Secondly Djon, how did you manage to escape that attack in your office and who the ghas was it?' Djon looked across at Terens and took his time answering.

'Well to be honest Djim, I have already left a timed message with your mother.'

'What! How the ghas did you know I would come on this escapade? That's ..' I spluttered to a halt not knowing how to continue. But Terens interjected into my apoplexy.

'As for how Djon escaped. He did not. It's just that I got him out first.' He did not look at me as he spoke but across at Djon. I was so incensed at Djon's audacity to assume that I would come with him that I did not pursue how he did it.

'It's the plan at how we get from here to the portal that we need to agree now.' Interrupted Djon. There was a further silence as I tried to calm down and the others thought of a plan to get us away from this light sapping moon. Perhaps it was the black moon that was poisoning my thought towards Djon. Perhaps it would be better to get away before deciding what to do next. Getting away from this dread moon became my highest priority now. It gave me an incentive to start thinking again.

'I have an idea.' I said finally. 'Often the unmanned freighters do drift out of the correct trajectory. They pull them back from the satellite and set them off through the portal. That will be the tricky bit, not going too far off course because if we do, they will send a drive unit over to pick us up and then our cover will be blown. I don't know if they do a visual check when a freighter drift happens, but judging by what Ruuth was saying I think it is unlikely. All we need to do is drop down from here to near the surface and then veer off away from the planet. With the transponder they will just pick us up and drag us to the portal.' There was another silence.

'It could work Djon.' Said Ruuth quietly.

'It looks as though we have no other plan. Will the pilots on duty notice anything?'

'No.' I replied. 'They will be too busy. I would not notice one odd freighter.' I felt as though I should be putting up more of a fight, but the will just vanished like mist in sunshine as soon as the thought arose.

'OK.' Replied Djon finally. 'We will go with that as we have no other plan. Will they notice us as we come round this miserable moon?' he asked no one in particular.

'I think if we can keep as close as possible as we come round planetside and head planetwards in a direct line we should be alright.' I said, but it was dubious. I was almost hoping we would get caught. That would show Djon. But then I thought better of it and decided that indeed it was the only way we would get to the portal without being seen and perhaps it was the best thing to do in the circumstances. It was possible he was right anyway.

'OK, let us make it happen.' Said Djon. 'The sooner we get started the sooner we can get away from here.' We all agreed with that sentiment and immediately everyone got up and set to work. Although we had only been together for a short while we worked as a team in a remarkably enmeshed way. But then we all wanted to get away from the moon, so it was hardly surprising. We got ready in record time.

*

When the forward vision enhancer and the other controls showed that take-off was now ready, I looked across at the others and Djon nodded. This would test if we had managed to make half decent repairs. The dull almost inaudible rumble of the anti gravity gyros was suddenly eclipsed by the roar of the drive. I could feel the power of the drive vibrating through the vessel as it tried to lift the huge bulk of our vessel from the surface of this accursed moon.

Then suddenly the drive cut out!

I could feel the drive powering down and the gyros slowing. Then my eye caught sight of a small red warning light blinking on the edge of the control panel. What had gone wrong now? As if listening to my though Djon asked. 'What is going on Djim? Why have you shut down the drive?'

'I haven't' I replied tersely. 'It shut down all by itself.'

'Why?' I did not even bother replying but just pointed to the warning light still blinking away.

'Oh.' He said. Then added. 'What does it mean?' I looked up at the forward vision enhancer and found the repeater data displayed and called up the details to be displayed on screen. We all looked as the details scrolled down the screen. It showed excessive stress building in the landing gear.

'Ghas.' I muttered.

'What does it mean Djim?'

'It means everyone I think our landing gear has sunk into the surface of this dreadful moon and the suction and surface tension is preventing us from taking off.' Ruuth immediately sprang into action and prepared the drone for a visual release run. Moments later as the drone powered away from the hull of our vessel the pictures from the onboard cameras appeared on the screen. At first it was blackness with a few stars moving across the view. The stars were not moving of course it was the drone rotating. Then the hull came into view. With a reference point I was able to lower the drone. The hull images slid silently up the screen to be replaced by the undercarriage and then the large feet. We all drew in breath simultaneously as we saw the feet. Even the large flat spreaders had not prevented them from being sunk unto the soft crust of the moon. The matt blackness oozed over the bright shiny metal effectively trapping us on the surface.

'No wonder there is never any evidence of asteroid impacts.' Muttered Terens quietly.

'What do we do now?' Asked Ruuth with just the hint of worry in her voice.

'We have to cut ourselves free.' I said. 'The vessel will not allow us to rip off the landing gear and leave it behind.'

'So, we have to go EVA.' Said Djon. 'Let us go then.'

'OK' I said rather dejectedly, 'an EVA is required.

'How long will this take?' Asked Ruuth.

'Why?'

'We will lose the window of darkness on the planet's surface if we are too long.'

'I know.' I said. 'But we do not know how long it will take. If necessary, we may have to wait until tomorrow or even the next day!' The thought of staying a second longer was complete anathema to me but we had no choice. Djon was already on the way to the suit room.

'No, Djon. I called. 'I'll go. I know what to do. I have been trained for this.' He stopped in mid stride and turned.

'OK.' He said. 'I'll help you into the suit, now come on we mustn't waste time.' I was up and out of the seat and following him in an instant. I needed no more encouragement.

In the shortest time ever, I was suited up and found myself standing frozen into immobility on the threshold of the external hatchway. My hands were gripping the edge of the hatchway in a vicious death grip. I had never experienced this before. But before me and without anything to block or interfere with the view was Erebus 421. While I had been looking up at the pitch black of space there had been no problem. But as soon as I lowered my gaze then something happened. Suddenly I had gone from comfortable warmth in the suit to a shivering sweaty state. In front of me was the completely smooth surface of the moon stretching without feature to the horizon. The light sapping blackness of the surface was not like the blackness of space, it just did not seem right that any moon should be so featureless and non reflective. It was impossible to locate yourself as there was absolutely nothing to focus on. It was like looking down into the proverbial bottomless pit of oblivion.

But others depended on me now so with supreme effort I looked up into the star filled blackness of familiar space and then jumped out of the hatchway. This was something that was instilled to never do when leaving a vessel, but I could do nothing else. Fortunately, with the gravity pull being only twenty percent of standard there should be no danger but as I floated gently away from the hull I had the nasty thought that maybe I had misjudged the distance I could fall before the arrest system slowed me down. With nothing to focus on there was no way of knowing how high I was above the surface. I had only the basic dimensions from the manual to go on to know the height to ground level. Then I began to slow down as the system began to slow me to a controlled descent.

It was very unusual to be in a gravity situation and outside a vessel like this. Although the gravity pull was not one standard pull it was still sufficient to make it awkward.

Finally, I found myself on the surface, it had come upon me suddenly and not unexpectedly without warning. I managed to turn my foot over as I landed and cursed loudly. That brought a worried response from inside which I managed to laugh off. I did not want them worried. I turned to the job in hand but could hardly think straight, this was the last place I ever had wished to be.

The feeling was very spooky indeed.

I was sweating inside the suit even though the temperature was set to normal. The matt black of the surface was barely distinguishable from the matt black sky of space and the dull surface of the vessel bulging out above me. It was only the absence of stars in the sky that gave any indication of the position of our vessel above me. The portable lights suddenly dropped down beside me and blazed into light. I grabbed hold of them and pulled the tripod legs out and placed them on the ground. The light illuminated a pathetically small amount of ground in front of me. It was as if this dreadful moon was sapping all the energy of the photons or converting them to darkness. This could not be I told myself. Just get on with the task.

I stumbled forward to the edge of the huge foot. The blackness oozed over the edge of the foot like treacle over a spoon. Then the enormity of the task hit me. The feet of the vessel were at least six metres long and there were three of them. It took all my will power to reach down and touch the surface of the moon. It felt very solid. There was no way that I could hack all this stuff off from around the feet in time. My shoulders drooped within the suit.

'You are very quiet Djim.' Came Ruuth's voice over the suit intercom.

'I think the task ahead is a bit too much. The crust of the moon has oozed over the feet and it is surprisingly hard stuff. Obviously geologically speaking it is very soft to allow us to sink so far in such a short time but to dig it away is going to be tough!' There was a long pause from the vessel. I felt very alone and vulnerable. I could feel the movement of the moon's surface beneath my feet. I was sure if there had been an atmosphere I would have heard it groaning as it flowed ever so slowly over our vessel. Gradually oh so gradually our vessel would be sucked into the interior of the moon until it vanished forever. I looked up at the landing gear. They were like giant versions of the feet on old fashioned sewing machines that fed the thread through. A massive pivot allowed the feet to take up the lie of the land. Then an idea struck me.

'Djon!'

'Yes, Djim.' Crackled his reply.

'Get me three of the explosive charge shells and the polymetal tape and lower them down.'

'Sure thing Djim, but what do you intend to do?'

'I intend to blow off the feet!'

'What!'

'Trust me Djon just hurry up and do it we do not have much time. The longer we stay here the worse it gets!'

'Sure thing Djim if you are sure.'

'I am sure, Djim.'

'Just give me a moment.' He added without further question. He knew to trust me, which was a great relief in this place and took a load off my mind. We needed to act quickly; a moment on this horrid place was like an eternity.

Eventually to my great relief a bundle descended on the wire. I grabbed it almost feverishly and tore open the container and ripped out the three charges and the tape. The suit seemed to make every move last ten times longer than it should be but eventually I had the charges fixed to the pivots and I was being winched back up into the vessel. I did not look down. If those charges did not blow those pivot pins out of their housings then we were doomed. Besides, I dare not look down at that moon again.

In fact, I never ever wanted to see it again.

Once inside I collapsed on the floor and lay there panting from the sheer emotional exhaustion of being out there on the surface.

'Right, back to the control room.' I finally managed to blurt out as I staggered to my feet. A worried Djon hurried along beside me. I ran into the control room finally back in control of myself and shouted out orders as I flung myself in the pilot's seat. The others thankfully leapt into action.

'Right, as soon as the anti-gravity gyros have the weight of the vessel, we blow the charges and then power up the drive. We must not let the legs sink into the surface or we will never get off here!

We gently powered up the engines and the anti-gravity gyros so that we were straining to get away. 'Now!' I shouted. There was a shudder from outside and sudden movement. At the same time I powered up the main drive.

Moments later the roar of the drive and the data scrolling down the screen confirmed that we had finally broken free of the moon. It had tried its best to trap us there for ever but had not succeeded. I breathed a huge sigh of relief as the data showed us moving away from the surface. We all cheered spontaneously.

'Let us get out of here.' I said as we ascended to orbital height.

When it was dark side on the planet below us, we ventured out from behind the moon. The air was tense in the control room as we watched the vision enhancer intently for any sign that we had been spotted from the surface below. The great curve of the planet's surface filled most of the forward vision enhancer and the thermal imaging highlighted any settlements or drive flares below. The surface was dark as all the habitation was on the other side of the planet. So far so good but this was a long journey and there was no cover. We headed directly back towards the planet. No one generally came anywhere near the parts of the planet where Erebus could be seen. It was mostly superstition but now I was really thankful for that. The hours slid almost silently by. They were some of the tensest hours that I had ever spent. We barely spoke to each other.

The trajectory numbers scrolled in the corners of the screen and the direction indicators hovered centrally. No one spoke. I hardly dared breathe. We watched the numbers and indicators to when we could start 'drifting' away from the planet. Then the settlement came into view on the surface below, highlighted by the thermal imaging and the indicators silently displayed the sudden radio traffic that was now detectable. We almost stopped breathing again but no drive flares headed for us and none of the sensors indicated any scanning of us even though we were expecting at any moment the lights to flash and the buzzers to sound. All remained quiet except for the sound of our laboured breathing. We dared not turn on the V20. Its operation could possibly be sensed from the ground and alert someone below that we were there. I was driving by other instruments and hoped I was on course.

My hands were shaking slightly, and I was perspiring by the effort and concentration. We would switch on the transponder that Ruuth had rigged up when closer to the normal cargo routes. The surface of the planet got closer and closer. Uncomfortably close it seemed. It filled the view ahead and the glows from the settlement got closer and closer. Surely someone must have seen us by now? The control room got more and more tense. We had to keep our cool. Without the V20 we could only see the dumb freighters by their drive flares. Then we saw two of them rising up from the planet's surface. That was not good news. Three freighters together may cause some suspicion. It was too late to back out now though, any attempt to change direction would give us away immediately.

We seemed to be getting impossibly close to civilisation and possible detection, uncomfortably close it seemed. I was hoping that the space flight traffic to the satellite was so normal that one extra flight would not be noticed. It was nerve wracking, and I was close to wrenching the controls to take us away from the lights ahead. Fortunately, the clique computer then decided it was time for us to start to 'drift'. The direction indicators started to move away from the centre of the screen, the numbers scrolled in negative. With shaking hands I followed the direction indicators to keep them lined up with the vector organiser.

'I just hope that the satellite controls will work on this ship.' Said Terens. His voice, even though barely above a whisper sounded like a claxon warning everyone down on the planet that we were there. Then we all realised that no one could hear us talk. We relaxed just a little.

'Don't worry Terens.' I replied. 'As soon as the satellite starts to pull us back we will make the right moves.'

'Won't they notice we are too far away?'

'We hope not.' Said Ruuth, almost to convince herself. She seemed to be speaking so close she was almost inside my head. I then noticed that we were all huddled together around the active controls like children around a toy box. 'They do not usually check that sort of detail. If they do then we are doomed.'

When we had almost given up hope that our plan would work there was a beep and a light flickered faintly on the control panel. We all started, and everyone pointed to it and then looked sheepish for being so silly.

'At least they have spotted us.' I said unnecessarily and began to change direction with the thrusters, hopefully just what was expected on the satellite. The direction indicators shifted back across the screen as Djon altered the vector and destination on the control panel. Without the V20 it was difficult to know exactly where we were going. We needed the vision enhancer to show up the satellite. I just hoped we were headed in the right direction. Then there was a sigh as it appeared on screen. I wiped the back of my hand across my brow to stop the sweat trickling into my eyes. We took it in turns to stare at the screen and keep the dim smudge of the satellite in the centre of the vector indicators. It was hard on the eyes. Then as it grew closer it became easier to see. The drives of the other freighters were two bright dots of light. Then one vanished as it went through the portal. Then soon after that the other one vanished.

'Get ready' I said, 'As soon as we get to the portal we will need to be quick or we will end up with the other freighters.' The others moved to their stations to enact the plan of action. I suddenly felt cold and alone as they moved away; it did not last long as the concentration required for the looming portal obliterated everything else. It was a vast ring of slowly rotating drones held together by a quantum-electro-magnetic force. This one was the exit portal. There was another identical portal for incoming vessels nearby. Was it the exit though? I had a sudden fear we were heading for the wrong one! Then I relaxed again. No, we had seen the other freighters disappear, that meant an exit portal. Then I remembered that an exit portal was indicated by the red shift in the spectrum as light was sucked away from us. The entry portal was blue shifted. There were strict rules governing vessel movements near portals and had we been heading for the blue portal then all Erebus would have been unleashed. Then we would have been noticed! Also, an entry portal would have the vessels drive flares suddenly appearing. In my panic I had forgotten all this.

As we went through we had to take control of our destination, which was not where the freighters were going. We were heading for a small planet near Fyrest Prime. We did not think it wise to head straight there. As soon as went through the portal we would need to switch on the V20. Instantly! If we did not, we would end up with the freighters. I would have to do it just a fraction before we went through-while we were still in the zone of influence- and hope no one noticed the brief signal.

The screen indicators counted down to the portal. The tension mounted again. Was anyone watching us? I could feel the skin on the back of my neck tingle as though they were.

'Ten seconds to go.' I was not even sure who spoke. Nine seconds later the 'zone of influence' meter swung over so I switched on the V20, one second after that the portal activation beacon sounded and the vision enhancer went blank.

The portal was designed, so they say, to reduce the distance between itself and the next portal to a few metres. Someone once tried to explain it with a balloon. 'It's like this.' He said, and pinched the sides of the balloon together so his finger and thumb were touching. 'This is what the portal does to the space time continuum.' It was called ND-space, for Non-Dimensional space. There were no dimensions to this space. No material dimensions anyway. Distance became nothing. We were about to travel light years without travelling in the normal sense of the word.

Then it seemed as though we were falling down a deep dark well through a viscous atmosphere. No one knew why this happened either.

The V20 thankfully was operational and the familiar globe of light had sprung into being. I could hear the others beside me but they seemed to be a long way away. I slowly tapped out instructions on the control panel. Then gradually the vision enhancer came back on line like a thick fog clearing.

The falling sensation had stopped, and the stars came out again.

'Where are we?' Asked Djon thickly, there was a sense of desperation in his voice.

'Just a minute.' I checked the V20. I could see our dot. I could see the planet nearby. I called up the details and letters and figures appeared by the planet. I relaxed. 'We are near Midnight Twenty.'

A whoop went up. We all laughed out loud as the tension ebbed away. Then we fell back in our seats, just too tired to speak again for a while. We opened the external cameras and could see much more clearly the Arachnid Looped nebula. It would be much closer when we reached Fyrest.

Our moment of relaxation was interrupted by a lady's voice, which leaped out of the control panel. Somehow, I was not expecting anyone to notice our arrival, which was stupid really – but then I had never been to another planet before.

'Welcome to Midnight-20. It is twenty two hundred hours and ten Thursday 7th of May. Do you wish to dock at geostationary control?' I wondered why she had given the time and date and then I remembered back to pilot school – every time an occupied vessel used a portal the receiving space flight control always gave the time and date as there was the ever-present possibility of a time delay going through the portal. Sometimes it was a few minutes or rather a few minutes should be the norm. Occasionally this extended to an hour or two and sometimes it could be a few hours or more. In a very few cases it has been a few days. The problem is, no one knows why this should happen. It was thought to be something to do with the ND space that occurred during the portal's operation. I heard that some of the best minds in the galaxy had investigated this to try and eliminate the problem but with no success. It was a hazard of portal use. It was however a small price to pay to be able to move throughout the galaxy in a very short space of time. It would not be possible to colonise the galaxy without the portals as the time taken to travel through normal space would be absurdly long. Communication throughout the galaxy would also be impossible as messages travelling at the speed of light would not arrive during a person's lifetime! Who had invented the portals? As far as I could find out no one knew! It seemed to be lost in the mists of time. I always felt that was strange. A universally useful object as the portal would have hailed the inventor as a true genius of the galaxy. My questioning of this had caused some problems at work. But enough of this.

'Are we stopping?' I asked, completely at a loss what to reply. Relieved only that we had arrived safely and without a loss of time.

'No, we will go straight on to Fyrest Prime.' Replied Djon.

'No, thank you' I replied to the space flight control lady. 'We are going straight on to ....'

'Stop!' shouted Djon and grabbed my arm. He shook his head and whispered. 'Don't tell her where we are going.' I switched off the communication device.

'They will know where we are going because of the next portal we will need. We cannot avoid that. We could give a wrong portal but that could be awkward. I'm sure they have to dial in the receiving portal.'

'OK then.' He released my arm.

'Sorry about that.' I said to flight control. 'We will be moving on when we have recharged. Can you please give us a flight window in about two hours?'

'Thank you.' Came the voice again. 'I have a slot for you at twenty-four hundred hours. I will put you in. Please state receiving portal.'

I made a face at Djon. 'Receiving portal is Fyrest Prime.'

'Thank you. Be at co-ordinates MT 300/400 by twenty-three fifty. Please place your payment card in the reader. The charge for using the portal is one hundred galactic dollars.'

'Ghas, I had forgotten about portal payment.' Cursed Djon as he fished his card out of his pocket. He placed it in the reader on the control panel. The charge came up on the screen as being deducted. A receipt was received, and the card popped up again.

'Thank you. Is there anything else you require in the meantime? We can get a supply vehicle up to you in half an hour.'

'No thank you. We are fully stocked. We will just be at MT 300/400 at twenty-three fifty as required. Where can we wait?'

'Just wait where you are for now. We will give you ample warning for you to get into position. Thank you for visiting Midnight space. Goodbye.'

'OK, so we just have to wait again.' I said to the others. 'I suggest we have someone on watch at all times and while we wait the others get some food and some rest.' We did not need to be reminded a second time.

'And!' Added Ruuth loudly. 'We still need to do some more repair work so set your alarms.' We all nodded our agreement. It was the first time I actually saw Terens with a disgruntled expression on his face. So, the man does get tired after all I thought. He seemed almost robot like with his apparently inexhaustible supply of quiet unassuming energy.

'OK, Terens and I will take first watch, you and Ruuth go first. You have done us proud Djim.' I saw Terens give Djon a black look, but he said nothing and sat down heavily in his seat again. Ruuth and I went to the galley where there was a table, fixed seats and cooking facilities.

'I'll get the food. What do you want?' She asked as she waved me to sit down.

'Thank you I'll have the 41.' I sat at the table and watched her work. It was then that I realised that she was really quite attractive. She had dark hair that was tied up at the back today in two small buns, blue eyes and a pale skin, which indicated that she had at least spent some time in space before. She even managed to make the standard flight suit look interesting. I could have watched her for hours. Again, I had the strange feeling that I had before but did not know what it was or why I should be feeling it. I had worked with many women before but never had such a feeling. I put it to the back of my mind and looked at something else.

'Where are you from?' I finally asked, embarrassed. She did not stop working as she replied.

'I was originally from Galilei, which is in the same group as Fyrest. Hence my name.'

'Oh, what is that then?'

'My full name is Ruuth-400-N421. N421 is because officially I am now from Enceladus in the 421 group. The 400 is because my mother died and my father ...' She paused. 'I don't actually know what happened to my father. But when I was still very young, I was sent to relatives on Enceladus, which is where we met. And you?' She placed the plates down on the table and sat down opposite looking intently at me. It made me feel nervous and I was suddenly overcome with a strange shyness. I coughed.

'Very unremarkable, really. I have always lived on Enceladus, my mother, sister and brother are still there, and they must be wondering what has happened. I hope they are all right.'

'I'm sure they are Djim.' She said and touched my hand

comfortingly. It was like a shock wave coursing through me. I tried not to make it obvious what effect it had. But I did not know why it should. What was going on?

'Thank you.' I muttered. 'I hope you are right.'

'You haven't mentioned your father.' She said as she took another mouthful.

'My father disappeared on a routine space flight about twenty years ago.' I paused. 'And do you know what on Erebus Djon meant when he said that faster than light travel prior to the colonisation has been hidden?'

'Even working in Enceladus governing body I could not find that out. It was partly that that made me become an originist like Djon. As for the space travel: well to travel at the speed of light is, we know impossible. Any bit of space debris at that speed would just go straight through the ship and anyone in it. After no time the vessel and the occupants would be like a colander. And dead. Also.' She added. 'It would take too long. We are after all about twenty-eight thousand light years from the other side of the galaxy! That would mean twenty-eight thousand years to reach here from there! So, for the colonisation to have happened they must have been able to skip the distance like we do now, but without the portals.'

'That's impossible isn't it?'

'That's what is believed. But so many things do not add up, and I am sure Djon has raised a few of them with you. The dire shortage of history of the galaxy is also strange. The draconian penalties for infractions of the law are another anomaly.'

'You have to be fairly strong with a pioneering populace or there would be anarchy and riots.' I trotted out the usual answer.

'I know there is very little crime on Enceladus, but it was not just the harsh penalties. Everyone is well supplied and comfortable for an outpost like our planet. But there is something else which I just cannot put my finger on. We must find Ultima Thule. I am sure that it will hold the key to this riddle.' She had become quite animated and agitated. 'I would also like to find out what happened to my father.'

'Same here. I would like to find some answers. I would also like to find out what he had done. It does not seem right that we cannot find out why he became so withdrawn just before he disappeared. I was also imprisoned for nothing! Surely after so many years of man's existence we should be much more civilised than that?'

'I know.' She said awkwardly and I did not know why. Perhaps she was not used to being asked questions about her family or she was not sure of me yet. We lapsed into a thoughtful silence for a while. I felt the faint vibration of the ship through the table as we ate. I dare not look at her although I felt tempted to. She was not attractive in the standard sense but had a radiant inner beauty that spilled out to obscure the physical flaws. That strength and personality so shone through that it made her extremely attractive. I felt as though I should be asking her something, but the thoughts would not form. Then my father's warning came to mind, after all I had only just met these people no matter how nice looking they were. Silence again.

'Do you have any other family? Brothers or sisters?' I finally asked.

'No. I am an only child. My mother died before she could have any more.'

'I am sorry to hear that. One should have siblings and parents.' I felt awkward myself now and decided to change the subject. 'How did you come by this vessel? It isn't easy to buy interstellar vessels just like that.'

'I know.' She looked relived that I had changed the subject, fortunately. 'It helped that I was working in such a high position. I was able to hide a few things and disguise the transactions. Terens helped too. As he was used to travelling between planets he could bring it without being questioned. He hid it behind Erebus for us. I went and got him in the moon hopper.'

'Why did you need me then?'

'Neither of us is good pilots. It was almost a disaster. There was no way I was going to try that again. We agreed that we needed a proper pilot. That is why Djon wanted you along, we just had to be sure ...' She stopped.

'Sure of what?' I asked. She paused, biting her bottom lip gently.

'Sure that everything was right before leaving.' I felt that it was not the original answer she was about to give.

'I found the moon hopper difficult to fly so you did very well to get up there and back again in one piece.'

'Yes, it was the most unnerving thing I have ever done. I very nearly did not make it. I was cursing Djon all the time.'

'I bet you were. How come you need me again though? Terens can fly too?'

'I've told you my flying is very basic and so is Teren's. He should not really be flying between planets. He took a mighty risk too. Normally he goes with a pilot. We just had no choice.' She bit her bottom lip again. It made her look very attractive. I looked away.

*

All too quickly it seemed our break came to an end and we went back to take watch while Djon and Terens took their rest. I took my place in the pilot's seat and checked the controls and the time. I also checked the view outside and then the V20. All seemed normal as far as I could tell – not knowing the traffic routes of the planet. Ruuth sat next to me and checked the vessels other systems even though we knew that Djon and Terens had just been doing the same. It was automatic after any time away from the controls of a space vessel, even for a 'droob' (which was an astronaut's name for someone who lives on a planets surface and does not go into space).

'It's a while yet.' I said to break the silence. 'Let us listen to the local voice traffic.' I turned up the radio volume and a chatter began to fill the control room. It was the usual stuff, flight control instructions as we had had earlier, requests for supplies, requests for landings or dockings. Then the radar sensor bleeped suddenly!

'What's that?' Ruuth asked worriedly.

'I'm hoping it is the normal checking of our position and nothing more. If it does it again quickly then it could be something more.' We waited tensely, watching the sensor light. The proximity sensor then bleeped a different tone.

'Now what's that?' Ruuth jumped.

'I'm hoping that is someone coming through the portal.' I replied with what I trusted was exterior calmness, which belied an interior concern. I did not want to worry Ruuth unnecessarily. Sensors were usually going off in planet orbits. I checked the cameras' screens. There was one vessel nearby, which was the only one which could have set off the alarm. I zoomed in closer on the craft. It was small and probably then only a local vessel so had not come through the portal. It could just be a supplier, but then again it could be the satellite authority drone checking up on the vessels in orbit. If it was, then we could be called on to identify our destination and flight plan. Normally that would not be a problem but in our heightened state any questioning of our presence was a worry, even though we had broken no law. At least we had broken no law that I knew of. There was no restriction on moving in space or between planets. Or was there?

I became concerned that our transponder signal may cause an enquiry or someone may wonder why we have had the V20 on for long periods. I was hoping that space traffic controllers had other things to worry about. The proximity alarm ceased sounding and the vessel kept moving on without pausing or changing direction. But even that made me think it was a ruse to put us off the scent. It was a worry just hanging there above the planet.

The rest of our watch was uneventful but still stressful as was our repair shift. Every small noise made us jump or a sudden silence would make us look behind. I found myself nodding off so Ruuth suggested I get some rest. She would stay on watch for the short time left.

Sometime later I was woken from my nap by Terens.

'We've been given the signal to move.' He said and left. Typical of Terens, he did not normally hang around for small talk. I quickly got up from the couch and headed for the control room. It was empty except for Djon and Ruth and was lit dimly. His big frame filled the pilot's seat and was silhouetted against the vision enhancer. His white hair a halo above his head. He turned as I entered the room.

'Good, you're up.' He said and left the pilot's seat. 'We need to move into portal readiness.'

'OK. No problem.' I sat down and checked the controls. The vector indicators were already alive on the screen, the flight commencement indicators were counting down from signals emanating from space flight control. I started up the drives and matched our speed and direction to the indicators on the screen. Finally, we were on our way again. The relief was palpable. A bright spot appeared on the screen as a vessel fired up its drives in front of us. We would be next. I let the clique flight computer keep us aligned with the portal entry vectors as we drew nearer and nearer. Any moment now would come the call to abort the skip and return to orbit around Midnight as someone checked up on us. But it never came.

Again, the sudden feeling of falling as the screen went blank.

– CHAPTER 4 –

FYREST PRIME.

It hung in the blackness of space in front of us and we all just took in the view of the big majestic planet. It was blue and brown with white clouds hanging in the atmosphere, which formed a halo around the edge of the planet's surface. We were looking at the sunlit side, or rather the sunnier side. Behind it and spread out across the space black sky was the Arachnid Looped nebula, it was so close here that it illuminated the other side of the planet so there was never a dark night. There was a bright normal day and a dull reddish lit night. I had never seen it up so close before. From home it was quite small. But here it was a hugely majestic sight. I had never seen such a dramatic part of the universe at such relatively close quarters. The reddish light from the nebula lit by a hundred hot young stars at its centre would make for an interesting night sky. The space flight control voice crackled into life to bring us out of our reverie.

'Please move to location D20-310/425. Do you wish to dock?'

'Moving to D20-310/425. Yes, we wish to dock.'

'Do you wish to visit planet surface?'

'Yes, we will be visiting planet surface.'

'We will bring you into dock 10, please let us take control of your flight drives.'

'OK, switching to remote control when we reach D20-310/425.' I set up the co-ordinates in the flight plan and we slowly moved to the location they wanted. As we neared I set up the remote control system. Then there was a small jolt as the remote took over and we began to descend to dock ten.

Most planets had a geostationary docking platform to

prevent the surface being cluttered with space vessels and the pollution from the drives. It also meant that vessels could be designed purely for space flight. The flight down to the planet could either be by private shuttle, which many deep space vessels had or by public shuttle. The latter was more common as only the largest and most expensive vessels had the room for a personal shuttle. The skies over most planets were also very full of flying vessels of all sorts so it was generally safer to use the public shuttle. They were very frequent.

Now in front of us was the satellite. It was the biggest I had seen, with fifteen rings of docks each with twenty spaces for vessels. Each ring was joined to the others by a central spine. Most of the docking spaces were taken. I could see the bright flares of moving traffic in the vicinity; shuttles, deep space vessels, supply vessels, maintenance craft and the like. It was the busiest space dock I had ever seen. Not having been in such crowded places before I had a sudden sense of panic. Strange that I should feel this way. It was not anything that I had encountered before. I dare not mention this to the others as I felt too embarrassed. So many people would be in these vessels and in the satellite, probably there were more people up here than on the whole of Enceladus! I concentrated on the flight vector lines on the screen and the approaching dock to take my mind off the thought of all these people. The true scale of the structure began to dawn on me. It began to fill the entire view on our screen.

'How are we paying for this?' I asked and looked at Djon.

'I have the card. The originists we know of have clubbed together to not only buy this spacecraft but also to fund our mission. They will be asking for the card soon actually.'

As if on cue the ladies voice again crackled into life from the control panel.

'Please place your payment card in the slot in your control panel. The charge is two hundred Galactic Dollars a day plus portal use. How many days do you wish to stay?'

'By ghas, Djon that is steep. I hope your fellow originsts have stumped up enough for this trip.'

'I hope so Djim. Here take the card and insert it in the payment slot over there. Let them know we will be staying for two days. I hope that is also enough.'

'I would hope so too.' I took the card and dropped it into the slot. 'We will be staying two days.' I informed the lady from space flight control. She sounded genuinely nice but without a picture link it was not possible to tell.

'Thank you. That will be six hundred Galactic Dollars. You must clear the dock by twenty-four hundred hours on Saturday tenth May. Thank you. Enjoy your stay on Fyrest Prime. Do you require anymore services?'

'No thank you.' By now we were so close I could not make out the shape of the satellite and I could now see windows, the number ten of our dock, the nervate appearance of the outer skin and even people spacewalking. The forward vision enhancer told me it was initializing the guidance views, not something I had seen before and I assumed it must be part of the remote-control system here. Our progress slowed as we began to come in between two other much larger vessels. I could make out the markings and the scars of much travel in space.

It would not be long now.

'I do not recognise the class these big boys are.' I said and nodded towards the views of the other craft. 'Do you recognise their ...' I stopped and a cold chill ran down my spine. There, drifting slowly past us were weapons oscula on the hull of the craft, and judging by the smears and carbonisation, they had been used!

'What's the matter Djim?' Asked Ruuth as she came and stood by me. 'What are you looking at? What are those slots on the side of that one?'

'Weapons oscula.' I said quietly.

'Quick.' Said Djon. 'Get the serial numbers, maybe we can find out who owns it. I have never seen any vessel with weapons oscula before. I cannot imagine why anyone would need them?'

'I've got the number, Djon.' Said Ruuth. Then there was a thud and a clunk and we were docked.

'Right, we had better get a move on; we've only got two days.' Said Djon as he stood up out of his seat with a grim determined look on his face that meant 'don't argue with me now'. Terens obviously did not notice.

'Yes, but we need to check the damage on the hull as well and see if we can get any repairs carried out while we are here.' He said sensibly.

'Good point!' I shut down all the systems and put us in hibernation mode and we left the control room. I pulled the remote out of its socket on the control panel and slipped it into the socket in my space flight suit. I checked that the remote had a signal link with the control panel and turned to go. We checked the rooms around the damaged part where a smell of burning still lingered and irritated the nostrils. It was testament to the design and the self healing systems that it could take such damage and still be intact. Only two small rooms were open to the vacuum of space, but the design allowed for such damage and therefore was not an immediate problem. Our original repairs had restored much of the damaged hull to a reasonable state so only a small area was now still holed. We could wait until we could reach some repair stations.

We returned to our rooms to change from space wear to planet wear, and pick up our bags, which we had ready, and move to the airlock. I made sure that the remote was again safely inserted into a pocket and the signal was still connected to the control panel. We had to wait for Ruuth while she did something extra in her cabin. Terens tutted under his breath as we waited in the galley, Djon idly nibbled on some snack bites from the dispenser as he waited.

The airlock was modern and mostly automatic; it only required the crew to confirm the opening for the system to operate the hatch and the receiving hatch. We stepped through into an empty corridor, which curved gently as it followed the shape of the satellite. It was not a big corridor as I was expecting but small and narrow. The floor was covered completely in a similar drugget fibrous carpet as Djon's office, the walls were a patchwork of hatches, marked cableways and pipework while the ceiling was also lined with pipework labelled and covered with security tags. There were only a few vessels to be serviced by this corridor so perhaps it was a sensible size. Vast numbers of passengers would not be flooding through this area. This was not a cargo dock.

A big arrow and a sign on the wall directed us the way to the planet-side transport. Another larger corridor branched off. We followed the sign and soon found ourselves in the central spine with a group of lifts. There were a few others waiting. We had no choice but to be engaged in a bit of chit chat. It seemed they were businessmen and women coming to make a deal. We did not delve and tried not to give away our reason for being there without looking furtive. My palms were sweating as they looked at us with what I took to be suspicious glances. They tried to find out our reason for being there but we kept not answering. I wished that we had agreed a good story before we had disembarked but it was too late now. I hoped that something would distract them from us. At that moment the large lift doors opened and fortunately it was crowded. Thankfully we pushed our way into the car and made sure that we did not stand next to them. As usual as soon as the doors slid shut there was silence.

We took the lift down to the reception lounge in the welcome silence. The lounge was the huge bulge at one end of the central spine. It was mostly a giant glazed dome in which the planet filled the greater part of the view overhead. Even that seemed wrong. A planet should not be just over one's head as it seemed. It felt as though any moment it would come crashing down through the great domed roof because something that big should not be able to be held up. In fact, we were hanging upside down, held in place by one gee gravity created in the satellite. Even that should not be thought about as it sometimes made people violently sick. It certainly gave a curious sensation to think about it. So I didn't. The rest of the view was taken up by the Arachnid Looped nebula arching out from the edge of the planet. It must be one of the greatest views in the galaxy.

The main room was sparsely populated with people milling around. Mostly they were travellers as they were carrying the type of travel bags only used in space vessels. There were also a few satellite staff in their distinctive uniforms of bright saffron yellow overalls. It paid to be noticeable in space. Overhead were large advertising signs and other information signs. One of them gave details of the planet and the nebula. I stood awestruck until Terens grabbed my arm and brought me back to the moment, he nodded to where the others were walking away. We followed and looked for a shuttle flight to take us down to the surface.

'Over there.' Pointed Terens. 'Gate four. There is a shuttle in half an hour.'

'But there is a shuttle in only a few minutes from this gate here.' Said Ruuth. 'Why don't we use that?'

'Just look who is in the queue for starters.' Replied Terens tersely. 'Besides the further gates are quieter and usually there is less chance of getting caught in awkward situations.' Now I realised why Djon had brought Terens along. Not only for his experience in weapons and planet lore but his experience in travelling the galaxy.

We followed where he was pointing and began to make our way towards gate four. I felt exposed and awkward as though everyone else was looking at me and thinking 'what are they up to?' For once I was wishing there were more people there not less. The shiny well-kept floor in the lounge seemed to want to shout out every footstep. Why were there not more people to hide behind?

When we reached the opening with a large number four over the lintel we left the large arena and entered a quieter room, this was again floored with the same fabric as the corridor. A large window showed the underside of the planet unmoving in front of us. As we were in geostationary orbit the spin was not visible, only the stars behind the planet's rim moved. The strange orientation made us feel odd for a few minutes while we adjusted to the view, after all common sense said the planet should be 'down'. Outside of the window we could see the side of a shuttle and hear as it docked. We sat down on some empty seats and waited with a few others although we tried to keep our distance so as to not get engaged in conversation. We listened to the murmur of speech and tried to make out any useful information. We could not. We spent the rest of the time reading a leaflet that Ruuth had picked up, which gave some information on Fyrest Prime, and discussing our plan of action. To maximise our usefulness we would have to split up, coming together to compare notes. I was given the library, if there was one: if not the nearest equivalent.

The sign over the door to the shuttle sprang into life announcing that we could now board. We gathered up our bags and joined the queue. A large lady in front of us got talking to Ruuth and soon we were all dragged into her conversation. She was coming back to see her daughter. We got a large chunk of her life history, which seemed to be as large as she was, and unfortunately it continued in the shuttle as well. Fortunately, she spoke so much we did not have to give much away. We all had to visit the toilet more often than usual that trip. It also meant we could not enjoy the view of the approaching planet. So, it was a surprise when we felt the landing and the call to leave the shuttle. We exited along the arrivals corridor into the visitor's hall where our bags were screened as we left the building.

We found ourselves in a watery dawn sunlight. Taksi firms hustled us for our custom but we waved them aside, or rather Terens did as he was a seasoned traveller, and we walked to the monorail system. I looked up and could just make out the nebula as the faintest of faint red clouds on the horizon even in daylight. We reached the monorail station. Although it was called a monorail it was more like a horizontal cable car. We assumed that this was because of the frequent earth tremors, which would have soon wrecked an ordinary train system. There were curving supports, between which was a thick cable that ran in a series of catenary curves away towards the town. We watched the cars arriving in a series of swooping boat like motions. As it came into the station it was caught between two rails and held firm, thankfully. We took the next train into town. We made sure that we had a car to ourselves. It took a while to get used to the ride, but having spent many years in hover cars it was not difficult.

The town, Ho-Dei-Da, was typical of most towns in the galaxy. It was made up primarily of prefabricated units, either as individuals or grouped into blocks. Like most inhabited planets in the galaxy Fyrest Prime was also a young planet, geologically speaking. This meant that there was still a considerable amount of tectonic shift resulting in earthquakes and volcanic activity. Almost anywhere on the surface would experience some form of earthquake although fortunately volcanic activity near Ho-Dei-Da was non existent, I hoped this was why the town was here. All this geological activity meant that almost every building was not quite square as the ground shifted and cracks were evident everywhere. There was evidence that these cracks were regularly filled in within the city limits. Beyond the town the cracks were left.

The volcanic activity also meant that the air was full of a fine dust most of the time. Just like home. The buildings that were not regularly washed were consequently covered in a good layer of the grimy dust, which was washed into streaks by the infrequent rain. It was not an uncommon sight therefore in the galaxy to see even important cities looking run down. The earthquakes made the monorail ride rather uneven even though the city evidently made some considerable effort trying to repair and straighten the lines. We finally pulled into the central station, which consisted of one platform and an arched canopy, which covered the track and platform. It was busy. People milled around as people have for time immemorial in such places.

We stepped out onto the dusty street and were immediately accosted by taksi drivers looking for trade. Terens waved them away too.

'OK, everyone to work. Meet at lunchtime here.' Said Djon and was gone. Terens also left without saying a word as was his usual way. Ruuth and I stood for a few moments to gain our bearings. I tried to remember the plan of Ho-Dei-Da from the pamphlet.

'Right, well I'm going this way.' I said and pointed across the street. Ruuth nodded.

'I'm heading over there. See you later.' And she was gone too. I was left standing on the street. It was not busy. Most people were using the sickies so the sky was busy and only occasionally a taksi or private flyer would drop down causing small clouds of dust to puff into the air. I set off to what I thought must be the library or what passed for a library here. I felt dirty already. I brushed the fine dust off my suit as I walked, but it was a fruitless exercise, I would be just as dusty in a few minutes. I stopped doing it. It would make me look like an outsider.

Then I was standing outside the library. It was open even though it was still early in the morning, in fact I would have been surprised if it had been closed. Throughout the galaxy as trade was almost continuous there was life and business going on continuously day and night. Almost everything stayed open twenty-four hours a day, even if there were more or less than twenty four hours in the particular planet's day. The library was in a group of the same prefabricated units, with the same dusty exterior.

I went in. Inside it was the same prefabricated library layout as at home. The same bright interior lit by large high-level windows. There was the usual counter and the usual librarian. I was taken aback slightly to see that she was different. Then realised how silly I had been, of course the librarian would be different! It was just the sameness of everything made me think I was back home or something. She looked up when I came in. She was dark skinned and attractive with short hair. I tried to look like a local who knew exactly where he was going. I was helped by the standard layout of the library. She looked back down, so far so good.

Two hours later I was getting nowhere. To relieve the boredom I decided to check up on the serial number of the vessel next to ours. I found no reference. That was odd. All information was freely available in the galaxy, or so I thought. This made me think otherwise. Then I thought I would see if I could find anything about the free-floating toroid interrogator. A small earth tremor made the screen shimmer, briefly. I could find no reference to the interrogator either, even more strange. I looked around. I took in the people in the library. The usual selection of people you would see on any planet, doing the usual things in any library on any planet. Except of course we had no library on Enceladus 241 that I knew of.

So then I decided to check on the colonisation dates of all the planets in the galaxy. This should show something. Another earth tremor made the screen shimmer again and a very fine shower of dust descended from the high ceiling and fixture hangers. Cleaners were one of the most populous employees on any planet as there was always cleaning required. I absently brushed some of the fine dust off the monitor. There were four thousand two hundred and nine inhabited planets listed in the catalogue. The next stage was more laborious as I had to tease out all the information of the colonisation dates – as this information was not listed in a useful way. After a while I got used to the format and began to get quicker and quicker. At each planet I separated out the date and saved it separately. I downloaded the information so we could check it later. But as I had found nothing on the vessel or the interrogator I began to doubt if all the planets were listed. I ran the list down the screen and quickly checked the dates of colonisation.

Something seemed wrong!

I looked up and checked the room, confident that someone was watching me. No one was. Perhaps there was a security camera watching me. I could not see one. I could not see anyone behind me watching either. I thought though at any moment a frisson bolt would blow my skull apart in a crackle of ionised air and a flurry of energised dust. It did not happen. I looked back at the dates, they were still the same. I just had to get back to the others but it was not time to meet yet. I had to control myself and bring my thought back to the task in hand. I would have to investigate further and make sure the information I had here was correct. Maybe there were other reasons for the anomaly. I needed some more corroborative evidence. I then checked all the portal co-ordinates. They should correspond with all the inhabited planets but I would need the V20 to check that so I downloaded that information too. I sat and thought for a while and while I thought I again checked the room to see if anyone was interested in me. It seemed not although I had a queasy feeling that I was being watched. I was not used to clandestine work, it made me nervy. I then called up the standard interplanetary flights, generally called the 'bus service' and downloaded them. It should all tie up. Then I looked up the inhabited planets sizes and day lengths. The information was not there! Either someone did not want us looking for it or it was not considered relevant. There was such a wealth of information to store and someone had to decide what to leave out. I realised that I was trying to convince myself and that really I thought the information should be available. Dare I ask the librarian? I thought not, at least not until the others were with me. I then typed in 'Ultima Thule' to see what happened. The answer came up on screen as 'an unknown far away region' so, just the dictionary definition then. Why did the originists think the original planet was called Ultima Thule? Where did that come from?

I checked the time; it was time to go. I pulled out the disc and closed the terminal. I checked the room as innocently as possible to see if anyone else was watching me or getting up to follow. They were not, so I picked up my things and left the library. As I stepped outside the dry heat hit me like an oven. The library had been air conditioned then and I had not noticed. I walked back to our agreed meeting place and as I walked I looked up to check the traffic flying overhead. Were any of the hover cars a police car? Were any of them following me? I could not tell and looking up into the sky made my eyes hurt anyway so I returned my gaze to the dusty street. I could see the familiar shape of Ruuth in the distance standing waiting. She was being accosted by taksi drivers who were not going away as they did when Djon was with us. I hoped my presence would deter them from staying. As I got closer Ruuth saw me, her face brightened, and she waved. Obviously pleased to see a familiar face. The men turned and saw me and reluctantly moved off.

'Hi.' She said. 'Am I glad to see you. I have been pestered everywhere I go. You would think no one on this planet has seen a woman before.'

'Obviously, there must be very few women here as pretty as you.'

'Oh, shut up.' She said, but I hoped it was not entirely meant. Fortunately, the other two turned up before it got awkward.

'Let us find a place to eat and talk.' Said Djon without ceremony and pulled out the pamphlet and looked for restaurants.

'There's one just down the road here.' I said, pointing to a group of buildings on the other side of the street.'

'I hope it has air conditioning. This heat is unbearable.' Said Ruuth, tugging at her clothes. Djon looked up and grunted. We crossed the street and walked a short way to the restaurant. We went in. It was a small place, more like a café, and there were very few people at tables. It looked clean and tidy. A small, neat lady with an apron over a pretty flowered dress saw us and came over. I wondered why she did not wear the more common one-piece modern dust protective suits.

'A table for four?' she said, which must be the most repeated question in the entire galaxy of eating houses.

'Yes please.' Said Djon. 'Near the window.'

'No problem. As you can see we are not very busy today. You're not from here are you?'

I froze. It was an innocent enough question but after being in the library I had become almost paranoid about our quest. I also wondered why Djon wanted to be near the window – we could be seen by passers by. Fortunately, Djon remained calm. I must remember not to become a spy.

'No, we are here on business. We will be off tomorrow. You must get a lot of visitors here?' Either she did not hear him or did not think it was a question for she did not answer but bustled around us as waiters do everywhere as we pulled back the bent wood chairs with fabric seats and sat at a small round table. It was covered with a clean tablecloth spread neatly over. Then she did reply. 'Yes, we get a lot of business-people dropping in, but most of them do not look like you.'

I looked at Djon. He remained completely unflustered. 'Trouble with an earth tremor.' Was all he said She looked askance but it seemed to satisfy her. She brushed back some stray hairs as she handed us handwritten menus on card. 'Wow, I haven't seen the like of these for years.' He joked.

'I know.' She said with a smile. 'It's my little hint to the past. I'll leave you now to choose.' And she was gone, checking up on the other few customers.

'Right let us choose quickly and then we can get down to business.' Said Djon. We picked something simple off the menu and ordered. She spent some time chatting as we made the order and we could not be impolite so we had to listen. Eventually she got our orders and went back. I felt guilty, she was a lovely woman and ordinarily I would have loved to pass the time of day in conversation, but this was different.

'OK, Terens.' Said Djon. 'What have you got?' Terens shifted in his seat. He sighed deeply.

'I have spent a fruitless morning. Found absolutely nothing.'

'Don't worry Terens.' Said Djon, resting a hand on his shoulder. 'That may tell us as much as anything.' He turned to Ruuth. 'And what have you found?'

'I went to the Trade Council as we agreed and tried to pass as a trader trying to move into the area. But it was strange Djon, they said that all trade was taken care of and they could not cater for anymore. There was no spare capacity. It took hours to even get that out of them. They made me wait for each person. I then spent the rest of the time trying to find out who the traders currently were. It seems, as far as I could ascertain, it is a consortium called the 'Fair Trade Dealers.' I could not find much about them though. All I could find was that they seem to be based on a planet called 'Geryon' in the Illyria Region.'

'Well, it is something. We may have to go there and have

a look. Djim?' I was just about to reply when the lady returned with our food. It looked good. We waited until she had returned to her station before continuing.

'I had a very productive time in the library.' I could see the others stiffen in anticipation, food halfway to the mouth.

'Keep eating.' Said Djon. 'Yes, Djim?'

'It took a bit of getting as the information is not clearly laid out but as far as I could tell from the details every single planet has been colonised! Every single planet has a date of colonisation.'

The others stopped eating again. There was a silence.

'Keep eating!' Hissed Djon. We did.

'That cannot be possible Djim.' He whispered. 'Not every planet can be colonised! We must have started from at least one planet.'

'I know. It just does not make sense. Who do we ask to find out why this should be?'

'With data like that we do not ask anyone.' Suggested Terens. 'If that is the case then Djon was right from the beginning. There is a conspiracy to hide the original planet. But why?'

We had no answer. So, we just continued to eat in silence for a while.

'Why?' Said someone again. 'Just what is the point?' It was Ruuth. 'Why hide a planet or planets if we did not originate from one?'

'It cannot be for a good reason.' Muttered Terens, staring out of the window. Black clouds were looming over the buildings opposite as if to confirm the gloom in our thoughts.

'It means we cannot ask anyone.' Said Djon. 'This means it is bigger and more dangerous than I ever imagined. We are on our own.'

'Would that vessel with the weapons oscula have anything to do with it?' Asked Ruuth perceptively.

'I checked that as well.' I replied, before anyone else could answer. 'There was no data. It made me think at the time, but now it makes me really worried that perhaps it is, and we are right next to it. It also came to me that if there is an original planet and it is hidden is it called Ultima Thule? Perhaps that is to put you originists off the scent. Perhaps the original planet is called something else. I am getting seriously worried.'

'Keep calm.' Said Djon. 'No one knows we are here or what we are doing here.' It began to grow dark outside to match the dark thoughts we were expressing. A few drops of rain made smears on the window as the lights came on slowly in the restaurant to compensate for the light level dropping outside. Then it began to rain in earnest and the water ran in dusty rivulets down the window glazing making the view outside distort into corrugations.

We all jumped as a dirty yellow taksi dropped down to the ground right outside the window.

'They're not supposed to do that.' Complained the lady as four large men jumped out of the taksi and ran into the restaurant. They were all dressed identically in dark one-piece suits of the planet fashion, which they shook as they came in to remove the rain. They were all wearing the goggles and face masks common throughout the galaxy. They finally pushed them up off their faces and onto their heads. Then the lady came forward.

'Table for four?' she said. They finally pulled their goggle units off their heads and banged the now sticky dust off them on their legs. Even I knew that was not etiquette. That should be done outside. I was not going to chastise them about it though. They were all big and gave me an uneasy feeling.

'Yes, mam.' Said the largest man, who had a strange hairstyle like a ploughed field. He nodded to a table near us.

'Time to go I think.' Said Terens quietly.

'The library is near, and dry.' I suggested keen to leave. The others nodded and finished up.

'The bill please.' Said Djon getting up and walking to the counter. We gathered together our belongings and waited by the door for Djon to pay. It seemed to take an age. The four men appeared to take no notice of us. The one with the 'ploughed field' hair had his back to us, there was one with no hair at all apart from a tiny bit under his bottom lip, and one had very short spikey blond hair which did not look natural. The last one had shoulder length brown locks and a fuzz on his chin. At least one of them was wearing a strong perfume that followed after them like a microclimate. It was a smell that I would not forget in a hurry, partly because very few people ever wore perfume or if they did it was so mild as to be completely unnoticeable.

Finally, Djon had paid and we could leave. Even the poor weather outside could not dampen our relief at getting out of the restaurant. We pulled our collars up and ran as best we could round to the library. In the lobby we shook off as much water from our clothes as we could and then composed ourselves before going in. It was much the same as before, the same lady sat at the desk. We went over to a free table and sat down.

'Let us get some books. It will look better.' Suggested Djon. We all got up and grabbed some books at random and sat down again. I found I had Titular's Legal Handbook. I opened it. It was really pleasant to handle a good old-fashioned book again after spending so much time with screens and the V20. I rubbed a page between my fingers just to feel the texture of the paper.

'What do we do?' Whispered Ruuth. I noticed that she too was just touching the paper in her book although she was looking at Djon while she spoke. The feel of a proper book made my thought go back to my childhood. I had one book only in my whole life. It was an instruction manual for a dust extraction unit at a ground station. I had no idea why this particular manual was in book form rather than clique computer disc. I treasured that manual dearly and in fact still owned it. It was somewhere in the back of a cupboard and this reminded me that I had not looked at it in a long time. By now it was so well thumbed that it was barely readable in places and the pages were ragged at the edges. I think it was my father that had found it for me come to think of it.

'I think we see if we can find the hidden planet.' Said Djon coolly.

'What!' Hissed Ruuth, and then looked round to see if anyone had heard. 'To hide a planet means big business and a reason to do so. I cannot think of a good reason to hide a planet that is not somehow bad. Who knows for what reason it has been done.' She was leaning across the table to get closer to Djon.

'It could just be' Interposed Terens quietly. 'It could be that one of the planets has not been colonised but has been made to look like it, just to put the likes of the originists off the scent.'

'That could be the case.' I said. 'But I have downloaded as much information as I could so some of that may corroborate that theory.'

'But we still come back to why?' Insisted Ruuth. 'Why hide a planet? It cannot be for a good reason.'

'What Terens says may be true though, Ruuth. It might just be disguised not hidden.'

'Even so, but why do that even? Either way it doesn't make sense.' She paused. 'Do any of you think those men in the restaurant own that vessel with the weapons oscula?' We all looked at each other and realised we had all been thinking the same thing.

Djon spoke for all of us. 'I certainly do.'

They are the sort of people who would hide a planet.' Said Ruuth. 'They frighten me witless.' I could not admit it, but they frightened me too. I had to wonder why, because they had never done anything bad that I knew of.

'If that is the case then we are definitely on our own. We cannot afford to annoy people like that.' Said Ruuth. I had to agree again.

'Perhaps we had better get back out into space.' I suggested. 'We should be safer there.'

'Yes, but where do we go?' Asked Djon. There was a long silence while we all thought of an answer.

'First off we need to find out if it is a hidden planet we are looking for or one of the existing ones which has been disguised.' Suggested Terens.

'The latter should be easier to discover.' Said Djon. 'All we need to do is find as much information on the inhabited planets as possible. Is there a gazetteer of the planets here?' He looked at me as he spoke.

'I don't know. I didn't look for one.' I felt awkward, as though I should have done. 'Shall I go on the terminal and check if there is an electronic version, or do you think we can be traced if I do?'

'This is a library Djim.' Said Ruuth. 'They cannot know who is on a machine. Do it.'

'Terens, can you look and see if there is a paper version too.' Said Djon. 'We'll wait here and look after our belongings.'

I returned to a different terminal than before, just in case and sat down. Soon I had up the index and searched for planetary data. I started with what I had before and would work from there. Something was different though I was sure. I could not put my finger on it but it did not look quite as I remembered it the first time. I must be imagining it though. I downloaded it a second time to check later when on board our vessel and quickly closed down the terminal. I got up and went back to the table where Djon and Ruuth were sitting.

'Let us go.' I whispered. 'Now! Something is different. I think 'they' have been checking up on what we have been looking at on the terminal. We ought to get a move on and get off planet as soon as we can. Get Terens.' The urgency in my voice put paid to any dissent and Djon got up immediately and went and got Terens away from the racks. We picked up our bags and headed for the library exit. Again, I had the feeling that at any moment a frisson bolt would rent the air and my skull. We got outside. Now it had stopped raining but that only made it hot and sticky. The dust that hade been washed off the buildings now had been swept into little piles at the edges of the road and in other corners. There was the usual smell of wet.

'Just walk normally.' Said Djon. 'We don't want to draw attention to ourselves. I am sure no one knows who we are or that it is us who have been on the terminal. But just in case just keep cool.' We walked as normally as we could and began to retrace our steps back to the central station. Once on the platform again and with a crowd we felt safer but even there I could not help but look behind. On the second time Djon took my arm.

'Don't.' Was all he said, and I knew what he meant. 'Look at the train information.' And he nodded up at the screen above us scrolling down information. 'Next train now' it finally said and on cue one came sliding into the station and came to a halt with a sigh. The doors opened and the usual flood of people poured out onto the platform. We got in and found a seat each. Within a few seconds it began to move off with hardly a noise and the station began to slide past our window. We relaxed a little. So far so good. Even so, the journey seemed to take an age. Finally though we drew into the station at the ground terminal. We were up and ready to disembark before the monorail came to a halt. We were out of the door as soon as it opened. It would be just a short hop to the ground terminal building and into a shuttle. We crossed the open space and went into the terminal building where our bags were screened. We looked for the sign for the next shuttle up to the docking satellite. The screen said ten minutes for the next one. We went to the right bay and joined a short queue, which was already boarding the shuttle. We put our bags in the locker and took four empty seats together. I could feel the drives powering up through the fabric of the shuttle and could imagine the take-off sequences being run through. I could then work out the time to take off. I checked the time on my galactic standard time watch. Two minutes to go. The shuttle filled up around us and the buzz of voices increased as people chatted to their new temporary neighbours. Then all began to fall silent as the distant roar of the drives increased. Almost everyone was quiet on take-off even after many years in space travel. The ground then fell away from outside our porthole and we were spacebourne. Very shortly clouds passed by which was replaced by a sunlit sky as always exists above the clouds. The hazy surface of the planet curved away below us. It was always a most beautiful sight to see a planet from the sky and then from space. Then the sky began to darken and finally turn to the blackness of space. The docking satellite came into view, or rather the sunlit part came into view as the unlit part was as black as the rest of space and was only visible as an absence of stars.

We docked and disembarked into the reception lounge with the large overhead information screens still robotically scrolling through their information schedule. We looked for one to tell us where to find dock ten. Then Djon pointed to one which gave us the information we needed. We headed for the lift lobby, threading our way through the throng of milling people who seem to inhabit places like these in the whole of the galaxy. From the lift we went round the curved corridor to the big '10' on the airlock door.

But before we went to our door, we looked through the viewport of dock nine. Even with this small view we could see that the big vessel was still there but this time we could see no weapons oscula.

'It must be a different vessel.' Said Djon. I took a look too.

'No, Djon, they are still there but now they are closed and almost impossible to see in this light. We must have caught them just right to see them open. Maybe they were doing some maintenance. Now we would not have noticed a thing.'

Djon swiped his card through the slot to open our airlock. Then when we finally boarded the Jergan and the hatch was shut we relaxed. I went to my cabin and threw my bag on my bed and then threw myself onto it as well. Boy was I exhausted after that tense visit to Ho-Dei-Da. I did not want to go through that again but reluctantly came to the conclusion that we would probably have to. Now we had started there was no going back. Not with the information we had. Then I remembered the disc and dragged myself off my bed and rummaged in my jacket pocket. There it was. I then dragged my exhausted body to the control room. It was empty. The lights came on as I entered and sat in the pilot's seat. I put the disc in a reader slot and let the menu appear on the forward visibility screen. The menu appeared as if hanging in space in front of our vessel. I had a sudden panic that anyone outside could see it! Then I realised of course it was just an optical illusion. I opened the first list of planet colonisation data and became aware of someone in the seat beside me. It was Ruuth.

'Hi.' She said. 'I wanted to sleep but couldn't. What are you looking at?'

'I am comparing the first of the downloads of the planetary colonisation data with the second that I got from the library to see if there is any difference or I am seeing things.' As I spoke I called up the second list and had them side by side on the screen in front of us. I then spent some time extracting just the colonisation dates from the huge amount of data stored. They appeared to be the same. Both had 4209 planets and they all had colonisation dates. I must have been seeing things in the library then, so what had made me think there was something different? I hoped I had not dragged them out of the library all for nothing. Then Ruuth pointed to the bottom of the screen. At first, I could not see what she was pointing at but then I saw. The first download had a much smaller programme size than the second. Had I spotted that without realising it? So, someone had tampered with the programme in the short time between my accessing it at the library terminals. That in itself was curious and what had been added to the second programme? It occurred to me that it may be something that allows more control of the users.

'I don't like that.' I said to her as we both considered the implications of the different downloads. 'I think we ought to get out of here.'

'I agree.' She said, not moving but still looking at the screen.

'Ruuth.' I said sharply. 'Get the others up. We need to get out of here.' I began the take-off programme as Ruuth finally left her seat and disappeared. Moments later she was back with Terens.

'Djon is following. He was fast asleep and needs a few moments to wake up.' She said.

'What's wrong Djim?' Asked Terens.

'We think the programme of planetary data has been

tampered with and there may be some risk that we can be traced because of it. We need to get away.' Djon stumbled into the control room bleary eyed.

'What's up?' He asked

'Djim and Ruuth recon there has been some tampering with the planetary data programmes that Djim downloaded and there may be some risk to us because of that.' Terens replied.

'We must be careful Djim.' Said Djon 'To leave early could also attract attention. What makes you think the data has been tampered with?' Ruuth pointed to the screen with the two sets of data showing the different sizes of the programmes. Djon nodded knowledgeably and grunted. 'We still need a good reason to leave to avoid attracting attention. Ruuth any ideas? Being an ex governing body person.' She winced at that but thought for a moment.

'Sickness.' She said, simply.

'Good one. But won't they want to help or inquire as to the nature of the problem, you know, that sort of thing?'

'Oh, not us, a close family member somewhere else.'

I called up space flight control and requested a departure time. Indeed, they did ask why we wanted to leave early but seemed very satisfied by our answer. They gave us an immediate departure time.

'That was quick.' Said Terens.

'They want someone else to come and pay the docking fee, that's why.' I replied. 'Get ready, we can leave shortly.' It was not long before I felt the vessel detach from the dock and we became free. The anti-crash system came on and its dial flashed into life on the panel as the electro-gravity magnets kept us away from the other vessels docked either side of us and it was a simple job to back us out of the slot. The planetary data had been turned off and the vector diagrams were online and scrolling as we moved off. I watched the unfolding information as we slowly eased our way out into free space. The 'permission to turn' indicator flashed on with allowable directions to move appearing as symbols and lines on screen.

'Where are we going?' I asked as I switched on the V20

and began to turn the Jergan to the exit portal. The trajectory indicted by a green line in the stabilizing orb. It was a simple matter to follow the line.

'What was the name of the planet you mentioned earlier? Why not go there? It is as good a planet as any.' Said Djon.

'Geryon.' I said. 'But it was Ruuth that found that one and wasn't that where those Free Traders come from? Isn't that a bit like going into the lion's den?' I paused 'What's a lion?'

'No idea.' Said Terens. 'I have been to many planets but never seen any thing called that. Besides if you are asking, what is a den?'

'I have no idea of that either. Odd isn't it that we have all these sayings but have no idea where they came from.'

'Lost in the mists of time I suppose.' Muttered Djon

'We don't know that the Free Traders are anything to do with this problem.' Said Ruuth, stopping our irrelevant wanderings at a stroke. We all looked across at her. She shrugged her shoulders.

'I thought you said it was a closed shop. Isn't that tantamount to saying that they are part of it? We have to assume they are until we know otherwise.' I said. 'But we might find out something. We certainly will not find anything by going to places like Enceladus. That's for sure.'

'Geryon it is then.' Said Djon. 'Wake me up when we get there.' And he was gone. Terens sat quietly in one of the rear seats. I set the V20 to guide us to Geryon. I then called up space flight control and asked for a window to use the exit portal. We were told we could have one in half an hour.

'Does every planet have a portal?' Asked Ruuth.

'Yes.' I replied. 'Well, I think so.'

'Are all the portals listed somewhere then?'

I had to think for a moment. It was such an obvious question. There must be a list in the V20.

'I'll have a look in the V20.' I said and called up the menu onto the screen. 'It's normally done by planets because that is where people want to go but the portals must be listed in there as well because that is what the V20 will be looking for.

The portal identification signal, that is. Here they are.' I called them up on the screen but it was not in a very user friendly format. It consisted of clique computer language.

'I don't think this will help. We need a machine to decipher this.'

'We have one.' Said Ruuth. 'I know about clique computers, I can write a programme to decipher it. Just give me some time. Can you download it into another clique for me?'

'Sure. Have that one over there.' I downloaded the data. Ruuth sat at the console and began rapidly typing on the keyboard.

'How long will you need?'

'Two hours maybe.' She spoke without stopping or turning round.

'Shall we go somewhere else then before going to Geryon?'

'It might be a good idea. We need all the help we can get before going in.'

'OK, shall we ask Djon?' I turned round to look at Terens still quietly sitting at the back. He shook his head.

'Right, I'll find the planet nearest to Geryon with a portal.' I checked the V20. 'Here we are. Ghandza. We'll go there.' I reset the V20 and minimised the data so I could see the vectors for the portal. They were inactive at the moment, so we were not due to join the queue just yet. The wait was getting tense. Was anyone aware of us out here? I checked the local traffic to help ease my mind. As usual there was nothing unusual. Then we received the call to join the portal queue and I fired the drives. It made Ruuth look up.

'Are we going now?'

'Just getting into the queue. We will be leaving shortly.' She returned to her programming. I returned to checking the flight vectors and watching the trail of the drive from the vessel in front of us. After a while it disappeared and I knew we were next. 'Two minutes.' I warned everyone. Ruuth stopped and strapped herself into her seat.

Two minutes later we were through. I checked our clock

against the time from the Ghandza portal clock as sometimes it was not always an instant transfer. It was not this time. For some reason we had lost half an hour. No matter how often the portals were used there was never any certainty of the time it would take to get through. No one could work out why it happened.

Ghandza space flight control called us. 'Welcome to Ghandza space. Do you wish to dock?'

'No thank you. Can we just take on some small supplies while we recharge?'

'What are you doing?' Asked Ruuth, cancelling the contact. 'We don't need anything.'

'I know, but it will look better if we ask for something rather than just turn up and then disappear.'

'Hm, good idea I suppose. It will give me more time to get this thing sorted.' She returned to the clique.

'Certainly.' Came the ladies voice again, as I re-established contact. 'We will send a supply vessel over shortly. Please advise on your departure time. The payment for portal use is now due.' I paid with Djon's card.

'We will let you know when we intend to depart. What is the departure delay at present?'

'There is no delay at present. Over and out.'

'We'll wait for the supply vessel and your progress on the programming. Can you include for the planet's size and orbit times?'

'Why?' asked Ruuth.

'So we can check the day times and also the gravity of each planet. The original one should be one standard day and one standard gravity.'

'Good one Djim. I will include it. Does the V20 have that information?'

'I think so. Yes, it must have the day times to be able to calculate where they are and where they will be.'

'Good. So, the original planet will be one standard year, one standard day, and one standard gravity. This should be very interesting. Why has no one done it before?'

'I have no idea. But no one ever thought we only came

from one planet. It was not important to consider. We also do not know if anyone did. Can I go and get some sleep?'

'Sure.' She said without looking up from her work. 'I will give you a call when the supply vessel gets here.'

I went and lay down on my bed. The next thing I was aware of was Ruuth's voice. I must have fallen asleep then.

'Djim!' Her voice was a disembodied voice hanging in the air of my room. 'Djim, the supply vessel is here!'

'OK.' I managed to croak out and stumbled out of bed. As I came into the control room the voice of the supply vessel crackled out of the speakers.

'No video link?' He asked. We had turned it off as we did not want anyone to know what we looked like.

'It's being repaired at the moment. We only need basic rations. Can you display some?'

'OK. Menu coming up. What's your frequency?'

'one oh eight.' Moments later the menu appeared on the forward vision screen and scrolled down. I picked a few things which I thought would look normal. He acknowledged our order and asked for the payment card to be inserted into the payment slot. After a few moments when the payment had been accepted he requested a docking procedure for the supply drone to deliver the goods.

'Your hull has taken a beating. Been in some trouble?' Asked the supply vessel captain.

'Ghas.' I swore. 'I forgot they would see that.'

'Why does that matter?' Asked Ruuth. Who had been working quietly away at her programming.

'Because it makes us memorable, that's why'

'Come on Djim, you are getting too paranoid. Who knows we are here?'

'OK.' I pressed the talk button. 'We met with an accident. We are on our way home to get repairs. That is why we are stopping here. We think it better to take short hops; we are hoping this will stress the hull less.' I released the talk button.

'I hope all goes well, I would hate to think of you being stranded out in space.'

'Thank you. The supply drone has docked successfully so I will sign off until it has been unloaded.' I went to the docking bay and unlocked the airlock door and drew out the supplies container and then relocked the airlock. While there I was able to use the remote to let the supply captain know that dedocking could take place. I released the drone and could hear the locks disengage and the slight vibration caused by the drone moving off. I used the video link to watch it depart. I then returned to the control room. Ruuth was asleep at the desk her head in her arms. I set the vessel's controls to sleep mode which would keep us in a safe position as well as let any nearby vessels know of our situation and then went back to bed. I was asleep in minutes.

I awoke some time later. All seemed quiet. I got up and had a shower and dressed and went to the control room. The others were standing in front of the vision enhancer screen looking at the result of Ruuth's work. Did none of them sleep? They were silent.

'What's wrong?' I asked and they all jumped.

'Djim!' Said Djon 'You're up, good, look at what Ruuth has managed to come up with.' He pointed to the screen as he spoke. 'Just look.'

I looked and at first could not see what has made him so animated. But then it suddenly dawned on me. There were four thousand two hundred and ten portal signals!

– CHAPTER 5 –

GERYON

What was showing on the screen meant that there was an unlisted unknown portal!

Why? No wonder the others had been standing so silently and had jumped when I came in. I found myself just standing there also trying to work out why.

'That must be it!' Said Djon, his face now radiant with joy. 'It must be the portal for Ultima Thule. It would make sense, in one sense. Well done Ruuth we have found our original planet.' He could not keep still for excitement.

'Is there a planet near the portal Ruuth?' I asked, not quite as confident as Djon that we had already stumbled upon our goal.

'I have no idea Djim. All I found is the portal signal I don't know if there is an inhabited planet nearby.'

'There must be Ruuth.' Said Djon, his excitement ebbing as he turned back to the control panel. 'Why have a portal with no planet? It's got to be it!'

'We must still ask ourselves why someone would want to hide a planet, our original planet. Why?' Said Ruuth, still standing looking at the data on the screen her hands on her hips. 'It bothers me.' Again, I had to agree with her, it did seem very odd. To have an unlisted portal made me even more worried but I could not focus any thoughts as to why that should be. There just had to be a sensible answer but I could not think of one.

'Do we know where this portal is?' Asked Terens quietly banishing the worries from my perturbed thought. He was standing also looking at the data but showing no emotion as usual other than idly scratching his chin, which he often did when thinking I had realised.

'No.' Replied Ruuth. 'I have managed to get the portal signal isolated but not the location. But as far as I can tell it seems to be near the edge of the galaxy.' She called up a model of the galaxy. 'Somewhere here.' She pointed to an area. There were no other planet portals so close to the edge of the galaxy. That though was no reason to distrust the information, after all there was no logical layout of the rest of the planets in the galaxy.

'Why don't we just go there?' Asked Djon, still radiant with excitement.

'Unfortunately, Djon, we need the coordinates to input into the V20. And that area that Ruuth has just indicated is about four hundred light years across!' I replied.

'But we got this data from the V20.' Said Ruuth. I had to admit then that she had a point but could not think of any way to get the coordinates. It did not make sense.

'So, the information is in there?' I said, pointing to the V20. If Ruuth had found the hidden portal from the V20 then if only four thousand two hundred and nine appeared the extra one was deliberately hidden but could not be totally obscured. It was the fact that there had been an attempt to hide it that was so worrying. Every V20 was not only picking up the information but also relaying it throughout the galaxy every time a portal is used it appeared.

'Something must be hiding that information then. So, the V20 has been tampered with! The whole system is corrupted!' I felt my whole world being shattered. Was nothing right? Was nothing as it should be? Was this what my father had found? 'If that is the case then maybe every time we use the V20 someone somewhere knows exactly where we are and where we are going!' I gasped. The enormity of it suddenly hit me! If what we had found was true, then there was no hiding place!

'We are not safe then.' Muttered Djon, now deflated. 'No matter where we go we cannot hide.'

'Let us not jump to conclusions here.' Interrupted Terens. 'This was the V20 that Djim's father had, it does not mean all V20's are the same. It does not mean they can be traced.'

'The programme with the portal data had not been touched.' Said Ruuth quietly. 'It looks as though it was normal. The hidden portal would appear to be the same in all V20's. But Terens is right there does not appear to be anything in the V20 that would alert someone else. I think. But if the portal was hidden then maybe something else is too.'

'So, all along we may have been sitting ducks. So why has no one come for us after the breakout?' I asked innocently.

There was a sudden awkward silence.

'Djon?' I probed. 'What's wrong?'

'Look Djim.' Began Djon. He looked very abashed and did not look at me. 'I am very sorry Djim but that....' He paused, fighting for the right words. '...That breakout was a fake.'

'What!' I exploded and leapt up from the pilot's seat that I had sunk down into and grabbed at his flying suit. Terens and Ruuth grabbed me.

'Calm down Djim!' Growled Terens. 'At least hear him out first.'

'Hear him out! Hear him out!' I shouted, struggling against Terens iron grip and Ruuth's surprisingly tough hold. 'What in Erebus do you mean by that? A fake? This had better be good, Djon.' I snarled back from the pilot's seat again where Terens and Ruuth held me down into. My hands were balled into tight fists of rage. After all we had been through the thought that I had been duped was hard to hear.

'Oh, it's good Djim, believe me.' He straightened up his flying suit. 'Look, there is no way you would have come with us if I had just asked you. In fact, I did ask you but you would not budge. It was important to get you away from Enceladus though. What I said about you being a marked man was true. What I said about looking out for you all those years was also true. Sooner or later you would have 'disappeared' or had an accident like your father. You were already beginning to look for the truth without even realising it. I had noticed it even if you had not. Sooner or later you would have drawn attention to yourself just as your father did. We could not allow that to happen. We lost one good man we could not loose another. It is just that this thing is a lot bigger than anyone of us could have imagined! We faked the whole capture thing to make sure you came with us, and also to see if we could trust you. We had to be sure you would not give us away. You did not. I am really sorry but it was for your own good, believe me. It was necessary for us as well.' He stopped, still not looking at me.

'You realise I cannot trust you ever again Djon. You realise then that we trashed a perfectly good moon hopper to fool…..who? No one that's who!'

'Not quite. We wanted to make sure it looked as though we had perished in an accident and not escaped. Hopefully, no one would then come looking for us. We also had to have you on board. We needed a pilot, and we could not trust anyone else. Remember what your father said? 'Trust no one'. We thought he was right and now we know why.' He pointed up at the four thousand two hundred and ten portal signals still displayed on the screen. Something inside me realised that perhaps he was telling the truth. I relaxed and sunk back into the pilot's seat. 'I just need time to take all this in. I cannot believe this.'

'There's something else as well.' Said Ruuth quietly. 'There are no inhabited planets in the galaxy with one standard gravity or one standard day.'

'Unless it is the one near the hidden portal.' Said Djon, glad of a subject change.

'What is going on?' I was just shocked at the moment; this was not what I was expecting. 'We must find a way to get the data unlocked from the V20. Do you know anyone who can do that?' I looked up at Ruuth standing over me still.

'No.'

'Do we go to Geryon still?'

'Might as well.' Said Djon. 'If anyone is watching they will know where we are.'

'But not why.' I said. 'Just a minute. If that whole capture thing was a fake, then no one is watching out for us.'

'Not quite. What I said about there being people on Enceladus that we did not know was true.'

'That is why we thought we ought to move out quickly. We did not think we had to move that quickly though so someone would have been on the lookout.'

'Why didn't they come and get us when we were behind Erebus then?'

'I don't know. Maybe they fell for our ruse, or they are hoping we will lead them to other originists. Or maybe they just want to see how much we know.'

'We cannot go looking for any of your friends then?'

'Correct. At least we found out before putting others in danger.'

'Why don't we sell this vessel and buy another?' asked Ruuth.

'I cannot see anyone buying this in the state it's in. Besides there is always the galactic sales register. We would be advertising our location just as much as if we keep it.'

'So, we just keep going then?'

'I suppose so. If we get found out we get found out. But before we do, we must make sure that the information we have is not lost. So we need some ideas as to how we can do that.' Djon looked round at us all for ideas. We sat impassively.

'That's it.' I said at last. 'That's our insurance policy.' The danger that we all appeared to be in seemed to dissipate the anger that I felt towards Djon for duping me into this. We were all now in the same boat and getting my own back on Djon now would put everyone at risk for nothing. I felt myself relaxing even though I thought that I should not be letting him get away with it so easily. My own safety was also of prime importance.

'How do you mean?' Asked Djon.

'Well, we put the information we know somewhere so that if we are imprisoned or killed even, the information will be spread throughout the galaxy automatically.'

'Yes. A good idea but how do we do it?' asked Terens.

'We could use the drone. If we set it free with a timer on board so that if we do not return and reset the timer a radio broadcast will relay the information we have.'

'How will a radio message reach the furthest parts of the galaxy?' Asked Ruuth. 'It will take thousands of years.'

'No, it won't.' I replied smugly. I had thought this one through. 'Every time the portal is operated here it takes any electromagnetic signal with it. So, every time a portal is operated it will spread the message very quickly. In this case the oldest form of radio signal is the best as it is transferred by the portal the easiest.'

'So, can we use that to identify the location of a portal?' Asked Djon.

'I don't know that. We can try with the one that is here or the next nearest. Ruuth can you get the radio direction finder to find that out?'

'Yes, no problem. I think. Anyway, I will have a go.' She got up and went to the room next to the control room, where the radio and communication equipment was kept. We heard her pulling the front cover off the equipment housing.

'How do we set the timer?' Asked Terens. 'And get the radio signal to operate?'

'Perhaps we don't have to.' Said Djon quietly, a thoughtful look on his face. 'All we have to do is make anyone who threatens us believe we have one.'

'Will that work?'

'I would hope so.' Said Djon, resting his chin on his hands. 'Would anyone who had this secret dare to call our bluff?'

'I would like to think that if anything happened to us, nefarious or not, then the message would get out. I would prefer therefore to have the actual threat.'

'Can you make it work though?' Asked Djon.

'I am sure between us we have the knowledge to do it. Well, let us try at least. If we cannot do it then we resort to the bluff. We have some time to do it so let us get going.' To reinforce this I got up. I poked my head into the room where Ruuth was crouched down surrounded by parts of equipment.

'We are going to try and get the drone to be our insurance policy.'

'OK.' She replied without looking up. 'I'll join you all

when I've finished.' I then followed the other two down to the drone bay. The corridors were very narrow on our vessel so we had to go in single file, stepping through airlocks which divided up the corridors. They would automatically shut in any emergency, as they had done when we had the accident behind Erebus. The drone bay was a small room containing the drone in its launch tube. We manually closed the outer airlock door by a remote and then opened the inner access door. There was a concave table onto which we pulled out the drone from its launch tube. The drone was a cylinder about the size of a large suitcase. I got the cover off and looked inside. There was very little room. There were two cameras in there.

'Aha.' I said. 'They can go. We won't need cameras.'

'What if we need to survey the hull again?' Asked Terens.

'We'll have to get another drone. In fact, it will make a good reason for us to go to Geryon. We can claim our original was lost when we received our damage.

'Good idea I'll get a radio beacon.' Said Terens looking at the storage lockers while I set about getting the cameras out of the casing.

'I'll see if I can get a timer then.' Said Djon and joined Terens at the lockers. When they opened the first one there on the shelf was the toroid investigator!

'And what the Erebus is that thing?' I said. They looked up and immediately knew to what I was referring. They looked at each other. Djon spoke.

'Sorry, Djim.' He stumbled over the words. 'We just needed to know if you would betray us and it was the only way to do it without you seeing us.'

'One ghas of a way to do it.' I retorted angrily. 'How does it work?'

'I'm not sure. It is one of Ruuth's toys. I think it is the motor out of a small hovercar with a speaker. It is very basic.'

'Jolly effective I can tell you.' I felt stupid to have been taken in by it.

Two hours later and we were still at work. Ruuth joined us.

'It doesn't work.' She said. 'The portal seems to disrupt

the signal somehow so it is not possible to pinpoint the source. At least I am not able to make it work. Someone who knows the portal operation may have a better idea.'

'OK, you tried. That is the main thing. Can you help us with this?'

'Certainly.' She squeezed past the equipment tables to join Djon and Terens. With her knowledge we made more rapid progress and soon had what we thought was a serviceable insurance policy.

'We had better test it first.' I suggested. 'With an innocent radio signal for now.' We tried it. It worked. We all had big smiles on our faces. 'Right, let us get to Geryon and release this when we get there.'

'What is the range of this thing?' Asked Terens.

'Infinity eventually.' I replied.

'No, I mean what is the range of our remote operator for it?'

'Oh, about a hundred thousand kilometres I think. At least that is the normal limit of these things.'

'How will we find it?' Asked Ruuth.

'Good question.' I thought for a while. 'We need to keep it within the range limit. What do we know about Geryon?'

'We could keep it hidden in here somewhere.'

'What happens then if this vessel is taken?'

'Isn't that a good enough reason for the message to go out?'

'I don't know. It depends upon who takes it.'

'What happens if we are taken and they threaten one of us by threatening the others?'

'Good point, a very good point. We must make a pact never to give in to such pressure. It is the only way. We must stand firm. Agreed?' We all agreed and held hands in a circle to affirm our resolve to adhere to the plan.

'We still need somewhere to hide this. I think it is better not on board.'

'I agree.' Said Terens. 'There is an old disused satellite still in orbit around Geryon. At least there was one last time I was there. We could easily hide it on that.'

'Sounds good, but how do we get it there without drawing

attention to ourselves?' Asked Ruuth.

'We don't, we use the drone's own engines. We removed the cameras though so it will be much more difficult to get it well hidden.'

'Can we fly by fairly close without drawing attention to ourselves?' Asked Djon.

'I don't know.' Replied Terens. 'It was a long time ago when I was last there and I did not take much notice of where it was. I have a feeling it is a long way from the current satellite docking station. It could even be on the other side of the planet.'

'That could be awkward. It would look very strange if we went all the way round there and back. It would draw attention to ourselves and the old satellite. There must be another way then.'

'Why don't we strap the cameras to the outside?' Said Ruuth.

'Brilliant!' I said. 'Let us do it.' I jumped up and grabbed the camera from the table. 'Come on, help me here.' The others got up slowly. Djon came over and opened up the drone again to find the camera connections. He then ran the wires to the outer casing and closed it up again. We strapped the cameras to the outside with elastic polymetal straps. It was then too big to fit into the original drone tube so we put it on the trolley and wheeled it with difficulty to the airlock. It took a while and we had a few laughs on the way. For a while we almost forgot why we were doing it and the danger we were heading for. When that was done we then carried out a few more repairs on the ship. We discovered we needed replacement fluids in various parts and we also discovered that we were right about the trips through the portals stressing the hull. Some major repairs were becoming necessary to the outer hull. We had to find a repair yard at Geryon. We decided therefore to get there as soon as possible. I made my way to the control room while the others made more running repairs as best they could. I called up Ghandza space flight control to arrange for a trip through the portal. We had only a short wait as they had originally said.

I warned the others and set the vessel on course for the exit portal. Soon we were through with the familiar feeling.

*

Geryon hung in the black void of space before us. A large blue-brown planet with white clouds in the atmosphere. Nearby in geostationary orbit above the only inhabited part of the planet was the large docking satellite. It was identical to the one above Fyrest Prime.

'Open the airlock, Djon.' I said. 'We can release the drone.' I felt through the fabric of the vessel the door open, I did not need the control panel indicators to tell me. I turned on the drone camera and fired the drive as the release of pressure sucked the drone out into space. Fortunately, it was on the side of our vessel away from the satellite so should not be spotted just yet. I would kill the drives before it came out of the shadow of our hull. I set it on course to circumnavigate the planet using its gravity to help reduce the amount of fuel and time needed. I hoped it would not be noticed. It was small enough to be considered as a piece of space junk. Then Geryon space flight control contacted us.

'Welcome to Geryon Space. Do you wish to dock?'

'Yes, please, and we wish to visit planet surface too.'

'OK, please go to coordinates N30/300/70 and allow us to take control of your drives.'

'OK, will do. We also require some repairs to our hull.'

'OK, in that case we will bring you in to dock R2. Please go to coordinates N30/70/80 thank you. We will bring you in.'

'OK, going to coordinates N30/70/80.' I set the drives to take us to the coordinates. Slowly the satellite slid across our screen. I could see where they were going to take us. At the opposite end of the spine to the shuttle dome was another dome, but this one was not lit and glazed like the shuttle dome but was dark and full of holes for vessels to enter for repair. When we reached the coordinates there was a jolt as Geryon took control. We started to turn towards the dark dome at the end of the spine. As we got closer we could see the familiar nervate appearance of the outer skin and the rings with vessels docked at regular intervals around them. As we moved the sunlight glinted off the facets of the vessel's hulls. Only half the docking bays were occupied. Closer still we could see the docking bay that was obviously for us. Geryon space flight control interrupted us again.

'Please insert payment card. Repair bays are five hundred galactic dollars a day. How long will you be staying? Thank you.'

'We only require one day in the repair bay. We may need another at a normal dock.'

'OK, will book you in for one day in repair bay. If you wish to stay longer call us.'

'Djon.' I asked. 'Payment card required.' He produced it and I placed it in the payment slot.

Closer still the repair bay lights came on illuminating the approach and the interior. It was full of cranes, cables, gantries and machines that I could not identify. As we got closer still we slowed and slipped gently through the open door. Once inside we stopped and settled on the supports. There were thumps and thuds as the restraint clamps grabbed hold of our vessel to secure us to the supports. I shut down our systems. The outer door to the repair bay slid shut with a vibration felt through our vessel. When the bay had been pressurised I opened our airlock. We exited to find a repair worker standing nearby. He was a big man dressed in the usual overalls that workers have worn since time immemorial, except these were capable of use in the vacuum of space. He had short hair and a stubble on his chin.

'What can we do for you?' He asked in an accent which belied his stature.

'We can do most ourselves. We cannot afford a full repair service. Can you supply the following items?' Said Djon handing him a small disc. The man took it in his large ruddy hands and put it into a reader. He checked his screen.

'No problems, we have most of the items in store. A drone as well?' He called the stores on his radio. 'Yes, we even have a drone. It is the SD100 model, will that do?' He looked at Djon, his fingers hovering over his keyboard. Djon looked at me.

'Yes, thank you that will do.' I replied. He then typed on his keyboard. 'What other service machines do you require?' He gave Djon a similar disc. Djon put it in his reader and selected a gantry so we could reach the hull all round and some other tools I was not familiar with. He gave the man his payment card and he put it in his reader and typed in some figures and then returned the card to Djon.

'OK, good repairing. We are here if you need us.' Then he turned and shot away in a cradle on the end of a long arm to a doorway high up in the bay wall. The gantry we ordered dropped to our floor level and the tools Djon ordered were in pods on the side. The replacement drone also then appeared on another arm. I had to go back in to open the drone bay door. Djon released the drone from its rack on the arm and I was able to call it in from inside our vessel. It was more difficult being in a gravity environment but between us we finally managed to get it in the rack in the drone bay. I then closed the outer hatch and returned to the repair bay. We climbed on the gantry and using the joystick control took ourselves up to look over the hull. We examined the whole hull to get a good idea of how much damage had been done. We then set to. The first thing was to make the hull airtight again at least. We could then repair the internal systems when out in space if necessary from the inside. As we worked we discussed what we should do. Unfortunately, every now and again I had to stop work and go inside to check on the progress of our insurance policy. I got so engrossed in the repairs that the last time I nearly did not make it in time. The old satellite was right in front of the drone as I got back to the controls. I hurriedly made corrections and tried to slow it down. I could see the tiny puffs from the forward thrusters condensing in front of the camera. Then I saw the hole in the hull of the old satellite. Not too big because that would invite someone to come looking. I moved in closer. Just right. A small hole not much bigger than the drone itself. I guided it as best I could but even so

I still managed to hit the side of the rent as it went through. It span the drone round as it hit and I lost control in the confined space. Fortunately, at such slow speed I was hoping it would survive. It wedged itself into a gap inside the hole. I had no idea if it was still visible from outside. It was too late now. I sent a test signal. At least it was still responding. I heaved a sigh of relief and went back to the others.

We finished in good time so that we had not even used up all our allotted time in the bay. We got on so well with the big man, who was called Perak, he even gave us a small refund for finishing early. We thanked him profusely. He seemed a genuine guy, so much so that we even agreed to meet him in the evening at his local drinkery. We thought this a useful contact. We then called up space control and asked for an exit. We were guided out and after moving to the original coordinates we were guided into a dock.

We exited into the familiar curving corridor with the same colour drugget fibre and the same numerals and signs on the wall. We went to the same lift lobby and went to the same domed shuttle room. It was difficult to know where in the universe you were sometimes if you travelled a lot. The shuttle room was not as crowded as the room at Fyrest Prime but it had the same overhead signs and the same information screens. For such a big place it seemed odd that there were not more people about. Fortunately, though it meant a very short wait for the shuttle, which was already docked. We boarded straight away and sat alone. There were a lot of empty seats. I felt more exposed than if it had been crowded. It was an uneventful flight down to the planet's surface. We stepped out into a similar shuttle hall as at Fyrest and to the same hustle from taksi drivers. Again, we took the monorail. It was an identical type to the one on Fyrest too, even down to the swooping ride. The station was the same design, which made the whole journey rather uncanny. We found ourselves in the capital Hai-Duk. This also was so similar, being made up of the same type of prefabricated units. The dust from the volcanic activity was a different colour here though. There was also a lot less of it. The place almost seemed clean by comparison to Ho-Dei-Da. It was getting dark and we needed to find the drinkery that Perak mentioned. It was not easy as there was no street lighting. It was not deemed necessary as there was so little crime, here as everywhere in the galaxy. Besides most people went by hovercar. It would also have meant overhead cables as it was not feasible to put them underground because of the tectonic shifts. We tried to follow his directions from the station. We had not brought any portable lights with us.

We finally found it by the illuminated sign hanging outside. We went in. It was not crowded but the barman said it would pick up later. We ordered drinks and some food. It helped being less crowded. It meant we would not have to wait for the order. We ate in silence watching the few people at the bar. It was typical in that there was a large bar, which took up one wall, with drinks hanging behind it, all illuminated tastefully. The floor was a light-coloured soft plastic compound divided into large squares all grained differently and was marked with constant use. There were round tables of some metal with tops made from a similar plastic compound but much harder to the touch and slightly warm. The seats were made from some woven plant-based material into curved ribbed seats which were full backed with small short legs. Around the edges were grouped dark coloured settees. The walls were a reddish colour illuminated by lights shining down the walls in triangular shaped patterns. The low ceiling was divided up into large squares by beams criss-crossing. Small points of light were carefully placed regularly along the beams making spots of light on the floor. There were pictures of faces on the walls. Circular columns broke up the space. The lighting was low and bordering on the red it gave a very warm and comfortable feeling. As we finished eating then more people began to arrive and the 'buzz' that you get in all good eating and drinking houses started. Perak arrived with a blond-haired woman. He saw us immediately and came over.

'My goodness, you guys have made it.' He said cheerily. 'People don't normally bother once their vessel is repaired.

By the way this is my sister, Karon.' We shook hands. She was obviously older than him but still very beautiful with a thick mane of blond hair rising from around her face to fall down to her shoulders in wild but controlled waves. She had dark brown eyes with long lashes. There were little laughter lines running from the corners of her eyes. She had dark brown eyebrows that curved naturally over her eyes. She had full lips highlighted with a red lipstick. She wore black. We made polite conversation. Perak wanted to buy us drinks, but we declined and insisted that we buy him and his sister drinks instead. He finally agreed and eased his large frame into the seat. Djon went and got the drinks and we got talking. It seemed that Perak had always been a mechanic on Geryon as had his father. His sister worked in the shuttle business. She was in the office on planet surface. She never went into space as she did not like it. In fact, she hated it even though there was artificial gravity and flights didn't usually take long.

We told Perak that we were looking for business opportunities. He did not seem too pleased at that. I looked at Ruuth and her look back confirmed my suspicion. I needed to know why he reacted that way. The time came when Karon went to the toilet and Perak insisted it was his turn to buy the drinks.

'We must be direct with him.' I said to the others. 'He did not like it when we said about the business deals. I think we must just try and just go for it. Tell him why we are here. We have nothing to lose.'

'What do you mean "we have nothing to lose"?' asked Terens. 'We have everything to lose if he tells someone why we are here.'

'I think I know what he means' Said Djon, quietly. 'We will solve nothing by not putting ourselves out on a limb. Perak is not high up in the echelon and should not therefore pose a high risk.'

'I agree.' Added Ruuth. 'We need to try and find out more, and the only way to do that is to ask questions. We are probably already in the firing line and the longer we hang about doing nothing the less we will find out and the sooner be caught.'

'So, we are agreed then?' I asked, looking around at the others as I saw Perak returning with a tray of drinks. The others nodded gravely. I could sense the feeling of anxiety, even though we had agreed. I felt strongly we had no choice. I hoped we were not jumping straight into a bottomless pit. I sat up straighter as Perak arrived back at our table. He was not as chatty as before. The others looked at me and nodded at me to say I should raise the subject. I was just about to begin when Karon returned also. It was now or never.

'I have something to say.' I began hesitantly. Perak and Karon looked at me with a look of fear on their faces. 'Ok, guys, we were not quite honest when we said we were looking for business opportunities. What we are actually doing is looking for the original pl...'

'Good ghas!' Erupted Perak and then lowered his voice conspiratorially. 'You're originists.' He leant forward over the table. 'What are you doing coming here with stupid notions like that? And what are you doing dragging us into it.' He then got up and took his drink and went and sat over with his usual friends at the other end of the room.

'I'm sorry about Perak.' Said Karon, surprisingly calmly. 'He lost his brother when the vessel he was on never returned from a flight. We never found out what happened. But just before he left, he had met with originists and Perak thinks there was a connection.'

I hung my head. Karon looked at me then at the others.

'Are you saying there is a connection?' She looked so worried it made me feel really bad. I looked across at the others. They were equally awkward and looked down at their drinks.

'Look.' I fought for the words. 'There is something very strange going on in the galaxy. It appears as though there is no original planet. At least there is no original planet that we can find. As far as we can ascertain it either does not exist or it has been hidden! Not only that but there are some person or persons unknown who want it to stay that way for reason or reasons unknown. I'm sorry but that sounds rather garbled.' There was a stunned silence for a while.

'What are you people saying?' She said finally, looking at me in a shocked state, her natural colour had drained from her face.

'I know this must come as a bit of a shock.' Said Ruuth, putting a comforting hand on her shoulder. 'It is as much as a shock for us too. We cannot go home.' Karon looked at her with wide eyes. 'Why don't you come aboard and see what we have found out.'

'Are you trying to kidnap me?' asked Karon in a small voice which seemed unnatural as her normal persona was one of confidence from experience. But this was experience as she knew it here on her planet in her normal environment.

'Of course not.' Laughed Ruuth. The sudden natural sound of her laughter seemed to break the mesmerism of the moment. Karon seemed to relax a little. After a while she came to trust us a little more. We talked a bit more about our problem.

'I don't think Perak will come.' She said finally. 'He won't go aboard a space vessel since our brother disappeared. I will come though, as long as you promise not to depart from the docking satellite.' Her natural confidence returning together with her obvious desire for knowledge.

'Of course, we promise.' I said.

'I will go and see if he will come then, but I don't think he will.' She got up and went over to where Perak was sitting with his friends. She took him to one side and they talked animatedly for some time. She returned.

'He wouldn't come as I thought.' She said, and then stunned us all by adding. 'Shall we go now?'

'Now?' Said Djon, taken aback. 'It's very late.'

'Sure, why not? If this information is as serious as you say then there is no time to loose.' I was taken aback by this sudden interest in our quest. It seemed as though this was no longer our own project but now belonged to others.

'Do you realise what you are saying?' said Terens. 'Do you realise what we have just said? There are people out there who will stop at nothing to keep a secret secret.'

'I know what you are saying.' She replied and seemed to

stand taller as she spoke. 'I have felt for a while that something was not right, as you have said. I am convinced that our brother's disappearance was not an accident. I had no proof and no evidence that it was not but just a gut reaction somehow. What you have said has just made me all the more sure that my feeling was right. I want to try and help if I can.'

'Ok, then.' Said Ruuth. 'Let us go.' And as if to reinforce her decision she got up and finished up her drink. We all got up and went to the door. Perak waved as we left but did not want to come over and did not seem to mind his sister coming with us. I found that quite amazing that even knowing us a short time he would let her leave with strangers. I was not sure I would have done the same. Karon called a hover taksi and would not accept our protests. She said it was late and there was no time to lose. She would not accept any monetary recompense either saying she could easily afford it and we deserved it. We soon found ourselves at the shuttle terminal and in a flight up to the satellite.

Once inside our vessel she was keen to see the information we had. We were also careful to make sure she knew of our insurance policy, but not its location of course, just in case. After all we had not known her long. We were taking a gamble and we all knew it. She seemed genuinely interested and genuinely concerned over our news. We asked her if she could help us locate the hidden portal. She said she would try.

Very late that night she left our vessel and went back to the planet. She would not accept any of us to accompany her back down insisting that she was quite safe. We all then fell into bed.

When we awoke next morning there was a message from Karon inviting us to go down to the planet and meet someone she knew. Did the woman not sleep I wondered? We debated whether to go or not but decided that if we did nothing then we would get nowhere. So, we left for the shuttle terminal on planet surface after breakfast. It was there that Karon had arranged for us to meet. It was becoming a familiar journey. I was apprehensive of what would await us. Was Karon a traitor to our cause? Was she friend or foe? We would find out soon enough I thought as the surface of the planet grew nearer and nearer. My insides grew ever more unsettled with the nearness of the planet surface.

Once in the terminal we went to the section she had said in her message and waited. She came to see us shortly. 'Good, you came.' She said. 'I have someone I would like you to meet.'

'Is this safe?' Asked Djon. 'We cannot trust just anyone in this.'

'I am fairly sure he is safe.' She replied a worried look coming over her face. 'He is the Deputy Gerent and knows my family well. He wants to see you all. He thinks he may have information that you will find interesting.'

'What is the Gerent?' asked Ruuth.

The planet ruler.' Terens answered for her. Now it was our turn to look worried. 'I am not sure of this. We all know this thing starts at the top.'

'I'm sure we can trust him.' Said Karon and as she spoke she directed us towards a door marked 'Private' and held it open for us to go through. We found ourselves in a corridor. 'Please.' She said. 'Follow me.' She led us down a wide drugget covered corridor with picture lined walls with a series of regular placed doorways, all closed. At the end of the corridor was a lift. She stopped and pressed a button. The doors slid open with barely a noise and she stepped inside the brightly lit mirrored interior of the lift car. We followed and the doors slid shut. The lift went up three floors and the doors slid open to reveal a similar corridor. The opposite wall was made of some obscured glass or plastic equivalent. In a recess off the corridor was a desk and a young woman sat at the desk surrounded by the equipment required by a receptionist, much as receptionists have for many many years I felt. She waved us to seats opposite. 'Mr. Tire will be with you shortly.' She said and returned to her work. I noticed that she did throw us curious glances when she thought I was not watching. We sat down on the well upholstered seats. We did not have to wait long. The woman opposite soon pointed to a door opening in the glass wall. 'Please go in.' She said and watched us enter the room.

We entered a large well-lit office with two large windows overlooking the city. All the ground stations in the galaxy were the same; the large cargo vessels grounded and turned into the first building on a planet. The huge cargo holds formed the public arrivals and departures hall and this room was probably the crew dining room I thought. It still even now had the original light fittings which adhered closely to the ribs of the vaulted ceiling. The two large vaults still had the perforated finish presumably for sound reduction or something or for air handling grilles. The windows would have been added after arrival and grounding. The walls were designed for it and the windows would have been carried as part of the cargo. Everything was geared for optimum effectiveness and ease of settlement. All this divided the room into two parts. Large deep beams emphasizing the division. One part held Mr. Tire and his desk; the other part held a round glass table with two identical soft settees facing each other. New lighting had been installed to illuminate the curved vaulted ceiling over the windows. The beams ended in columns which framed the windows. The windows ran from a beam down to the floor giving a light bright interior to the office as well as giving a superb view out of the city. On the table was a vase with artificial plants and a couple of old objects.

Behind a large desk sat a small thin man with black hair that fell forward from a central parting. His head was shaped like an upside-down pear, large at the crown and small at his chin. His nose was thin and long and deep creases fell from it to the ends of his thin straight lips. But it was his hair that struck me most. It was one of the great revolutions of the galaxy to be able to prevent or cover over realistically male pattern baldness. This was one of the better jobs, but I could still tell it was not his original hair, even though I did not know why. And why pick such an odd hair style? He wore black.

'Sit down.' He said in a rather nasal voice and waved us to sit on the settees. 'I trust that Karon has looked after you well. Thank you all for coming. Karon tells me you have something of interest to tell me.'

'Yes, we do have something which we have found.' Said Djon rather slowly and carefully. 'But we need to know your interest in us as well.'

'What do you mean? Do you think I am somehow against you or your enemy in some way?' He said as he rose from behind his desk to join us at the settees.

'I mean that the information we have may put us in danger and possibly yourself as well.'

He laughed and rocked back in his chair. 'Danger!' He said finally. 'What a quaint idea. And from whom would I be in danger?'

Djon looked rather awkward. 'We don't actually know'

'That is rather awkward then, not knowing your enemy Mr er...' He faltered to a stop.

'Djon is my name.'

'Thank you, Djon. So, tell me then what is this information that is so dangerous to you and me?'

'We are trying to find the original planet.' Said Djon rather levelly. Mr Tire looked askance.

'That is not dangerous, Djon, just misguided. There is no original planet, we all know that. Only a certain rather deluded group of people think there possibly could have been. This is not dangerous information.'

'I agree, but in looking for the original planet we have come across some anomalies that we could not account for.' Went on Djon carefully. 'We discovered that indeed there is no original planet because we could not find one with one standard gravity or one standard day which would be the original, otherwise why do we have such a standard with no planets with those qualities. But we did find that there is one portal that is hidden for some reason. Not only that but when we looked for the information then the programme was tampered with after we looked at it. We do not know why. We also know that the colonisation is only 200 years old but before the portals space travel would have meant that it should have taken about 14,000 years assuming a central start that is. Unless of course space travel at faster than light or in some form like the portals existed before they were set up. We cannot find any way that could have been possible. There is surely no way of knowing where you will end up with no receiving portal?' Djon then ran out of steam and stopped and looked at us for support. I nodded to him, he looked drawn.

The man Tire looked at us for a while as he absorbed what Djon had just spilled out. It obviously was nothing like he was expecting to hear. 'A hidden portal you say. A discrepancy in the colonisation dates. Are you sure the information you have is correct? Is it not possible that there is a corruption of your data?'

We were then stumped, he made us feel we were stupid. Was our data correct? I began to doubt it under his stare from his deep-set blue eyes cast in shade from his hair. 'Do you have a copy of this data?' He asked finally.

'Yes.' Said Ruuth. 'We have a copy here, see for yourself.' She took out the small disc and placed it on the table in front of Mr Tire. He took it, got up and returned to his desk and placed it in the reader. The data sprang into life in front of him. He looked at it carefully and the room fell very silent. He then broke the silence with. 'Very interesting. You seem to have some unusual data here. But again, how do you know it is correct and not corrupted data?'

'We don't.' Said Djon again. 'But it is sufficiently odd for us to continue searching for the truth behind it. Especially if we can find a hidden portal.'

There was a pause again as Mr Tire thought. 'I wish to show this to some colleagues, will you come back tomorrow?' He looked at us. We looked at each other.

'We are not sure we can afford to be docked here for another day.' Said Terens.

'Ah, I see. No problem. I will give you a dispensation for the day. Go and enjoy yourselves. See something of our planet.'

'Why thank you, we will come back tomorrow. What time and where?'

'Same time, same place tomorrow. Karon, you can show them in again?'

'Yes, sir.'

'I will see you all tomorrow, and hopefully we will be able to see what can be done.'

'Thank you.' Said Djon. We all got up and Karon showed us to the door and then back out to the arrivals hall.

'See you guys tomorrow. I told you he would help.' Said Karon, while still holding open the staff door, half in and half out.

'Thank you. I hope this does not cause trouble for your brother.' Said Ruuth. Karon dismissed it and ducked back into the staff area with a cheerful wave. The door shut with a soft click and we were standing alone. Well, not so much alone as the hall was filling up with travellers but alone with our thoughts. We stood without moving for a while until Terens said. 'Let us go get a coffee or some other local drink.' And he headed off to the parade of shops that lined the edge of the concourse. We dumbly followed him to a café. It was not the best location being off the busy, noisy concourse with no frontage other than a wide opening. Tables spilled out of the café onto the hall floor. We sat at the empty table under the canopy which projected out of the hall wall and gave some sense of place amidst the huge open area. It tried to make the café more intimate but without success. The tablecloth was clean though. We ordered drinks and sat and silently drank for a while longer. We had a good view and watched the cavernous space with the information screens and the tall pillar of lights that moved slowly around the central open space. We assumed the latter was some form of art, for we could see no other purpose for it.

'Do we go back?' Asked Terens after a while.

'I think so.' Said Djon absently. 'We will find nothing if we just run away all the time. We have no way of finding out any more information without a little risk.'

'What if it is a trap?' Asked Terens again. 'What if they lock us up? What then?'

'Then our insurance policy comes into play.' I said.

'Yes, OK, but what if they don't fall for it?'

'Then at least we will know that the information we have will be spread throughout the galaxy and our sacrifice will not be in vain.' Said Ruuth into her coffee.

'Shall we leave one or two of us on our vessel just in case?' Suggested Terens.

'No.' said Djon surprisingly sharply. 'Remember what we said? We all stick together.

'OK.' Said Terens and went back to staring at the throng of people milling about.

'There are still some repairs that need doing.' Said Ruuth quietly. 'Perhaps we should go back and get the vessel in a more spaceworthy condition.'

'Yes, you are right.' Said Djon. 'Do we all need to go, or can we be doing something useful to find more information from town?'

'We could try and find the location of the unknown portal.'

'We came to find the 'Fair Trade Dealers.' Reminded Ruuth.

'You are right as usual.' Said Djon brightly. 'Are you happy to go looking for that? You and Terens maybe?' I had hoped he would have said me and not Terens but he did not.

'OK.' She said. 'When I have finished my drink.' She looked at me quizzically as I stiffened and then shrunk down in my seat, my hand up to my face. 'What's up Djim?' She asked, a worried look now spreading across her face.

'Don't look round!' I hissed, emphasising the first word. Then the man that I had seen was gone. 'I have just seen one of the men we saw in the restaurant on Fyrest Prime.' I said. The others looked at me frowning.

'Are you sure?' Asked Djon, just a note of concern entering his voice as he did not quite think his question necessary.

'Yes, there is no mistaking them is there. I have not seen anyone quite like that in here, or anywhere else at all.'

'Right, follow him then. Now!' Said Djon quickly. 'Let us see where he goes.'

'Me?' I stuttered.

'Yes, you! Now get going.' He replied leaning forward

over the table and speaking quietly but firmly. I stood up in obedience. His age and years of being a surrogate father making me immediately fall back into child like acceptance of his authority. I kept an eye on the man as he reappeared in the crowd. It was not easy as I set off as he kept disappearing behind other travellers, but fortunately reappearing again. He was heading towards where we had just come from not long before. I had not taken more than a few steps when he reached the door through which Karon had taken us. He did not stop but opened the door and disappeared through it. I stopped, turned round and returned to the others. They were looking at me askance.

'Well?' Said Djon. 'What went wrong?'

'He has just gone where Karon took us just now.' I replied as I sat down in my old seat. It was still warm. We all looked at each other with bemused expressions on our faces.

'He certainly didn't look like a member of the establishment to me.' Muttered Terens, more under his breath than to anyone in particular.

'We need to speak to Karon about him then.' Said Ruuth pragmatically.

'OK. We will do that tomorrow. We cannot do anything about him now and I suggest it would be best if we avoided him anyhow. Now, what are we going to do today?' Said Djon almost all in one breath.

'Well, Terens and I are going looking for the 'Fair Trade Dealers' if you remember.' Said Ruuth with a wry smile on her face.

'Which means then.' Replied Djon without noticing the jibe. 'That Djim and I are on repair duty. OK, let us go then. We will see you guys back on board later today.' He stood up as he finished speaking. Ruuth continued to finish her drink. Terens as usual sat impassively with his own thoughts, staring at the people. They both nodded as we left.

*

Later that evening Karon and Terens returned, obviously exhausted. 'Well?' Asked Djon. 'What did you find?'

'Not a lot.' Replied Ruuth as she threw herself into the nearest seat. 'We found what appeared to be the main office of the Fair Traders. The lady on the desk was most unhelpful at first. We eventually got someone to come and talk to us but he was just as unhelpful. They would not accept that we wanted to join up and become a member. They said there were no vacancies in the organisation for any new staff of any kind.'

'What!' Said Djon. 'Dealers not wanting more people to help trade? Strange.'

'Quite.' Ruuth carried on. 'So, then we went to the ground station to see if we could find any way to gain access to the information there. The security there is nothing like on Enceladus. It was so tight we could not even get to the office. So then we went to the library to see what we could find there. The references to the Fair Trade Dealers just mentions that it is the largest dealers in the galaxy. We then looked up the next largest and could find nothing.'

'You mean they are the only dealers?'

'It looks that way. We tried everything to find out other dealers or traders but could find nothing. Nobody was willing to talk about it either. Then…' Ruuth hesitated. 'Then we were stopped by security and asked what we were doing. They would not accept our explanation and more or less told us to leave or face the consequences. They were not very specific but they made their position very clear.'

'Oh.' I said. 'Maybe that means we are onto something.'

'It looks like it. But what do we do? And what are we onto?'

'I don't know, but tomorrow we go and see Mr. Tire. Well, we can do nothing now so let us have some dinner. Any requests?' I was met with a barrage of various suggestions for dinner. 'OK, you are getting what I want then.' I set off for the galley. More basic space rations rehydrated for dinner. Boring but nutritious. It was a little later when Ruuth came by the galley and asked if there was time for a shower before dinner. After a while as I heard nothing I went looking for her, she was flat out on her bunk fast asleep. Obviously the day had taken its toll on her. We ate without her, saving her dinner for later, it made no difference to the taste much. We then just sat and talked for a while, too tired to do anything much. Even Terens looked tired which was unusual for him. We then went to bed.

– CHAPTER 6 –
GALILEI

The next morning, we were back in the arrivals and departure hall waiting for Karon to let us into the staff area. We stood uncomfortably watching the passers by, half expecting to be hustled off somewhere. I had an uneasy feeling of being watched but even though I looked around could see nothing out of the ordinary. There was the usual apparent random movement of people filling the space with their presence and hubbub. The tower of lights was a long way off and not moving this time. I could see no cameras but as they can be very small that was not surprising.

Fortunately, Karon suddenly appeared from behind the door and ushered us into the now familiar corridor.

'Karon.' I said. 'Yesterday we saw someone we had seen on Fyrest Prime come into this very same corridor. He is a big man with...' Karon stopped me in mid sentence.

'I'm sorry but I have not seen anyone I do not know in here. He must have arrived when I was off duty. I'm very sorry but I cannot help you.' She was awkward I felt and perhaps knew more than she was letting on, but I did not want to confront her with my suspicions. She turned and led us silently on. She took us up to the same office as before and we were shown straight into the office. It was empty. She pointed to some seats and we sat down in silence.

'Karon.' Said Djon. 'Who are the people that Mr. Tire is speaking to?' She held up her hand.

'Mr. Tire will explain everything.' She replied. She did not seem her usual self. Although we had only known her a short while I would swear that she was not comfortable with the situation.

'How…' Began Djon again but he stopped when I looked at him with an expression that said stop. He did.

'Thank you.' Said Ruuth. Karon turned and left.

'He won't be long.' She said as she left.

'Thank you.' Called Djon after her. We looked at each other.

'She was not keen to talk about things today was she' Said Ruuth. 'It was not like her, even though I do not know her well.' She continued.

'I agree.' I added. 'Do we go through with this or do we go now before we are clapped in a containment field.'

'We said we would go through with this.' Said Djon. 'We will find nothing by running away.'

'She also said she would try and find the missing portal for us too.' I added 'but I don't think she will now somehow.'

'You're right.' Said Terens absently. 'I …' We were interrupted by Mr. Tire entering the room with his secretary, whom we recognised from the day before. She was carrying a tray with drinks. She placed it down on the table and left the room. Mr. Tire sat down behind his desk.

'Please.' He began. 'Take a drink, and then we shall begin.' We duly stood up and took the drinks from the tray on the table and sat back down again on our seats facing the desk.

'I have shown the data that you presented me with to our experts and unfortunately they have come to the conclusion that as I originally thought that the data is not correct. We suspect that it has been corrupted. Perhaps you should return to your own planet and resume your lives.' He paused. 'There is no such thing as an original planet. We all know that, and your data actually confirms this by not producing any clear evidence of such. We have all developed across the galaxy as it is recorded. There is no hidden portal and our experts have examined the data for this and found it is not correct. The so-called hidden portal is no more than a shadow produced when portals are activated and sometimes confuses the V20. This is what sometimes causes flight errors and the loss of space vessels. If you had let the V20 work normally the anomaly would have resolved itself as it does every day.' He stopped and took a drink. 'I am so sorry to have to say this, but your mission is fruitless.'

'Excuse me.' Said Djon. 'But the data we collected was from a library. It clearly shows that none of the worlds in the galaxy have one standard day, or time, or orbit. It makes us suspicious that the standard galactic day, hour and even...' He paused slightly before continuing. 'The standard galactic gravity of 'one' does not appear on any planet.'

'You do not seem to understand me. The data that we have is not very exact. We suspect that not all the data for the planets has been collected or is even correct. Certainly, libraries have been known to store either outdated or incorrect data on the planets. We have been concerned for some time that data is being corrupted somehow and cannot be trusted. We do not know how or why. There was, many years ago near the beginning of the colonisation an agreement on the standard galactic days and units etc. It was the only way to manage the vastness of the galaxy and keep costs within bounds and also make space travel a reality. It would not work if we were all using different units. It was decided to use units that did not relate to any one planet to avoid favouritism.' He stopped and looked at us. His hair no longer seemed funny. 'Now, we have been very generous with our hospitality but now we suggest you return to Enceladus and resume your lives. We will even repair your vessel for you. What do you say?' He looked at us again. His look suggested we accept his suggestion and there was no argument.

'I think we need to discuss this amongst ourselves for a short while.' Said Djon. 'But before we go Karon said yesterday that you had some interesting information for us.' Mr. Tire looked awkward and shifted uneasily in his large office chair. 'I think she must have been mistaken, I'm afraid.' He replied, finally. 'I may have thought originally so but after seeing this data that you have presented I am convinced there is no more to say.' He rested his chin on his touching fingers.

'You have indeed made a very generous offer and we thank you for it.' Said Ruuth diplomatically. 'We will return to our vessel now and let you know shortly what we intend to do. I suspect we will take you up on your kind offer, but you will agree that we have the right to at least discuss this first.'

'Thank you, but please do not take long as we need the docking space. Goodbye and good journey. 'He pressed a button on his desk and his secretary reappeared in the office and held open the door. We got up to leave.

'My secretary will give you my personal communication details so you can contact me direct.'

'Thank you.' His secretary entered the room and showed us out. At her desk she gave Djon Mr. Tire's personal communication address. We left the way we had come escorted by his secretary and not Karon.

Back in the arrivals and departure hall I said. 'Why didn't you mention our insurance policy?'

'I didn't think it would do any good.' Replied Ruuth. 'He has been got at I think.'

'Really?' said Djon.

'Yes. His complete turn around from yesterday, and that man from Fyrest coming here makes me think so. I do not think there is any point in pushing him further. The only way we will get anywhere is by looking to people like us. I suspect the problem is from the top down and not from the bottom up. That means people like us are less likely to be part of it.'

'But people like us do not know what is going on and have no access to power. Look at you two and the Fair Traders. You got nowhere.'

'I know, but now we know that we will have to be more careful and devious.' We headed back to the shuttle bay.

*

Later on, we were back on board and sitting round the control room table. We had been discussing the situation for some time and getting nowhere. We all agreed that Mr. Tire and Karon had changed since our first visit. Djon was annoying me by dismissing their arguments out of hand. He would not listen to any other point of view but his own. Finally I snapped.

'Well Djon.' I said. 'You have dragged me halfway across the galaxy; you have lied to me and put all our lives in danger by tampering with standard flight equipment. And all for what? Some stupid harebrained scheme to find the original planet which has never existed and never will exist!' I slammed my hand down on the table. 'What on Erebus possessed you to drag us all into this? I cannot believe you would put my mother through all this stress for some stupid idea. Now those two have been threatened. All you have managed to do is get us caught up in some nasty business that is not going to help anything. All you have managed to do is stir up a viper's nest and put us all in danger.'

'I must agree.' He began contritely, which immediately took the wind out of my sails. I stopped mid thought to ask myself what sails were but he continued and the idea evaporated. 'It would appear that I was wrong. But I assure you all it was no harebrained scheme. Your father, Djim, also felt the same way as me. But we cannot carry on if we have nothing to go on. We either need to get the information corrected or confirmed. I have to say again that it was not....look I believed what your father and Terens had found out.' He stopped, sweating profusely. It was the first time I had seen him so stressed. It unnerved me. He had always been such a tower of strength to me and my mother. Now he looked like a frightened child. I looked at Terens.

'I still think something is wrong in this galaxy.' He said, as impassively as ever. 'I think that guy back there was lying. I am not phased by being threatened, It just makes me more determined.'

'I agree.' Added Ruuth.

'Really?'

'Yes.' She looked more determined than I had seen her before. Her jaw was set and she had a grim expression. 'I will prove our data is correct.'

'Can you prove it?' I asked. Strangely I wanted to believe she was right. Even though I had been angry at Djon I wanted to believe that all this was based on fact not fiction.

'No.' She said after some thought. 'The information came from the V20. It is one that has been tampered with so no one would trust any information from it. We would need corroborative data from another V20 at least. I don't think we can trust the library information anymore either though.'

'Oh, why?'

'I think somehow someone somewhere is able to infect it.'

'It is always these mysterious faceless 'someones'.' I said. 'After all this time we still have nothing!' I wanted to throw something at someone but all space vessels were free of loose objects, especially in the control rooms.

'Well, we tried.' Said Djon in a rather dejected way. I did not like to see him in this state. What has he done to me I thought, now I want to believe his harebrained view of the galaxy! What was the matter with me? Had I lost all sanity? At least if we could find no way of proving our data perhaps at last I could go home and resume my job and take up the threads of my life once more.

'OK, then we go home.' I said matter of factly.

'You still don't understand do you.' Said Djon. 'We cannot go home. Do you forget so easily..'

'Look you.' I retorted angrily. 'Don't forget that you lied to me about my kidnapping! How am I supposed to believe you about these strange faceless people that want me and you done away with? How can they do it without being found out? There are laws and protection for people you know. You cannot just go around the galaxy just disposing of people! And besides now we have nothing to support your theory either. Just a load of conjecture and 'funny feelings', well that will not do. I want to go home and go back to my life. You can carry on with this harebrained scheme if you wish but I have had enough.'

'Don't forget your father, Djim.' Said Djon, some of his former strength returning.

'Proof, Djon, proof! That is what we need, not this vague conjecture!' I got up to leave the room, but then thought better of it and sat down again. 'OK, so who is for going back to Enceladus then?' I put up my hand. We looked at each other.

They looked down at their hands. Terens continued to rotate a small recording disk. Finally Djon spoke.

'OK, I agree with Djim here.' He said. 'I think we have no alternative but to return to Enceladus. If we try and go elsewhere then we can easily be followed by the V20 trace. It would look bad if we did not return. Besides, where do we go from here?'

The airlock sounder chimed loudly into the awkward silence. We stiffened and looked at each other. No one moved.

'Use the video link.' I said finally breaking the mesmerism and nodding to Djon, who was nearest the airlock video link. This link enabled occupants of docked vessels to speak to visitors at the docking station airlock door. Djon quickly got up and pressed the intercom button.

'Hello.' He said as the video link screen sprang into life, but instead of showing the dock corridor it showed a blank screen. 'It's not working.' He said.

'Yes, it is.' I replied. 'Look, the screen is active. There must be something over the lens.'

'So, someone doesn't want to be seen.' Added Ruuth. Now I wanted to scream! Yet another faceless 'someone' another faceless entity but yet this one was not of Djon's making. There was someone out there who did not want us to see them and that raised the question of why?

'Let us go and look then.' I got up quickly and made for the doorway.

'Just a minute.' Said Terens quietly but firmly as he grabbed my arm; stopping me in my tracks. 'If someone out there does not want to be seen we could be walking into danger. We need a weapon and two of us to stay in the control room. I will go and Djim will come with me. Ruuth man the airlock link and if there is any sign of danger you flush it out.'

'That will kill you if you are in it!' She cried.

'It will also kill anyone else too. Better that than all of us being taken out. Lock the hatch behind us. Just wait while I get a weapon from the locker.'

'What sort of weapon?' I asked. 'We cannot risk doing damage to our vessel.'

'That rules out a frisson bolt gun.' Said Terens.

'OK, take an E.N.D.' Suggested Ruuth.

'What's an E.N.D?' I asked. 'I was hearing a lot of new things on this trip and they weren't all Djon's cranky ideas.

'An E.N.D.' Replied Terens as he was half out of the door. 'Is an electrical nerve disrupter.' And he was gone.

'It's much safer.' Added Ruuth. 'It will not damage the vessel but it will damage anyone else. It is not always lethal but it will give us enough time to reseal the airlock and prevent anyone getting in.'

'Unless they are carrying a G.F.S.' Said Djon enigmatically.

'Oh, ghas.' I swore. 'I don't believe it. Now what is that?'

'Sorry Djim.' Said Djon. 'I forget you are a parochial. 'A G.F.S is a generated force shield. It protects the wearer from most discharge weapons.' Terens returned then gripping a black object which had a small dish like a tiny black radar dish on the end. It did not look very threatening.

'OK, let us go Djim.' He led the way out to the airlock. When we reached the airlock chamber Terens stood aside.

'I'll cover you. You open the door and step aside.' I spun the circular manual handle to open the inner door, thus saving valuable energy in the onboard systems and pulled the hatch open. Terens peered round the door.

'OK.' He said and waved me on. I stepped through into the link corridor that separated us from the docking satellite. I was always acutely aware that we were only millimetres away from the cold vacuum of space. It was not a place I liked to linger. It was an irrational fear based on no real evidence at all. I quickly reached the satellite airlock door and pressed the open button and stood back. Terens tensed as the lock swung open. As it did so a small metal disk clattered to the floor. Terens stepped over it and looked carefully into the familiar curving corridor. He visibly relaxed. I followed him into the corridor. It was empty and quiet. I checked the video link system and found a piece of sticky tape over the camera lens. I peeled it off.

'Working now?' I said into the speaker.

'Fine now.' Replied Ruuth, her grainy image from the airlock chamber facing me on the tiny screen. It was a shame they still used such poor-quality equipment for these links, but had to admit there was no need to use any better really. They did the job. Then I realised that Terens had disappeared back into the vessel. I then remembered the first rule of space flight, "always stay on board unless absolutely necessary". Should anything happen it would be better if as few people as possible were lost. It was not unknown for a vessel at dock to break free. I went back into the link corridor and picked up the disk. Why hadn't Terens picked it up? Then I remembered that he had been very tense looking out for anyone waiting for us and had probably missed the tiny disk fall to the floor. I looked at it in my hand, it was similar to the one that Terens had been playing with just moments earlier. I put it in my pocket and returned the way we had come. The others were waiting for me in the chamber. Terens returned from locking away the E.N.D.

'Well?' asked Djon.

'This was all that was there.' I said, holding up the recording disk. Ruuth took it out of my hand.

'Let us look at what it says then.' She said and disappeared out of the chamber. The others followed her as I shut the hatch and then followed them. When I got back to the control room the disk was already playing. It was a series of DNA profiles, except none of us knew what DNA was.

'What on Erebus is DNA?' Asked Djon.

'I don't know.' Replied Ruuth, distractedly. She was trying to get the readout to scroll down. 'I am hoping it will give us some more information. Ah.' As she spoke an explanation of DNA appeared in the text. We all stood reading it.

'Wow.' Said Ruuth. 'It appears that we all carry this imprint that can not only identify us but also track our ancestor's way back in time and identify from whom we have come.'

'Strange.' Said Terens. 'Why would any....' He stopped and the sentence hung unfinished in the air of the control room as we all at the same time understood the significance of the information scrolling before us. The profiles were DNA from people from almost every planet in the galaxy. But what was really significant was that they were all of the same base. Throughout it all someone had helpfully highlighted the relevant data with little cryptic comments for the uninitiated in DNA profiling. Even though there was the huge diversity the highlighted data was showing unequivocally that the entire human race in the entire galaxy was not derived from different planetary sources! It would have been an impossibility for such an event to have occurred, even with intermarrying. At least that was the deduction the little cryptic notes were saying. People from all over the galaxy could be linked by the XX and XY chromosomes with types such as M20, M173, M96. We could not find out the significance of the microsatellites information although this also seemed relevant in some way.

What it meant though was that we were all related!

That was the only deduction to be had from the data still unrolling in from of our eyes. We did not originate from different isolated worlds. All mankind had come from one related source! That could only mean one thing.

We had to have all come from one planet!

Ultima Thule had to exist as Djon had said all along!

'Now we have something to show that Mr. Tire.' Said Ruuth brightly.

'Of course not!' I snapped. 'I'm sorry.' I added as I saw her shocked expression. 'I shouldn't have been so quick there. We cannot go to him with this. What do we say? 'Excuse me Mr. Tire, someone stuck this on our airlock door.' If he did not believe our last offering he will poo poo this one for sure. If he thinks our other data was corrupted or not to be trusted he will say the same about this. Especially the way it has arrived. It cannot be trusted. How do we even know it is true? How can we verify it?'

'Djim's right.' Added Terens. 'Without some form of legitimacy this also useless.'

'Can we add this to our insurance policy?' asked Djon.

'I can, but it may reveal the location of it.' She replied. 'Also, we need to be sure this is accurate. We need corroboration somehow.' She turned off the data. 'Also, what happens to our insurance policy when we return to Enceladus?'

'What do you mean?' Asked Djon.

'I mean, how do we stop it sending out the information until we are ready?'

'I think we can use the portals in the same way that communication is used throughout the galaxy. The portals take in and emit signals as well as vessels as they operate. In fact, they spread everything throughout the galaxy at each operation. I don't think anyone will notice one extra little signal going through especially if we used a narrow beam signal and fired it straight through the portal.'

'Will it be a narrow beam signal when it leaves the exit portal?' Asked Djon.

'No.' Replied Ruuth. 'I am sure it will be spread by the portal into a normal radio type signal. Fortunately for us, otherwise our insurance policy would not work from home.'

'But it will work from anywhere in the galaxy with a portal nearby. So, we don't need to go home.' Said Djon. I groaned. He looked at me but carried on. 'We might as well go on. If anyone is looking for us they will find us wherever we are. So, we might as well try and draw them out by going on.' I had to inwardly agree with his sentiment but was not going to voice it. I still wanted to go back home. As nobody spoke Djon carried on. 'OK, we will go and see Mr. Tire and tell him about the DNA and also that we will go home. But we will not go home and then we will see what happens then. Agreed?' He stopped and looked at us all. I watched the others nod in agreement one by one so I nodded too, even though something inside of me was screaming at me to not be so stupid. I just could not help but nod.

'Just one thing.' I added. 'No one seems to be concerned over who put this information on our hatch or why?'

'Oh, I had thought of it Djim but the information it contained rather put it out of my mind for a while. But you are right of course. Someone wants to help us. That can only be a good thing. It means we are not totally alone. There are people out there willing to help.'

'Karon is the only person who knows why we are here.' Said Ruuth.

'And her brother.' Added Terens slowly.

'True, but he has not seen much of us and he did not show any interest in our quest. She said she would try and help. But obviously she does not want us to know. So, I suggest we let her keep it that way and not embarrass her by bringing it up.' Continued Ruuth. 'It may be very dangerous for her too.'

'Let us go and try and find this unlisted portal then.' I found myself saying but at the same time wishing I hadn't. 'Let us also forget that slimy man down on the planet. I can see no point in returning to see him. He and his 'friends' will only find something wrong with the DNA data.' My palms were sweating now, and I did not know why.

'Yes!' Said Ruuth loudly. 'We can triangulate the position by using a sub-atomic radio location detection from here and a couple of other places.' She was animated now and some of her normal vigour had returned. We all seemed to have a rejuvenated sense, except Terens, who was always the same laconic self who showed very little emotion or joy. He spoke.

'Won't there be traces in the V20 from the places we have already been?'

'Of course, Terens.' Beamed Ruuth. 'Of course, I will check it out now.' She leapt up from her seat, pleased to be doing something positive again. I sensed she did not want to return to Enceladus again. Maybe I was the only one who wanted to go back home. Suddenly this little disk seemed to have given this harebrained scheme another lease of life and kick started it again. I stared down at the minor imperfections in the top of the control room table.

'Shall we dedock now and then be ready to leave in the morning?' Asked Terens again.

'OK.' I agreed. 'That sounds like a good idea. It may also make the authorities here think we are ready to go home. We can call Mr. Tire in the morning and tell him we are going home. It will give Ruuth some time to work out the coordinates of the unlisted portal.' I went to the pilot's seat to begin the dedocking procedure. Before I could begin, the airlock entry sounder chimed again. Immediately Terens was out of his seat and heading for the airlock before anyone else could move. His laconic and slow speech disguised a man whose physical movements could be swift and explosive. Had I not known him it would have come as much more of a surprise. I suspected that I would never quite be unsurprised by his ability to move. I immediately reached over and turned on the video link, but as before it was blank. Djon had left the control room after Terens to man the airlock on our vessel and be a backup. It was like a well-oiled machine working. I felt the airlock hatch open and close and then the video link screen sprang to life as something was removed from the camera and Terens face appeared. He smiled and his face disappeared. I felt the hatch open and close again as Terens returned. He came back into the control room brandishing another recording disk, Djon was behind him. He placed a long metal rod on the table as he returned to the control room, the only weapon he could find. Terens took some risk going out there unarmed after our last discussion.

'Is that all you found?' Asked Ruuth. 'This is getting rather silly. Shall we put a notice on our hatch saying, 'place things here.'?' She added jokingly.

'Yes, that is all that was there.' He handed it to me. 'And there was no one in sight. I even ran down the corridor but could find no one. There was some more tape over the camera as well. I have it here in case we can find some information from it. I'll put it in the lab.'

'I'll put this in the reader.' I replied, taking it from his hand. 'But first we need to dedock. Then we'll read it.' I began the dedock procedure and opened a channel to space flight control. 'Space flight control this is Jergan EN4-31 seeking permission to dedock.'

'Jergan EN4-31 this is space flight control. Permission granted. Do you wish to leave Geryon space?'

'Not until morning please. We wish to remain in orbit until then. Please give us your holding coordinates.'

'OK. Please go to coordinates N30/290/90 for holding until morning. What time do you wish to leave?'

'About oh ten hundred hours standard galactic time please.'

'Thank you. At nine fifty please be at coordinates N30/300/100. Dedocking commencing now.'

'Commencing dedocking. Anti gravity gyros primed, anti crash programme operational, purging airlock docking link.' I watched the telemetry readout. 'Link purged. Ready to be released.'

'Commencing to release vessel Jergan EN4-31 from dock ten. All vessels clear.'

'Thank you. Dedocking now. Anti gravity gyros at release speed.' I felt the docking clamps withdraw from our link and the slight shudder as the link spiralled back into flight location. The forward vision screen was now dimming to allow the head up display to be more easily read. The various different instrument readings were slowly beginning to appear. I fired the forward thrusters or rather the clique computer fired them for the correct amount on my command. The numbers on the screen began to scroll up more quickly, the virtual dedocking procedure showed our vessel slowly begin to move away from the dock. In the virtual world we could see how small our vessel was against those on either side. The space flight control was keeping us away from other objects. It was like moving along rails, there was no sideways movement detectible. Gradually the dock became the familiar curved shape and nervate appearance as we withdrew. Soon we were in free space and able to move independently.

'Space flight control, this Jergan EN4-31 taking control of free flight.'

'Jergan EN4-31 confirm can take control of free flight.'

'Moving to holding coordinates.' I then took control and moved us to the coordinates. When we were in our holding position I turned on the disk reader. I called the others from the various parts of the vessel that they had migrated to see the contents of the disk. We stood in silence again as the information scrolled up the screen.

'This is the official gazetteer of the planets of the galaxy.' Muttered Djon. 'Who could have obtained this?'

'And why give it to us?' Asked Ruuth.

'Is it a trap?' Asked Terens, ever the cautious one.

'Why do you think it is a trap?' Asked Djon.

'It is not normally information held by the general public. It could be a way of putting us in a containment field for having restricted information. Just a thought.'

'It's not that restricted. After all, we got the same information from the library.'

'Yes, but Djim.' Said Ruuth. 'This clearly shows four thousand two hundred and nine inhabited planets and portals. It still leaves us with the unlisted portal.'

'Isn't that this echo that our Mr. Tire was talking of?' Terens asked.

'I don't think so.' I replied. 'There are certainly echoes of portals and I have seen them before. In fact you do have to be careful in setting up the V20 coordinates to ensure it is not an echo or a mirage as they are sometimes referred to. It can send you out to nowhere space with no hope of getting back. But the information we had was different. It did not look like a portal echo or mirage. Would you agree Ruuth?'

'Yes.' She said guardedly. 'But I will check it again before I go to bed. Just to be sure. Just as soon as I have checked the V20 data to see if I can find the location of the unlisted portal. I should be in bed by midnight.'

'And Djon.' I said. 'Now who has put this on our hatch?'

'I have no idea Djim. But two people have decided we need help and that is very encouraging. It has given me renewed hope. These will be ordinary people like us with considerable courage I suspect.' His eyes were shining again with a new zeal like I had not seen for some time. I felt that going back home was now just a fading dream. I had mixed feelings. The appearance of these disks by two persons who wanted to help gave me renewed courage as well. But at the same time I still felt we were on a wild goose chase that was taking me further and further away from home.

'Do you need me for anything?'

'No. you can go to bed.'

'OK, then see you in the morning.' I turned to leave.

'Djim.' Ruuth's clear voice pulled me back. 'Do you think your father went looking for the unlisted portal?' It was the question I was dreading but somehow new had to come sooner or later. Fortunately, it was Ruuth who had asked it. I think I may have been less generous if either of the other two had asked me, especially this late in the day.

'I really don't know. Djon said he wanted to talk about something but disappeared before he could....' I was unable to go on. Ruuth saw my rising distress and stood up. She came over and put a comforting hand on my shoulder.

'I know how you feel, Djim.' She said. 'Just get some rest, it will help. I'm sorry I asked.'

'No, it is all right, really. I should not be this emotional after all these years. But I will take your advice and get some rest and will consider it in the morning. It is silly isn't it? My father has been gone all these years.....'

'Djim. I know. It is just all this is putting doubts in your mind and raking up old unfinished memories. Do not worry. Just get some rest.' I wanted to give her a big hug but decided it was best not to.

'Thanks. See you in the morning.'

'Oh, seven hundred sharp.' She said with a big smile.

*

In the morning I was up and showered in the finejet shower, listening to the sucking of the recycling pump taking up the water and cleaning it for reuse. Then I was dried with the dry air jets with the air-conditioning unit sucking out the warm moist air and drying it out and sending the water for reuse again. I then dressed and had breakfast by oh seven hundred hours. When I got to the control room Ruuth was already there.

'Don't you ever sleep?' I said cheerily. Ruuth had been right, I felt much better this morning and ready to talk if necessary. The rest had done me good.

'Oh, yes. It didn't take me long last night.' She looked back as a crack and a bang somewhere in the vessel indicated that the suns rays had caught our fuselage and was warming it up unevenly. 'I never get used to that.' She added.

'Well, what did you find last night?'

'I'll tell you when the others get here. Don't want to have to say it twice.' She sat in the co pilot's seat. I sat in the pilot's seat. I fired up the external cameras and sensors to check our surroundings while we waited. All seemed normal. The planet was still hanging in front of us with the sun beginning to appear from behind it. The docking station was still in its geostationary orbit and the usual collection of vessels were coming and going. We did not have long to wait. The other two came in shortly after. We greeted each other in the usual time-honoured fashion.

'Right Ruuth, what have you got?' Asked Djon without further ado.

'I checked the data last night and all the evidence points to an additional portal and not a mirage.'

'Well, well.' Muttered Terens.

'Do you know where it is?' I asked excitedly, much more excitedly than I should be feeling. I wanted to go home, not set off again on this escapade.

'Sort of.' She replied slowly. 'I checked the V20 and can place it...' She leant forward and switched on the V20. The familiar bluish orb sprang into life. It showed the whole galaxy. She pressed another button and on the edge of the galaxy a grey smudge appeared. 'That smudge shows approximately where the portal should be.'

'Why is it on the very edge of the galaxy?' I asked.

'Who knows.'

'Call up the planets.' Said Djon. I pressed some buttons on the V20 pad and the tiny red dots appeared.

'It is not very close to any inhabited planet.' Muttered Terens again.

'What is the nearest planet?' Asked Djon again. I pressed another button and data began appearing by each dot in turn.

When it appeared by the smudge, I released my finger pressure and the last data hung by the red dot.

'Galilei.' Whispered Ruuth. 'My family planet.'

'Co-incidence?' I asked.

'I hope so. You're not suggesting that I am somehow involved in this are you.' She turned her steely blue piercing eyes upon me. The gaze was withering.

'No. No I am not. Sorry.'

'Well, that's where we will go then. Can we manage with one skip or not?'

'Hold on.' I said as I called up our present position. A green dot appeared beside the red dot of Geryon. It was close.

'It's the next portal.' Said Djon.

'Why is the unlisted portal so difficult to pinpoint?' I asked no one in particular. It was a thought that just escaped into vocalisation.

'It is intended to stay hidden I would say.' Replied Ruuth. 'The signal appears to have been deliberately blurred to prevent it being discovered. It will always look like a mirage, never quite being anywhere in particular. It is only because we were looking for it that we reduced the area to that grey smudge.'

'What is in that grey smudge?' Asked Terens.

'What do you mean?' Queried Ruuth.

'Any planets, any inhabited planets any supernova. That sort of thing.'

'There are no listed inhabited planets.' Said Ruuth. 'As for the rest we don't know. But there is a portal there so it is intended to be used we assume; by whom and what for we will just have to find out.'

'Do we need to add this information to our insurance policy?' Asked Djon of Ruuth.

'I think we should.' She said. 'Just before we leave we can send a pulse signal with the information encoded. I will set it up ready. We have an hour left to wait.' She set to work immediately; with a determination I had come to admire.

'Well, I suppose we had better tell this Mr. Tire that we are going home.' I said.

'Oh, yes, I had forgotten him. 'Replied Djon. 'Go ahead.'
'Verbal or nonverbal?' I asked.

'Nonverbal.' Said Terens tersely. He said it as if there should be no argument. I looked at Djon, he shrugged.

'Nonverbal it is.' I called up the text signal generator and began to type a message. It appeared in a corner of the forward vision enhancer.

'There. Will that do?' I asked. They looked across and read my message. There was a general grunt of assent.

'OK, I will send it.'

At nine fifty hours we moved to the coordinates allotted to us and got in the queue. Ruuth sent the signal. It was going to be a tense few minutes as we hoped no one would pick up on our signal and start asking questions. Fortunately, just before a portal journey there was always a lot of signal traffic between vessels and space flight control. Hopefully, it would just get lost in that. We watched the bright spot of light of the drive in front of us. Any moment now we would be at Galilei.

Then suddenly the proximity sensor shrilled its warning and simultaneously an abort signal flashed as someone tried to call and stop us leaving! They had left it extremely late, dangerously late to be trying to stop us. A cold shiver went down my spine.

'What do we do?' Asked Ruuth wide eyed.

'Let us just get out of here.' Muttered Terens in his usual clenched jaw kind of way.

'We can't do that!' I shouted back, much louder than I intended. 'Sorry, I didn't mean to shout. We do not want to draw that much attention to ourselves. If we leave now, we will be hunted down for sure.'

'OK, OK.' Said Djon. 'We abort.'

Then everything happened at once. Geryon flight control wanted to know why two vessels were in the portal exit queue. The vessel near us was hailing and wanted an answer. The portal exit beacon wanted confirmation of exit or abort. The vessel behind us in the queue also queried two vessels in front of it. I aborted the exit procedure and punched the abort button.

More sounders screeched into life. We accelerated through the now unoperational portal and I veered us off out of the zone of turbulence from the next ultimate event singularity that followed a portal activity. The other vessel followed us but did not go through the portal but took the short cut passed it.

'Geryon flight control this is Jergan EN4-31. We apologise for aborting the portal exit procedure, but we have been hailed by another vessel.'

'Thank you Jergan EN4-31. Confirm aborted portal exit. Please note that a new exit will require additional costs. Please advise if you still intend to leave Geryon space.'

'Thank you. We will be leave after contact with hailing vessel.' I signed off. 'Djon, have you answered the hail yet?'

'Yes, Djim. They are now online.'

'This is Jergan EN4-31.' I began. 'Why have you made us abort our exit procedure?'

'Hello Jergan EN4-31. This is taksi GN32 I have a passenger for you. They wish to board now. Please proceed with docking procedure.'

'A passenger!' Djon spluttered.

'We can't take on more people.' Grumbled Terens. 'Besides who on Erebus wants to come aboard?'

'Well, there is one way to find out.' I said as I began the docking procedure. The docking link spiralled out ready for the taksi. We locked docking programmes and slowly the two vessels were drawn together. I felt the slight judder as both vessels docked followed by the sharper vibration as the docking clamps snapped close. I did not flood the link as it would be too demanding on the vessel's resources for such a short dock.

'Taksi GN32 This is Jergan EN4-31. Docking complete. Link not atmosphere. Repeat link not atmosphere.'

'Thank you. Confirm link not atmosphere. Passenger ready to board. Prepare reception airlock for passenger.'

'Confirm airlock ready to receive. Ready to transfer.' There was a pause. I watched the telemetry confirm the passenger had left the taksi airlock and entered ours.

'Confirm passenger transfer complete.' Came the taksi voice.

'Confirm passenger transfer complete.' I asserted. 'Prepare to dedock.'

'Preparing to dedock.'

I checked the airlock that the passenger was indeed safely on board. 'We have a passenger folks.' I said. 'Do we have any weapons ready?'

'Of course.' Replied Terens showing me the E.N.D. discharge weapon in his hand as he left the control room for the airlock. I began the dedock procedure and withdrew the docking link.

'Whoever it is will have to pay the portal abort fee.' Muttered Djon.

'I agree.' I said. 'Confirm dedocking complete.'

'Confirm dedocking complete.'

'Right let us see who we have on board. Where's Ruuth?'

'She's backing up Terens.'

'Impetuous woman.' I had to admire her even though I was not sure how effective she would be in a fight. I had a sneaking impression she was actually tougher than she looked. I heard voices coming along the corridor. I thought I recognised the second voice; it was a woman's. I looked at Djon and saw in his face that he also was thinking the same thing. Ruuth came into the control room first followed by Karon! She was obviously agitated.

'You.' Stuttered Djon.

'I thought you wouldn't go near a spacecraft in flight.'

'You are so right.' She said and obviously looked very worried to be where she was.

'What on Erebus are you doing here then?' Asked Djon not too kindly. He was getting worked up about his project getting out of hand I suspected.

'I just had to get away and we must leave now.' She sat down, her face white and drawn. 'I will explain but you must get back in the queue and go!' The urgency in her voice made me return immediately to the controls. No one else tried to stop me or query her. I called up space flight control and obtained another exit time and coordinates.

'OK, we are on our way. We will be leaving in half an hour.'

'Are you sure about this?' Asked Ruuth.

'Yes, yes, just go. Everything seems to have changed since you came to see Mr.Tire. After you left the first time he was concerned about your claims and called the…. Well, it doesn't matter but this resulted in some big guy who didn't give his name turning up just after you had gone and had some words with Mr. Tire. I didn't see it, but his secretary was so concerned that she actually came and told me that she had heard raised voices in his office and when the man had left she went in to see Mr. Tire and he was as white as a sheet. He did not speak for some time and she got very worried. He eventually told her not to worry and everything was all right. She knew it was not, she knew Mr. Tire very well having worked for him for many years. Later on, Mr. Tire called her in to send messages to everyone that you were misguided fools and not to be trusted and possibly were even spies. He instructed her to tell the council that the information was seriously flawed and possibly intended to undermine the galaxy. Then things began to change but I could not find why. It was an unseen change, but I could feel it. I was told my job would have to change. Normally open people became distant and unhelpful. And finally, there was an attempt on my life!'

'What!' Stormed Djon.'

'I can't be sure, but what with one thing and another I could not ignore it. I felt my flat was also being bugged.'

'How can you be sure?'

'Again, I cannot be sure, but I feel it. I feel watched. I feel uncomfortable now.' She paused before continuing with her harrowing tale. We just stood amazed at how quickly a whole society it seemed had become dangerous overnight.

'That's how I felt back on Enceladus.' Said Ruuth finally and she looked at me.

'When I finally got to see Mr. Tire he had changed.' She continued. 'When I tried to ask about you and your information, he became very agitated and told me to forget it. He said if I didn't then I would lose my job. I think I was followed home too, but I could not be absolutely sure of course they seemed to be very good. I got so scared I just decided to leave. They don't know yet so go before they find out.'

'Why did you leave that data disk for us without....?'

'What data disk?' She asked her brow furrowing.

'You didn't leave a data disk on our hatch?'

'No.'

'Oh.' Said Djon. 'That makes it even more of a mystery then. So, who else would do that?'

'Or even know why we are here.' Added Terens.

'Mr. Tire did talk to some people before that man came.' Said Karon.

'Do you know who?'

'Sorry, no.'

'OK, guys let us get ready to go. Into your seats please and belt up.' I turned my seat round to face the controls and prepare for the exit. It was so tense I could hardly concentrate. Karon began to cry.

'I've never done this before. What is going to happen? What does the portal do?'

'Well.' I began but then stopped as I was not sure myself. I used them but did not know how they worked. Ruuth stepped in.

'Have you heard of macrocosmic quantum physical metaphysics?'

'Sort of.'

'Well, the portals make use of the principles of macrocosmic quantum physical metaphysics by creating an elemental subatomic electromagnestatic macrocosmic quantum manifold using a quantic homogenous function utilising the Dirac constant modulation which produces a ubiquitous ultimate simultaneous harmonic singularity displacement event in the spatio-temporal fabric. Then...'

'Thank you.' Said Karon. 'But what does that mean in galactic English?'

'Well basically.' Said Ruuth, completely unfazed. 'We are

in normal space and time. The portal creates an event horizon which is a sphere in which time and space... well, we become everywhere at once and then we chose which place to return to normal space time. So, we can travel light years without moving in effect. Does that help?'

'Thank you. But what will I feel?'

'Not a lot. A strange feeling of falling and as though the universe has become thick and viscous. It does not last long. It is a metempirical experience.'

'I don't know much but I know that must be a contradiction in terms.'

'Yes, that about sums up the whole thing. It is a contradiction, apparently. You cannot be in two places at once. You will be OK. Just sit tight.'

'Thank you. But what I have never understood either is why the portal has to be way out here in space?'

'I know that one at least.' I said proudly, before Ruuth could answer. 'If it was on the surface of a planet it would suck up part of the atmosphere as well as probably part of the planet. Or rather, the portal creates a bubble which everything inside is at one place than at another so if it was on a planet it would do that to the atmosphere and everything else. It also creates a large electromagnetic pulse which would fry electronics around it as well as cause poor weather conditions. It is safer up here.' I looked at her.

'It does no't create an EMP for us then?'

'No, not for those in the portal. It would be difficult for us if it did. All our cliques would go down. I think the V20 would stop working too and that could be awkward. It is only outside the bubble created by the portal that the EMP is created.'

'Thank you.' She stopped. 'Do you think that abort will have alerted anyone?' She asked me.

'Almost certainly knowing what we know now. It is very unusual. It will eventually get back to someone.'

'Will they follow us?'

'It depends upon who gets the information and when.'

'Mr. Tire will be looking for us to leave and go home so

it will go to him. He may already have the information and be wondering why we aborted. Then the taksi will be found and quizzed as to the passenger. Then he will be checking with Enceladus N421 to see if you have returned home. When you do not return then questions will be asked. Then it will go to that man who turned up I am sure. They will not assume we have had an accident.' She began crying.

'We have already had one there.' Said Djon.

'Pardon?' she looked at him.

'Yes, we faked an accident when we left. As far as Enceladus N421 is concerned we did not leave we died. Space flight control suddenly came online.

'Jergan EN4-31 we require additional payment for the earlier portal abort. Please place your payment card in the slot.'

'Ghas!' Ejaculated Djon. He reached into his pocket and fetched out the payment card and placed it in the slot. They then confirmed payment had been made.

'OK.' I said. 'Get ready everyone portal coming up.' Karon began sobbing into her hands. Ruuth tried to comfort her. Then we were falling, the sky went blank. I could hear Karon moaning.

– CHAPTER 7 –

V20

The stars came out again and a planet swam into view. A beautiful blue-brown planet with white clouds not streaked with the ubiquitous dust as on most other planets. It looked clean and inviting like I felt all planets should be. The familiar satellite blinked in the distance. Gallilei space flight control burst into the awkward silence. Karon had been shocked into silence too.

'This is Galilei space flight control. It is Monday twelfth of May and the time is....seventeen hundred hours. Please identify yourself and state your reason for your visit.'

We sat in stunned silence, and then Terens spoke for us all. I have never heard that before. I have been to many planets and never heard that.'

'What do I say?' I asked. The others shrugged. 'Hello Gallilei space flight control this is Jergan EN4-31. We are on en-route to Midnight Twenty. We just need to recharge and then we will be moving on. We do not need to dock, and we do not wish to visit planet surface. Thank you. Please give a recharge holding coordinate. We will need about an hour or two.'

'Thank you Jergan EN4-31. Please go to coordinates GL100-100 and place your payment card in the payment slot for portal use.' Djon did so and the money was deducted. 'Thank you. Enjoy your trip.'

'Thank you, we will.' I switched off the communicator. 'I hope they bought that.' And then I paused and added. 'Where on Erebus does the word en-route come from? It seems to be such an odd word which doesn't fit with other galactic English words.'

'You're right.' Said Djon. 'I have not used the word much but you're right it doesn't fit.' He paused as a thought crossed his mind, I could tell by now that something else was coming. 'There is another reason for this trip.' My heart fell, why did I have to open my big mouth? Now here is another reason for Djon to continue with his harebrained quest and I have just given him a boost in that direction. I vowed to keep quiet in future.

'Where are we?' Came Karon's small voice.

'Gallilei.' Said Ruuth absently. She was staring at the planet filling the forward vision enhancer, the reflected light from the planet's surface brightening her face. I looked out too. The sun was shining almost full on the visible surface of the planet. I could see a large amount of blue water covering a lot of the visible surface. It shone in the sunlight. I suddenly felt a deep desire to see my own home planet again, even though Enceladus looked nothing like this from space. Enceladus had much less water covering the surface and the clouds were very rarely white and were mostly not true clouds but dust from the mines or volcanoes. Gallilei looked somehow more graceful and peaceful. I hoped it was.

'How far is it?' Came Karon's small voice again. I suddenly realised that no one was taking any notice of her.

'From Geryon you mean?'

'Yes.'

'About twenty light years.' I said. Karon burst into tears again. This jogged Ruuth out of her reverie and she went to comfort her. 'Do you want to go back home?' She asked her.

'No.' She managed to say between the tears. 'Not now. It has changed. There is something not right and I think you may be onto something.' Ruuth looked at Djon who was staring back at Karon. A smile gradually appeared on his face. I knew then that his resolve had returned, I groaned inwardly. I was not going home. Then Karon suddenly sat up. Her eyes began to dry. 'Don't be put off. Do not give up. There is something not right.'

'I thought as much.' Muttered Djon. The smile had given way to a determined look, much like he had way back in his office when he first raised the subject.

'I thought as much too.' Added Terens. 'For years. Nothing that I could put my finger on though. And you were willing to go home.' He turned to Djon.

'We had nothing Terens. No proof. We still only have circumstantial evidence. So, there is a hidden portal. It does not prove anything. So, we have DNA that proves we are all from the same source. It does not prove there was originally one planet.'

'Oh, yes, it does!' I retorted and immediately realised that I had again supported this scheme only minutes after telling myself to keep quiet. I realised then that Djon and Terens were staring at me. Ruuth had gone back to staring at the planet and was not listening.

'You're right Djim.' Said Djon. 'You are so right. It does prove there was an original planet. There must have been for all mankind to be related.' He whooped and stabbed the air with his fist but then stopped and his shoulders sagged.

'What's up Djon?' Asked Terens.

'We still don't know where the original planet is.'

'And if there is an original planet why do some people not want that fact known.' Added Ruuth, now having dragged herself away from the view outside.

'There must be something to hide.' I said

'Precisely.'

'What day did she say it was?' asked Karon suddenly. Interrupting our train of thought.

'You mean space flight control?'

'Yes.' I thought back for a minute.

'Monday twelfth May.' I said. 'Good ghas! We have lost a day in the portal.'

'Is that a lot?' She asked.

'Yes, I suppose it is.' Although it was nothing to take a day to travel twenty light years it always seemed as though someone had stolen a part of my life when it happened. It was always a strange feeling.

'I have lost a week once.' Said Terens. 'Now that is scary. A whole week! You really begin to wonder where you have been.'

'But it is always just a few moments as far as you are concerned?'

'Oh, yes. It always lasts the same for those going through the portal.'

'Why does time take longer outside then?'

'No one knows.' I said. 'I don't know anyone who knows exactly how the portals work anyway. Ruuth here has given the most technical term for it I have ever heard. Do you know how they work Ruuth?'

'No. I have read about the theory. The rest of the explanation made no sense to me.'

'Oh, well. They just do work that is all we need to know. The time taken can vary from a few moments to... as Terens says, a week. Not bad though considering we have just covered in normal space ten light years!'

'I've never been so far from home before.' Said Karon.

'Neither have I. 'I said, giving her a big smile which I hoped would help put her at ease.'

'Really?'

'Yes. Even Geryon was the farthest I had been, let alone Gallilei. But if you think about it, in some ways we are closer. It would not take long to get back.'

'Why are you not going back to your home planets?'

'We consider that we will find nothing if we go back. At least if we go on we might find out what we consider is wrong with the galaxy. It is risky but the only way. It looks as though it is going to be dangerous too. Do you still want to come?'

'I have nothing to go back for now. If I was to return, then I fear for my life now. I am just concerned about Perak. I hope they won't take it out on him because of me.'

'I think if that happens then people will start asking questions. This thing seems to survive on being unseen. Even so, we have our insurance policy to protect us.'

'Your what?'

'We have something that will spread what we know throughout the galaxy if we are killed. We are hoping this will stop people killing us because if they do what we know will become known to the rest of the galaxy.'

'Why don't you just tell the galaxy now?'

'Good point but I think that may be premature, and besides if we do that, we have lost our bargaining chip.'

'Oh, good point.'

'Karon.' Said Ruuth. 'Would you like to take a rest? Or have something to eat? We have got a spare cabin haven't we?' She asked the last question of Djon.

'Yes, of course Ruuth, there is the very small cabin back by the heads. It's a bit untidy and the decorations are shot because of the moon hoppers drive blast but it is still perfectly useable.'

'OK. Karon – by the way do you have any luggage?'

'Yes, it's still down by the airlock. I couldn't bring much though I thought it might look suspicious.'

'Come on then.' Said Ruuth, gathering up the woman and ushering her out of the control room. As they left Terens shut the door and Turned on Djon. 'What are you going to do now?' He asked him in a hoarse whisper.

'What do you mean?'

'I mean – she could be a plant a trap or an informer.'

'She could Terens, she could. I do not think we have given anything away. OK, we will not give her any information until we are sure. Go and discreetly tell Ruuth not to either.' Terens immediately turned and left the control room.

'Ruuth won't give anything away.' I said.

'I know.' Replied Djon. 'It gives Terens something to do though.'

'We need Ruuth up here to get another fix on that hidden portal.'

'Ghas, you're right.' Said Djon. 'I'll go and remind her, having Karon come aboard has put it out of thought.' He got up and also left the control room, leaving me alone with the big screen and the sounds of the local space flight control and other vessels quietly muttering in the background. I watched the planet spin slowly in front of the screen and the satellite blinking in the distance. I never ceased to be captivated by the beauty of the universe. I could see down on the surface of the planet the evidence of a past volcano eruption that must have been huge to be seen from up here. I checked the recharge dials to see how much longer we needed. I was brought back from my reverie as Ruuth came into the control room and fell into the seat next to me.

'Boy, am I tired.' She said.

'You OK to make the fix on this hidden portal?' I asked.

'Sure. For that I am ready. I might need to go and have a nap afterwards though.'

'Anything I can do to help?' I asked. She thought for a while as she set up the instruments to get another fix on the portal.

'No.' She said finally. 'There's nothing you can do, sorry. Well actually there is something you can do.'

'Yes.'

'Can you get me a drink? Long and cold.'

'Sure.' I got up and fetched her a drink from the galley. I got one for myself while I was there.

'Thanks.' She said as I returned to the control room and placed the drink in the holder. It was dangerous to have fluids slopping around on board, so all drinks had to be in sealed containers which were clipped securely into place while not being used. I returned to my work.

'How's Karon?'

'She'll be alright, I think. She is made of stern stuff. It is all a bit of a shock for her at the moment. She plucked up enormous courage to come aboard and then after that she realised what she had done. If she can get some rest, I am sure she will bounce back. And before you ask, I am sure she is genuine. I'm sure she is not a spy or a plant.'

'You read my mind. But I must admit I do agree. Still, I think it best we do not give anything away just yet.'

'Sure thing.' She was talking absentmindedly to me while she worked on her fix. I went back to my standard checks. She did not speak again for a while. The silence was shattered by Karon stumbling into the control room. 'I forgot to tell you something!' She gasped. 'I'm sorry, it slipped my mind.'

'What is it?' Asked Ruuth, turning from her work and half rising from her seat as Karon stumbled on towards us.

'Something I overheard down on Geryon I don't know what it means but the man who came to see Mr. Tire said something at one point, which I am sure I was not meant to hear. About.. well he said something like....I don't quite know...'

'Karon.' Said Ruuth firmly. 'Calm down. Sit down and tell us slowly.' Ruuth had got up now and gone over to Karon and sat her down.

'Right, right.' She said. 'I'm sorry I should have said earlier.'

'Look, it's all right. Just calm down and tell us.'

'OK.' She took a deep breath as she dry washed her face with her hands. Ruuth was standing over her placing a comforting hand upon her shoulder. Karon looked up at Ruuth with a pale face. 'That man said something about some sort of infection that could be brought aboard without us knowing. Except he didn't use that word he used another word like it.'

'Do you mean virus?'

'Yes, that's it!'

'But that won't matter.' Said Ruuth Calmly. 'The self healing programme will deal with any virus or faulty programming or anything not right.' She looked at me.

'I'm sorry.' Said Karon. 'I thought it might have been important.'

'Don't feel bad, I would rather you told us and there was no danger than the other way round.'

'Of course.' She replied thoughtfully. 'So, if there is no danger then why did he have an awful smirk on his face?' Ruuth looked at me again. I shrugged. She appeared to be thinking hard.

'Perhaps it is a virus which is not intended to damage the computer. If it were innocuous then the self-healing programme would not be triggered!'

'But what would be the point?' I queried, at a loss as to why they would want to do such a pointless thing.

'The only thing.' Began Ruuth. 'It could just alter slightly the way our computer operates. That also would not trigger the self-healing programme if it were linked to the safety programmes in some way!'

'Oh, ghas!' I said, a cold shiver running down my insides as I looked back across at Ruuth. She had gone white. 'The second download of the information from Fyrest Prime.' I said. Ruuth obviously knew what I meant. Karon looked at us both.

'You know what it means? So, I was right to raise it after all?'

'Sorry. Yes, we do. Yes, you were. Thank you. Thank you.' I gave her a big hug which surprised her and me. 'But now I think we have work to do. Thanks.' I went to the control panel in a panic; my fingers fumbling with the adrenalin rush and desire to get to the information quickly. I went to find the second download of the planetary data from the library. It was soon spiralling up the screen. Ruuth had by now joined me at the control panel and she reached across and took control of the data. Her clique computer knowledge far outreached mine, so I stood back and let her get on with it. All I could do was stare in amazement as her fingers flew over the keys. She got into the programme data somehow and started searching for anything unusual. At the same time, she had called up the original download and was displaying them both side by side to look for any difference between the two.

Djon and Terens returned.

'What's going on here?' Asked Djon lightly. 'You up again Karon.'

'I remembered something.' She said quietly.

'What?'

'We think, Djon.' I said. 'That there was something in the second, or even the first load of planetary data that we downloaded from the library on Fyrest Prime. That's what Karon has remembered.'

'What!' said Terens, very loudly for him.

'Shush.' Said Ruuth. 'I need to concentrate.'

'Sorry.' He said and I ushered them all to the back of the control room.

'Ruuth has taken over the search for any hidden or dangerous data in the download. Karon overheard the man who came to see Mr. Tire on Geryon mention something to him. She has just remembered and come to warn us.'

'That's right.' She added. 'I'm sorry I didn't remember sooner.'

'That's OK.' Said Djon. 'You did remember. So, thanks. Do we know what it is yet?'

'No. Ruuth has just started.' I said. We all then turned our attention back to Ruuth who was still intently working on the programmes. I turned to Karon. 'Why not go and get your rest now Karon. I do not think there is anything you can do here for the moment. We will wake you if there is any news. You will be better for a good rest.'

'OK, I will, thanks.' She turned and left. We just stood and felt like spare parts as Ruuth worked furiously. It seemed like an age before she suddenly appeared to find something.

'Got something at last.' She confirmed proudly. We stumbled over each other in our haste to see what she had found. Unfortunately, it was a clique computer language, which I did not understand. I knew Terens had no idea of clique computer language either and suspected that Djon was equally ignorant.

'Look there.' She said, pointing to lines of text. 'We will need to go through all our systems to check. I am not sure what this programme is supposed to do but I am hoping that as we did not open it for too long it may not have got very far. I am not a virus expert, so this is pure guesswork. I also do not know quite how to protect us from it either. Fortunately, it does appear to be very sophisticated. It is also not destructive. It looks as though it is intended to go unnoticed. Close down everything that is not essential to be open or operational and I will go through the systems. I will also write a quick disablement programme to stop it getting any further. We can then open it without fear of further infection.'

I began to close down whatever I could as Ruuth continued to work furiously at the console. 'Aren't all vessel systems designed to prevent any corruption?'

'They are. This is clever in that it is not intended to corrupt. I wish I knew what it was supposed to do. It does not make sense. It must be intended to do something, but I cannot yet work out what. I need more time to study it. I'll tell you what.' She said finally. 'I'll show you all what to do with each system programme. We can then get through it much faster.' With that she sat us down and went through the process of checking the programmes; what to look for and what to do. I felt that I was having an advanced clique computer lesson here. Some time later, I was not sure how long, we were interrupted by Gallilei space flight control.

'Jergan EN4-31 this is Gallilei space flight control. You are well past your recharge time and have not requested onward...'

'Ghas.' I interrupted, blotting out the rest of the message. 'I had completely forgotten about that!'

'.....Is there a problem? Do you require assistance?'

'Can I turn on the communication system, Ruuth?' I asked.

'Sure – actually I've already done that one.' I turned on the system and replied.

'Hello Gallilei space flight control. Yes, we did have a problem, but we have already fixed it now. No assistance is required. We will be ready to leave shortly. Is there any delay in the portal queue?'

'No, there is no delay in the portal queue; you may leave at any time. We will await your call.'

'Thank you. Jergan EN4-31 out. Have you got a fix on the portal?' I asked Ruuth after.

'No, not yet.' She sounded annoyed, and I realised why. We had been spending a lot of time trying to rid the vessel of the clique computer virus. I immediately felt stupid for asking.

'OK. I'll finish off with the programme de-virus if you can finish the portal fix.'

'Thanks. That is more like it. Here I have got to there in this programme. It is nearly done. There are only a few left. Not all the programmes are affected. It seems the virus is very selective.'

'That's good isn't it? It means we could possibly work out what it is supposed to be doing?'

'Possibly. It may also have a decoy in it to put us off. Right, now to finish this fix on the hidden portal.' She left me at the console and left the room again. She returned almost immediately.

'I just need to input the data into the V20.' Her fingers flew over the keyboard as she went back and forth from the console to the V20. It was not long before she finally stood up. 'Done.' She said with obvious pride and turned on the V20. The familiar bluish orb sprang into being. She typed some more commands and the grey smudge grew smaller and smaller until it was a large dot.

'Well done.' I said.

'I just hope its right.' She replied. 'It's a long way if we are wrong. We will not be able to get back. It looks to be about four hundred light years from here. If it is not there, we will die out there.'

'Good point. I think we had better have a talk about this and see what we do. We cannot skip without Karon's consent. She may not want to stay on planet here while we go. We may not all want to go. In fact, it might be sensible to leave someone behind just in case.' I added finally, looking into Ruuth's bright blue eyes.

'I'm going.' She said with a finality that took me by surprise.

'Really, just like that?'

'Yes.' She stood up and looked directly back into my eyes. 'For me there is no going back. I don't know why it's true but it just seems as though we are finished if we go back.' I looked from her to the V20's galaxy glowing above the control panel to the screen and the shining planet slowly turning as I weighed the options in my mind. I found myself saying. 'I agree.' And could not believe it! We could be going to certain death. But somehow even though I had only known this woman for a few days it just seemed natural that I expected her to say she was going. What was more unexpected was that I was agreeing with her! I just could not work that one out. There had been some odd things happening, but it just did not seem logical to be doing this.

'Let us have something to eat and then have a chat about it.' She said and we turned to find Djon and Terens sitting in the back seats looking intently at us.

'You two seem to have forgotten we were here.' Said Djon with a big smile on his face. I had not seen him smile like that for some time. In fact, none of us had smiled for some time. Or rather it had felt like some time but had again been only a few days. All the same it was good to see it again.

'I'm glad you want to include us.' Added Terens in his usual dry manner, but even he had a wry grin.

'I agree with you both as it happens.' Said Djon. 'And I'm glad to see you do at last Djim.' Terens looked askance at him.

'Really?' he said. 'You agree that we should go on? So do I.'

'Well, it looks as though we don't need much of a chat then after all.' Said Ruuth.

'It's only Karon then that we need to get a decision from.' I added last. 'But first we need to find out how big that dot is that locates the portal and get some co-ordinates for it.'

'I'm on to it.' Said Ruuth and set to work again. I was amazed at her tenacity and capacity for sustained work. It was not long before she had some figures. 'Well.' She said with her satisfied way. 'It looks to be about a million kilometres across approximately. How fast can this vessel go?'

'I think we can get up to about thirty thousand kilometres an hour in an hour or so.' I replied. Djon nodded.

'OK.' She continued. 'I suggest we get back out into normal space right on the edge of the dot there and then go in under normal power. We can cross it in a couple of days. If there is no portal there then we need to get our vessel based one up and running. I must admit that that frightens me, we have not even built it yet let alone tested it.'

'I know.' I added. 'But we have no choice. I am sure there is a portal there. We will be OK. Right, let us get some food and then we will get Karon. I suggest we stay here tonight and leave early in the morning.' The others agreed and the two men got up and we went to the galley to get something to eat. We were surprised to find Karon already in the galley looking for something to eat too.

'Oh, I'm sorry.' She said guiltily. 'I still couldn't rest and then I got hungry.'

'That's OK.' Said Ruuth. 'Sit down. We are all going to eat now anyway.' Ruuth then rummaged through the food storage and suggested some ideas. We soon found something that we were all happy with and she quickly prepared one of the standard space ration meals. Nourishing but not really exciting. We had a quiet meal together seated around the galley table, the first time ever if I recalled correctly.

After we ate, we discussed the options with Karon. Surprisingly, she wanted to go on to the hidden portal in the morning and we could not dissuade her. With that sorted we then just sat around the table chatting. It was a great moment and we got much closer together as a group. Maybe it was because we may all be dead shortly if the portal did not exist, or if these faceless someones decided we knew too much. We then got on to the subject of parents, and naturally my father came into the conversation. I don't know how it happened, but someone managed to ask Djon how he knew the V20 beacon could be turned off.

'I just looked on the set-up menu and there it was. Don't all the V20's have that facility?'

'No.' I said. 'You are not supposed to be able to turn it off.'

'Do you think it was your father then that adapted this V20?' Djon said to me.

'I don't know. I was very young when he disappeared. 'He told you more I assume. He told me nothing.' I had a growing feeling that I had not known my father; or rather that he had been living two lives; one the loving father and the other a clandestine person creeping unseen throughout the galaxy gathering information which it seems normal people should not know. I found myself thinking back to when I was young with the addition of hindsight. Could I find any oddness to my father's behaviour? Unfortunately, I could not. All I could remember were good times when he was at home; playing games, going to see his place of work, the usual father child relationship.

'Do you think he did anything else to it then?' Asked Terens.

'I don't know, he disappeared before he could tell me anything.'

'Shall we have a look then?' Said Ruuth, getting up from her seat and stopping any chance of a negative response. We all followed her back to the control room. I started up the V20 and called up the start up menu with a little help from Djon as it was not something I did normally. Funnily enough it was not part of pilot training and for the first time I wondered why. Instead of the normal bluish orb of the galaxy a grey sphere appeared and within it a list of instructions scrolled up to hover in mid air. Each one had a number beside it. None of them was a beacon on off instruction. I looked at Djon. He did not say anything but leant across and pressed the two buttons that formed the bottom of the vee of buttons and held them down. Nothing happened for a moment or two and then slowly the list of instructions rose higher in the bubble and at the bottom in the gloom where the sphere was created was another instruction. It read beacon on and beacon off with the appropriate commands. Djon smiled at me and released the buttons he was holding.

'Well, that should not be there.' I said.

'Did he do anything else then?' Someone asked. I studied the list that was now squeezed up at the top of the ephemeral sphere and mentally went through the list in my head from pilot training. I could find nothing. Then Ruuth, who was standing at the back of the group crowded round the V20 pointed. 'What is that?' I half stood to look down into the base of the sphere under the on off beacon instruction and saw another dot half hidden in the interference at the base. There was nothing beside it. I used a cursor to scroll down to the dot. As it came to the dot seven small white dots appeared beside it.

'Well, what's that then?' There was no answer. We all looked at it trying to work out what it could mean.

'Does it mean there is some sort of code required to open it?' Said Ruuth hesitantly. 'Seven letters or seven numbers. What would he use?'

'His own name. Rojer?' I suggested. 'No, that is only five letters'

'What if we convert his name into numbers?' Asked Ruuth.

'That's only five numbers though.' Djon called the table down and we swivelled the seats round to sit at it and wrote down numbers and letters.

'Your birthday?' Suggested Djon.

'No. That's only six or eight numbers.' I said. We went back to my mother's name, birthdays, family names, but none of them seemed to fit. Even the seven letters or numbers we could think did nothing. It was getting late when Karon suddenly asked, out of the blue. 'What about Djon?'

'That's only four letters.' Djon said dismissively, but Karon was unfazed. 'What if the letters are their positions in the alphabet, like D is.' She thought for a moment. 'The number four.'

'That would make.' Djon also thought for a moment. 'Four, ten, fifteen and fourteen. Seven numbers!' He jumped up as we all did. Ruuth reached the V20 first and tapped out the seven numbers and to our surprise a message from my father scrolled up in the ephemeral sphere.

– CHAPTER 8 –

GALAXIES ARE VAST

The message read: Djon, I am hoping it is you reading this. If it is you then please type in my usual phrase.

'Ha. I know that.' Said Djon and typed something into the V20. Another series of headings scrolled up in the sphere.

'What was his phrase, Djon?' I asked. He looked at me a while before answering.

'I'm sorry Djim I was debating whether to tell you or not.'

'Why ever not?'

'In case we are caught. What you don't know you cannot divulge.'

'I think Djon.' Put in Terens. 'We are all in this right up to our necks.'

'I know we are all in it together Terens but if we are caught and someone finds this then you cannot tell them if you do not know. It is safer that way. You can truthfully say you do not know. I will tell you all later when the danger has passed.'

'If it ever does.' Muttered Terens but grudgingly accepted Djon's reasoning, as we all did.

'Right.' Said Ruuth. 'Let us work through this data that Djim's father has left you.' She sat down in front of the V20 and we all crowded round the orb glowing above the control panel as she began to work through the data. It was the same information that we already had. The number of planets and the hidden portal, the DNA correlation, the settlement dates and comments about them all. Then came something about the Fair-Trade Dealers. It listed the galaxy wide trade and there was a huge discrepancy between what was transported from planets and back to the planets. Vast quantities of valuable minerals, metals, gold, silver etc simply vanished from the galaxy it appeared. My father commented that this might have something to do with the hidden portal.

'I thought something was not quite right!' Spluttered Ruuth. 'When I was working for Enceladus Governing body I came across details of trade figures. I was not supposed to I might add. And there seemed to be much more leaving than returning.'

'They told me.' I interjected. 'That it was because the raw materials leaving were bulkier than the products arriving. I knew something wasn't right either.'

'And that, Djim.' Said Djon calmly. 'Was one of the reasons you were a marked man. You were always asking questions.'

'I didn't realise. It just seemed normal to me to question things. You cannot take everything at face value.'

'And that is what got your father into trouble too.' I felt a cold shiver run down my spine. What was the matter with this galaxy?

'Look, this isn't getting us any further.' Said Ruuth. 'Can we get on with the job in hand please.' She pointed us back to the V20. We looked again at the shimmering orb. At the end of the list my father wanted Djon to type in his phrase again. Djon did. This time came scrolling up in the orb instructions to construct a vessel-based portal!

'Wow. I didn't know a portal could be vessel based.' I said. The others agreed. We looked at each other. What was going on in the galaxy? Why was this information not readily available?

'If we had this information then no vessel could be lost in space. There would always be a way back.' Commented Ruuth.

'Who would hide this?' I asked, horrified. If my father knew this then he should have been able to get back from wherever he went.

'I am wondering if this is what your father wanted to see me about. Said Djon. 'Perhaps this is what he found out just before he disappeared and maybe someone knew he had the

information. The coincidence is just too loud to ignore I think.'
Djon slumped down in his seat. This had hit him hard. Harder than it had hit me it seemed. I felt I had to help him out. After all I had said about his harebrained scheme it now seemed he had been right all along. I felt small and humbled.

'So, what do we do with this information?' I asked, in an effort to jog Djon out of his apparent despair.

'We add this to our insurance policy.' Said Terens.

'Insurance policy?' Asked Karon, a frown creasing her brow. We all stopped and realised that our plan to keep it secret had misfired badly. Terens obviously realised what he had said and was trying not to give the impression that he had said anything wrong. He also looked imploringly at Djon for support. Djon shrugged. No one was answering.

'Our insurance policy is a hidden.' I stopped. 'I'm sorry, but I think it best we do not tell you. Just as Djon was saying about my father's phrase what you do not know you cannot divulge.' I hoped she would be satisfied with this.

'Yes, I see what you mean.' She said.

'I agree with Terens.' Said Ruuth. 'We should add it to our insurance policy.'

'Definitely.' I added. I looked across at Djon. He was still looking at the portal instructions trying not to laugh.

'Right.' He said finally. 'Let us see if we have any of these items in store. Ruuth can you patch the list through to the store. Visually please. We don't want anything left in the clique computers.'

'Certainly Djon. Shall I also add this lot to our insurance policy as well?'

'Of course. That is vital.' He was up out of his seat and heading out of the control room as he spoke. The rest of us remained in the control room. We all felt independently that perhaps Djon would prefer to do this alone. I went back to looking at the instructions to build a portal as Ruuth busied herself doing a visual link to the store and then sending a coded message to our insurance policy. It looked too easy, but I knew we would not carry the components needed. We would have to go down to the planet to get them and that could be very risky. How could we explain why we needed such parts? That would be the biggest challenge, for as far as I knew a lot of the parts were not seen in anything else.

Sure enough Djon came back shortly with a list of things required that were not in store. He put the list on the table. 'OK, we need this lot, but I don't know where we will get it from.'

'Is it all available from Galilei?' asked Terens.

'Who knows? But as there is a portal here then it must be I assume. I suspect spares must be required occasionally. Djon, you work in space, are spares needed for portals?' Asked Ruuth.

'I've never known it. The portal technicians were a breed apart and never mixed with anyone. I never met any or knew where they came from. It is a bit strange now you come to mention it. I never thought about it before but now…' He trailed off, deep in thought staring out of the forward vision enhancer at the planet in front of us.

'Karon.' Said Ruuth. 'Would your brother be able to get this stuff from his stores? If we paid him of course.'

'I don't know, but he must be in the best position out of all of us. Unfortunately, I have no idea how to contact him or get the parts here or pay him.' She added.

'It is a problem, that is for sure.' Muttered Terens. 'If we send a normal signal someone may pick up on it, especially on Geryon.'

'Will they be able to trace the call back to us?' Asked Djon of no one and everyone in particular.

'It would take quite some time as the portals confuse the signals as we know. It could possibly be weeks – or hours. I really don't know; it depends upon the quality of their equipment.'

'I do not recall anything very sophisticated.' Said Karon, which made us all sit up. Perhaps it was worth a try after all. We just needed some way of getting to the equipment.

'Can we trust him?' Asked Terens.

'I think if I am here, we can.' Said Karon. 'He will not agree with me leaving or joining you, but he would not put me in danger.'

'Will he think we kidnapped you?' Asked Ruuth.

'He might. I did leave him a note, but in the circumstances, I will try and persuade him that it was all my idea to leave and join you.'

'OK, let us do it then.' Said Djon. 'So, how do we contact Perak and not everyone on Geryon?'

'And how do we do it without putting him at risk. After all he will have to account for the equipment, and the paperwork etc.?'

'Why, how considerate you lot are.' Said Karon, her face beaming at long last.

'Thank you. It is a good point.' I said. 'Do individuals order such equipment? Would it look odd on the inventory?'

'Let us just ask him, shall we?' Suggested Karon. 'He may have some ideas of his own.'

'OK.' Said Djon, in a final way, which we all new meant the discussion was at an end and action should begin. 'Djim, can you set up a text only call to Perak? Coded of course unless that would arouse suspicion.'

'I'll see what I can do. Ruuth, do you have any ideas?' She looked up and smiled as I spun my seat round to face the control panel.

'Karon.' Continued Djon. 'Please send your brother a message and see what he says. Djim will set up the sender.' He then got up and left the control room while I set up the message system. Ruuth stood over me and gave some hints and tips as I worked. Then over the internal communication system came Djon's mechanical voice. 'Djim.' He called from somewhere in the vessel. I waited for more of the message, but it never came so I made my excuses and left Ruuth finishing the message system. I left the control room and went to find Djon. I finally found him skulking outside the galley in a suspicious manner.

'Come in here.' He said and dragged me into the galley.

'Just make sure there is a delay on that call. We need to check it before it is sent.' He hissed leaning back out into the corridor to check if it was still clear. It seemed almost comical.

'Don't worry Djon.' I said, calmly putting a reassuring hand on his shoulder. 'I have already done it. We need to be sure of her first. We all were agreed on that.' He visibly relaxed.

'You really are just like your father.' He said with a big smile. We were interrupted by a call for me to return to the control room and send the signal. We then agreed it was finally bedtime. When everyone was leaving the control room, I made an excuse to just stay and set up our vessel for an automatic night shift. I also called up Gallilei space flight control and asked for a night-time holding place and to let them know that we required spare parts to be able to continue our onward flight. They tried to get me to book into their repair bay but I managed to talk them out of that but was not happy that they fully accepted me. At the same time, I checked the message to Perak that Karon had written. It was fine. I tried to see if I could find anything that looked like a coded message but there was nothing. As I returned to my bed, I put my head into Djon's room to put his mind at rest, and let him know of our predicament about leaving. He was very relaxed and agreed to deal with it in the morning.

*

I woke early in the morning and went to get some breakfast. Ruuth and Karon were already there. Djon and Terens joined us shortly after. I put everyone in the picture regarding our lack of moving on. I was concerned that this might have caused suspicion. I suggested we try and see if Gallilei will accept we have a problem and need spare parts but not requiring their help. It would help as we could legitimately be getting a delivery. We would need a good reason though to not be using the repair bay in the Gallilei satellite. I told them that I had tried to do this last night. I did not have an excuse which sounded too plausible though. Karon eventually suggested we just almost come clean and say that her brother can get the parts for us at cost. We decided it was worth a try so after we had eaten, I contacted Gallilei space flight control and explained our situation and the reason for getting parts out of the solar system. They seemed to accept this, so all we then had to do was wait for Perak's reply. It was not long in coming. He started by ranting and raving at Karon mainly but also at us for taking her away and wanted her back. Karon sent another message saying she was not coming back, and it was not our fault but could he help. We waited patiently for his reply again. This time he seemed to have calmed down and eventually agreed to get the parts for us. He gave us the costs and the payment code. He wanted the money up front. It was a lot of money and we debated hotly whether we should pay up front or not. Karon convinced us that Perak would keep his side of the bargain because of her. By Djon's and Terens looks I could see we also had a bargaining chip – Karon. We agreed and sent the list of required parts with the payment. All we could do then was wait and see what happened. All we could do was wait and see if the equipment came through. It was a worrying time just hanging in space above the planet, not knowing who or what was watching us or who was observing our transaction. I constantly kept checking outside our vessel to see what other vessels where about. I also kept checking the visual and aural communications. As far as I could ascertain everything was normal. Still, I was worried. I hated just hanging about.

Later on that day an incoming message made us all jump. It was from Perak telling us that the equipment was on its way. He gave us the shipping number. I called Gallilei space flight control and asked for instructions to pick up the shipment. We were surprised and annoyed at having to pay an import handling charge. They then said they would let us know when it arrived. Two hours later Gallilei freight handling called to say the shipment had arrived and was ready for collection. They gave us the docking coordinates. I began the vessel wake up procedure and sought a trajectory and docking time for the collection. When this arrived, I commenced the flight path procedure to take us over to freight collection dock. The freight satellite was separate from the human transport satellite and was usually further out from the planet. It was also much bigger. It was identical to the one at Enceladus that I was used to docking at. It was a huge cube of docks with a series of vast storage bays. There was a very small living compartment on one corner. Each corner had a small observation dome for checking vessels docking. As we got closer, I realised just how small our vessel was compared to the freight vessels arriving and departing. They were packed together tightly when docked, their anti-crash systems preventing any collisions as they manoeuvred. When we docked however there was enough room for another Jergan either side. It was easy therefore to bring us into the dock. We locked onto the freight airlock. It was a special airlock to allow transfer of goods to a vessel such as ours. Most freight vessels storage holds were not atmosphered, so an airlock was not necessary. We waited as the airlock cycle completed and then prepared to go and get our equipment. We decided to leave Ruuth and Karon on board while we collected the crates just in case and also asked them to be separate as well. Ruuth in the control room and Karon in the workshop. We also decided to set up hidden cameras by the airlock so Ruuth and Karon could watch what was going on. We felt very vulnerable and wanted as much help as possible. Djon, Terens and I went down to the airlock and fixed the camera. I looked into the lens of the camera and spoke to Ruuth. 'OK, good picture and sound?' I knew the camera was there but anyone else would not spot it I felt sure. Karon's tiny tinny voice responded from the intercom speaker.

'Loud and clear Djim. We are ready.' Once that was done, we looked at each other and then opened it up. It opened directly into the cargo bay in the freight satellite. My eyes took a moment to adjust to the lower light levels in the bay. We stepped out into the dimly lit storage chamber. This was the smallest storage chamber in the freight satellite. I knew the main storage chamber was a vast unlit space with no gravity and no atmosphere. It was a vacuum. Inside the freight crates

– some of which could be the size of a small vessel would be stacked into neat piles and secured against movement with huge magnetic clamps. Throughout the space were huge handling gantries that would very slowly manoeuvre the crates to the correct docks for the freighters. It had to be done slowly as the crates still had the same mass although weightless and if allowed to gain speed would become vast weapons of kinetic power and could easily burst out of the side of the satellite. Consequently, this had to be done by computerised machines as humans would not have the patience. As a consequence, the vast space was unlit and almost pitch dark, machines do not need light. I had never been in this smaller chamber before although I had seen it from the other side at Enceladus. Even this space was not lit brightly. It did not need to be. Once my eyes had become accustomed to the lower light level I could see two men dressed in the standard freight handlers' overalls standing just a few metres from the airlock. I spotted our crates stacked and locked into place nearby. I knew they were ours because they were the only ones in the chamber that were uncovered, and I recognised the Geryon freight handling logo. It was rather amusing in one way seeing this tiny pile of crates in the large space. And this space I knew was tiny compared to the main freight storage hold. The two men did not appear amusing.

'Good afternoon.' The larger of the two said. He had dark skin and a big chest that pulled his overalls tight. I thought nowadays it should be possible to have well fitting overalls, in fact I could not remember the last time I had seen ill fitting clothes. His voice was thick and full, not the sort of voice to toy with, it commanded respect. The other man was much smaller, but then I realised that it was purely an optical illusion as he was standing next to the bigger man. He was thin with dark thin hair and looked nervous. My gaze was drawn back to the bigger man as he spoke again.

'Please sign here to say you have received your freight and paid the handling charge.' He held out his inventory pad.

'Certainly.' I replied. 'We will sign that we have received

the freight when we have, and it is in our vessel. I know nothing of a handling charge. I have never heard of this before.' The big man did not look pleased at this, but I had become very wary recently and wanted the freight on board before signing anything. Djon stepped up and put a hand upon my arm. I was shaking like a leaf, I hoped he did not notice.

'We will pay the handling charge.' He said, producing his payment card. 'But we will not sign until we have the freight in our vessel as my friend here has said.' The big man looked like thunder but eventually took Djon's payment card and slipped it into the payment slot on the top of his inventory pad. It clocked up a large amount of money and again I was not surprised. He withdrew the card and handed it back to Djon but before he could take it dropped it on the floor. Terens moved forward but Djon stopped him with a slight gesture that I nearly missed.

'Oh, sorry.' The man said. 'Sign when you have your freight on board.' He nodded to his thin companion and then they both turned and disappeared into a polyglass walled office I had not noticed before. The blinds snapped shut. I went and got our anti gravity hauler from our storage hold and manoeuvred it out into the freight chamber where Djon had picked up his card and was releasing the first crate from the magnetic clamps. I clamped it onto the crate and began to manoeuvre it into our hold. It quickly became obvious that our six crates were only five. One was missing. It also became obvious that our freight was not the only objects in the space. There were other crates and mysterious objects covered by protective shrouds. We knew from Perak that there should be six crates. This had us worried, either someone knew the contents, or they were stealing our crate. That gave me a strange feeling inside, as crime was almost non existent on Enceladus it was not something I knew how to handle. We worked slowly to give ourselves time to search the gloomy space, visually at first then quickly looking under the shrouds when Terens indicated the men were not watching. He was loitering near the door of their office pretending to guide our hauler. Djon soon found our crate covered up nearby, our delivery note removed.

'How do we get that last crate?' I asked as we moved the fourth crate into our hold.

'I don't know. Terens, get Ruuth and tell her the situation while Djim and I get the fifth crate.' Said Djon. Terens nodded and left the hold.

'What can Ruuth do?' I asked as I unhooked the hauler, slower than we normally would. We needed time.

'We'll see.' He replied enigmatically. 'Now let us get the fifth crate into our hold. Nice and slowly of course.' We manoeuvred the hauler back out into the gloomy space to collect the crate. As we were bringing it into our hold Terens returned with Ruuth. She was carrying a shoulder bag and had a short black rod in her hand. 'Keep behind her.' Muttered Djon as we clamped the crate into a secure position. As we returned to the gloomy space the two men left their office and came over.

'Now sign.' Said the big man.

'I'm sorry.' Said Djon. 'But we still seem to have a crate missing.'

'Now don't be silly.' Said the big man, his small companion smiled unpleasantly. 'You have your goods now sign and leave. We don't want any trouble do we.'

'No, we don't so give us our last crate.'

'I'll say this once more. You have your goods now sign and leave.'

'No.'

'I'm sorry then.' He reached back into a pocket, but before he could move much more there was a bright flash of piercing white light. My mind went immediately back to Djon's office. I felt weak and dropped to my knees. I then felt Djon grab my arm, lifting me up. Fortunately, the feeling soon passed.

'Come on Djim. Wake up!' I struggled to my feet. 'Come on Djim, we need to move fast.' He thrust the hauler controls into my weak hand and ran over to the last crate with Terens. They threw off the shroud. He grabbed the hauler and clamped it on. I just about had the ability to control the hauler with my shaking hands while Terens and Djon guided the crate into our hold. Djon shouted instructions to me all the time. It sounded as though he was calling from a long way away, I could barely hear him. I could not see Ruuth. In fact, my vision was still poor and blurred from the flash. I felt I was looking at the world through a fog. My mouth felt dry and I was shaking as though cold. As soon as the last crate was secured by Djon, Terens already closing the airlock I dropped the controls. They fell with a clatter to the floor. Djon and Terens rushed over to grab me by my arms and half drag me half push me I knew not where; I was in such a state. I heard Djon giving instructions as we stumbled along the corridor. I was dropped into the pilot's chair and someone poured a cool refreshing drink of water into my mouth. It revived me considerably. My normal senses returned quickly.

'Come on Djim, we need to leave, quickly.' I heard Djon say. 'Call up space flight control and get the first available portal window out of here.' I leant forward but it ended up as more of a slump onto the control panel. I called up space flight control and asked for a flight window.

'Certainly.' Answered the space flight controller. 'May I have your delivery collection number.'

'Ghas!' I swore. 'We did not sign the....'

'Hold on!' said Ruuth as she returned to the control room. 'I did sign the pad and got a number too. Here.' She handed me a copy of the delivery collection sheet. There was a scribbled signature.

'I don't know what we would do without you Ruuth.' I said managing a weak smile.

'I don't know. I'm sure you would muddle along somehow.' She paused. 'On the other hand....' She did not even bother finishing the sentence.

'Space flight control.' I continued. 'This is Jergan EN4-31 we have the delivery collection number.' Space flight control acknowledged our call and took the number. There was a pause. My palms were sweating now. We needed speed above all else to be away from here before those two men woke up again and raised the alarm. Now we really were outlaws running from the scene of a crime. It was not exiting at all. It was frightening. We were finally given the co-ordinates to go to for the portal queue. The relief in the control room was palpable. We joined the queue but still all the while expecting to be called out and the skip aborted.

'Set the V20 for the hidden portal co-ordinates as we agreed.' Said Djon, his voice was shaky and thin, not at all like his normal full voice.

'We've already done that.' I said. 'We did it when we agreed where to re-enter normal space. There was nowhere else we would be going next.' I watched the bright dot of light in front of us disappear. 'OK, we are next.' We got closer and closer to the portal, the screen displaying the approach diagrams and vectors with numbers scrolling down indicating the approach speed, distance, time to enter the portal and a whole list of technical details. Lights flashed as clique computer programmes we activated and then as the numbers all reached zero the screen went blank and with it the familiar feeling of falling and a thickening of the atmosphere. I switched the V20 to take us to the hidden portal co-ordinates.

*

The stars did not come out again! The screen in front of us was dark with just a few smudges of light.

'What's happened?' Asked Djon groggily after a few minutes recovering from the skip.

'I'm not sure.' I said also recovering slowly. 'Just a minute while I get the V20 going again.'

'Where's the portal?' Asked Terens.

'Oh, we didn't skip straight to it.' I said. 'Hopefully, we should be a day or so's journey away from it. I didn't want to be too close until we knew what we were heading for.'

'Good idea.' Muttered Djon.

'Well, I'm not so sure.' Muttered Terens darkly. 'You don't know what you will come out of ND space into doing that.'

'An acceptable risk.' I said as I got the V20 going again. The familiar bluish orb was empty apart from the red dot indicating our position.

'Oh, ghas, where are we?' Someone said.

'I don't know.'

'Just a minute.' Said Djon. 'There's one star – look there. Just zoom out.' I did so and saw it then as a tiny dot of light emerged from the fuzzy edge of the orb. I zoomed out to maximum. A few more stars appeared. Of course, we were right on the edge of the galaxy so there would be very few stars. I called up the star and portal details. A few numbers and letters appeared by the dots.

'We seem to be right on the edge of the galaxy.' Muttered Terens again.

'Where's the hidden portal?' Asked Ruuth. I typed in the hidden portal co-ordinates and a small grey smudge appeared right beside our red dot. We were on target. 'Why put a portal right out here?' She asked. No one replied as no one knew the answer.

'Who knows?' I finally managed to say, breaking the silence. 'Why hide it? Why disguise the fact that we came from an original planet? Why? Why? Why? That is all we get. Questions and no answers.'

'Well, let us go and find this hidden portal and maybe we might just get some answers.' Said Djon.

'OK.' I replied and began the sequence to fire up the main drive. 'By the way Ruuth?' I added.

'Yes, Djim?'

'What was that thing that makes the bright light and knocks us out?'

'Ah, that.' She said and looked across at Djon.'

'OK, Djim.' Replied Djon. 'It's a little something your father also gave me. I do not know where he got it or what it's called because I have never seen one before. But after a bit of detective work we managed to operate the thing. We don't know what else it does but the brief instructions we have only refer to the capacity to render human beings unconscious for certain periods. It says it is perfectly harmless otherwise.'

'It's what you used on me, isn't it?'

'Yes, sorry Djim. We didn't know what else to do.'

'Really?'

'Believe me Djim, we had to get you off the planet.'

'So you say. But so far you have offered no proof of that, or why.' The main drive warning alarm sounded, and we sat down facing front. Then there was a punch in our backs and a dull grumble from the rear of the vessel and a subtle vibration coming up through the structure. When the green light finally came on I said. 'Come on then let us have a look at our equipment. We have not yet had a chance to look at it.' I felt that it was not worth pursuing the reasons for Djon's actions on Enceladus. He must have either been deluded or had a good reason for his actions. Besides, we were here now and harking back to the past was not going to get us out of this situation or put anything right. I was beginning to want answers for the questions we now had and see if I could find any more out about my father too. I stood up. It was time to check the quality of our goods.

'They didn't have it long enough on Gallilei to do anything.'

'We hope.' Muttered Terens.

'Quite. Now who is willing to stay in the control room while the others go checking the freight?'

'I will stay.' Volunteered Ruuth. The other two left for the hold while I stayed and gave Ruuth a quick lesson on normal space flight control. The vectors were set in and the course determined. She acknowledged her capability and I also left for the hold. The storage hold was the largest space in the Jergan and was vital to prevent occupants getting mental problems when cooped up in confined spaces for long periods. Now of course this space was taken up by the crates. The other two had done nothing by the time I arrived.

'Check the seals first.' Said Djon. 'It will determine if the crates have been opened or tampered with.' All crates for space travel are airtight and sealed to keep the contents safe from the vacuum of space and the effects of zero gravity. The seals also ensure the contents are not tampered with or spoilt as a safety measure for sender and recipient. They are located so that they can be seen even when the crates are stacked one upon another. It was a simple job to do a visual check and then a sonic check with a sonic pencil which checked the internal matrix of the seal. They were all sound.

'Well, that's good.' Muttered Terens, looking at the readout of the last crate. 'I suppose we had better check the contents against the list we sent Perak. I know Karon trusts him, but I would be happier if we also knew we had everything.'

'It's a bit late if he didn't send everything. If this portal is not here, we cannot get back without a full load.' I said.

'We had better keep that thought to ourselves in that case.' Said Djon. 'We cannot scare Karon with that idea.' I could see in their faces that Karon was not the only one who was scared at that thought. We all were. I had a cold feeling in the pit of my stomach at the thought that there was not a complete portal in the crates. We were light years from any assistance. We stood still for what seemed an age.

'Right.' Said Djon finally and went and called up the inventory of goods we requested and displayed them on the wall panel. 'We'll start with this one.' He pointed to the top crate on the nearest stack of two. I got the hauler over and the four hooks automatically were guided into the lifting lugs in the top of the crate by the magnetic guides. With apparently no effort it lifted the crate and gently put it down on the floor in the open inspection area where floor bolts locked it into place. We broke the seal and recorded the breaking in the log before lifting the lid. We looked inside at the neatly and professionally packed contents. Perak had done a good job so far.

'Hm.' Muttered Terens, looking from the inventory list to the contents. 'That looks OK. I trust these things are what they say they are because I do not know. I've never seen anything like this before.'

'Neither have I.' Added Djon. I had to agree with him. Half the stuff on the list I did not know. There were a lot of sealed components the contents of which were not explained. We began to unpack the contents of the first crate. It was a slow job as the contents were very tightly packed together with a vacuum and weightless resistant packing material. We became so absorbed in the job that Ruth's worried voice over the internal communicator made us jump. It was much later than we thought.

'There's something coming up on the screen.' She said. I immediately got up from the floor where I had been trying to open a set of small components and headed for the control room.

'You don't need us do you?' Called Djon after me.

'No. You carry on with what were doing. I'll call you if we need help.' I called back to them over my shoulder. As I ran up to the control room I was thinking what on Erebus could be way out here? As I came into the control room Ruuth left the pilot's seat and I threw myself into it. Then I heard the familiar beep of the UFO alert. What ever it was, was still far away then. When the alerts come more frequently it would indicate the object was getting closer. I switched on the V20 and zoomed in until we got a flashing dot about two hundred thousand kilometres away from us. The V20 gave us a UFO signal too, meaning it was unable to identify the object. It was not heading for us. It appeared to be stationary as far as I could tell. I switched on the long-range telescope but not with much hope of seeing much. The telescopes on vessels like these were pretty poor. It was too small to see it other than a meaningless dot. The V20 then began to show some figures and numbers beside the dot. I read what it was trying to tell me.

'Have I brought you up here for nothing?' Asked Ruuth.

'I don't know yet, Ruuth.'

'I'm sorry if I have. I'm not used to this yet.'

'You did the right thing. I would rather you called me than left it and we collided with something. That's odd.'

'What is?'

'Look. The V20 readout.' I highlighted the readout and put it up on the forward vision enhancer screen. There was the usual data for a small object out in space but with it was something else.

'The object appears to be emitting a signal.' Said Ruuth carefully.

'Yes, it does. But way out here on the edge of the galaxy. What on Erebus could be doing that and why?'

'Not another of your unanswered questions Djim.' She said smiling broadly. 'I tell you what. It is a long way away. I will keep an eye on it and call you when it gets closer. We are not going to collide with it are we?'

'No. Judging by the data the V20 is giving me we should pass it by at about five thousand kilometres distance so nothing to worry about. OK, I will go back and help Djon and Terens. Thanks. By the way what time is it?'

'Well according to the ship's timekeeper it is midnight on May thirteenth. But do not forget we have not emerged from ND space anywhere near a planet for them to update our timekeeper. We could be way out of time.'

'That's a good point. We will just have to go by ship's timekeeper for now. We'll work for a bit longer and then get some shut eye.' I got up and left the control room. 'How long have we got until we get to the object?'

'Just a second.' She said and tapped on the keyboard for a moment. 'We have about six hours.'

'OK, we'll get some sleep now and get up early to check it out. Where's Karon?'

'She's in bed already. It has been rather stressful for her. She looked as though she needed the rest, so I sent her to bed.'

'Good idea. I'll see you later.' I finally left the control room to go back to the storage hold. When I got back Djon and Terens had yet more stuff out on the floor and the workbench.

'No trouble then?' Said Djon with a big smile as he struggled with the packing on a large piece of equipment. He had called up the instructions to build the portal and they hung eerily in the middle of the open space in large letters over twenty millimetres high. Terens walked through it, though to him it would have been by me. It was much like the proverbial rainbow, always out of reach. It another of the new clever technological innovations.

'I'm not sure. It was small and unidentified, but it also appears to be emitting a signal.'

'Really?' Djon stopped what he was doing and looked up. Terens also stopped what he was doing and looked over.

'Ruuth is keeping an eye on it for the moment but as it is midnight, we thought it better to get some sleep and get up early when we are closer.'

'When will we meet it?'

'About oh seven hundred hours ship's time.'

'Right. Let us get some sleep then and get up early.' Said Djon and started to secure loose material for the night.

*

I was up at oh five hundred hours after a fitful sleep and went straight down to the storage hold. Djon and Terens were already there!

'Hi.' Said Djon. 'Good morning.'

'Oh, hi. Why are you up so early?'

'Neither of us could sleep much so Terens got down here at oh four hundred and I was here half an hour later. Had to get on and do something. Do you know how any of this works?' He held up a piece of the equipment. 'Because neither of us can make head nor tail of it.'

'I couldn't either.' I had to admit.

'None of the components make much sense.' Added Terens from the other side of the hold.

'It must be the interaction between the V20 and the portal then.' Said Djon, trying to fit two of the components together into the cradle.

'But the transport drones do not have a V20.' I remarked as I reached into a crate and lifted out another well wrapped component. 'If it needs a V20 then they wouldn't work. Unless they have a component in them that interacts.' I ticked off the component against the inventory with the interactive schedule on the screen.

'How do you know where it is going if the unmanned drone does not have a V20?' Asked Djon.

'Good point.' I said and stopped what I was doing. How did the portal work? Ruuth had given us the technical name for what happened. What did she say it was? I thought for a moment, yes that was it she said it was an elemental subatomic electromagnestatic macrocosmic quantum manifold using a quantic homogenous function utilising the Dirac constant modulation which produces a ubiquitous ultimate simultaneous harmonic singularity displacement event in the spatio temporal fabric. I had tried hard to memorise it and hoped I got it right. So, there must be some form of electromagnestatic element to it. Electromagnetic I understood. The static part floored me. Perhaps the satellite has some way of directing traffic to the right portal. I went back to the original question as the portal operation mechanics had me stumped. I relaxed again, fortunately we had a V20 to direct us, or we could have found ourselves stranded out here light years from anywhere. I looked again at the inventory. How did those components manage to reduce the whole of the galaxy into a small ball the size of a portal? I looked again at the list of components. There was nothing there that I could see that could shrink light years of space to nothing. It just did not make sense. Still, it was all we had and now we were light years from anywhere, so if it didn't work and we didn't find the hidden portal we were dead. It suddenly hit me. How did we know it would work? Had my father actually used it? If he had one, why did he not return? Was it all a joke? Had someone else got hold of this information and sent us to our certain death? I felt like I was trapped in a bubble of despair while the others messed about in ignorance. I felt like I was suddenly in a different world from the others. I looked across at Djon and Terens busying themselves with the components and felt as though I could not touch them – as though they were light years away. Then a voice broke the grip this thought had on me as Karon came into the hold.

'Hi.' She said, her voice a little shaky. 'I was getting a bit worked up.' And then I noticed that her eyes were red rimmed from crying. Her hair was in disarray and she was wringing her hands. She was putting on a brave face of being cheerful but underneath she was frightened still, I could tell. My inner desire to hep a maiden in distress took over from the despair that had hold on me and I immediately went over to her. The other two had not noticed her other than a quick glance over and a nod. They went straight back to their work bent over some complex arrangement of components lost in discussion. I put a comforting hand on her shoulder.

'What's up?'

'We're lost, aren't we? We are going to die out here.'

'Hold on there. We are not lost Karon, we know exactly where we are.'

'But we are so far from anywhere.' She then burst into tears putting her head on my shoulder. The other two finally noticed and came over.

'What's the matter?' Asked a concerned Djon.

'She's frightened.' I said quietly over her sobs. I indicated that they should carry on while I sorted her out. They went back to their work but kept looking in our direction. I sat Karon down and talked her through. I had to push my own fears to the back of my mind. She finally began to calm down again.

'Ruuth had suggested I come down here. She said the bigger room would help and also if I started doing something useful it would also help. I feel so useless, like a spare part not wanted.'

'You're wanted all right. Doing something would help. We need help with this portal.'

'I don't know anything about portal electronics.'

'We don't know anything either.' I suddenly realised that was perhaps not the best thing to say. 'I mean to say our knowledge of space hardware is excellent, but we are also learning this as we go along. You can help as much as anyone. Just sit here a second while I talk to the others and we'll work out something for you.' I went over to Djon and Terens and spoke quietly. 'We need to pretend we know more about this than we actually do. She is very frightened and if she thinks we know nothing about this it could send her off again.' The others nodded. 'We need to find something she can do.'

'No trouble Djim. There are seven of these identical pods. Once we have one it is just a question of building the duplicates. Send her over we'll get her working don't you worry.'

Ruuth's voice then came over the internal communicator. 'Djim. We are within range.'

'Coming!' I called back as I went over to Karon. 'OK, Djon will give you something to do. We could do with an extra pair of hands down here. I must go to the control room; I'll be back shortly.' I got up and ran back up to the control room. Ruuth was standing looking at the telescope image. It was poor as I expected, these vessels had very poor telescope resolution. It was not something that was considered important in their design. I went and sat in the pilot's seat and turned on as many sensors as I could think would be useful.

'It appears to be round.' She said.

'It is definitely issuing a signal too, like white noise. It makes it difficult to locate it or get a good fix.' I tried various screening programmes. Suddenly the data came together. 'It is man-made!' I said. 'It is sending out a screening signal. It is not moving as far as I can tell. It is about as big as a house maybe more. What on Erebus could it be doing way out here?'

'The only other thing out here is the portal.' Said Ruuth. I looked at her.

'Of course. It must be screening the portal. So, it is deliberately hidden then and not just lost or something. We had better be careful. I will go and tell Djon. Let me know if it has any defence mechanisms or locks on any radar or something.'

'Sure thing. I'm not letting this out of my sight.'

I got up and ran back to the storage hold where the other three were working away. Karon was indeed much better getting stuck in and lost in her work.

'Djon.' I called. He looked up and I beckoned him over. He gave me a puzzled look but came. The other two also looked up and stopped what they were doing.

'It's OK.' I said. 'I just need to have a word with Djon about some vessel mechanics with which I am not familiar.' I called across, hoping they would not query me. Fortunately, they did not and went back to work as Djon came over giving Karon some last minute instruction.

'What's all this Djim?' He said quietly. He knew me well

enough to know it was not vessel mechanics that I wanted. I turned him around and walked him away from the others.

'The object that Ruuth spotted is man made and is hiding the portal.'

'What!' He immediately realised he had spoken too loudly and quietened down again. He became conspiratorial. 'Are you sure?'

'There's nothing else out here Djon. What else could it be doing?'

'Fair point. But let us not jump to conclusions just yet.'

'No. but we had better be extra careful. If it is intended to hide the portal, then it means that definitely someone does not want this portal found. That cannot be a good thing can it?'

'No.' He became pensive, stroking his neat white beard thoughtfully. 'Better tell Ruuth to close down any external signals, let's go into stealth mode. Shut down any drives and hopefully we will just look like another piece of space debris.'

'OK, will do.' I returned to the control room and we shut down all external signals and anything that would give us away. Ruuth continued to look after the control room while I returned to the storage hold. It seemed like only minutes before Ruuth's voice again came over the internal communicator. 'Djim' I was expecting more but it did not come. I stood holding the component I was trying to fix while I waited for more.

'I'll just go and see what she wants.' I told the others and left, carefully placing the component on the workbench locking clip.

'Djim.' She said as I entered the control room. 'I finally have a good fix on the hidden portal. Once we were past the object back there it suddenly cleared.'

'So that object definitely was obscuring the portal then.'

'Definitely.' She asserted. 'But look, there is something else besides the portal.' She turned on the V20. 'Don't worry Djim the beacon is still turned off. Look.' She pointed to the dot representing the hidden portal. It even had a reference number hovering beside it with the co-ordinates. But next to it was another dot.

'That's too small for a planet.' I said.

'I know.' She replied. 'I have been looking for a planet nearby for some time but there is not one there.'

'Djon said to not give us away by using external signals or anything.' I chided.

'Oh, don't worry it has been purely visual. I have been using the optical telescope. I know it is not very good but it is enough to find a planet. What I cannot work out though is why there should be a portal located right on the edge of the galaxy so far from any star system or planet. This cannot be Ultima Thule after all. It looks as though we have come on a wild goose chase.'

'The whole thing may be a 'wild goose chase' as you put it. What on Erebus is a wild goose anyway?'

'It's nothing. It is just a saying meaning a pointless search.'

'It's that all right but this might be a very dangerous search. This portal has still been hidden for some reason. We must be very careful we cannot afford to use the drives to slow us down or it will be seen.'

'In that case we will just go straight past at thirty thousand kilometres an hour. What good will that do?'

'We'll see who is there. If it is deserted, then we can slow down and return. Yes?'

'I cannot think of anything better.'

'Well, this more or less puts Ultima Thule out of the question. We have come to the edge of the galaxy and not found even a planet, let alone our original planet. This makes Djon's whole premise rather weak. He has kidnapped me and dragged me halfway across the galaxy only to find that the whole thing is what I kept telling him it was.'

'I know Djim, I know, but that does not explain in any way why this portal is hidden way out here!' That I hated to admit was a good point. Maybe one idea was wrong but there was another that needed explaining. I was not about to admit it just yet though.

'Hopefully then we will find an explanation when we get there.'

'As long as we are not killed in the process.'

'Yes, that is now a very worrying possibility. Have you spotted any other vessels out here?'

'Not yet, but I cannot use anything that would give us away though. I can only use passive means and that is not so useful.'

'All we can do is keep looking. How far away is the portal?'

'Let me see.' She entered some calculations. While she was doing that, I put the optical telescope image onto the forward vision enhancer. Two tiny dots appeared. There were no stars to see as we were actually not only on the edge of the galaxy but heading away from the centre. All we could see in front of us was the portal and the other object and the blackness of intergalactic space. There were however the faint smudges of other galaxies close to ours as well as tiny dots of more distant galaxies. It was not anything I had ever seen before. I had never been this close to the edge of the galaxy before. I felt as though we were heading at full speed to the edge of a cliff with no brakes, and no way to stop! There was of course no sensation of speed to go with this. The image of that large, scarred vessel with the weapons oscula swam back into my thought. Was it waiting for us by the portal? Was that what the second dot was? No, the second dot was far too big an image to be a vessel. It was too small to be planet so what was it?

'Right.' Said Ruuth. 'It seems we are about three hundred thousand kilometres away and closing at thirty thousand kilometres an hour. That's relative of course.'

'Portals are usually stationary. I assume his one is. Well at least I can work that one out. It will take us ten hours to get there. We will be there about nineteen hundred hours tonight ships time. Right, I will go back and help Djon. Are you happy to continue up here?'

'Sure thing.'

*

After lunch we were satisfied by a good meal and we all sat around in the storage hold on various crates and chatted. For the first time I saw us all in a relaxed state surrounded by the partly completed portal. Since we had not had any sign of any other vessel, we had relaxed a little and a whole morning of no surprises had made us complacent. The seven big egg-shaped containers filled the storage hold. Some lay opened with their incomplete innards exposed. It had been hard work even with the mechanical assistance of the hauler. It was therefore hard to stop talking and sitting and get back to work.

'What do we do when we get to this portal?' Asked Karon suddenly as she eased herself slowly up off her uncomfortable crate to stretch.

'Well, that depends upon what we find when we get there.' Said Djon unhelpfully.

'It could just be a dead portal.' Added Terens in his usual style.

'There is another object near the portal.' The others, except Ruuth stopped getting ready to go back to work.

'Well?' Said Djon.

'Ruuth and I saw two traces on the optical telescope. So, there are at least two objects there, and no Djon, the second object is not a planet, it is too small.' His face fell.

'What is it then?' Asked Terens.

'We could not identify the second object.'

'When was that?'

'Earlier today.' Said Ruuth.

'So, if we are still travelling at thirty thousand kph we should be much closer now. Could we identify it now?' Asked Djon. I looked at Ruuth.

'It is possible Djon.' She said. 'Do you want me to go and have a look and see if it is clearer now?'

'Yes, please Ruuth.' Said Djon. She then pushed herself up from lying down on her crate and stood up. As she did so the proximity alarm went off!

– CHAPTER 9 –

'Ghas! What is that?' Said Karon, dropping a tool on the floor with a loud crash.

'It's the proximity alarm!' I shouted as I put down the component I was about to complete, now really annoyed with myself for allowing us all to become so complacent that we had left the control room untended. Had someone stayed there we would have had more warning. I could see in my minds eye the warning light flashing unseen on the control panel long before the proximity sensor going off. Why had I not linked the controls down to the hold? Even as I thought it, I realised that had we seen something coming there was not a lot we could have done. I just hoped it was not a vessel but just some asteroid careering through the galaxy, except that I knew there would be no asteroids out here. There was nothing out here. I looked round at the others as I set off for the control room. Karon had her hands up to her face, a very worried expression lining her face, Djon and Terens looked concerned, Ruuth was already on her feet a determined expression on her face.

I turned back and headed for the control room as fast as I could. Hopefully, the anti-crash programme would have kept us from colliding with any space debris. Once in the control room I threw myself into the pilot's seat and silenced the alarm which had been ringing through my head. The red lights continued flashing in the corner of my eye as I switched on the forward vision enhancer. I dare not switch on any radar or active external sensors for fear of announcing our presence. The two dots of the portal and the unidentified object were all that appeared in the screen. I switched on the other external cameras and a series of pictures began to appear down the side of the screen. One of them showed the hull of a vessel uncomfortably close. I had a sudden cold chill in the pit of my stomach. The vessel was so close I could see all too clearly weapons oscula, and they were open!

The others stumbled loudly into the control room and stood there silently looking at the one camera picture that was filled with the hull of the vessel. The numbers and figures scrolling down the vision enhancer with the arrays showing the relationship of the two vessels and all the other data a pilot needed were ignored. I could not work out how they had managed to get so close without setting off any of the alarms earlier; I felt I had let us all down.

'By Erebus, what is that?' Said Karon in a small querulous voice. She had managed to pick up on our expletives in only a very short time of being with us.

'It's a vessel the like of which we have seen near your planet.' I found myself saying. 'It may even be the same one for all we know. It is so close it is impossible to see enough to identify it for sure. All I know is it is not out here on holiday, nor is it lost. This vessel must be something to do with the portal. The question is why did they bother to come and greet us?'

'I bet it won't be welcome committee.' Muttered Terens.

'Well, this can only mean one thing.' Said Ruuth.

'And that is?' Asked Djon.

'It can only mean that the portal is not derelict but operational and someone does not want visitors.'

'I have to agree.' I added. A voice then crackled over the intership communicator.

'Jergan EN4 – 31 be ready for docking.' There was no niceties or introduction. We looked at each other but all knew there was no alternative. The voice had been determined and we felt that they meant business.

'What right have they to...' Began Karon but stopped and fell silent when we all looked at her. She had a sudden realization why she had left Geryon and her family and friends and come with us. 'Is this it then?' She added. 'We are light years from any help.'

'If they had wanted us dead, they could have vaporised this vessel from afar without even raising a sweat.' Added Terens.

It made me feel better. He was right, there may be hope yet.

'Do I comply?' I asked, but now knowing the answer. They all nodded.

'Of course we do.' Snapped Djon. 'Look at that thing. It may not be as fast as us, but those weapons sure will be. I don't think they would hesitate to use them either.' I had to agree with him too. Even with the poor resolution of the camera equipment on the Jergan it was possible to easily see the array of weapons oscula which indicated the types of weapons lurking inside the other vessel. Terrible terrible weapons and out here in the vacuum of space it would not take much to destroy us and if they were particularly unpleasant, they could do it in a slow and painful way. I looked up again at the black shiny curve of the other vessel, it did not reflect any light. There was of course very little light out here to reflect. That made it all the more ominous.

'OK.' I said and with shaking hands opened a channel. 'Jergan EN4 – 31 to ... unidentified vessel.' There was nothing coming up on the screen as any form of identity signal or any other data. They were screening themselves. How did they know us? They must have some way of hacking into our systems as our identity signal was also turned off as was every external signal. No doubt they will comment on that. 'We are preparing for docking. Can you please give us reasons for ...?'

'You are in a restricted area with no identification showing. Be ready to dock when we say. Make no course changes. We shall make all the manoeuvring necessary.' I acknowledged the call and began the docking procedure. Although it was a procedure I knew intimately I was moving slowly and deliberately. I was in no hurry to dock.

'Why didn't you have the radars, or something turned on?' Asked Terens gruffly.

'I didn't want to alert anyone we were here, that's why.' I snapped back.

'If they had been on, we could have got away from them.'

'Oh, really? Well, we may have got away from the vessel itself but not their weapons. We have no defence mechanisms.

We cannot outrun a kinetic dart even.' Teren's shoulders sagged visibly; I did not see him in this state very often.

'What's a kinetic dart?' Asked Karon.

'It's a very fast spinning very fast-moving solid weapon. It has no explosives as it does not need them. Its speed and spin plus a rear section that disintegrates just rips a great hole in a vessel. It does not need to do any more. The internal pressure and the vacuum of space does the rest.'

'Oh, it sounds horrible.'

'It is.'

It was about half an hour later when we were standing in front of the screen watching the hull of the vessel approaching docking. It now filled the screen, and the size and shape could no longer be determined. The docking vector diagrams heralded the moment when the two vessels would be locked together in a deadly embrace. I had never in my whole life as a pilot not wanted to dock as I did now. There was a tightness in my chest that would not go away. I looked across at the others standing staring at the approaching hull, the reflected light of the vector diagrams making their faces unreal. The numbers were counting down to the moment of locking on. Then there would be no escape until we were released or killed, it would be one or the other. It was a sombre moment for all of us; no one dared speak what we all felt. It seemed as though it was all over now. Then ominously there was a clunk and clicks transferred throughout the vessel which heralded the completion of the docking procedure. It was accompanied by a slight shudder of our vessel which echoed our own shuddering like it knew fear as we did. There was a shiver down my spine and a cold feeling in my stomach. Who were we going to come face to face with? Then came the foreboding call to commence disembarkation. I looked at the others worried faces and began the airlock cycle. All too soon came the green light indicating that it had been completed.

'You will now leave your vessel one at a time. Bring no weapons with you.' Came the disembodied voice over the intercom. Silently we all walked slowly to the airlock chamber.

'I'll go first.' Said Djon when we reached the chamber and he manually unlocked the hatch and it irised open. No light flooded in from the other chamber. A voice, cold and hard, called 'one at a time'. He looked at us and then stepped through. I heard an unfamiliar voice. 'Put your hands up and stand against that wall.' Then there was silence again. Then the voice again. 'Next!' Terens then stepped through and then the girls and finally myself. I found myself in a similar small room with a hard flat floor and curving walls ribbed with structural members curving over uninterrupted into the ceiling which was the same as the walls. It was gloomy and underlit. The others were stretched out on the floor like common criminals, their hands outstretched in front of them. There were two large men dressed in standard flight suits standing over them with frisson bolt guns in their hands. They were not supposed to be used on humans I thought. They also wore dark screens covering their eyes. They did not smile or appear to be very friendly, in fact it was the exact opposite. They looked like the sort of person who would shoot you without a qualm. I became aware of the difference between our vessel and theirs. In here although there was the usual background hum there was a stillness that I had never felt before in any space vessel. Then there was the smell. Almost every vessel that I had ever been in had smelt of polymetals and other substances. In here the smell was sweet, not overpowering, just a slight pleasant background smell unlike any that I had smelt before.

'Hands up and lean against that wall.' Said a voice from behind me. I did so and was searched all over. It was not done aggressively but rather with a ruthless proficiency as though this was all in a day's work. 'Right, now on the floor as the others.' I obeyed and stretched myself out on the metal floor.

'What...' I heard one of the girls begin to say but she was cut short.

'Do not speak.' And she squeaked. I tried to get up to see what they were doing to her but something pushed me back down and held me down on the floor. It felt like someone's foot. 'All lie still, and no harm will come to you.'

I heard instructions given to remove us one by one to secure rooms as a bag was placed over my head and pulled tight. Then I was hauled upright and guided down what I imagined were the corridors of their vessel. I tried to imagine the shape and distance and match it with any vessel I knew. I could not. Then I was sat down, and I heard a door slam shut. After a few minutes I reached up and pulled the bag off from my head. I was in a very small room that had the bed I was sitting on and nothing else. There was a dim light to see by and the room appeared to be a standard small bedroom of a space vessel. The door was different though. It had no handle on the inside. For the second time I was a prisoner left only with my thoughts for company. One of my thoughts was expecting to hear the sound of the drives powering up and sending us away from here or the sound of our vessel being dedocked and then the sound of a kinetic dart being fired. I heard none of them. The one thing I did hear was a small hatch open and a tray of food and drink appear. I looked at it for a moment and then realised that I was very hungry. I took it and ate the lot. It was very good, hot and tasty and unlike anything that I had ever tasted before. It had much more flavour than any food from on board a vessel or even from Enceladus for that matter. I felt much better when I had finished. Then nothing happened for what seemed a long time. I got up and went to the door and put my ear to the surface to see if I could hear anything. I could not. I did the same to the walls and the floor, but it was the same. All I could sense was a feeling of size and power to this vessel that I had never felt in any that I had been in before. There was a quality about it too. I felt the walls and ran my hand along the joins. It was definitely of good quality, very good quality in fact, which was not apparent from the outside.

*

I was awoken by a bright light shining on my face. I had not realised I had even fallen asleep. I felt as though I had let down the others by not keeping a proper vigil. A large man was standing over me; there were silhouettes of other men standing in the corridor. He wore a flight suit unlike any I had seen before. It was already in defence mode, the fabric stiffened. He was holding a light that was shining in my face. It meant that I could not make out his features too clearly. He was wearing something that smelled sweet though not unpleasant, again like the smell that pervaded this vessel. He appeared to be unarmed but I knew the other two were; besides he was bigger than me and as his suit defence mechanism was already activated I would stand no chance of doing him any harm. He knew that, I could tell even though I could not make out his features clearly.

'Get up.' The man said. I groggily got to my feet and immediately a bag was put over my head and I was ushered out into what I took to be a corridor. After a short walk I went through a doorway and was sat down. The bag was removed. I found myself in a large room unlike any I had ever seen in a space vessel. It was richly decorated, there were even pictures on the wall, and a drugget on the floor that had swirling patterns and deep colours. The lighting was subdued but cheerful, it gave a sumptuous air to the room. There was a large desk and seats that had patterned covers, gold glittered from fine lines on the furniture. I had never seen anything like it before. I was sitting on one of the elegant seats. Sitting behind the desk was another large man with olive coloured skin that shone in the light. He had dark black hair pulled tight back from his large face that also shone. On his fingers were rings of what appeared to be a gold metal that contained sharp clear stones of some kind that sparkled brilliantly in the light. He wore similar small sparkling stones in the lobes of his ears. He had some dark screen across his nose that covered his eyes and rested on his ears, similar to the type that the men had been wearing when we first entered this vessel. He was wearing a suit the style of which I had never seen before. At each end of the room on either side stood two more large men. I could not see their faces clearly. They also held weapons. I knew someone was behind me, but I resisted the temptation to turn round. I looked back at the man behind the desk. He leaned forward.

He removed the dark screen from his face so I could now see his dark eyes, so dark that I could not make out his pupils.

'Mr Stone.'

'Yes.'

'You and your friends have given us some trouble recently.'

'I don't follow you.'

'Now don't be stupid Mr Stone. What are you doing here?'

'We thought there was a portal here that was not listed.'

'And what were you going to do?'

'We hoped it would lead us to Ultima Thule.' The man smiled and leaned back in his seat.

'There is no Ultima Thule. There is no home planet. We come from a range of planets around the galaxy and have formed a loose association of trading partners. But that is not what is at issue here. What matters is that you and your friends here left Enceladus in a real hurry. Why?'

'Who are you to be asking questions of us? You are not police.' The smile vanished from his face.

'Don't try and be clever Mr Stone. I have the authority to be asking the questions and you do not. Now, why did you leave Enceladus in such a hurry and then sneak around the galaxy causing trouble?'

'It was not my choice to leave Enceladus at the time.'

'Well that at least ties in with your friend's statements so I am inclined to believe you on that point. But you have been asking too many questions and causing too much trouble in the galaxy since.'

'Are my friends safe?'

'I ask the questions, you do not. You have no authority to be here or to ask questions. Now what were you doing here?'

'We were only trying to find Ultima Thule.'

'No one leaves a job and family to go sneaking around the galaxy just to try and find a fictitious planet. You were obviously planning to create a revolt in the galaxy.'

'No! That is not true.'

'Why should I believe you?'

'Because it is the truth pure and simple. We were looking

for Ultima Thule and made no secret of the fact. We were concerned that someone was trying to kill me.'

'Really? And who might these people be who were trying to kill you and why?'

'I don't know, but it might have something to do with my father.'

'What had he done then?' I realised then that I could not say what my father had told Djon or what we had discovered. I faltered. I hoped he did not pick up on it.

'We felt that my father's disappearance was not an accident but did not know why.'

'So, you think someone killed your father and then waited twenty years before trying to kill you? That doesn't make much sense does it?'

'No, I suppose put like that it doesn't.' I began to feel foolish. In the warm light of this room the idea did seem preposterous.

'Where did you get your vessel from?'

'That I don't know.'

'And why is that?' I could not find any way of answering him without putting the others in trouble, not that I knew where the vessel had come from.

'I was not involved in the procurement of the vessel. It was already at Enceladus when Djon..' I paused. Could I tell him that Djon had kidnapped me? 'When Djon decided I should leave the planet. He did not give me any time to go home first.'

'And you went along with this?'

'I had no choice.'

'What do you mean by that?' I felt a bigger and bigger hole opening up before me. I had no choice but to tell the truth. I just hoped that I was not putting the others in danger.

'Djon kidnapped me.'

'Really?' He leant back in his chair and looked at me. Had I done the wrong thing? I felt a sudden feeling that perhaps I had now put us all in even greater danger than before. 'He is your family friend, and he kidnaps you?'

'Yes.'

'That does seem a very strange thing to do? Is your friend in his right mind do you think?'

'I wonder sometimes.' I replied and then wished I had said something different.

'He does seem to have a complex.' He leant forward. 'How did you find the portal?' A cold chill ran down my spine. How could I answer that without incriminating my father and the others.

'All portals give out a signal. We just followed it.'

'That is not possible.'

'Oh, why?'

'I ask the questions not you.' His manner became cold and hard in an instant. Then he relaxed again. 'Why did you take Karon from her planet?'

'We didn't. She joined us voluntarily.'

'Why?'

'I assume she was unhappy with her life. People do want a change sometime, an adventure. Perhaps she saw us as a chance for adventure.' I had no idea what the others had said or if it conflicted with their stories.

'What were you doing here?'

'I've told you, we were looking for Ultima Thule.'

'That I do not believe. Is it your final answer?'

'Yes.' He turned to the person behind me.

'Return him to his room.' Immediately a bag was placed over my head and I was led away again to my room as before and the door was shut with a soft thud. I went and lay on the bed. At least they did not torture me or take us all and set us adrift in space without a suit.

I did not know how long it was but some time later the door opened again and the same man as before came in and put the bag over my head and I was led away. Again, we entered a room and I was sat down as before. This time however the others were there. I smiled at them relieved at seeing them all there. They smiled back, but they were forced smiles. We were all in the same room and the same men stood back against the walls well away from us and still armed.

'Thank goodn...' Began Djon.

'Be quiet!' Said a strong no nonsense voice from behind us. We were all sitting in a row and could not see behind. 'Do not look round.' We did not. We sat in silence for what seemed an eternity. Then a door opened and the same man who had spoken to me earlier came in and sat down behind the ornate desk.

'Well, you people have been giving us some trouble.' He began.

'We..' Started Djon again.

'Be quiet!' He retorted. Djon stopped and his shoulders slumped. 'As I was saying you people have been giving us some trouble recently and that gives us a problem as to what to do with you.'

'May I speak?' Asked Djon quietly.

'Go ahead.'

'I must just say that should you decide to get rid of us we have, how shall I put it? All we have found I stored safely and will be broadcast if we do not report back within a certain time.'

The man smiled. He picked up a small remote from his desk and pressed a button. A wall screen behind him flashed into life. I was horrified to see our drone lying in a cradle in a store room. I looked across at the others. Their faces also looked shocked.

'Is this what you mean?' He said mockingly.

We all sat in shocked silence staring at the screen. All except Karon of course who did not know what it was. I hoped she did not ask. Fortunately, she had enough sense to keep quiet. The man tapped the remote gently on the ornate table as he watched us and thought. He then switched off the screen and leant forward.

'The problem as I say is what to do with you. The information you have is very damaging to the cohesion and smooth running of the galaxy. Your subversive ideas could be very disruptive. We cannot just let you continue or send you back to Enceladus.' I felt another cold sensation in the pit of my stomach. Now perhaps we were to be sent spinning out into space. Djon had been right all along. There was something in the galaxy that these people did not want us to find. We were obviously getting close. I felt really irritated that I had doubted Djon all this time and now we had got so close but failed at the last fence. I suddenly found myself wondering what a last fence was and was surprised to find myself thinking it.

The man continued. 'You have proved to be far too inquisitive and persistent, and this gives us some worry. You are too dangerous to be let loose again.'

Karon broke down and began sobbing. 'What are you going to do with us?' She managed to say between the sobs.

'This woman knows nothing.' Said Djon, trying to protect Karon. 'you can safely let her go back to Geryon.'

'That is very touching Mr Djon Twenty. Unfortunately, she has been with you long enough to know what you all know.'

'Are you going to kill us?' Asked Terens in his usual terse way. 'If you are, just get on with it will you.'

'We are not animals Mr Terens-D-D2. We do not go around killing people. Now Mr Stone here, his father was also troublesome and caused much disruption and dissent in the galaxy. Fortunately for us he suffered an accident in space and was lost.' I had a funny feeling down my spine at the mention of my father. I did not entirely trust this man, and his inappropriate remark about my father's disappearance being 'fortunate' made me distrust him even more. How did he know of my father and why did he mention him? 'Mr Stone here seems to be carrying on where his father left off. As you insist on proceeding with your quest and will not be put off.'

'We won't tell anyone.' Said Karon.

'Oh, dear. That I am afraid I do not trust. I cannot allow you to just return with what you persist in trying to spread in the galaxy.'

'By what authority do you tell us what we can and cannot do?' Asked Ruuth. The man looked at her with a cold hard look. He did not answer for a long time.

'As usual you all have found a little discrepancy and made a whole conspiracy out of it. And also, as usual you all have managed to get close to the truth but not made the right assumptions. Unfortunately, you have got so close to the truth that it is now very dangerous for the whole galaxy.' I knew Ruuth would be really annoyed that he was not answering her question. He continued 'I am left with only two choices and one is not very palatable.'

'You have not..' Began Ruuth.

'I ask the questions here not you.' His cold hard eyes flashed at Ruuth. It was like seeing a snake suddenly appear from the body of another animal. It was a frightening moment. He was used to being obeyed and not questioned. His authority was obvious, but why? Where did he get his authority from?

'She.' Started Terens rising out of his seat. A hand appeared from behind and pushed him back down into his seat as the man spoke again.

'I say again, I ask the questions. You give the answers.' He calmed down again and seemed to gather his thoughts. 'You leave me no choice in the matter. Wait here.' He got up and left the room. We looked at each other. Karon sat crying gently into her hands. I felt so sorry for her; she had given up her life on Geryon for this. Had she only stayed she would probably be all right. Had Perak betrayed us? I hoped not.

After a while, the man returned and sat down.

'I have spoken to my superiors and we have agreed to be lenient with you.'

'Th..' Began Karon. He stopped her just by raising his hand and shooting her a hard look.

'As you have been so persistent and troublesome, but have not been causing dissent in others or told others what you know, we will give you the chance to redeem yourselves.' He paused for an effect or maybe a question. As none came, he continued. 'As I say you got very close to the truth but not quite. What I am about to tell you must not go any further than this room.' He looked around at us all. We all nodded that we agreed to his terms. 'There is indeed something wrong with the galaxy, but it is not what you thought. About one hundred years ago our galaxy was visited by aliens.' He stopped as Terens snorted his disbelief. 'You seem to disagree Mr Terens D-D2.'

'There are no aliens.'

'Indeed, and how do you know this?' Terens stopped, unable to formulate a reply to this. I myself could not come up with a categorical denial that aliens existed even though none had ever been encountered in the entire inhabited galaxy. I had occasionally wondered why mankind was the only sentient life form in the galaxy. Why did I believe so strongly that we were the only intelligent life form? As Terens tried to come up with an answer I also tried to formulate one as well. I could not. As we did not reply the man went on. 'As I was saying, about one hundred years ago our galaxy was visited by aliens. They were visiting us because their own galaxy had become devoid of useful minerals and substances required for their life. In the same way that mankind was beginning to explore the galaxy for new sources of minerals, metals and non-renewable resources. They were looking for new sources of wealth and life requirements which no longer existed in their galaxy. Fortunately, they did not come here with all guns blazing. They came and talked with our ancestors. We learned how to communicate with them and them with us. That is how it became obvious what they wanted. It also became obvious that they would stop at nothing to get it.

If we had stood in their way, they would have annihilated the human race.

Fortunately, again our ancestors were good at negotiating with them. The aliens agreed that we could stay here unmolested by them if we gave them what they wanted. Part of the deal was this should remain confidential. No one was to know what was going on for fear of upsetting the delicate balance. This required a firm hand in making sure that no one discovered what was going on. You were in danger of doing just that and possibly destroying this delicate balance with your hidden drone. We could not allow that to happen.' He paused.

'Why are you telling us all this? Asked Ruuth.

'Good question. Your persistence has made us think that you may be more useful to us alive than dead. In fact, you may be more useful to the whole human race.'

'You were planning to kill us!' Squeaked Karon. The man looked slowly in her direction.

'Unfortunately, had you stumbled upon the truth we could not allow you to continue living and possibly spreading this secret throughout the galaxy. The fate of the whole human race depends upon us keeping this secret. Did I not make that clear? The aliens do not want this arrangement to be known'

'Why is that?' I asked.

'We do not know the reason why.'

'How often do they contact you?' Asked Ruuth

'Another good question. We receive text messages irregularly – and before you ask.' He added quickly. 'Each one ends with the same order to keep this secret. There is no voice contact. We have a special dedicated receiver to receive messages. I see your Terens-D-D2 still does not believe me.'

'Show me these aliens and I will.' He replied tersely.

'Well, you were wrong about what we knew.' Said Djon, fortunately taking the attention away from Terens. 'All we were doing was looking for Ultima Thule. We would never have come to the conclusion that you are now expounding. By telling us you have put us in a situation we would not have found ourselves in otherwise. I find that rather distasteful.'

'Oh, believe me; you would very soon have stumbled upon the truth once you arrived at the portal here.'

'So, what happens now?' I asked, curious to know where this was leading. Had they wanted us dead presumably they would have done it while we were separated in our individual rooms.

'Another good question. As I was saying your persistence has become obvious to us and that is a useful trait that we think we can use. Certainly, you cannot go back into normal society with what you now know. We have a proposition to make to you. It is highly dangerous and one you may not return from, but we feel that you deserve as much. What we want you to do is be sent to where the aliens have their reception portal for our goods and gain as much information as possible that we can use to defeat them and end this awful tyranny. Needless to say, this is a very risky venture but your behaviour so far indicates that you might just be the people to do this.'

'Why don't you do this?' Asked Terens darkly. 'You know a lot more about these aliens than we do?'

'We cannot. We are already fully occupied in trying to keep them off our backs. If we divert our energy to trying to infiltrate them then all is lost. Failure of our operation would entail the failure of the human race. We needed someone not part of the status quo.'

'What are these aliens like?' Asked Ruuth. 'How advanced are they?'

'Excellent. We have not seen these beings for about a hundred years. It was our ancestors who dealt with them and only a few of them were ever seen. There have been no records kept of the aliens, as they demanded, except what they were capable of doing.'

'So, you do not know what they are like?' I asked.

'We are not sure. We understand that they are similar to us, perhaps a little larger. They may have two legs and arms similar to us but are stronger. Their capabilities we also understand are also not recorded but.' He paused. The pause went on, Terens looked at the ceiling.

'As far as we can ascertain they were capable of destroying planets.'

There was a shocked silence in the room. No one dared speak. I had an awful foreboding that the reason that we could not find our original planet was about to become clear. He began again. 'It looks as though they actually not only were capable of destroying whole planets but did destroy one, our own home planet!' He sat back in his chair.

'What, completely?'

'No, it still exists as a barren lump of dead rock but no longer orbiting a sun.'

We looked at each other. I felt a cold feeling in the pit of my stomach. No wonder we could not find Ultima Thule, it no longer exists! How could an advanced civilisation behave so cruelly to another race? He sat foreword again. 'We think this destruction was to show mankind that they meant business and to make sure we did not renege on the deal. In that it was very effective. Our ancestors realised that it would be pointless trying to challenge them, so they agreed to the deal. They managed to make the aliens agree to keeping out of our galaxy and letting us get on with our lives as best we could under the circumstances. That has been the case ever since. We cannot allow the status quo to be affected in any way. It is also why you would not be able to find our original planet and also why we cannot allow you to discover that and then the reason why it no longer exists'

'What do you want from us then?' Asked Djon.

'Yes, good point.' He sat back again as if in thought. 'During the intervening years we have been lucky that certain people have got close to the truth and have agreed to our terms.' He looked at me as he continued. 'Your father, Djim Stone, was one of them. What we require of you is to be sent near to where the aliens receive our goods and find out what ever you can about them. Particularly their weaknesses of course. We need to find anything we can that may help us rid ourselves of this awful millstone about humanities neck. That is our terms for your continued living. You will have to do whatever you can to help humanity against these aliens.' He looked at each of us in turn.

'How do we let you know what we find?' Asked Terens, I knew from the tone of his voice that he did not believe all this.

'Another good question. We will give you a device that the aliens gave us to enable us to communicate with them. You will be able to use that. But be careful, they may be able to locate its use so be circumspect in using it.'

'If they do discover us won't they then know that the status quo as you put it has not been maintained.'

'Another good point. I am glad that you are thinking this

thing through. Your story, if you are caught is that a portal malfunctioned, and you do not know where you are. You will also not say where you come from. There may be other inhabited galaxies and in fact that must be your main story. Hopefully, this will have them looking in other directions other than back here. As a last resort you must destroy your vessel and yourselves to avoid any comeback on the rest of society. You must agree to this.' There was another lull as we all considered this final horror.

'How will we get back?' Asked Ruuth.

'Another good question. There is the reception portal that the aliens use to receive our goods. You will have to find a way to use it to get back. The aliens send back the cargo vessels that we send the goods in so it should be possible. Unfortunately, no one has yet been able to do it as far as we know. It is a very risky venture indeed. Now, no need to answer straight away. Follow me.' He rose from off his seat. I could see now that his clothes were unlike our normal wear. The fabric looked different, more sophisticated somehow, the cut of the separate jacket and trousers appeared to be very fine. The colours more vibrant. As he moved his jewellery sparkled. His shoes shone. I had never seen anything like that before either. He opened a door which I had not seen as it matched the walls and only a small handle declared its presence. He led us into a large room that contained a long table in the centre. The walls were also covered with pictures that were not made from light but coloured pigments and appeared to be very old. They had ornate gold-coloured frames. I wondered how on Erebus they managed to keep them safe on a space vessel. The table was covered in a clean white cloth that had sharp creases regularly along its length. On the table was a pair of ornate curving stands that contained long white waxy sticks that each had a flame dancing on the top. A flame on a space vessel! I could not believe what I was seeing, such a flagrant abuse of all space safety standards. At one end of the table there was a series of plates covered with hot steaming food. There were five empty plates, white with a delicate gold edge, and a knife and fork alongside.

'Please.' He said and gestured towards the table. 'Be our guests and enjoy some dinner while you contemplate your reply to our offer.' He was gone before any of us could answer. I did not even hear the door shut or hear if there was the sound of a lock sliding into place. We stood looking at the table like stuffed dummies not moving. Finally, Terens spoke.

'Well, there is no point in standing around and wasting this lot.' He stepped forward to the table. We looked at each other and did likewise. I realised then just how hungry I had become. The food was good and hot but unlike anything I had ever tasted except in the room on this vessel. It had more flavour and variety and certainly was not normal space fare. I felt that it was not just hunger that gave me this impression. It did not appear to have come from vacuum packed containers. We ate heartily before trying to speak. When we had satisfied our initial hunger and our eating had slowed, we began to discuss the issue.

'This is a most amazing room to have on a space vessel.' Said Djon, looking around at the décor.

'I thought that too.' I said. 'Especially these things with naked flames on. In a space vessel! It goes against all safety standards.'

'Too true, too true and those pictures too. I have seen nothing like these either.' He got up and went over to one. It depicted a young woman dressed in a most sumptuous dress richly decorated and sporting an amazing hairstyle. I too rose from the table and joined him at the picture. The surface was covered in tiny cracks and was not smooth. It looked very old, but I had no idea how old or where it could possibly have come from.

'What is that man suggesting?' Asked Karon, making us turn round and drawing us back to the table. 'I did not like him or trust him.' She added.

'What he is suggesting Karon.' Replied Djon. 'Is that we go on a mission to where these aliens are and find out their weaknesses or we face certain death I imagine.'

'I think we would.' Added Terens.

'Do we have any choice?' Asked Ruuth.

'I think.' I added returning to my seat. 'That we have no choice. If we do not do as they ask, we are dead. At least if we accept their offer then while there is life there is hope. We can find some way of coming back.'

'We cannot come back.' Said Terens. 'They have managed to find our drone and follow us across the galaxy. How can we return without being discovered and eliminated?'

'Is he telling the truth about the aliens?' Asked Karon.

'I cannot see why he should lie.' Replied Djon.

'Maybe there is something else they are trying to hide.' Suggested Ruuth.

'That may be the case.' I said. 'But they hold all the cards. The sooner we get away from them the better I say. We can do nothing cooped up in here. At least if we are in our own vessel and well away from them, we stand some chance of doing something. We either find out he is telling the truth, or he is telling a lie. That gets us nearer our goal. We may even be able to return somewhere without them noticing. After all there are many planets in the galaxy, and they cannot watch them all.'

'Good point.' Said Djon. 'Ok, I for one agree with Djim and we accept their offer. After all we have…' I stopped him before he could mention the portal. I sensed that this vessel may be bugged, and I did not want them knowing we had a portal on board. We had already said enough for them to know we were not entirely taken in by them and still looking for ways to outsmart them. But I still felt that we ought to keep quiet about the portal. I was not quite sure why, but an inner voice suggested we do not divulge it. With a few hand gestures I tried to convey all this to the others. I was also hoping those people would not search our vessel and even if they did, they should not know what we had on board. After all none of us could actually work out what the components were for! I made another gesture to try and tell him not to mention the portal and that the room may be bugged. Eventually his face lightened as he understood my gestures as did the others. 'We have nothing to lose.' He added with a smile. The others also agreed. All we had to do was wait. We continued eating the fine food and drinking the fine drink. It would be hard going back to normal space fare after this.

When we had finished, I finally managed to drag my satiated carcass up off the well upholstered seat and into a standing position. I began to look around the room. Finally, I went and closely examined another one of the pictures.

'This appears incredibly old.' I said, almost to myself.

'What makes you say that?' Asked Ruuth and she came to stand with me.

'Just look closely at the surface, it appears to be dry and cracked from old age. I do not know what the pigmented medium is made from. And the clothes. Look, I have seen nothing like that....' The door opened again, and a man entered. He beckoned us to return to the original room where we were interrogated. We dutifully rose and followed him into the room. We sat in the row of seats facing the grand ornate desk. The man returned.

'Well.' He said, as he sat down. 'What is your answer?'

'We agree to your offer.' Replied Djon for all of us.

'Good. A sensible choice.'

'What do we do?' Asked Terens.

'I have already explained.' The man replied. 'We send you to a location near where the aliens receive our goods, and you do the rest. We do not have any more information than that. We know nothing. Hence your valuable but risky trip.'

'Once again, how do we send back any information we find?'

'As I have already explained we will give you a communication device that the aliens allow us to use to communicate with them over the intervening light years. It allows us instant communication. Do not lose it or allow anyone else to take it. Destroy it before losing it. Is that clear?'

'Yes, thank you.'

'OK. Take them away while we prepare for your trip.' He nodded to the men standing behind us. Immediately a bag was placed over my head. I heard someone cry out. The man ordered quiet, and that this was a necessity. I soon found myself back in my small room. I was well fed and quietly confident that all would be well.

I don't know how long it was but eventually the door opened, and a bag was placed over my head again and I was led out. After a while I felt that I was back in the Jergan. I recognised the faint smell of our vessel. I was sat down, and the bag was removed. I was sitting at the table in the control room. The others were already sitting round it. The man who removed my bag walked backwards out of the control room. A voice came over the intercom.

'Prepare to dedock.' I turned my seat round and faced the control panel. I sent my reply.

'Preparing to dedock.'

'Well, Djon.' Said Ruuth. 'There is one good thing.'

'Yes.'

'You were right after all, Djon. If this man is telling the truth, then Ultima Thule did exist. If he is lying, then he is probably hiding something which may be Ultima Thule.'

'Good point Ruuth, thank you.'

We spent the rest of the dedocking procedure in silence. It was a relief to finally be free from the big vessel and I felt the whole Jergan feel different once we were free. I finally switched on the V20 and the forward vision enhancer. The shock in the control room was palpable as the view appeared before us. We were directly in front of the hidden portal! It was a standard portal after all but beside it were three of the storage vessels. Standard cubes hanging in space some distance from the portal. Also, there were a number of drones and other vessels like the one that captured us together with a host of cargo vessels, some manned and some were unmanned automatic vessels.

'That would explain the other image we saw.' Said Ruuth finally, breaking the mesmerism of the moment. It was a very busy place. The amount of stuff that must be being sent to the aliens appeared to be colossal. No wonder there was such a discrepancy that we had found. If they were not telling the truth though then where was all this stuff going? It appeared to be enough to keep a whole planet in luxury.

'Set your course for the portal.' Came the voice over the intercom. It made me jump, it made the others jump as well. I began to set the course. The voice began again. 'We have already programmed your V20 for the correct exit point. This will not be the receiving portal naturally. It will be as close as we dare put you within the tolerances of non portal exit. The programme will be erased once you skip. We needed to do this to prevent the information being captured by the aliens should you fall into their hands. You are on your own now. The whole human race is depending upon your success. Remember what we told you and good luck. We look forward to hearing from you. Do not call too early or your location will be revealed. Goodbye. End of transmission.'

'Thanks a bundle.' Muttered Terens.

'Look at that lot.' Said Djon suddenly. 'The amount of stuff they must be moving must be colossal.'

'I know.' I said. 'And if they are not sending it to the aliens then where is it going?'

'You don't trust him?'

'No, Djon I don't. I will reserve judgement until we come across the aliens and see where all this stuff is going.'

'I agree.' Added Karon.

'Really?' Said Djon. 'Then let us hope we find these aliens. If we don't then what?' There was silence again as no one wanted to answer that question. I sat and watched the portal approaching and the data scrolling down the screen heralding the imminent 'skip'. Skip was a good word to describe the method of traversing the universe as no travel was involved – we skipped that part being in one place and then another.

I kept to myself the discrepancy in that man's statements regarding my father. There was no point in bringing it up now. There may have been other factors of which I did not know.

'OK, people here we go.' I said as the portal finally approached. The screen went blank, and I felt the falling sensation which this time seemed to go on for ages. Then finally the screen .... stayed blank!

I rubbed my eyes like a foolish child or a cartoon character but to no avail. The screen was still blank. Then I noticed that the data had reappeared on the screen showing the vessel's status. All was well with the vessel as the data faithfully showed. I looked at the V20 which had been on when we went through the portal. It was still on. There was the familiar bluish orb, but it too was empty!

'What's happened?' Asked someone. 'Are we dead?'

– CHAPTER 10 –

I switched off the forward vision enhancer and opened the front window to get a natural look at the universe outside. It was the same black nothingness that the vision enhancer had shown.

'Djon!' Said Karon. 'I'm frightened. What is happening?'

'I wish I knew.' Said Djon. 'Djim, do you know what is happening?'

'As far as I can tell Djon, there is nothing out there. Just a minute while I reset the forward vision enhancer and run some tests.' I switched on the vision enhancer again and waited a moment while it came online. The view was the same – nothing.

'Just a minute.' Said Ruuth. 'Look carefully there.' She pointed at the screen and we all looked at where she was pointing. There was a faint smudge of light and as I saw it, I then noticed other smudges of light.

'They are not stars.' I said.

'I know.' She said. 'But, they are something.'

'The V20!' Said Djon suddenly. 'Look.' I looked and it was as empty as before.

'Do you mean there is nothing in it Djon?'

'Yes, there is nothing there'

'I know. I noticed it just now. I will just switch it off and on again and see if that clears it.' I did so in the correct way, it seemed an absolute age for it to run through the close down and restarting procedures. As the familiar sphere sprang into life again, I hoped it would show something. It did not it was as empty as before. I felt a cold feeling run down my spine.

'Where are we?' Asked Karon with a very small voice. She was shaking visibly. Ruuth went and put her arm around her shoulder.

'I'm not sure where we are at the moment Karon, but we will find out shortly. I've got something for us to do anyway so come with me.' She led Karon away but over her shoulder she gave us a look that said 'find out where we are'. I nodded back at her as she left. Terens returned to the control room. I had not even realised he had left.

'Everything appears to be in order.' He said with quite a bit of surprise in his voice. 'I thought they would take something or at least nullify our weapons, but they haven't.'

'Well, that is something.' Said Djon.

'OK, so where are we then?' Asked Terens, coming and sitting down beside me. He stared quizzically at the V20. 'Why is there nothing in the V20 then?' He added without waiting for a reply to his first question.

'I don't know yet.' I said still trying to see if the V20 was malfunctioning or something else was. As far as I could tell though everything was working normally. I began to get more worried. If none of the instruments was faulty then what could account for the total lack of any sensor readings or stars in the V20? Why were there no stars outside? My mind began to play tricks on me and slow down. I could no longer think straight. I slammed my hand down on the control panel beside the V20 perhaps that would make it work. All I succeeded in doing was make the others jump.

'What was that?' Asked Djon.

'Sorry, Djon. I was just getting a little frustrated because I can not get this V20 to work properly, and the other instruments don't seem to be recording either. I don't know what else to do to make them work properly.'

'Could the portal have done anything?'

'I have not known it before, but then anything is possible it seems.'

Ruuth returned to the control room.

'Ok, so, where are we?' She said.

'What have you done with Karon?' Asked Djon.

'Oh, sorry, I have put her to work on something to keep her mind off things. So where are we then?'

'I don't know.' I said dejectedly. 'I cannot get the instruments to work.'

'Let me have a look.' She said and sat down on the other side of me and started to check out the instrumentation. After a while she grunted.

'What's the matter?' I queried.

'All the instruments appear to be in order.' She replied slowly as if not sure of what she was saying.

'Which means?' I asked again. She looked at me for a long time.

'Which means, Djim, there is nothing out there! If we take that to its logical conclusion then we are no longer within the galaxy!'

'What!' Stuttered Djon. 'What do you mean?'

'I think the V20 is reactive and not containitive.' She replied enigmatically.

'What does that mean?' Asked Djon rather frustratedly.

'I think it means that the V20 responds to its surroundings. It picks up the portal signals which contain the galaxy information. Once we leave the galaxy there is nothing for the V20 to pick up. It does not hold any information in itself. It is more like a radio than a clique computer. That can only mean we are well beyond the range of the galaxy portals. That is only possible if we are well outside the galaxy. That is the only explanation I can come up with. Which is also why the other instruments are also not picking up anything, there is nothing to pick up!' The cold feeling in my stomach increased to a cold knot of fear. I then recalled something my father had said as I began my pilot training. He had said, 'make sure you don't rely totally on the machine.' I had ignored him and now I really wished I had not. What had he found out and why had he not told us before?

'Where is the alien portal then?' Asked a worried Djon.

'That appears to be the problem.' I replied quietly. 'Either there is no portal out here or our instruments are on the blink.'

'Let us hope it is the latter then.'

'I had better see how Karon is getting on.' Said Ruuth

finally getting up from her seat. She kept looking though at the screen as if doing so would magically make the instruments come back online. 'Djim, can you see if you can get the thing working properly again there may be something I have missed. We cannot afford to be stuck out here with no instruments. And let us not give Karon the impression that we are completely lost I think that might be a bit much for her at the moment.' She finally left the control room as we nodded that we agreed with her sentiment. I returned to the communication seat and tried again to see if I could get either the V20 to work properly or the instruments to register the portal. Eventually I pulled off the front panel under the control panel to see if I could find anything in there that had come loose or was not connected. Perhaps our 'friends' had done something. I could find nothing wrong. I began to get more and more worried.

'How far are we away from the galaxy?' Asked Terens.

'Good question Terens.' I replied. 'I haven't even tried that for one good reason. Sorry two good reasons.'

'Oh.'

'Yes, I have been trying to get the V20 to work properly and also trying to get the instruments to work as well. I will get to where we are when we have something to be able to do it with. There is one other problem though.'

'Yes?'

'I don't think our instruments on board are capable of finding out how far we are from the galaxy. They are all geared to working within the galaxy with the information provided by the V20. If the V20 has nothing, then we have nothing to go on. What you could do is go and do a visual check from a porthole and see if you can find anything, such as the galaxy.'

'What is wrong with the view of the forward vision enhancer?'

'I do not know if it is working.'

'OK.' He needed no further reason and immediately got up from his seat and left the control room.

'Djim.' Said Djon, there was a worried note to his voice as he was checking something on the control panel.

'Yes?' I said as he did not continue immediately.

'How long would we normally have in space?'

'What do you mean?'

'How long could we normally survive in space before needing to recharge the air and water?'

'Goodness, that does not normally come up as most flights don't last long. They have reduced the amount of time as a result. I would estimate that we would probably have about a week.'

'According to this here Djim we only have two days left.' He looked at me, concern etched into his ruddy complexion. He stroked his now slightly ragged beard with agitation. I leant over to check the atmosphere controls. He was right. The readout confirmed that according to the calculations of the numbers on board and usage of the air we only had two days left. That was odd. We had full capacity before we met our 'friends' at the hidden portal. I had a very nasty suspicion rising in my thought. Had they tampered with our life support systems? It was most surprising that they had not touched anything onboard. Perhaps we had found something at last.

'Give everything a good check over Djon and see if anything else is out of order. It may be part of the general problem with our other instruments. I hope it is because the alternative is too worrying to contemplate.'

'What do you mean?'

'I mean that someone has tampered with our life support systems while we were on board that vessel.'

'Why would they do that?' The look on his face changed as he finished his own question and realised what he had said and implied. 'They don't want us to survive. Let us hope it is the instruments then.' He went back to running his checks. 'Let us hope it is the instruments.' He muttered to himself again as he worked.

Two hours later saw me exhausted and out of ideas. As far as I could ascertain the instruments were fine. That finally only left one alternative. Ruuth was right after all there was no portal out here. There was nothing out here!

Terens returned to the control room and he too had a worried look on his face. 'I have tried to find the galaxy but...' He trailed off.

'Yes?'

'I don't know what the galaxy looks like from outside is one thing. The other thing is there appears to be more than one galaxy nearby. When I say nearby of course I mean in light year terms.'

'Oh.' I said with a sudden realisation that I too did not know what the galaxy looked like from the outside. Without the V20 to tell me where I was, I was lost. I then realised how little I knew of the galaxy and the surrounding universe. 'Is there nothing that you can identify?' I asked hopefully.

'No. I spent some time doing a visual look. I could find smudges of light in various places which I can only assume are galaxies but as I have never been outside the galaxy before I cannot be sure what it looks like. We have nothing on board that could tell me how far we are away either.'

'We're coming back!' Called Ruuth loudly as she entered the control room with Karon who now looked much calmer. Ruuth's little deception appeared to have worked. I felt awful as we now had nothing good to tell her. 'How are we doing?' She asked cheerily. There was an awkward silence for a moment before I could decide what to say. Ruuth caught the tension and her face dropped. She looked at me imploringly.

'I have checked all the instruments.' I finally managed to say. 'As far as I can ascertain they are all functioning normally.'

'That's good'. said Karon.' Totally unaware of the implication of that statement. 'So, have you managed to locate the aliens? Have they spotted us yet?'

'No, we have not found them, and we hope they have not found us. In the meantime, I suggest we try and finish our vessel based portal. Ruuth can you take Karon and Terens and get the portal finished.' I looked hard at Ruuth as I spoke. She got my meaning.

'OK.' She said, with a good imitation of cheeriness and got up from her seat. 'Come on guys let us get this portal finished.' Terens looked hard at me as Ruuth grabbed his suit as she passed. He also got up and looked back at me again as he left the control room. Once they were clear I turned to Djon.

'Right.' I started. 'I think we had better try and contact those guys on the vessel. Can you get the communication device they gave us please?' Djon got up without a word. He returned moment later with a large metal box about 600millimeters by 600millimeters and 300millimeters thick. It had a handle on the top and simple combination locks. He placed it on the table in front of me. I turned it round so the combination locks faced me. I turned the tumblers to the number we were given, and the catches flicked open. I opened the case fully. Inside was a simple black box with the normal radio type controls, a tiny keyboard and a long lead. 'It looks as though we need to plug it into a power source.' I said as I pulled out the lead. Djon took it without a word and plugged it into the external power socket on the control panel. Tiny lights flickered into life on the top of the box and the dials and controls illuminated. I turned the dial to the frequency we were given. They had told us it did not work on an audio band and that we had to type our messages. They also told us we had to direct it back to the portal as it 'fired' a message in a pinpoint narrow beam. All we could do was point the arrow on the case towards the largest smudge of light and hoped it was our galaxy.

I began to type out on the tiny keyboard – In normal space. No sign of portal. No sign of aliens. Need help Please give our position and new location required. There was a simple send button. I pressed it. There was a satisfying beep, and a message came up 'message sent'.

'All we can do now is wait for a reply.' I said. 'Let us get some food ready and then help the others with the portal, at least with that we can get out of here. Let us hope this message doesn't alert the aliens.'

'I'm agreed with that.' We got up and went to the galley. We needed to get the portal built so we could get out of here. But where was here and where to go? I did not have that answer.

After a good meal we all felt a little better even though

there was a nagging feeling at the back of my thought that would not go away. Even though I kept checking the communication device there was no reply. The longer it went without a reply the more concerned I became and the more the nagging thought stayed in my thought. I tried to put it out of thought by joining the others who were trying to build the portal.

Unfortunately, the nagging feeling at the back of my mind would still not go away any more. Like the dim distant glow at the end of a long tunnel it drew my attention back to itself constantly, no matter how much I tried to push it away.

Why was it there? What was causing this nagging feeling?

In the few quiet moments we had between chores and assembling the portal I endeavoured to get to the nub of it all. But then another nagging thought popped up to compound the issue. There was something about the portal itself!

I did not know enough about subatomic quantum physics to be able to dissect the portal and then know how it worked. But that, I decided was a side issue to divert me from the first problem. That distant glow would not go away but rather grew stronger and then brighter by the hour.

Something was not right!

I had to find out what it was. As I worked and ate and rested my mind was going over the last few days. I had no idea what to call this thought or why it should appear to come from nowhere.

Then the light grew from a glow to a point of light.

Then the point of light grew to a charging rushing almost blinding realisation.

The implications of this charging, rushing, deafening, wailing light were horrendous. No one should be subjected to such a .... Such a .... Words, thoughts failed me. My thought had suddenly been zapped into a numbed state of shock. The tiny glow had become an all encompassing white-out stopping all thought processes in their tracks.

Then sensation, feeling, anger rose in its place. The upwelling anger was almost as numbingly stultifying as the original charging, rushing light.

Numbness was finally replaced by action.

Finally, I could stand it no longer and I left the others finishing off the portal as I went back to the control room. As before, there was no reply on the communication device. I took it out of the case and paced it on the table and then closed up the metal case and snapped shut the catches and picked up the case. I stood looking at the small black box on the table holding the case at my side. Then in one swift motion I brought the case up over my head and down onto the device. At the same time someone shouted. 'Djim! What are you doing?'

The case smashed the device easily sending a spray of sharp pieces of some metaplastic material flying around the control room. Ruuth staggered backwards with her hands covering her face to protect herself from the shards.

'What have you done?' She said, a panic in her voice. I did not answer her but only picked up the cracked top of the device and turned it over in my hand. On the underside was a very small solid state circuit board about the size and complexity of a small cheap calculator. There was nothing else in the remains of the device at all! By this time Ruuth had run round the table and grabbed my arm.

'Djim!' She said again. 'What on Erebus are you doing?' I turned the piece over so Ruuth could see it. She let go of my arm and took the piece of the device out of my hand and looked at it closely. Her face changing from anger at me to a look of horror. She then started scrabbling around trying to find other pieces of the device.

'Ruuth!' I said sharply, trying to stop her fruitless search. She did not stop. I knelt down beside her on the floor beside the table and slowly took her shaking hands. Tears smeared her face which had now turned red from fear. 'Ruuth, it's no use. The device is a fake.'

Slowly, ever so slowly she began to relax again until finally she sat back on her feet. She pulled away her hands from mine and pushed her hair away from her face and dried it with shaking hands. She looked down again at the piece of the device with the small useless circuit.

'Why?' she said finally picking up the piece again and turning it over in her hands as if the very act could make it more useful. Then she threw it against the wall. 'Why?'

'I'm not sure.' I said. 'The only thing I can think is that this whole thing is just a way to get rid of us.' Then the enormity of it hit her and she burst into a flood of tears allowing herself to rest her head on my shoulder as she sobbed uncontrollably. I had never seen her like this and was surprised; I thought that she would have been the strongest of al of us. I just held her as she cried herself out; there was nothing else I could do. Then I saw Karon's face appear over the edge of the table, concern etched into her eyes.

'What's up?' she asked. I looked at her for a while, not knowing how to answer her. Then she took in the smashed device with a look of growing alarm. Then she knelt down and took Ruuth in her hands. 'It was a useless piece of junk wasn't it?' she said to me.

'Yes, Karon, it was. We have no way of contacting anybody.'

'Then we had better finish the portal.' She said matter of factly which surprised me. I thought she would be the one to break down and not Ruuth. 'I'll look after Ruuth, you go and finish the portal.' I did not have the heart to tell her that even if we finished the portal, we would still not have any idea of where to go. Not only that but we still did not know how to operate it or direct our way. I got up from off the floor and left the two women in the control room as I went down to find the other two.

They were huddled over the last pod to be finished as I came in. They stood up. A look of concern came over their faces. I walked through the instructions hanging in space in the room and went over to them. That is how it would have appeared to them. To me the instructions always kept at a readable distance sliding around the room.

'What is up, Djim?' asked Djon.

'The communication device those people gave us is a piece of useless junk.' I handed over the part. Djon took it and turned it over in his large ruddy hands.

'Is this all of it?'

'It is all of it that had anything on it.' I replied flatly. Djon handed it to Terens.

'Are you sure?'

'Yes, absolutely.'

'It is junk then.' Added Terens, throwing the piece onto the bench. 'That circuit certainly is not alien and of no use for communication.'

'Why?' Asked Djon, his face grown pale.

'There can only be one reason Djon.' Said Terens darkly. 'The whole thing was a sham from the start. There are no aliens and no portal. They are obviously hiding something else.'

'Yes, but what?'

'Let us get this portal finished and hopefully we can get out of here and find out.' I just hoped they were right. These things contained twenty thousand unknown components all of them untested and untried. Most of the components were sealed units which had test markings on them which was a relief but also gave no indication of how the thing worked. We had followed the instructions to the letter but had no idea what we were doing. The only good thing was that everything appeared to fit well and go together as indicated. Each pod was slightly different in their content which was odd to say the least, but then the whole thing was odd. But at least the planet-based ones worked.

It was a tight fit inside the pods, and it made working more and more difficult as the insides were gradually filled up with components. There were also long wiring looms to be connected and looped round the interior. It gradually came down to only one person being able to work at any one time.

Then it came. The time when all the pods were complete. We stood up and scanned the instructions to check. Then Djon picked up something for off the bench.

'What's this?' He queried handing it to Terens. He looked at it quizzically too and then handed it to me. I had no idea what it was. We had finished but there was still one component left. I looked over at the instructions and groaned. We would have to go back to the beginning and check through them all over again. It would take hours. Hours we did not have. We might run out of atmosphere before we could finish building the portal.

'OK. Let us take this in three parts. One each and go through the instructions again. See if we can find where this bit goes.' I placed the component on the bench and went to the controls. The instructions split into three different shimmering virtual screens hanging in the air. I began to read at once. We had no time to lose.

Half an hour later Karon and Ruuth came into the bay. Ruuth's appearance had improved so that she almost looked her old self again. I was glad at that.

'OK.' She said. 'What can I do?'

'You can tell us what that is for a start.' Replied Djon, pointing to the last component on the bench. She went over and picked it up. I stopped reading and went over. I needed a rest from reading, it was quite a strain. She turned it round in her hand.

'It looks familiar somehow.' She said. 'Look, there are pins for connection into something else.'

'You're right.' I replied, annoyed at myself for not seeing it earlier. Then something clicked in my thought. 'Just a minute, wait here.' I grabbed the component and raced out of the bay for the control room, but in my haste, I tripped and fell over something on the bay floor. The component flew out of hand and bounced across the floor. Something flew off it as it hit a crate. 'Ghas!' I cried as I came to a rest looking across at the component lying on the floor. I struggled to get up as Terens walked over to it.

'What the Erebus have you done?' he asked as he bent down to pick up the bits.

'I'm sorry. I did not intend to damage it. I just had an idea I had to try that was all. It was an accident.'

'Did you have to be in such a hurry?' Asked Djon.

'Perhaps not, in hindsight. I was just keen to try it that was all.'

'Try what?' Asked Ruuth. Terens had by now returned the pieces to the bench. She turned to look at them. She picked up the pieces and tried to put them back together as I finally got up and joined her.

'How badly is it damaged?' I asked, fearing the worse.

'Fortunately, it's not too bad I think. It looks like it is just the casing that has broken.'

'Thanks. Let me try it then.' I tried to take it out of her hand. She snatched her hand away.

'Not before you tell me what you are going to do with it first. I think you have already done too much damage to it.' She continued to hold it out of my reach as I stood looking hard into her eyes. She looked back with a determined look in her eyes. I finally relaxed and sank down onto a box.

'It looks as though it should fit into the V20, that is all.' I looked up at her. 'I'm sorry, there was no reason for me to go charging off like that. I just got so excited that is all. I felt it might fit.' I felt really stupid now. There was no reason for me to get so excited and damage the component. I could have done a lot worse. I felt a hand on my shoulder.

'Don't feel too bad.' Said Ruuth. 'It could have happened to anyone. But we must try and be much more careful. This is our only way out of here.'

'I know.' I said. Looking up into her eyes. 'I know. That is why I feel so stupid. It could have been my fault that we could be stranded here.'

'Come on then. Let us all go and see if your idea works shall we.' She said and then added. 'Slowly.'

'OK.' She held out her hand. I took it and she pulled me up with a firm dry grip. She handed me the component. 'I won't drop it this time.' I led the way to the control room as the others followed me in grim silence. In the control room I switched off the V20 and waited for the bluish orb to vanish and the system to power down to safety. I then looked into the small bowl shape that the orb normally sat in. At the bottom was the same number of pin holes in the same pattern as on the component. With trembling hands, I delicately tried to put the component into position but there was no room for my fingers as well.

'We need something to hold it. There is not enough room for my fingers.'

'What do you need?' Said Terens coming forward to look at the problem. 'OK.' He added when he had seen what was required and disappeared out of the control room. While he was gone, I tested the instruments again in the hope that I could find something wrong. I could find nothing wrong. I looked up at the forward vision enhancer at the blackness outside.

'We are outside the galaxy.' I finally said. 'There is nothing wrong with any of the instruments.' A cold feeling ran down my insides to sit in my stomach. How far away were we? Where was our galaxy? I then again realised how little I knew. Everything was done by the V20 and we knew nothing about the galaxy or what was beyond it. How stupid! But then normally we did not need to know. We skipped safely from one portal to another. There was no need to know what was beyond the galaxy as patently there is nothing here for us to come for. I just wished I did know what our galaxy looked like from the outside though. Terens had said that there was more than one smudge of light which could be other galaxies but there was no way of knowing how far away from any of them we were. To know how far away we were we needed to know how big they were. I knew the size though of our galaxy. All we had to do was try and find which smudge of light was our galaxy and then we could find out how far away we were. It was a glimmer of hope, something to hang onto. It was the vast expanse of nothingness in between the galaxies that was the most terrifying. An impenetrable, total, nothingness it seemed. I had a nasty feeling that the portal would not work out here. There was nothing. How could it compress nothing into....? Terens came back into the control room. He was holding what can only be described as a rather ham-fisted concoction. It was a small gripper that required two to work it.

'I made this up.' He said as he handed it over. Considering the time he had to make it it was very clever even though it did not look much. I clipped the component onto the little gripper claws and Terens pulled it tight to maintain the grip. I held onto the shaft to direct it into place. It took a few goes to get it right. We had to smile at our feeble attempts. Then finally it seemed to click into place but as soon as Terens relaxed the grip I removed the gripper it did not stay in place. On the third attempt I got annoyed and very nearly stamped on it but fortunately stopped myself in time. That would have been a very stupid thing to do. I picked it up and looked at it. Then I looked at it closer.

'Ghas!' I cried suddenly. The others jumped as they were getting tired of watching us try and get the thing into place. Djon was almost out of the door and banged his head as he was startled by my cry.

'What is it?' He asked rubbing his forehead.

'There's a bit missing! The little pins. They must clip into this thing somehow and when I dropped it, they must have been dislodged. We need to go and find them. They are very small though.'

'Just stay here Djim.' He said. 'We will go and find them. We know where it landed.' He disappeared. The others followed. Terens gave me a very hard look as he left. I felt such a fool. If they could not find those pins, we were lost and it would all be my fault. I put my head in my hands. I stayed like that for what seemed like ages ruminating over my stupidity but then came to my senses and decided that such behaviour was not going to get us out of this mess. A better idea would be to try and find our galaxy so we could find our way home. I turned on the telescope and cursed the poor quality of equipment on this vessel. It showed very little, and I realised now just how difficult it had been for Terens to try and locate our galaxy. I panned around the sky and then realised that it was not 'sky' I was panning around but just light years of nothing. Then I found the image filled with tiny distant stars. Even on maximum zoom it was not possible to get more detail than tiny points of stars crammed together as though there was no room to move between them. Was that our galaxy? Was it a galaxy? It had to be. I panned around as much as I could and found about seven or eight different smudges of light that appeared to be galaxies. Only one was bigger than all the rest. That then had to be our galaxy. To make sure we would not drift off course or be spinning round I inputted as many star groupings as possible into the computer to lock the giro compass onto. Hopefully, that would keep us facing in one direction. The more I looked the more galaxies I found but they were much further away. Or were they? I had no way of telling distance I realised. They could be just much smaller. Then I realised that they were further away as the stars were smaller and closer together which must indicate distance. Then Ruuth returned to the control room.

'We finally found it.' She said, handing me the tiny piece of the component. I managed to smile broadly.

'Thank you.' I said, taking the tiny piece from her hand. 'Where are the others?'

'It's really late, according to the vessel's timekeeper.' She said. 'They have gone to bed.'

'Oh, right. Can you stay and help me locate this before going to bed too?'

'Sure.' She sat down beside me as I picked up the component. We needed the gripper to be able to locate the tiny pin piece into position. We then located the component into place in the V20. It went home perfectly first time and locked into place in a very satisfying way. I knew it was right the way it went home.

'Right then. Bedtime.' I said and we left the control room together to go and get a snack. 'But we had better not sleep for too long though.'

*

I woke very early in the morning. Except was it morning? The vessel's timekeeper had stopped working! I leapt out of bed and hurriedly dragged on some clothes and then ran to the control room. What else had gone wrong? Had I overslept and all the vessel's systems were finally winding down? I stumbled into the control room which was already lit. Ruuth was sitting in the pilot's seat. She turned round as I entered.

'Good morning.' She said.

'Is it?' Was all I could manage as I threw myself in the seat beside her.

'Ah. So, you've noticed the vessel's timekeeper as well have you?'

'Yes. I wanted to come and check if there had been any system failures.'

'Ahead of you already.'

'You always are. So, what's wrong?'

'That's just the problem. I can find nothing wrong.'

'Then how do you know it is morning?'

'There is a caesium clock that starts running when the vessel is built. It provides a constant against which the vessel's timekeeper is set. It is still running, and I ran a few calculations and if we discount any time loss due to the portal skip then it is the morning of the seventeenth of May.'

'I'm sorry, I have let you all down. Instead of working to get us out of here I have been asleep.'

'Don't worry, Djim.' She put a comforting hand on my arm. I was taken aback for a second as I had not had much human contact of the comforting kind. 'You only slept for three hours and I only make it oh five hundred hours. I think we have all got up early.'

'How long do we have left of our life support?'

'One day left.' She said it very matter of factly, but it sounded the death knell. If words could ring in space like a huge gong, then those few words would do it. I could almost hear the echo coming back from the galaxies (even though I knew that the distances would make that impossible). I began to feel the impenetrable darkness outside the vessel creep into the control room. The absolute nothingness outside began to take on a solid oppressive substance. I had to stop such thoughts before I became too depressed to do anything. Fortunately, Djon came into the control room still eating.

'Hello.' He said. 'What's the matter with you two?'

'The timekeeper seems to have stopped working.' I said

with as much cheerfulness as I could manage.

'Really. Why?'

'We don't know.' Said Ruuth.

'What's the matter with it?' All Ruuth did was to point to the timekeeper readout. Which was blank. Djon stared at it for a moment.

'Is it like the V20?' He said finally.

'How do you mean?'

'Is it.... what was that word you used for the...?'

'Containitive!' Shouted Ruuth. 'Of course. Do you mean it also picks up the time from the portals, so when they are not there it has nothing to register?'

'Er, yes, something like that. Just like the V20.'

'Of course.' She pushed back her ragged hair from her face. 'How silly of me. We will have to rely on the caesium clock for timekeeping. I'll mark now as a reference point.'

'Right.' Said Djon, with an air of finality. 'We need to get this portal up and running so we can try and get out of here.'

'Can I join you later?' I asked. 'I am going to try and see if I can find out where we are and how far we are from the galaxy.'

'Sure thing. We need to know where we are going. The other thing you can do is try and see if you can find out how this portal works. We don't have another one to aim for.'

'I know. That was the other problem. I'll join you when I have made some progress.' Djon slapped me on the shoulder as he left, taking another mouthful of his breakfast. 'Where's Terens?' I asked Ruuth as she too got up to leave.

'He's already down with the portal. He knows he can do nothing about navigation and the like.' She too slapped me on the back as she left. I returned to the control panel, but my eyes were drawn again to the utter blackness outside punctured only by the few smudges of light from the distant galaxies. I suddenly realised what I was doing and dragged my concentration back to the matter in hand. The galaxy was thirty thousand light years across. That was my starting point. Now I just had to pick one of the smudges of light which was our galaxy. It had to be the biggest I felt sure. The others did not have the same classic structure. I could just about make out a typical three bar spiral shape. All I had to do next was to subtend the angle to find out how far we were. It had to be accurate to have any chance of giving us any form of accurate position. I knew the baseline to be the size of our galaxy so with a little bit of geometry I should be able to work out the distance. But first I had to try and remember some basic geometry. Natural tangents. That was the clue, but where could I find the tables of natural tangents? Did we have them on board? I began a search through the vessel's data basis to see if I could find anything that looked like a natural tangent table. As the time dragged on, I realised that we had so little time left. It began to cloud my judgement and I constantly had to drag my gaze away from the blackness outside. Finally, though my perseverance paid off, I found the tables. My relief was palpable It was then an easy thing to take the base line of the galaxy and divide it into two and then get the angle. I cursed again the crude technology on the vessel as I tried to get a bearing on both sides of the galaxy. I cursed again as the galaxy was infuriatingly fuzzy at the edges. It only took a few minutes once I had taken what I considered were the best bearings of the galaxy's width. It meant we were approximately twenty thousand light years from the galaxy! The shock went through me like a cold knife. I had never been so far from any portal or any destination before. It took me a few minutes to gather myself together to go and face the others.

I was greeted by an upbeat and cheerful crew. I sensed it was partly to allay fears about our predicament. The portal was complete, and all the pods were closed up. Terens was already in a space suit and ready to go outside. The instructions were hanging in space as usual. It stirred something in the back of my mind.

'Hi.' Said Ruuth. 'So, how far are we from home?'

'Well.' I began. They immediately picked up on my hesitation.

'What's the matter?' Demanded a worried Djon.

'According to my calculations we are approximately twenty thousand light years from home.' There was a long silence as they all stood looking at me. Their faces were drawn.

'Twenty thousand light years!' repeated Djon.

'Yes.'

'That's an awfully long way.' Came Terens mechanical voice from the suit communicator.

'I know.'

'How far can this portal send us?' Asked Djon.

'In theory Djon.' Replied Ruuth. 'There is no limit to the range if I have the idea correctly.'

'That's rubbish.' Retorted any angry Djon. 'There is no way this gadget could compress the entire universe into nothing.'

'Space is nothing.' I added calmly. I had spent far too long looking out of the forward vision enhancer and checking the instruments not to have noticed this. The instruments had picked up nothing for the last few hours. There appeared to be no atoms of anything out there. If there were no atoms of anything then there was nothing. Nothing could not have any dimension. So Ruuth should be right but somehow, I could not quite bring myself to believe it. Yet we all needed to believe it otherwise this portal would not be taking us home. If it could not take us twenty thousand light years in the next few hours, then we would be dead. Then I remembered that we would be dead sooner if we did not close down the instructions.

'Close the instructions, Djon. Quickly.'

'Why? We need them.'

'I know, but we must close down the instructions and use a small screen. I have just remembered that they use up air molecules!' There was a scramble as Djon ran to close them down. The ethereal wording then vanished.

'Thanks, Djim. How did you know that?'

'I read it somewhere when it was first brought out. As pilots we are introduced to all new technology as part of our continued training.'

'Come on!' said Karon. 'We won't be going anywhere if you don't at least get the thing set up. Chop chop.' None of us had seen her come into the bay. We had stopped, relieved at helping to reduce the air consumption. It was what was needed just then though. It galvanised everyone into action again.

'Don't just stand there Djim.' Called Djon, suddenly the master of ceremonies again. 'Get yourself into a suit and get out there to help Terens. He cannot do it on his own.' He was waving at the suit store.

'I'll help you.' Said Ruuth, taking me by the arm and guiding me to the suiting bay. The modern suit was easy to get on and soon I was ready to go EVA with Terens. Ruuth ran the pre space walk tests and declared everything OK. I went with Terens to the airlock. We stood there as it went through the cycle and I got a knot in my stomach as the outer hatch irised open revealing the blackness of intergalactic space. Pilot training obviously included spacewalking, but it was very rarely required during normal space flight these days. As far as I know no one had ever gone EVA outside the galaxy. I just hoped we would all survive to benefit from the novel experience. I had to slow my breathing and stop catching my breath as we walked to the edge. As the vessel had almost one gravity walking to the edge of the doorway with thousands of light years of nothing below it was a scary moment even though there was no 'down' out there. The effect of the artificial gravity stopped at the outer edge of the hull and one had to be ready for the transition to weightlessness. It always caught me out and I remember my tutor at pilot college shouting at me to get it right. I never did, but I tried hard to remember the technique. I noticed Terens stop at the lip.

'I've never liked this.' His voice came over mechanically in my earpiece. It was always a shock the first time to hear so clearly.

'Don't worry, you'll be OK. Just do as I do. We'll talk you through it.'

'OK guys.' Came Ruuth's voice direct into my ear. That again was an extraordinary experience to get used to hearing someone so closely and clearly even though they were not in sight. I had to stop as well to get my bearings and concentrate on my reply to start with. 'We are ready to eject the first pod.'

'Thank you Ruuth. We are just getting used to the idea of going outside. Neither of us is used to this. Give us a few moments to get our spacelegs.'

'OK. Let us know when you are ready.'

'Let us go.' Came Terens voice. It was odd. There was no stereo effect from either of their different positions. The sound always came from the same place.

'OK.' I said. 'Lets go. Ruuth. We are going EVA so get ready. We will let you know when we are in position.' Terens disappeared out of the hatchway and I found myself yet again frozen in the opening with my hands gripping the jambs. This was not normal space. Thoughts flooded into my mind from pilot training.

Suns are very big.

A typical main sequence sun is typically over a million kilometres in diameter. This means a volume of over five hundred thousand million million cubic kilometres of helium and hydrogen. These constituents are being ripped apart by thermonuclear fusion at fifteen million degrees Celsius to give a luminosity of almost four hundred quintillion megawatts. This vast body is the central mass of a solar system capturing planetary bodies with its huge gravitational power. This vast body also fills the solar system with light and a solar wind which spirals out of the sun for about fifteen billion kilometres.

The light travels the universe, theoretically for infinity.

The solar wind, which is likely comprised mostly of protons and travels at around five hundred kilometres a second fills any solar system but is dispersed by the ionized and neutral gases in interstellar space. Although this can be deadly there would be no indication that a living being had been subjected to a lethal dose of radiation. No wind would be felt. All appears still and quiet even in the turbulent space of a solar system. Even outside a solar system or a galaxy there is still no safety from deadly bursts of radiation. Fortunately, the magnetic fields of iron based planets forms a protection from this solar wind for planets based life forms.

Stand outside on a clear night and look up into the night sky. All appears still and quiet and beautiful. No solar wind can be seen no terrible sounds can be heard. Sound does not travel in a vacuum. Most planets have only a very thin atmosphere and the thickness of that atmosphere depends upon the gravitational pull of the planet. Although looking up into the night sky it appears to be just a few miles above your head it is of course not. What appears to be something is in fact nothing. Those tiny pinpoints of light are something. They are stars. The blackness of the night sky is the vast emptiness of space. How come it appears to curve like a dome above your head? Jump high enough and you could touch it? It is all an optical illusion.

Solar systems are also very big.

A typical solar system, depending upon the size of the sun at the centre, could be in the region of six billion kilometres across. Once away from a planet it becomes a very empty and lonely place. It is exceedingly difficult even to grasp the size of a solar system. Actually of course a solar system is not an actual thing as more of a concept. It is the area or volume within which the planets orbit the central sun. Most of the mass in a solar system is in fact found in the central sun. This means that the rest of the solar system is a very empty and lonely place. It would be very difficult to find anything in it at all. Very difficult. The analogy of looking for a needle in a haystack will no longer work because the distances in the sheer volume of nothingness are so considerable, together with the fact that everything is moving. Some planets can be moving at about fifty thousand kilometres an hour! You need to know where you are and where everything else is (and where it is going) and without good equipment to do that then your chances of finding anything is practically zero.

The universe is even more vast.

The universe is so vast in fact that the human mind is barely capable of comprehending the vastness involved. In fact, it cannot. There are no words big enough to adequately convey the size. The normal units of measuring distance are so puny that to be able to make measurements of the distances between suns, stars and galaxies, new methods of measurement are required. Hence the light year, the parsec, the astronomical unit. Even the latter distance is difficult to comprehend as a distance. Light, as we know, travels approximately two hundred and ninety thousand kilometers in a second while in a vacuum; which means that in a year it has travelled approximately nine and a half million million kilometres....so far that even the phrase 'light year' has very little meaning to the human mind. Just try and imagine nine and a half a million million kilometres. Even if you can imagine how far that is it will not even get you halfway to the next nearest star. Even the light year soon became too small a measurement to adequately be used to locate objects within the further reaches of the known universe.

The universe is vast.

The universe is so vast that that the numbers become colossal. There are estimated to be ten to twenty billion stars in the galaxy alone! And each star is generally a few light years from the next resulting in a huge volume of space required to contain even this small part of the universe. There are many countless other galaxies, some of which contain two hundred billion stars! There are some that which contain more. So, the volume of space enclosed by all these stars and galaxies becomes unbelievably huge.

There are millions of galaxies!

It soon becomes impossible to calculate meaningfully the actual number of stars or volume of space even in one local group of galaxies.

The universe is vast.

The universe is a vast and inhospitable place for a planet living air breathing animal. There exists around inhabitable planets a very thin layer of liveable atmosphere; beyond that it becomes a cold and airless vacuum where any animal or human has only seconds to live unless encased in a portable atmosphere.

The universe is also beautiful, but only from a distance of course. Up close the beauty vanishes much like a rainbow, as it is always at a distance and never near and never reachable; except perhaps for some planets which have a varied and disparate beauty depending upon their constitution or atmosphere. Some of the beauty of course could be deadly, as some of the gas giants for instance have unbreathable or oppressive atmospheres. But any planet or any solar system is infinitesimally small compared to galaxies or groups of galaxies. Even these are small compared to the known universe. Galaxies have been identified as being ten billion light years away!

Even between galaxies in the extreme vacuum there are deadly radiations that can strike without warning if there is no detection equipment to herald its arrival. Once detected then a safe place is required to hide from the radiation. Supernovae release hard gamma radiation that travels the universe possibly for ever. A living being would not know it had passed until too late. All would appear empty and still and infinitely lonely.

It was originally thought that to reach other stars then space travel would have to be at the speed of light, if not faster. But, even at that speed it would still take too long to reach anything other than the nearest of stars. It was soon discovered that travel at the speed of light was also not a feasible option. The trouble was, at speeds approaching the speed of light any object would be very vulnerable to any other object in its way, no matter what its size. Much like a typhoon can send a straw through the trunk of a tree purely because of the speed it is being propelled, so it would be for any vessel travelling at such high speeds in space. And contrary to popular opinion, there is a lot of matter out there in the galaxies. Some of it is large enough to see, some of it is not. Micrometeoroids are a typical example of the latter being generally less than one tenth of a millimetre in size and a microgram in mass. At the speed of light, they would have enough mass to penetrate any substance. The hull of a space vessel or a human body for example. Also, if anything went wrong, then any vessel would be a long way from help. A long, long way even within a single galaxy let alone between galaxies, so far in fact it is not possible to grasp how far. It is much like an oemeba trying to understand the principles of mathematics.

Galaxies are vast.

Galaxies are vast and they contain millions or billions of stars. There are also millions of galaxies. The galaxies are also so colossally distant from one another. No one still quite knows what is out there between the galaxies. There is so much volume of space in between the galaxies. There is more in between than there are galaxies. It would be a mind numbingly lonely place to be stranded, between the galaxies. It would be far worse than being left far from home on a cold wet winter's night in the remotest part of an inhabitable world. Even in the remotest places on inhabited planets neighbours are within an understandable distance, even if not reachable, and there is ground beneath the feet.

In the space between galaxies there is nothing except ionized helium and vast clouds of unseen hydrogen, in all directions. Unseen because the atoms are transparent after having been split apart by energetic quasar radiation. Anything solid that had been there had been sucked into the gravitational maw of the nearest galaxy, leaving the space in between swept mind numbingly clean of anything tangible.

A vast, uncomprehendingly vast volume of nothing that the mind can see!

It happens sometimes, so they say, that a vessel goes astray and is never heard from again. With all the best safety checks and balances there is always one that will get away. It is an unfortunate thing with chance. There is always the chance that something will go wrong. In space travel any accident is likely to be tragic. No help will be able to be given as the distress signal, without the portals, could take thousands of years to reach the rescuers. Even if they could find the distance and direction of the distress call it would still then be too late. And here we were alone and out of range of any help.

'You OK, Djim?' came Ruuth's voice again snapping me out of my reverie. I felt awkward and stupid.

'I'm fine thank you, just taking in the view.' And with that I checked my restraint line was secure and stepped out into..... nothing. Suddenly I was no longer heavy but weightless. The abrupt change took my breath away again and I cursed myself for not being more prepared. Now there was no up or down. I turned to face the hull of the vessel to give me some orientation and then pulled myself along the hull with the rails inset into the hull between the solar panels for just such work. They were all colour coded for direction and position. I ran through the colour system in my mind. Fortunately, I had learnt that well and it came flooding back. 'OK Terens?'

'Right behind you Djim. Stop worrying and just get on with the job.' I had to smile. I also had to stop myself from looking away from the vessel to try and see if I could see some stars. I knew they were not there. We came to the workshop bay airlock which was already open, and a pod was ready. Now we had to be careful. Even though the pod would have no weight when it came out of the airlock it would still have the same mass. We needed to move them slowly so they could not build up any kinetic energy. It would not be a quick operation but we did not have much time either. We needed to get nearer a star again to recharge the systems. I hoped Terens had remembered to bring the EVA hauler out with him. I need not have worried; he came up beside me with it expertly. We swung it round and clipped it onto the pod and drew it out. It trailed the carbonised polymetal wire restraint which would secure it to the hull. As the electric current flowed along the wire restraint, it would stiffen to a rigid rod. We hoped anyway. I took the end with the sprung clip and followed Terens as he slowly backed up the hull to the place we had decided was the most likely to give us the best chance of seeing this thing work. We had to get the centre of gravity within the ring of pods. Reversing my thinking I counted back to the correct locking hoop set into the hull. As we got close I looked closer to check the exact reference number of each hoop as we came to it. Then I found the first one.

'Here we are Terens.' I called and then realised I did not have to speak loudly.

'No need to shout Djim.'

'Sorry. I have just remembered. Here we are.' Terens

slowed up the hauler and brought the pod to a halt. I took the clip and secured it to the hoop. 'OK.' Terens nodded and began to pull the pod out to bring the wire taught. He then detached to EVA hauler and we returned for the next. We would have to repeat this seven times for all the pods. It went well until we came to the only remaining part off the hull that still had not been properly repaired. The last hoop was missing! This was difficult as we needed to make sure all the pods were secured in a perfect circle around the hull. Or so we thought. This required a new hoop to be fixed in the hull. I called Djon what we needed and asked him to see if he could fashion one for us and some way of fixing it to the hull. I showed him the situation with the helmet camera.

'I need something more accurate Djim. The fixing must be in the right place. Without the hoop reference number I cannot locate it.'

'OK. I will give you the coordinates from the nearest remaining hoops.' I began to inch my way to the nearest hoop. Then without warning the thought 'what is an inch?' came into my mind. I did not have an answer, so I put it out of thought and kept on. I found the hoops and their reference numbers and relayed them to Djon and then measured to where we thought the last pod should be fixed. Because the hull had been so badly damaged the computer could no longer create an image for that area. At least the longer I was out here I was not using up the vessel's atmosphere. It was a very small contribution, but anything may help. It may come to us all using the suits for the last moments. I hoped it would not come to that. I began to make my way back to the workshop bay lock. Terens had temporarily fixed the last pod to a hoop and had returned before me. I stopped on the way and looked up, hoping to see stars. There were none, only the faint smudges of the galaxies with what looked like stars beyond them. I knew they could not be stars so they had to be yet further galaxies. The blackness in between was so black it was unreal and unlike any sky I had ever seen in the galaxy. It seemed almost solid, oppressive, life sucking. Instead of being nothing it appeared to be trying to crush our vessel. I began to get a growing fear inside me and that I needed to get back inside the vessel before the life was squeezed out of me. Then I had another growing fear that even inside it would not protect me and the vessel would be crushed like a fragile egg. I began to move quickly before I could control myself and bring my actions under control again. Moving too quickly out here could be very dangerous.

Then I had the funny feeling that I was being watched. Out here! Although the idea seemed preposterous it would not go away. I found myself turning round to look behind me. This is not an easy thing to do in an EVA suit. They are still big clumsy things with large air cylinders on the back and multi layers – mostly for redundancy. In space I was glad of a good proportion of redundancy.

Everywhere I looked it was the same, apart from the clouds of glowing galaxies, there was an empty blackness. I knew the empty blackness was in theory infinite, or at least so infinitely huge as to be beyond comprehension. But this did not stop me feeling as though I could reach out and touch it; as though we were inside a dark sphere not much larger than our vessel.

It then began to feel again as though it was getting closer. A ridiculous thought, or was it? Each time I looked up it seemed to happen again, the sense of crushing infinity. I found myself sweating and not working. I must pull myself together and stop being mesmerised by the empty void in which we found ourselves. I tried directing myself back to the task in hand. I found myself shaking. The more I tried to stop it the more I shook. I just had to stop and close my eyes and think of something beautiful from home. Gradually I felt calmer so much so that I could continue even though at a slower rate than normal.

'All OK?' Crackled Terens voice over the communicator.

'Yes, all OK.' I replied hoping the nervousness in my voice did not register with them. I took a deep breath. 'Do I need to come back in Djon?' I asked. Not knowing how long he would be in producing the last fixing.

'No, I should be ready soon. Are you all right out there.

Not getting lonely are you?'

'I'm OK.' I lied. I could not let them down now. We needed to get this finished. The others lives depended on this. I had to really take hold of my thinking and stop myself from dashing back into the bay.

'You sure you are OK?' Asked Ruuth although I had to think for a moment whose voice it was as the suit speaker tended to make everyone sound very similar. 'The telemetry from your suit is showing some stress levels.'

'I'm OK, Ruuth, thanks. It is just the effort of working within this suit. I'm not used to it.' I hoped that would allay her fears.

'OK. Just try and keep calm Djim.'

'Will do.' I took some long slow breaths and dragged my eyes from staring at the blackness of the all-surrounding sky to the darkness of the solar panels on the hull. I tried to concentrate on the patterns in the panels and the other hull attachments. It helped and my breathing slowed and the sweating reduced. The suit atmosphere controls also slowed down as I calmed down. The remaining time readout began to climb again giving me longer out here. That was also a relief. The longer we had in the suits the longer we had to live.

Djon's voice snapped me out of my deep thought. 'Ok, Djim, ready when you are.'

'Ready. Coming over.' I made my way to the bay airlock. There was a strange pile of what looked like junk. 'Is that it?'

'Stop being cheeky. That is it. I have numbered the fixing points to match the hull hoops. It should be simple enough to fix once you are in the right place.'

'OK.' I picked up the pieces and pulled myself back to the damaged part of the hull. I studied the parts to try and find the numbers that Djon had stamped on it. In the poor light it was difficult I needed the suit light to give me a chance of reading them. When I found them, it was relatively easy to fix to the correct hull fixing hoops. Djon had included a tensioning device as well to bring the system taught. He had marked where the last pod was to be fixed as well. I retrieved it from its temporary position and fixed it in the correct place. 'All done. I will move back to the airlock. When there we can run the set-up test before I come back on board.'

'OK.'

I returned to the airlock and positioned myself so I could see the pods. They were dim shapes surrounding the dark hull. It was difficult to see either the hull or the pods. I felt the panic rising again as though I was being crushed, no not crushed but stifled by a big black pillow over my face.

'Ready. Run the test.'

'OK, Djim. Running test now.' I was sure that was Djon's voice. There was a very slight vibration running through the hull. Had there been air I might have heard it. Very gradually the pod restraint wires began to straighten out and then lock into place. As far as I could tell in the gloom they appeared to be all correct and uniformly positioned. I turned on the suit light but it was fairly useless, the emptiness seemed to sap all energy from the beam. 'How does it look Djim?'

'As far as I can tell it appears to be OK.'

'OK. Return inside.'

'Returning inside now.' I went to the airlock and closed the outer hatch manually to conserve power. I waited as the airlock ran though the cycle. Then the inner hatch was opened by Ruuth. She signalled that she would help me out of the suit. It was not necessary as suits were designed to be operated by one person, in case of emergencies. The thought was appreciated though. The ship atmosphere though smelled funny. She noticed my expression.

'I know.' She said. 'The atmosphere is beginning to get a bit rough. I had to alter the control panel to compensate. I turned off the alarm. I didn't think that would be too helpful.'

'Good thinking. We do not need that. We have some time left even when the alarm starts. It has a fair margin of safety.' I looked up. There was a definite humming sound.

'That's the portal.' She said. 'Let us go to the control room with the others. We need your V20 experience.'

'Sure, lead the way.' I followed her to the control room. I

could not help but notice that she had lost a little weight. Perhaps we all had. The worry of the last few days must have had an effect on us all. The others were crowded into the control room. They moved out of the way to let me get to the pilot's seat. I sat down. Someone had already turned on the V20, the empty blue orb was silently glowing, but the very emptiness seemed to shout distance at me. The silence was almost an unbearable noise that made it difficult for me to think. My actions seemed to be slowed by a dense fluid. What I needed was my calculations of the distance from our galaxy. I found it difficult to think straight. What was it? Twenty thousand light years? So how was this going to work? I stared at the V20 hoping it would give me an answer. It did not. But it must. There was that tiny component that we had added to the V20 it must do something. Suddenly I knew what to do. I called up the V20 contents list and sure enough at the bottom of the list was a new item. It did not say portal but did have six small asterisks beside it. Perhaps it needed to be told what the new addition was? I hoped not, I hoped it was just the title that was not automatically added because I had no idea how to add a portal to a V20. I scrolled down to the portal icon and pressed enter. Fortunately, a series of further instructions sprang into the orb. I could sense the relief in the room. I studied the new instructions carefully. There was the usual command lines looking for the input of coordinates for the start and end of the skip. Unfortunately, not being within the galaxy we had no means of inputting coordinates. We did not know where we were or where we needed to be. Not being within our galaxy we had no idea of the end coordinates. I looked down the list and was relieved to find at the bottom a way of making a straight-line skip of a certain distance. At least that was the way I read it. I looked up at Djon and pointed to the last instruction. He bent down and looked carefully at it and then straightened up. The atmosphere was getting worse by the hour and it made thinking more difficult. We were all taking longer and longer to make decisions or even make decisions at all. He nodded.

'That looks like the one Djim.'

I returned to the controls and picked the last instruction. I then had to look up how far I had calculated we were from the galaxy and typed in the figures. I looked up at Djon again. He shrugged.

'I have no idea.' He said. 'Just go with it and let us hope it is right.' He turned and sat in an empty seat. The others were already seated, and their seats locked into place. When we were all ready, I pressed the agree button. Up came a start icon. I pressed the accept button and the familiar feeling of falling thankfully descended on us all and the screen went blank.

I looked up at the forward vision enhancer and waited for it to come back online and show the glory of our galaxy. It remained blank. I heard a groan.

'Where's our galaxy?' moaned someone.

– CHAPTER 11 –

My breathing was becoming laboured, and I was not sure whether it was the poor atmosphere or whether I was panicking because the forward vision enhancer was staying blank. The vessel was also becoming eerily quiet as the automatic systems were shutting down unessential power drains to help preserve power. We needed all the power we had to maintain the last of the atmosphere. I had never been in a vessel where this had happened. We were taught about it of course but feeling it was something else. This was no practice; this was for real. I did not know what to do next. My mind was not working properly. There was no galaxy, but there should be!

I powered up the telescope to see if it would show anything different. There was a haze in front of us which appeared to be the galaxy but taunting us by not getting closer. What was happening?

'Is the portal working?' Asked Terens.

'I don't know.' I said struggling to find the words.

'Just do it again then.' Said Ruuth.

'I don't know if we have the power to do another.' I replied.

'If you do not we die if you do we die as well so let's just do it.' I looked around at the others. No one had got up from their seats. They just sat there looking drawn and tired. I lifted my hand which was beginning to feel heavy. The glowing orb of the V20 was getting fainter but there was still the same instruction from the last skip still defiantly showing. All I had to do was accept again. I did so and again felt the feeling of falling. I slumped into my seat not having the energy to do anything else.

I kept staring up at the vision enhancer for our galaxy to reappear, but it did not. The haze in front of us did seem to be brighter and filled the screen. I looked down at the V20. It did not show anything of our galaxy, all that was in it was the last instruction still taunting me. What was happening? Why were we not in our galaxy? I did not know what to do. I was sure that I had made the correct calculations, I could not be that wrong. I wished that I had asked someone else to check them while we were still feeling normal.

'Again.' Came Ruuth's slurred voice from somewhere near me.

'I don't know if we have enough....' I began.

'Just do it. We will die if we stay out here for sure.'

'OK.' With supreme effort I pulled myself up and managed to press the button again. I felt the feeling of falling and then blacked out.

*

There was a bang.

I awoke with a start.

I thought I was at home and then realised slowly that I was not as the control room swam into consciousness. I then realised that I was alive, or was I? I looked around. The others were still slumped in their seats so perhaps I was still alive.

There was another bang and I looked up at the forward vision enhancer and saw a bright sun beaming joyfully back at me. Then I realised that the vessel was sounding normal again. The automatic systems had brought everything back into operation again. The atmosphere was not good but was better than had been. That glorious sun out there was supplying our systems with wonderful, radiated energy. Then I realised that the bangs were the vessel heating unevenly so we were fairly close to the sun. A readout gave us as about one hundred and forty million kilometres from the sun. Not bad. But which sun was it? I looked down at the V20 which still had the last instruction glaring back at me. I cancelled it hoping to see the galaxy spring into view. It did not. The orb of the V20 resolutely stayed empty! What was happening? We were in the galaxy, but it was not showing. Perhaps the lack of power had affected the V20 and caused a programme failure. I hoped

Ruuth would come to so we could test it. I did not have the energy to get up and check the others just yet. My whole body ached, and my limbs would not fully follow my instructions. I could certainly not yet stand up. I tried to wake the others by calling but my throat was so dry I could only make a whisper. I sat back and just let my eyes feast on the view of the sun in front of us. It was such a glorious sight I cried. It was a main sequence star giving out a white light. There was evidence of planets orbiting the sun too or, so the instruments were saying. If they were working, then surely the V20 should be working too. I tried to get up to see if I could rouse Ruuth but all I managed to do was stumble a few steps and fall in a heap on the floor. I lay there and just laughed and laughed and laughed. We were back in the galaxy and we were near a sun which was powering the vessel's systems back up again. I laughed again and just revelled in the joy of it all. The galaxy and a sun. I had not realised just how stressed we had all been when outside of the galaxy.

Then I stopped. What if those characters who had lied to us knew we were back in the galaxy? They seemed to know where we were before. I had to get up and turn on all the defence systems so we had a chance of getting some sort of early warning of an approaching vessel. My laughter turned to concern again so soon. Why? What had happened to the galaxy? All I wanted was a quiet life doing what I had done for years. This stress was not good for me at all.

I struggled to my feet and pulled myself back into the pilot's seat. I turned on the proximity micro radar system and all the other passive and active systems. I also turned on the visual recognition system which normally we did not use. I also turned on the cameras and put their pictures up on the screen as well as small pictures down one side. I wanted everything on so I could both hear and see anything coming.

Then someone groaned. It was Djon struggling to get himself awake. He was almost immediately followed by Terens stirring uneasily in his seat. Then everyone was groaning and wriggling in their seats.

'What's happened?' Asked Djon in a groggy hoarse voice. He coughed to try and clear his throat. I knew how he was feeling.

'Welcome back everyone. We are back in the galaxy!' I said as cheerfully as possible.

'Pardon?' Said Terens. 'I'm not quite sure what is going on.'

'We are back in the galaxy!'

'At last.'

'And there is a sun too!' Said Ruuth, pointing to the screen her voice sounding thick and unnatural. There was a thump followed by a curse as Karon obviously tried to get up. Everyone laughed freely much as I had earlier. Terens reached over and helped pull her back up and into her seat. She glowered at us all but then once seated again began to see the funny side of it and smiled back at us. I hated to spoil the moment, so I decided not to tell them yet that now we were back in the galaxy we were possibly already in the sights of our earlier captors. I kept nervously looking at the screens and the defence systems readouts. All was clear.

'What is wrong with the V20?' asked Ruuth suddenly, bringing me out of my daydream as I let the glorious view of the sun wash over me. One of the best things about the forward vision enhancer I had just decided was the ability it gave you to look straight at a sun. I looked round at her.

'Pardon?'

'What is wrong with the V20, it is not showing anything?'

'I don't know Ruuth. Can you have a look at it for me? It is a bit worrying.'

'Is there anything else not working?'

'I don't think so, not as far as I can tell anyway.'

'That's odd.'

'Why is that?'

'It is odd that only the V20 is not working.'

'Perhaps it is something to do with portal we are carrying.' Suggested Djon, now more wide awake. Still, no one had got out of their seats.

'That is possible I suppose. I will have another look at it.

In a minute though, I still feel very tired. Has anyone got anything to drink?' Everyone shook their head but at the same time suddenly realised just how thirsty each of us was. Karon was the only one to struggle to her feet.

'I'll get some drinks. I cannot do anything else as I know nothing about this vessel or the way it works. I'll get the drinks you get us to civilisation.' She managed to stay on her feet and worked her way slowly to the door. When she had left the control room Djon spoke.

'What's up Djim, you are noticeably quiet and pensive?'

'Oh. Well, I didn't want to say anything to dampen the spirits but.' I paused, looking for the right words. 'Now we are back in the galaxy it is only a matter of time before our captors realise we are back in the galaxy and come looking for us.'

'Oh dear.' Said Ruuth, looking up from her work. 'Can we defend ourselves?'

'No. This vessel has no defensive weaponry. All we have are the personal weapons in the store. They are no good against another vessel.'

'Can we hide somewhere?'

'Once you can get the V20 back up and running then we can find out where we are and possibly find somewhere to hide. We will have to be quick and get rid of this vessel though. I am sure they will not be able to find us once we are on a planet or something.'

'You hope.' Muttered Terens.

'Do we have anything on board that could identify this star?'

'A light spectrum analyser for example?' I suggested.

'Yes, something like that. Is there a list of the stars in the galaxy and their qualities?'

'There is but I am not sure we have one on board. You got this vessel Djon was there one included in the inventory?'

'No idea. We never imagined that we would need anything like that. Do you recognise any of the star patterns?'

'Good point. I was just so glad to see this sun that I had not even thought of that.' I reached forward and turned the view from the sun to a part of the sky unaffected by the sun's light. As my eyes became accustomed to the different light level the stars appeared. We all looked intently at the view outside. There were many stars and a great belt of pale light stretched across the sky.

'Well?' Asked Djon, looking at me expectantly.

'Sorry Djon, I don't recognise any of the groupings of stars at all.'

'Can you see the Nebula?'

'No, not in this view.' This was another occasion when I rued the fact that we relied so heavily on the V20. It had never occurred to me that it could malfunction and leave us stranded. I scanned the sky all round, looking for something I knew.

'Is that grouping familiar?' Asked Terens at one point. I stopped and looked for a minute.

'I don't recognise it. I am familiar with the groupings of stars around Enceladus but not from other parts of the galaxy. I don't recognise anything so far.' Ruuth sat back and sighed. I put a comforting hand on her shoulder. 'What's up?'

'I can find nothing wrong with this V20.' She said, obviously tired and dejected. Then Karon returned with a tray of drinks fixed to a tray.

'Drinks everyone.' She put the tray into its holder on the table and handed us all a drink. It was the best drink I had ever had. I wallowed in the feeling as the cold liquid ran down my throat. A sun and then a drink. When I had finally taken as much enjoyment out of it as I could I turned back to Ruuth.

'If it is working then where are all the stars?'

'I have no idea. I can only assume it is working unless I have missed something.' She stopped and took another sip of her drink obviously trying to think of why the V20 was not working.

'OK.' I said. 'We have two choices. Either the V20 is working, or it is not. If we take the second one and it is not working, then we don't know where we are in the galaxy or where to go. So that puts us still in danger of running out of supplies before finding civilisation. If we take the first one, then where on Erebus are we? Because if the V20 is working then we are not in the galaxy.'

'Or it could be that those characters fixed our V20 to not respond any more.' Said Terens darkly.

'I had not thought of that one.'

'Is anyone hungry?' Asked Karon, beginning to brighten up, seemingly quicker than any of us. Perhaps separated from the mechanics of the running of the vessel meant she had less worries to bring her down. It was a welcome relief though that someone was willing to look after us.

'I definitely am.' I said and the others quickly joined in with that sentiment.

'Right then, don't go away and I will go and get something to eat for all of us.' I had to smile at her little joke. She had done very well considering this was her first time in space and we were well and truly lost and possibly being hunted down by ruthless killers at this very moment. That made me look again at the proximity alarm and all the other warning systems. All was clear. There was nothing within range. Unless. A very nasty thought crossed my mind that those very same killers had not only tampered with the V20 but other vessel systems as well. I looked across at Ruuth. She was still working hard at the control panel going through system programmes of some sort.

'Has anything else been tampered with?' I asked her, not really wanting to hear the reply.

'Well, that is the funny thing.' She said, stopping and looking straight at me.' I can find nothing wrong with any of the systems so far. The seals are all in place and there is no evidence of tampering, either mechanical or programmable.' That was not the answer I was expecting, but it was a relief of sorts.

'Maybe there has been a breakdown in the portal system, so we are not getting any signals. Or maybe just the nearest portal has a problem, that would stop us receiving the information too.' Said Djon, stretching his hands up as high as he could and then holding the back of his head as he spoke.

'I've never known it.' I replied.

'I suppose it is possible those people put a shield of some sort onboard.' Muttered Ruuth half to herself. 'I'll run a check and see if I can find anything. Keep looking Djim and see if you recognise anything outside. We need every help we can get however small.' She went straight back to the control panel.

'Sure thing.' I said and went back to the screen view. No matter how much I looked at the star patterns though I could not make out anything that looked remotely like any star pattern I knew in the galaxy. Then I felt really stupid as I suddenly remembered that all vessels carried a paper star chart in case of emergencies to give a rough idea of where you were in the galaxy should there be a systems failure. I put my head in my hands.

'What's up Djim?' Asked a concerned Djon.

'Sorry people.' I said looking up at the ceiling. 'I have just remembered that every vessel carries..'

'A star chart.' Finished Terens. 'I have just remembered too. Do not worry Djim we all should have remembered. I'll get it.' He pushed himself wearily from his seat and left the control room. He was soon back with a small book in his hand. He threw it nonchalantly over to me and sat back down. I opened the book. I then realised the enormity of the task. Not knowing where we were meant that there was a huge number of permutations of views of the galaxy to try and match with the view outside our vessel.

'Right then. This could be a long job.'

'Don't worry Djim.' Said Terens. 'We are not going anywhere for a while, take your time.' He laid his head back against the seat and blew his cheeks out with a long noisy breath. Karon came back shortly with a tray full of food. Djon brought the table down and everyone turned round to have a break from the tedium of looking at star patterns or vessel programmes.

'Thank goodness.' Said Ruuth. 'I really need this. I have found absolutely nothing wrong with any of the vessel's systems and I can find no evidence of a shield either.'

'That's odd.' Said Djon, his mouth now full of food.

'I know.'

'So what's..?'

'Excuse me.' Butted in Karon. 'But what's that?' She pointed at the V20. We had all ignored it for a long while. I looked back at the V20 but could see nothing. Then I realised that Karon was standing while I was sitting. I stood up and gasped. There in the V20 was a tiny dot. There was a scramble as everyone leapt up to get a closer look at the dot in the V20. What was it? Was it a star or a portal signal? There was no identification beside it just a tiny dot.

'What is it?' Asked Djon breathlessly.

'I don't know.' I said as I sat down in front of the orb on the control panel. I typed in some instructions, but nothing happened. 'It has registered something, but I cannot get any information on it for some reason.' I said, mystified. I sat back and scratched my chin while I thought.

'Well at least it shows it is working.'

'After a fashion anyway. But why is it only registering this one.' I paused trying to think what it was registering. 'This one star or portal.'

'Should we not try and find the nearest planet?' Asked Terens. 'We could at least hide near it and not be so exposed out here.'

'What a good idea. Why didn't I think of that before?' I said, kicking myself inwardly for not thinking of it sooner. I investigated the mass gravitometer for signs of planetary bodies distorting the fabric of space nearby. There was one not more than a million kilometres away, but it would take us a long time to get there by normal means. I wondered if we could do a small skip with the portal. That would require a lot of power so I then checked the power levels and put the parameters into the clique computer to calculate how long we needed before the vessel could allow the power to be used for the skip. The answer soon came back as eight hours. That was along time to sit out here exposed in the galaxy. I began a search to see if there was anything nearby that we could possibly hide behind but even if we found something the firing of the main drive could also alert anyone nearby of our presence. It was possible that just remaining here might be the best thing to do. The galaxy is vast, and a silent vessel would be difficult to spot. That last thought gave me some sense of peace. I returned to the food that Karon had brought us and thankfully tucked in. I kept one eye on the V20 though to see if anything else appeared in the bluish orb. It did not, the lone dot remained all alone, a silent enigmatic beacon of something that we did not know. I then thought it might be better if we cut all the active defence mechanisms we would become even more invisible. It would be a dangerous thing to do but might make us more difficult to find.

'I have an idea.' I said. The others looked up from their meals expectantly. 'What if we shut off all the active external defence mechanisms? That will make us more invisible to anyone looking for us. What do you think?' I looked around at them.

'That is never recommended Djim.' Replied Djon. 'It would leave us vulnerable to any natural impact let alone any other vessel approaching. It will leave us with no way of knowing if anyone is coming for us.'

'I agree.' Added Terens. 'The last thing we want now is to be smashed to pieces by a lump of rock.' The others agreed.

'OK, we will leave them on. I think we ought to run a shift pattern of watches though rather than relying totally on the automatic systems.'

'I agree wholeheartedly with that.' Said Djon.

'What day and time is it?' Asked Karon out of the blue.

'We don't know exactly.' Replied Ruuth. 'But I can find out what the vessel's timekeeper recons the day and time is.' She turned her seat round and examined the timekeeper controls. 'I just need to make a calculation from the vessel's built date.' She muttered more to herself than us. I finished my meal as Ruuth made her calculation. 'Aha.' She said finally. 'I make it the nineteenth of May at ten pm.' She looked round. 'We may have been out for some time.'

'That is good.' I added. 'It means we can spend most of the

night recharging for a skip to the planet. I suggest we work out our rota and then get some proper sleep ready for the morning.' The others agreed and Ruuth wanted to take first watch. No one disagreed with her. Although I had been unconscious for some time I still felt as though I needed a good night's sleep. Karon would not accept any help clearing up the food and sent us all off to our rooms. No one disagreed with her either.

Once alone in my room I sat on the edge of the bed for a while too tired to have a shower. I could not stop thinking about the V20 and why it was not working properly. I had never known a malfunction like it before. I tried to think of all the possible things that could go wrong in a V20 and then realised how little I knew about them. We were taught at pilot training how to check for the obvious malfunctions, but this defied all the known reasons. Then there was the lack of known star patterns. I got up and left my room looking for a viewing window. Perhaps if I looked directly at the stars from a window it might look different. I found a darkened storeroom and shut the door to keep out the light and went and stared out of the window. The sky was full of tiny points of light in patterns that I did not know at all and I did not know why. It was no good. Even seeing the stars directly, I still could not recognise any patterns I knew. It was so odd it was like we were somewhere else altogether. It could not be possible. We must be in an uninhabited part of the galaxy hence the unfamiliarity.

A sliver of light fell across the wall of the room highlighting the storage cabinets lining the wall and then vanished again. Ruuth came and stood close beside me and looked out of the window.

'I saw you come in here and you did not come out again. Are you OK?'

'I think so. I am just concerned that the V20 is not working, and I cannot recognise any of the star patterns. I thought it might be different if I saw the stars directly from here.'

'And is it?' She turned and looked at me in the dark.

'No.'

'Oh dear.' She looked out of the window again. 'I don't recognise any star patterns either but then I am not a pilot.'

'It doesn't look the same.'

'What do you mean?'

'The galaxy doesn't look the same somehow.'

'I still don't follow you. The stars are there.'

'I know it sounds silly, but the galaxy doesn't look right. As though something is not right. I cannot put my finger on it. I think there may be some connection to that and with the V20. I wish I knew what it was. I don't like not knowing where I am.'

'I know, neither do I.' She fell silent and we stared out of the window hoping against hope to spot a pattern that we knew. We had never spent any time together before and it was a very pleasant feeling. I did not want it to stop but knew it had to very soon as we could not stand there forever. I could feel the gentle heat of her body and smell the faint odour of her delicate perfume that she wore. It was a brief interlude of normal human closeness that we had not been able to enjoy for what seemed like eternity but had in fact only been a few days at most. It was extraordinary what had happened to us all these last few days.

'Have you ever been married?' She asked suddenly.

'No. Pilots are not allowed to marry until later in life. I should be eligible in a few years t...' I stopped.

'What's the matter?'

'We are no longer on Enceladus. What rules apply to me out here? I have no planet no job and no prospects? I should say that all of us have no planet and no job and our prospects are very uncertain at this stage. What about you, have you been married?'

'No. In the government even women had to wait until later to marry and have children.'

'Do you know, I didn't know that?' I put my arm around her shoulder. She did not protest but just put her head on my shoulder.

'We will be alright, won't we?' she asked, sounding like a

small girl all of a sudden, her voice tiny and unlike her normal forceful self.

'I hope so. We have come this far. I just need to find out where we are and then we can do something about it.' We fell silent again just looking at the stars.

'Are you wondering where you father is?'

'Yes, how did you know?'

'Because I am as well. My father I mean.' She added with a smile. I could just about make out her smile in the darkness.

*

I was woken what seemed like only moments after going off to sleep by a shrieking alarm. I leapt out of bed immediately as my pilot training snapped into action. I found I was still in my clothes of last night. Or was it still the same night? I had no idea. I could not remember what had happened. I remember talking with Ruuth in the dark and then catching a late-night drink in the galley. I did not remember going to bed. I ran to the control room and found Djon obviously still waking up.

'Sorry Djim!' He cried. 'I'm sorry I must have fallen asleep. What is going on?'

'It's the proximity alarm again Djon, how could you have fallen asleep?'

'I'm really sorry Djim. Ghas I feel so awful. Is it the same people again?'

'I don't know.'

'What do we do if it is?'

'We fire up the drive and just ram them.' Came Teren's dry voice from behind us. I had not heard him come into the control room. It was not a thought that had crossed my mind, but it seemed a great idea. If we were to die, then what better way to do it but in a blaze of exploding vessels taking at least some of those nasty people with us? After the way they had tricked us it seemed all they deserved.

'What is it?' Asked Ruuth. 'Is it another vessel or a bit of space debris?'

'I don't know yet.' I replied breathlessly and I checked

the proximity alarm details scrolling down a side panel in the screen. Something was heading straight for us. It would be very unusual for space debris to be heading straight at us, the chances were infinitesimally small. I checked the other sensors to see if anything else showed up. It was obviously another vessel. I looked round at the others and took in their worried faces drained of colour. We all knew that if it was a vessel then it must be the people that took us at the hidden portal. 'It is another vessel.' I said tersely and watched their faces fall.

'How long before they reach us?' Asked Ruuth surprisingly calmly.

'I would estimate that we have about half an hour standard galactic time.'

'Turn and face them then.' Said Terens. 'Are we agreed that we just ram them as soon as they are too close to do anything about it?' I was amazed at the calmness that Terens was showing while talking about the deaths of all of us. I was more surprised that everyone else agreed with him without a qualm. He looked at me last and I had to nod my consent too but with a cold lump in my stomach as I did so.

'I'll turn us around then.' I said and began the calculations to find their direction and how much to turn our vessel to face them. I punched in the calculations with a delay programme and the thrusters began to turn us round slowly. I made sure that the thrusters were facing away from the approaching vessel to help disguise the fact that we were moving or had seen them. It would take a few minutes for the manoeuvre to take place. While it was happening, I calculated how late we could leave it before firing the main drive to ram them. We had to make sure they had no chance to change direction so we would miss them. Then we all spontaneously began to hug each other and even the normally reticent Terens joined in. Ruuth hugged me the longest and I did not want to let go but unfortunately had to. We looked into each other's eyes for a moment before having to break away. I could not bear to look much longer knowing that it would be me that would have to fire the drive to plunge our vessel into the approaching craft. In fact, I could not look at the others either so I concentrated on the vessel's systems and the approaching craft. I felt we ought to do something to mark our final moments but could not think of any suitable action to take.

'Djim!' Said Djon suddenly, dragging me out of my melancholic daydream. 'Do we have a copy of the information that we downloaded into our insurance policy?'

'Yes, I think we have.'

'Then let us broadcast it to the galaxy. I know it is a forlorn hope but at least the signal will be out in free space and those vicious people will not be able to put it back in the bottle. Eventually someone will pick it up and hopefully act on it.'

'Good idea.' Muttered Terens.

'I agree.' I said. 'I will look for it now and get it broadcast.'

'Thank you.' Replied Djon with a look of relief on his now lined and worried face.

I returned my attention to the control panel and tried to find the information. Fortunately, I found it very quickly and sent out the data in a compressed signal stream. I just hoped that someone would find it before too long.

'I've done it.' I said without turning round. I still could not face them. 'We have about fifteen minutes until I must fire the main drive and plunge us into the oncoming vessel. Are we still all agreed that that is our plan?' I heard nothing. I did not want to turn round. 'I cannot hear your answers.' I added.

'Sorry.' Said Djon. 'I nodded; didn't you see me?'

'I cannot look at you because it is my finger on the button.'

'Ah.' Said Djon. I felt his hand on my shoulder. 'I understand. I agree.' There was a pause. 'Do you others agree?' There was another slight pause. 'They all agree Djim.' He kept his hand on my shoulder and then gripped me in a show of support. Then there was another warning call from the proximity alarm. There were two more objects moving towards us!

'What's that?' Asked Karon from somewhere.

'We have two more objects heading our way.' I said. 'I will just run a check to see what they are, hold on.' A quick check proved that they were also man-made vessels and not space debris. 'Oh.' I said.

'What's the matter Djim?' Asked Djon, coming up beside me again.

'There are two more space vessels and not just debris and they are heading our way. What do we do?' This time I did turn round and look imploringly at the others. We could only take out one of them and possibly not even one as soon as we fired up our drive one of the vessels would shoot us out of space before we could pick up any speed.

'What do you mean?' Asked Terens. 'We still carry on as we were. We ram the original vessel. We at least take one of them out. I suggest we leave it just a little bit later so that if we are taken out then there should still be enough velocity and mass left to do some real damage.' He looked around at us for support for his idea. I was stunned that he should still be thinking like that. There was a pause.

'I suppose we have no alternative.' Said Djon. 'It must be better than what they are likely to do to us.'

'Why?' Asked Ruuth. 'If they wanted to kill us why haven't they shot at us already?'

'They don't know who we are yet. We have no identification beacons online. They won't know until they dock.'

'OK then.' Said Ruuth. 'I go along with Terens. I can see no alternative. They tricked us last time, take them out!'

'What if it isn't them?' Asked Karon. Such a simple but obvious question that made us all think. How did we know it was them? 'We could be destroying an innocent vessel.'

'What do you suggest we do?' I asked.

'You could try asking them.' She retorted sharply.

'It is the only sure way.' Added Karon after a moment's reflection. 'We cannot kill innocent people.'

'Shall I ask them then?' I asked. Even Terens nodded. I turned back to the control panel but before I could do anything a message sounded in the control room.

'Unidentified vessel, this is the police! Do not attempt to flee or change direction. Prepare to dock.'

'What shall I do?' I asked. 'Shall I ram them now?'

'Wait a minute!' Cried Ruuth, grabbing my arm. 'What did they say?'

'They said do not attempt to flee.' I said.

'No, no who did they say they were?' That threw me; I had not registered who they were. Finally, Karon spoke.

'They said they were the police.' She said calmly, as if talking to a small child. That fact had not registered with me and I had to admit I had never even thought that the police would be out in deep space. There would be so few vessels out here as most people used the portals.

'How can we be sure they are the police?' Asked Terens. He was asking the question that was running round in my thought. Why would the police be out here where no one was normally?

'I have no idea.' I muttered. 'Anyone can say they are the police out here though.'

'It is a bit risky to try anything if they are.' Said Djon. 'Let us try another tack. Can we rig up something to blow up this vessel after a short…'

'I know.' I butted in. 'I can arrange for the main drive to fire after a predetermined time. If we were still docked then that would give them a real problem. It might not destroy them, but it is safer than trying to find a time bomb. I don't think there is time for that.'

'Don't forget what happened last time you attempted to get a drive to fire remotely.' Said Djon.

'Excuse me.' I retorted hotly. 'It was that dreadful moon hopper that you had butchered that caused the problem. My…' I was stopped mid flow by Ruuth who put her hand on my arm.

'Calm down. There is not time for this. Just do it!' Even Djon nodded and smiled at me.

'Unidentified vessel unless you respond we will have no alternative but to fire a disablement shot.'

'Oh, ghas!' I cried and opened up a communication channel. 'This is Jergan EN4-31 we understand. We will not change direction or speed and will prepare to dock.'

'Commencing docking approach and procedure.'

'They certainly sound like the police.' Said Ruuth.

'And what is that supposed to mean?' Growled Terens.

'They sounded like the police I have come across before. That is what I mean.' She scowled at Terens. 'It is the way they speak.'

'So those people that captured us at the hidden portal were not police?'

'They did not speak like any police that I have ever met. Now get on with it.'

'OK, I will set up the drive to fire after a while Djim, just in case. You can easily cancel it can't you?'

'Sure, it is not a problem. OK, I will arrange for it to fire an hour after we dock. We should have a very good idea if they are the police by then.'

As the image of the vessel grew closer in the forward vision enhancer, I took the time for docking from the data scrolling down the screen and added an hour and then set the drive to fire automatically and to keep firing until the fuel was spent. If they were not the police, it would give them a real problem. It would also be more difficult to find than a bomb.

'It is done. Now let us see who they are.' I spent the rest of the time watching the hull of the approaching vessel get larger and larger. I also wondered just how my mother and family were doing. What were they thinking after I disappeared so abruptly and Djon's office had a large hole in its side? What did the rest of the planet think? I had a nasty feeling that maybe someone may have covered up the whole thing, so no one knows what happened. But why I should think that I had no idea. I then found myself wondering just how far we were from Enceladus 421 and that made me feel homesick for my old home planet and guessed that the others must be feeling the same. It was strange, but up to then I had not really felt homesick. I had certainly missed my old home planet but that was to be expected. It would be wonderful just to be able to go home and give my mother a big hug and return to normal life. Now I ached to see home again. What had happened to the galaxy? Why did we have to hide? Why were the police boarding us?

There seemed to be even more unanswerable questions than before.

Why was the V20 not working either? Everything else seemed to be working perfectly so I could not understand why the V20 should fail. The one single dot still hung tantalisingly in the bluish orb but still no details appeared. Then another dot appeared!

'Look.' I said. 'Another star has appeared in the V20.' The others stopped looking at the forward vision enhancer and looked at the V20. As they did so another dot appeared and then another. Then dots began to appear rapidly. Then details appeared against the first dot.

'Oh look.' Said someone.

'Oh.' Said Djon as the details were not meaningful but gibberish. 'That's odd.'

'The whole thing is odd.' Added Terens. 'why can no one recognise any star groupings and why does the V20 not work properly?'

'I don't know Terens.' I said. 'I wish I had an answer to that.'

Then the docking alarm chimed, the relevant dials and controls lit up, as the final approach began. I returned my attention to the screen and the docking data. Then there was the slight bump as final docking took place followed by the smaller thumps as the clamps snapped into place to lock us together.

'Move away from the control room and prepare to be boarded.' Came the terse command from the other vessel. We duly got up and left the control room and headed for the airlock bay. As we got there the airlock lights were flashing awaiting confirmation to open the hatch.

'OK, guys this is it.' I said as I lifted my arm and pressed the open hatch button. There was a hiss as the seals unlocked and the hatch irised open.

'Stand away from the hatch.' Came a harsh mechanical voice from the other vessel. In the gloom through the hatch opening, I could see dark suited inhuman looking figures move towards us. Although they appeared to have two arms and two legs their faces were strange goggle-eyed artificial masks. Were they human? Perhaps we had finally stumbled across the aliens? That would change things completely. I felt strangely awkward and rather frightened. My stomach tightened and my legs began to shake.

'This is the police.' Came a voice and then there was a flash of light.

– CHAPTER 12 –

I awoke in a small unfamiliar room. "Not again" was my first thought. This was the third time in as many days it seemed. It took a few moments longer for me to come round fully but the strange feeling of sickness hung on longer. I was able to get up and stand holding myself steady by placing a hand on the wall. I looked around the room.

It appeared to be a standard small room in a vessel except this one had a strong room look to it. There was no ornamentation and only a single bed but on the opposite wall there was a small basin and a toilet. That was an improvement on the rooms before. There was a very strong looking door but again this was different as it had a small, barred window in the upper part. Light streamed into the room from this window. It was a warm pleasant light and not the usual hard light of the smaller vessel. I worked my way rather unsteadily round to the door and looked out through the small window. There was a narrow corridor outside with a similar door opposite that was also closed. Above the other door there was a large painted number which was peeling and faded. I needed a drink. I looked round the room and noticed that the tap above the basin was marked 'drinking water'. Thankfully, I made my way round to the basin and drank deeply from the running water. Very quickly I became more stable on my feet and stronger. I stood up straight and stretched. Where was I? Then memories came flooding back. The flash of light – again!

I went back to the door and called out. I heard familiar voices call back. It seemed that we were all there and safe. Then footsteps sounded on the rubberised flooring. A young blond-haired woman came and stood in the doorway. She was short and stocky and was wearing a dark navy-blue uniform. There was the word police on her left breast pocket. She was definitely not an alien.

'Yes?' She said without ceremony.

'Why are we locked up like this?'

'You have been found in restricted space without any form of identification. You will all be questioned shortly.'

'We have our rights.'

'Not out here.' She said curtly and then turned and disappeared out of view. I heard Djon call out to be patient. Terens had already been called for questioning and had returned unharmed. They would work through us all in time. He was right. We talked as best we could and Djon said to keep quiet. I asked him if we should mention that we had timed the drive to fire. He cursed loudly and agreed. He told me to get someone immediately as he did not know how long we had been there. I called out again and kept calling until the blond-haired woman returned.

'You must let me back on board our vessel. We set the drive to fire after an hour and if I don't disarm it there could be serious trouble.'

'Hold on.' She said and disappeared. She returned shortly with two big, uniformed police officers.

'Get away from the door and face the wall.' The nearest one said. I did so. I was grabbed from behind and my hands shackled and then led out of the room. I was taken at a very quick pace back into our own vessel. It seemed odd to be back in such circumstances. I was rushed into the pilot's seat in the control room and the shackles unlocked. The two officers stepped back behind me.

'Do not try anything. We are armed and will fire at the slightest provocation. Now do what you have to do.'

'OK, OK. I just need a few minutes to disarm the drive.' With shaking hands I ran through the disarm procedure. I was sweating profusely as I had no idea how much longer there was. As I finished sat back and wiped the sweat from my forehead. The free part of the polymetal shackle banged against my head. 'I have finished. It is OK now.'

'Stand up and put your hands behind your back.' Ordered one of the officers. I did so and the shackle was locked again.

I was then returned to my room. There was food on a tray on the bed. After I had stopped shaking, I ate it all. Then I called to the others and told them it was disarmed safely.

After a long wait there was the sound of multiple footsteps that stopped outside my door. There was a thump as the lock and seals disengaged and the door swung open. Two large, uniformed police entered the room.

'Turn and face the wall.' Said the first. I did so and as I was standing there my hands were grabbed from behind and shackled together. 'Come with us.' He added and led me out into the corridor. I was eventually taken into a small office that contained a table and two seats one on each side of the table. There was nothing else in the room. I was seated in one of the seats and the shackles secured to the seat so that I could not get up again. I realised then that the seat was fixed to the floor and did not move. Someone else entered the room from behind me and came and sat down in the seat opposite. He put down a recording device on the table.

He also wore the dark navy-blue uniform but had extra symbols on his shoulder straps. He had a hard narrow face with a small but full mouth. His hair was orange brown and obviously had some form of substance on it to make it sit rigid on his head. It was combed very smartly and neatly and was short. He had a prominent side parting. His eyebrows were also orange brown and went straight across his face above dark blue eyes. The eyes stared straight at me in a searching way, they penetrated deep inside me. He wore his authority with a calm confidence. He did not speak for a while. I decided to remain quiet too.

'Why had you set the drive of your vessel to fire?'

'We didn't know who you were and were frightened.'

'We told you we were the police, and your sensors should have informed you of this.'

'Sorry.' I replied, and then added puzzled. 'What sensors are those?' He again looked at me quizzically without speaking for a while. He then must have decided that I was telling the truth and continued.

'All vessels have police identity sensors.' Was all he said.

'I'm sorry.' I said again. 'I have been a pilot for some time and have never heard of this.'

'Don't play the innocent with me!' He barked and banged his hand on the table. It made me jump back in my seat, restricted only by the shackles.

'Look.' I said, when I had managed to calm myself again. 'I am telling the truth. I have never heard of such a sensor. You may inspect our vessel and if you find it then please show me.' He sat back again and looked at me. He again seemed to be weighing up the situation. He sat forward.

'You set your drive to fire, that could have killed us all.'

'I know. We were prepared to give our lives if necessary.'

'Why?'

'We didn't know who you were or what you were going to do to us.'

'So, you keep saying. You at least were prepared to disarm the drive and that will stand you in good stead. Now, what is your name?'

'Djim Stone N421.'

'Unusual.' He said genuinely perturbed, or so I thought. 'Why the 421?'

'The galaxy is so big you need some way of knowing where people come from.' I was a little worried by his need to ask that question. No one else had ever questioned this, but there again I had never been questioned by the police before. Perhaps it was a standard response. He noticed my hesitation and looked at me for a long time.

'Do you have a job?'

'Yes, as I said, I am a pilot.'

'Oh, a good job. Was that on this Enceladus 421 planet?'

'Yes. This is the first time that I have left it.'

'Your family are from there?'

'Yes, my mother still lives there.'

Now what were you doing here?' He asked finally.

'We were lost. Our V20 was not working so we did not know where we were.' I decided not to say too much just yet as I could not be sure how far away our original captors were or how reliable these police were.

'So where were you going then?'

'I was just trying to get back home again.'

'And where is your home then?'

'Enceladus.' I knew immediately that I had said it that he did not believe me. 'Enceladus 421.' I added, hoping this would make him believe me. His expression did change but I still knew he did not fully trust my answer. He sat back in his seat looking at me quizzically then his face broke into a wry smile but not one of humour.

'You people amaze me.' He said. 'I cannot understand you at all. You must think I am stupid to believe that?'

'Not at all. We were completely lost.'

'That at least seems to be consistent with your colleagues' stories. But why you were lost concerns me.'

'I'm not sure I understand what you mean?'

'You were a long way from any portal in a restricted area of space.'

'We were completely lost and had no idea where we were or how we got there.'

'So, you keep saying. Why did your friends tell you not to say what you were originally looking for?'

'Pardon?'

'Don't pretend you don't know. We have listening devices in the cells, so we heard all that you have been saying.'

'Oh.'

'Are you going to tell me?'

'No.'

'I am sorry to hear that. If you are innocent, then you should not be withholding information.'

'We have done nothing wrong. You say we were in restricted space. There was nothing that we could see to tell us it was restricted. We did not know where we were so we could not find out how to get home. Perhaps you could tell us where we are.'

'I am not at liberty to give you that information, besides;

your sensors again should warn you that you are entering restricted space.' I opened my mouth to speak but decided against it and shut it again. He continued. 'And you are not in a position to be asking questions.' He leant forward again. 'What is the ring of pods surrounding your vessel?'

'It is a vessel-based portal.' I could see no reason to lie about it. They would soon find out what it was when they called in some experts. I knew enough that police could do that.

'Oh, really, and where did you get it?'

'We built it from parts that we obtained.'

'You built it?'

'Yes.' He pursed his small mouth even smaller until it became a circle and then he relaxed it again, so the colour returned to his lips. 'Your vessel is also damaged. Why?'

'It was an accident with another vessel. The main drive fired prematurely before we could gain a safe distance.' He sat impassively and gave no indication if he believed me. I felt uncomfortable.

'Why were you not showing any identification?'

'We thought there were people after us.' I realised as soon as I had spoken that it could give the game away. 'We had felt threatened and wanted to be sure we were safe before declaring our position.'

'Who were these people that you thought were after you?' He seemed more interested in this and had sat more forward his hands intertwined on the table. I was not sure how to answer, mainly because I had no idea who those people had been who had imprisoned us. It became rather odd that I did not know who they were. Djon seemed to know.

'I have no idea who they were or why?' He seemed extremely disappointed in my answer and relaxed his shoulders.

'What makes you think they were after you then?' I was digging a hole here and could find no way to get out. How much could this man be trusted? I had become very wary.

'I know it sounds daft and sitting here in your vessel it does now seem very silly but at the time it was very real to us. I did not know who they were and looking back it was probably just our imagination. In space you can get strange effects.' He seemed to be satisfied by the last statement and also rather disappointed again. He sighed.

'How did you get the Jergan?'

'I don't know. Djon obtained it before we left.' I was sure that answer would not put the others at risk. I knew Djon would not say anything stupid.

'Right, we will have to take you back to Gonfalon Royal for further questioning.' He said suddenly.

'I've not heard of that.'

'I'm not surprised.' He looked up to behind me. 'Return him to his cell. Thank you, Djim Stone, if that is your real name.'

'It is. Here; there is proof.' I pulled my pilot's licence out of my flight suit pocket and handed it to him. He looked from my digital likeness to me and then back again. He had a puzzled look on his face again.

'That seems to be your picture. I shall keep this for safe keeping until we planet. Thank you. Now return him to his cell.' He spoke the last line to the officers behind me. The shackle was unlocked from the chair and I was lifted off my seat and guided out of the room.

'Let me know if there is anything else you want to tell me.' The man called from behind me as I left the room. I was returned to the cell. I refused to call it my cell, as it was not. After I had been unshackled and the officers had left, I went and called to the others and gave them a brief idea of what happened and how they were listening to us. Djon said he had suspected. Then I went and lay down. It had been very tiring.

*

I awoke with a start. What had woken me? I sat up and listened. There was a quietness, but I could still discern the faint vibrations I knew were landing or docking manoeuvres. That must have been what woke me. I had become so attuned to a vessel's motions that the variations had even got through the state of sleep. I rubbed the sleep from my eyes and swung my legs out of the bed grabbing my clothes as I did so. I had not been given any night clothes. I quickly got dressed and staggered to the door. The view outside had not changed at all. I called out. Djon answered.

'What's happening Djim?'

'I think we are landing or docking. That's what it sounds like.'

'Do you know where we are?'

'He told me he was taking us back to Gonfalon Royal. Have you heard of it?'

'No, I haven't. Do you know any more than that?'

'No, not a thing. It looks like we will just have to wait and see.' There was not any more to say and it was difficult to hear what Djon was saying. I went back to the bed and lay down again. It would not be long before we would disembark.

I was right as very shortly there was a disturbance in the corridor, and I could hear Terens muffled voice moving past my door. I leapt up but could see nothing as the window in the door had been covered by a screen. I jumped back as the door seals hissed open and the lock thumped open. The door was opened a bit and a familiar voice called out.

'Move away from the door and face the wall!' I did so. My hands were shackled behind me and a bag was put over my head again. I was gripped by my arms and ushered out of the room. I tried to work out where I was or what was happening but as it was so unfamiliar, I was unable to. I eventually just had to relax and let the situation unfold.

I knew at one point that we were on a shuttle of some description for a short journey and then straight into another room. I knew at once that we were now on a planet even though we had not been outside at all.

'Face the wall.' Said the familiar voice. As I did so the shackles were removed, and the bag taken from off my head. It was such a relief to be able to breathe properly again and feel the cool air on my face. I shook my head to settle my hair. I heard the door shut behind me and no seals hissed shut! I spun round. I was in another cell!

It was square with no window and two doors, one with a tiny viewing porthole set deep into the upper part of the door. There was no handle on that door but other did have a small round knob. I went over and immediately tried it. The knob turned freely in my grip and I pulled open the door. All I found though was a tiny room with a toilet and a small basin. I shut the door again. The only other object in the room was a hard looking bed covered with sheets and a thin blanket. I was so annoyed at being shut up in a cell again that I threw myself onto the bed and covered my head with my hands and just lay there for a long while.

Eventually I calmed down and finally turned over to stare at the ceiling. I could not believe that after all this time we were still being locked up. We had done nothing wrong! I would not mind if we had done something wrong. Had the galaxy gone mad?

The police had not given anything away and had not said why we had been incarcerated except for the odd business about being in a restricted part of the galaxy. Surely, we had not gone straight back to the hidden portal? No, there were no police in that area, only the lying people who had sent us out into space. Things just did not make sense. Then I found myself looking for patterns in the marks and stipple finish of the ceiling. There was an old man with long wispy hair, or so it appeared.

I sat up. I was feeling very odd and then realised again that I was no longer on the vessel but on a planet, no wonder I felt rather heavy and lethargic. I lay back down and listened. It was very quiet. Very quiet for a planet. I could not hear the winds or the constant rumble of drives powering vessels up to the portal or any other various noises. In my job I had heard of a lot of the planets but never this one. What was it called again? I could not remember now. Then I became concerned where the others were and what was happening to them.

I heard a noise coming from outside the cell. I tried to make out what it was but without success. It was a slow quiet hum.

A light in the ceiling above the locked door came on, making a pool of bright light on the floor in front of it. A mechanical voice also sounded from a hidden speaker.

'Move away from the door and lay on the bed.' I knew then that they did not have any surveillance cameras in the room as I was already on the bed. I smiled to myself as it gave me a small bit of knowledge that may help me later on. The lock snapped open, and the door swung slowly open on well oiled hinges. I sat up on one elbow to see what was going to happen next.

A bright light flooded the room as the door opened and meant that I could not see what was outside. A long thin table slid silently into the room. It looked hard and was only just off the floor being supported on four small wheels. Behind it was a man in a full suit but not any I had seen before. It had a large headpiece with a big window for him (or her?) to look out of and it was all of one piece. I could not see into the headpiece because of the backlight.

'We need to carry out a medical inspection as you have been discovered in restricted space and were unable to say where you had come from. Before we can let you come in contact with others you will need to be examined to ensure that you do not bring any infection with you. Please lie down on your bed face down with your hands behind your back. Thank you.'

'Why do I have to do that?' I asked, almost knowing the answer but I did not want to just do as I was told.

'To protect the doctor and to protect you. We cannot take any chances with prisoners.'

'I will not try anything.' I knew it was a waste of time but tried it anyway. There was a pause.

'Do as you are instructed, or you will face a prison sentence for failing to obey a police officer!' I decided that perhaps I had better now do as I was asked.

The figure in the doorway stood impassively, watching me. I slowly turned over and did as I was told. I heard movement behind me, and my hands were shackled. A hand was placed on my head and it was pressed down onto the bed. Something metallic was placed against the back of my neck and there was a sharp pinprick and then a warm glow throughout my whole body. Then something else was placed against my neck and held there for some time.

The next thing I knew I was laying on the thin hard bed near the floor. I looked up. The room was empty. I did not know how long I had been unconscious. My hands were no longer shackled. I sat up and went back to the other bed as it was more comfortable. I felt the back of my neck and could only feel a tiny spot. My mouth felt dry. It was then that I noticed the drink and food on a small table by the door. I ate and drank until satiated.

What had that all been about I wondered? I had never heard of such a treatment before. We travelled the galaxy without any need to check for infection.

There was another thing too; the police uniform did not look like any that I had seen before. Not that I had seen very many! I wish I had looked closer at them so I could remember something about them. I vowed to look much closer next time I saw one.

I then found myself thinking of my mother and what she was doing and how she was feeling. I just hoped that she was alright. If any of those people tried to harm her, I thought, I would do anything to find them and bring my own form of justice to them. How I was going to do this I had no idea. I lay back and immediately fell asleep.

I was woken some time later by the metallic voice again.

'Move over to the door and stand in the light.' I immediately got up off the bed and went and stood in the light. It felt warm on the top of my head. The lock on the door snapped open and the door swung slowly open. There was no one outside only a bright corridor with a cage around the opening.

'Step into the cage.' Again, I was obedient and as I did so the door to the cell closed silently behind me. I then saw that I was not in a corridor but on the sheer face of a wall covered with doors. How had they got me here without me remembering? I had no idea how. As nothing was happening immediately, I had time to look around. There was another wall opposite about the same distance again as the width of the cage I found myself in. I looked up and saw a ceiling a few floors up. Looking down as far as I could see the walls gradually disappeared into an unlit gloom. The only light came from the roof of the cage I was in.

There was a quiet beep from somewhere and then the cage started moving down the wall past other doors identical to the one that was on the cell that had held me. What a depressing place to be. The cage moved slowly but smoothly on well greased runners set into the stone wall. I noticed how damp the wall looked, and every crack had a green slimy growth protruding from it. The air had a slight damp smell to it too. After running down the wall for some time passing any number of floors it finally came to a stop at a floor level. There were soft mechanical sounds, and the cage began moving horizontally, again quietly and smoothly. It then stopped by another door which slowly opened onto another cage but this time there was a larger well-lit room beyond. I stepped through the doorway into another identical cage and the door closed quietly behind me. I was surprised to find I was in one of a number of cages and in each one was the rest of the crew. Djon was next to me. He put is hand through the bars to grab my arm.

'Good to see you again Djim. Are you alright?'

'I am fine apart from being annoyed at being shut up in a cell again. What about you, and the others?'

'I am fine and so are the others.' I could hear them all call out to me.

'Where are we Djon, I don't know this place at all?'

'I have no idea, and neither does Terens and he has travelled extensively throughout the galaxy, so I was relying on his knowledge. He has not seen nor heard of anything like this before.'

'Why are the police holding us like this, what have we done wrong?'

'I wish I knew. All they told me was that we were in restricted space without any identification beacon. I have never heard of any restricted spaces in the galaxy before, and neither has Terens. Hopefully, we should find out soon.'

'You don't think they have sent for those people who captured us before do you?'

'Sorry, Djim, I have no idea. Let us wait and see. At least with the police here we can hopefully get some proper justice.'

'I hope so too.' I began to take in the room. The cages were at floor level which was some hard material in a very subtle checkerboard pattern. The room was not large, maybe four metres wide but much longer, I assumed so it could hold more of these cages. There were definitely a large number of criminals in this part of the galaxy. Something I had never even heard of before. I thought crime was almost unheard of, so this was even more bizarre. The room was not high maybe three metres with a glowing white ceiling which was presumably the light source. There were a series of doors in the opposite wall and a long table in the centre with a row of seats behind it with tall backs that had a motif set in them which I could not identify.

'What is the motif on the seats Djon?'

'No idea. And neither have the others seen anything like it either.' We fell silent again and then one of the doors opened and the policeman that had questioned me came in. He was quite short I realised then and it was heightened by the man who followed him into the room. They both wore what were obviously policeman's uniforms, but the latter had even more decoration on the shoulders and other parts of the uniform. He was not only tall but held himself erect and had a presence and was sure of his position in society. He had very dark skin, a narrow face with full lips. He wore a thin black moustache well trimmed with another tiny tuft below his bottom lip and another bit of well trimmed hair on his chin. His eyes were what took the attention, being very dark. So dark that the pupils could not be discerned, the whites of his eyes had a yellow tinge. His black eyebrows curved down close to his eyes at the nose which gave him an almost sinister look. His black hair was cut short.

The first man with the reddish hair sat at the table and a screen popped up from the table surface. The light from the screen gave his face an unhealthy hue. The tall dark man came over to the cages and I lost sight of him as he went to the far end. I could hear him walking towards me and soon came into sight walking slowly along the line of cages. As he came closer, I could see that he was behind a screen of glass material that stayed directly between him and the cages. He finally stopped at me and gave me a penetrating gaze then turned and walked back to the desk and sat beside the red-haired policeman.

'What are ....?' Began Djon but he was cut short as the dark-skinned policeman raised his hand for silence. The two policemen talked quietly together for a few moments with the dark skinned one looking up at each of us in turn. The first one then got up and left. The dark-skinned policeman finally spoke to us in a rich strong voice that was guttural at the same time. It was as if he was not speaking his own language.

'Good morning. I am Chief Inspector Abba Bin Mclaad, head of the Force Here on Gonfalon Royal. I am informed that you were found in restricted space without any form of identification beacon and that you did not have any reasonable answer to your being there. I ask the pilot.' He paused. 'Djim Stone, to give me the reason for your presence there.' He looked at me with the dark penetrating eyes. I looked cross at Djon.

'We could not give any answer for fear for our lives, not knowing who you were or how reliable you were.'

'I asked why you were found in restricted space.'

'I am sorry. We did not know where we were. We had only just managed to get back into the galaxy. We had no means of knowing where we were or how to accurately direct our flight. The equipment we were using was very new to us and we were unsure how to use it.' He looked at me again with a penetrating stare. Then he spoke again.

'You say you were in fear of your lives. Of whom were you afraid?' I looked back at Djon.

'Just tell him the whole truth Djim. We have nothing to lose now.'

'We do not know their names and do not yet trust that they will not outrank you and force you to hand us over to them.'

'That is an even more obtuse answer. No one has the power here to force us to do anything and no one outranks me here. I am not about to hand you over to anyone. I am the authority here and I uphold the rule of law. I have the power to have you punished for withholding information from the police.' I looked at Djon again. He told me to give the whole story. I did. I began with Enceladus and the moon hopper and then the Jergan, going to Midnight twenty and then Fyrest Prime. How we went to the library on Fyrest and then left to go to Ghandza but then straight on to Geryon where we met Karon, and she joined us after getting fearful of the strangers. Then I told him about finding the hidden portal and then being captured by the people who did not give us any names but told us about the aliens and then sent us out into space, but we suspected that it had all been a lie and they had sent us out to die because we knew too much of something. Then we put together the vessel portal and managed to get back to the galaxy but because the V20 was not working we did not know where we were. Then his policemen picked us up. The inspector sat impassive throughout the whole story listening intently.

'So, you say that you three come from Enceladus 421 and that Karon comes from Geryon and Terens here is from Dardanus-2?'

'Yes, that is correct. Why?'

'We find this very odd because there are no such planets in the galaxy!' He looked at us. I felt a shock of cold in the pit of my stomach. What was going on here? I looked across at Djon and could see by the expression on his face that he was as surprised as me.

'There must be some mistake.' Said Ruuth from somewhere down the line. 'I lived and worked on Enceladus 421 for some time.'

'So, you say.'

'Look.' I said. 'Just get a V20 and we can show you where we come from.'

'You do not tell me to 'get' anything.' He replied with some force.

'I'm sorry. What I mean is, if we had a V20 we could show you exactly where we come from.'

'What is a V twenty?' He replied. That threw me completely. Where were we? Everyone had heard of a V20, it was the standard piece of space equipment.

'A galaxolabe.' I added.

'Ah, a galaxolabe.' Understanding dawned upon his thought. 'I think we can obtain one of those.' He looked back to the screen then back at us. 'Yes, we will have one shortly. Now, while we wait tell me about these people who captured you. Can you describe them?'

'Yes, most definitely. The ones we have seen have had a 'ploughed field' hairstyle, there was one with no hair at all apart from a tiny bit under his bottom lip, and one had very short spikey blond hair which did not look natural. The last one had shoulder length brown locks and a fuzz on his chin. They have all generally been large men with brown coloured skin and sometimes an oily look to the skin. One even had clothes that did not appear elsewhere in the galaxy and had small shiny beads in his ears. They also carried frisson bolt guns and looked as though they would use them on us if necessary.'

'Thank you. That is a brief description and to hear that these people carry frisson bolt guns is indeed bad news as they are banned for use against humans.'

'Yes, we know; that was why we were so concerned.' A door opened and another police officer came in with a silver box in his hand. He placed it carefully in the centre of the table and obviously was trying to get it to fit into a socket of some sort. Finally, it went. He stood up and left the room after nodding to the inspector. As soon as he had gone the familiar bluish orb sprang into life above the table. Then it grew and grew and grew until it was at least one and a half metres in diameter! I had never seen a V20 orb that big before. The stars suddenly appeared as millions of tiny dots held within the orb.

There was the usual list of numbers and names beside some of the dots.

But it did not look right!

I looked across at Djon to see what he was thinking. He also was staring at the galaxolabe with a puzzled expression on his face. His mouth was silently saying 'what'. I could not see the others but guessed that they were as bemused as us.

The galaxy in the orb looked different!

'Now, give me the portal reference code for your Planet Enceladus.' Said the inspector, looking up at me, his hands hovering over the galaxolabe controls.

'Something is wrong.' I replied. 'The galaxy does not look right.'

'OK, we will come back to that after we try and find your portal. Let me have the portal code.' Tentatively I gave him the code. He typed it in, and a red cross appeared in the instruction box indicating a mismatch. Something was wrong!

He looked up at me and then across at Karon. 'And where did you say you came from?' He asked her.

'Geryon.' She said quietly. He looked at me for the portal code. I gave it to him and again he typed it in and again came up the cross.

'No!' Said Karon. 'There must be something wrong. Where is my home?'

'Do you still stick to your story?' He asked, looking at Djon.

'Yes, of course, why would we change it? Look, it is the truth and not a story. What have you done to the V20?'

'I have done nothing to the galaxolabe. Perhaps if you gave me the region of the galaxy your planets are in it might help?'

'There are no regions in the galaxy.' I said. 'The portal and the planet are all that is needed, there is nothing else out there to be a region of.'

'You cannot even point to me where you think your planet may be?' He again looked at me surprisingly not with any anger or rancour. He genuinely seemed to want to help us.

'I'm sorry.' I replied. 'I am unable to recognise the shape

of the galaxy. Can you rotate the image for me? Perhaps that would help.'

'OK.' He did so, and the image rotated slowly above the table and I stared intently at it looking for anything that I recognised, but there was nothing! I could not believe this, what had happened to our galaxy? Perhaps this was a bad dream, and we would eventually wake up? It eventually came back to where it started and there was nothing recognisable at all!

'Ghas! I don't believe it!' I cried. 'By Erebus what have you done to our galaxy?'

'I have done nothing to the galaxy. What are those strange words you use too?'

'Sorry, which ones?'

'Gas, and erebus.'

'They are swear words. Ghas I do not know the origin of, but Erebus is the black moon orbiting Enceladus 421 and is very depressing hence using it as a swear word.'

'This is all very interesting, but does not get us any nearer to finding your planet.'

'Perhaps if you brought the V20 from our vessel it would explain something?'

'That is indeed a good suggestion.' He looked into the screen and nodded. 'While we are waiting perhaps now would be a good time to discuss the results of your examinations.' He looked back at the screen and then back at us. 'I am pleased to say that you are all in good health and do not carry any infection that we can detect. There is one thing however that does concern us. All of you have in your bloodstreams a chemical that we cannot identify. We are not sure why it is there.'

'All of us?' Said Djon.

'Yes, all of you have the identical chemical.' He looked at us intently. I looked across at Djon, he looked back at me and shrugged his shoulders.

'What is it?' Asked Ruuth.

'We do not know for sure at present but are running tests. The nearest thing that I can equate it to is some form of truth drug.'

'A what?' Asked Terens from somewhere down the line.

'Have you never heard of a truth drug?' He said, turning to Terens.

'No.'

'And have any of you others heard of such a thing?' We all shook our heads. He looked surprised. 'It is not of course but very much like it. It is more like..' He stopped unsure of what to say next. 'No, a truth drug is the nearest thing. We are not sure what effect it has but it is definitely not a natural chemical found in the human body. It has been introduced and for some time we would deduce. Who would have done such a thing and to all of you?' There was a silence.

'No one we know would have done anything like that. The only people who would have done such a thing were the ones who sent us here.' I said finally.

'It has been in your bodies for some years so think back further than the recent events.' He looked up as someone came in the room with our V20 and placed it on the table next to the other.

The inspector studied it for a while and then typed in some commands. The familiar bluish orb sprang into life but now seemed tiny by comparison. I was amazed to see that it was now full of tiny dots just like it used to be. But what had happened to it? Was it our V20? Perhaps as it had appeared so quickly it was not actually ours but a substitute. For what purpose they would bother to substitute our V20 I could not fathom. The dots though were not identified by the usual lists of planets and portals. There were just the dots. It was as if the V20 did not know what to make of the information it was receiving.

Then gradually I became aware that there was something wrong with our V20 as well although at first, I could not put my finger on it. Then suddenly it became all too obvious what was wrong. Our V20 was showing the same star patterns as the giant V20 beside it!

'No!' I cried, clutching my head in an almost comical expression of horror. 'What has happened to our V20?'

'What do you mean?' Asked the inspector, an expression of concern on his face.

'Our V20 is showing the same star patterns as yours!'

'Of course it will, all V twenties as you put it, will show the same star pattern as we are all in the same galaxy.'

'But it's not our galaxy.' He sat up when I said that, and it surprised me. He looked intently at me for a long time before looking back at the screen and talking quietly for a moment. There was a pause.

'I will make an exception for you people.' He finally said and I did not know what he was talking about. But suddenly there was a loud clunk on the cage and the front of it swung away from me! 'Come and join me at the table.' He said waving his hands to the chairs ranged along the long table in front of him. 'Do not try and be clever.'

It took me a while to step out of the cage because I still could not quite believe that it was now open. Eventually tentatively I stepped out into the room and walked cautiously to the table. The others were with me and together we pulled out the seats and at down opposite him. I looked across at Djon to see that he had just the same puzzled look on his face too. The whole atmosphere of the room seemed to have changed. What had happened?

'I trust that you are all telling the truth.' He began. 'This means we have a slight quandary here if you insist on saying that you do not recognise the galaxy. What is your galaxy called?' I was stumped at that one and could not answer straight away.

'It's just called the galaxy.' Said Ruuth finally.

'Really?' He said slowly and paused for a moment. 'Are you sure there is no other name for it?' There was another silence.

'No.' I said finally. 'As I a pilot I would know if there was another name.' He looked at the screen beside him again and then back at us in turn.

'Have you ever heard of the Milky Way?' Another long pause.

'No.' I said for the group.

'That is very odd for that it what this galaxy is called, and not only that, but it is also the only inhabited galaxy in the universe that we know of.'

I felt my whole world suddenly collapse around me. It was as if someone had taken my most favourite dream and smashed it before my eyes laughing. My whole sense of existence had become a lie. If that was the case, then what was going on?

He continued. 'Which in that case brings us to the question of where you people have come from?' He leaned forward and smiled at us.

– CHAPTER 13 –

'What do you mean?' Asked Djon.

'I mean.' Replied the inspector patiently. 'That your answers are inconsistent with what we know of the galaxy! For instance, Enceladus is a moon orbiting Saturn in The Solar System and is uninhabited.' I could not believe what I was hearing. Who was this person to tell us where we knew we came from. But at the same time there was a nagging thought at the back of my mind that I could not quite get hold of. A thought that somehow knew what he was saying.

'But we come from Enceladus 421. I can assure you of that and it definitely had the 421. I am unaware of any other planet of the same name.'

'Interesting.' He looked intently at me for what seemed a very long time. 'That is then very interesting indeed. We do not know of any planet named Enceladus 421. We also do not know of any names that have number suffixes as do yours. The only people we know who have numbers are prisoners!'

I looked across at our V20 still resolutely showing the same star patterns as the big galaxolabe but without the reference numbers. Something began to stir in my thinking, but I could not get it to form enough into a cogent thought or argument. I knew it would come eventually so I relaxed again hoping that the idea, if allowed room, would be able to formulate itself into rational thinking.

'Are you saying?' Asked Karon suddenly from down the line. 'That someone is deliberately introducing a drug into all of us?'

'Most definitely yes. There is no doubt that the chemical is not natural, and you all have similar amounts of it in your bloodstreams. How it got there we do not know.'

'Do you know how long it has been inside us?' Asked Ruuth.

'It would appear well entrenched which gives us to believe that it has been administered a long time.'

'For all of us?'

'Yes.'

'In that case.' Continued Ruuth, and I knew from the tone of her voice that she was onto something. 'It is much bigger than you think, because Karon comes from a completely different planet to us and only joined us a short while ago!' The inspector sat up, suddenly interested.

'That is very interesting indeed. If what you say is true, then this drug is not just limited to one planet.'

'The chances of us coming across another planet also with this drug is.... what?' Asked Djon.

'I would imagine very small. Even smaller would be the chance of taking on board the only person on that planet who has the drug. So, we must deduce that at least two planets have this as a matter of course but for what purpose?' He sat back again deep in thought. 'And where are these planets?' He was not asking us a question but more talking to himself. He looked at the giant galaxolabe as if it held the answer to his question. 'Djim Stone, tell me more of your home planet.' He looked back at me expectantly. I told him what I knew of Enceladus and the mining, the raw materials that I delivered up to the portal and the food and water that I brought back down on the return journey.

'Water!' He said suddenly. 'Why do you have to have water delivered?'

'Because the water on Enceladus is undrinkable.' That surprised him. He turned to the screen again.

'May we examine your vessel?' He asked.

'Of course you may.' Said Djon, for all of us. I knew we had no choice in the matter actually.

'Thank you.' He again turned to the screen and nodded again. He must be communicating with someone else via that screen I thought.

We spent the best part of the day in interrogation, seemingly getting nowhere. No matter how we tried we could not make sense of the questions and the inspector could make no sense of the answers. Then he surprised us by asking 'Do you swear by your God that your answers are the truth?' His question was followed by a pause. None of us spoke. 'Well?' He asked.

'Sorry.' I replied. 'What is this god you mention?'

'I do not believe you people. You seem to know of nothing. Well God is the supreme creator, the infinite ever present mind and power of good. Does that answer your question?' We were again stunned into silence.

Finally, in exasperation he said 'Who is ready for an evening meal?' He asked out of the blue. There was an immediate chorus of agreement here was something we could all agree on. 'Right then, follow me.' He stood up.

– CHAPTER 14 –

One of the doors opened and two police officers entered and stood on either side of the doorway.

'Please come with me.' Said the inspector and went out through the door. We all followed, Djon in front with Ruuth and Karon behind him and with Terens and me bringing up the rear. The two policemen fell in behind me. I found myself in a narrow corridor which appeared to be made of rock. The walls certainly appeared to be formed from rock which had been hacked out to form this corridor. It was not dark as there were many tiny pinpoints of light in the ceiling. The floor of the corridor appeared to be made out of well compacted earth, which was now firm and shiny with use. It seemed very surprising, going from the well-appointed room with all the modern appliances to this crude corridor. The light at the end of the corridor quickly grew into what I knew instantly was sunlight, but different to what I was used to.

We stepped outside onto a large area paved with huge flat stone slabs neatly jointed with the tiniest of joints. In front of us was the most amazing vista of mountains blue and pale in the distance. I could tell that we were high up, perhaps on the side of a mountain. The paved area was bordered with a stone wall that had large pockets that contained tall trees rustling gently in the breeze. It was a warm and pleasant breeze, clean and dust free. I found it difficult being outside and not wrapped up as was normal. The inspector turned and immediately noticed our reluctance to move further away from the doorway.

'What is wrong?' He asked returning to us as we stood huddled together like frightened animals.

'This is very odd to me.' I said. 'At home we never went outside without the dust suit and goggles, even the doors here do not have dust seals.'

'Really?' He was genuinely surprised again at our answer. 'We will discuss this further over dinner if you can manage to drag yourselves away from the rockface. It is not far. Just around the corner in fact.' I looked to where he was pointing, a small flight of stone steps that disappeared down and round the corner over to the left where the rockface ended in a sheer almost vertical edge that went up and up. I followed the edge of the rock up into the blue sky until I saw a metal lip at the top. Over the edge of the lip was the hull of a space vessel. Our vessel! I knew it was ours because of the damage to the hull which I knew intimately after spending all those hours repairing it on Geryon. The steps seemed to lead off down into nothing as all I could see was the edge of the rockface and the edge of the paved area on which we were standing. There was another wall of rock, but it was about two hundred meters away from the edge of the area. I plucked up courage to follow the inspector. He had already started walking towards the steps encouraging us to follow. The others also moved after I set off but kept close to each other. Only Karon strode off purposefully after the inspector. He disappeared down the steps followed by Karon. As I reached the steps I could see that the gap between the rock faces was not as deep as it appeared. The steps ran down to a wide green area between the rock faces and was set back in a sheltered cove. The rock faces curved round behind the green area and were in fact just one continuous wall of jagged rock. It took only moments to be down on the green area. The green was a small, short plant that covered the floor of the cove entirely. In the middle was a long table with a white cloth covering it that billowed gently in the warm breeze. The heat radiated off the face of the rock.

Surrounding the area were trees of more differing types. This was so unusual to see trees of different types on one planet!

I knelt down and touched the short green tufts of the plant. I could see it was made up of tiny individual green shoots packed densely together. As I walked past the trees to the table I noticed the leaves of the trees. They were of different shapes and colours. I looked around in wonderment as I walked slowly to the table, just unable to quite take in all this novel information.

The table was covered with plates and cutlery and dishes of steaming food obviously just put out. There were clean glasses sparkling in the sunlight.

'Please sit down and enjoy the food while it is still hot.' Said the inspector. 'We will talk.' He took his own advice and sat down. We needed no second invitation and joined him. There was not much talking at first as we ate and drank. Again, the food reminded me of the food on that hateful vessel. It made me stop.

'Is something wrong Mr Stone?' Asked the inspector.

'No, it's just that this food reminds me of the food we had in that vessel.' The others nodded in agreement. The inspector looked at us with an enigmatic look. 'And why is that?' He asked. I looked around at the others to garner support as I tried to formulate the reason in my thought.

'This food and the food on that....vessel are very much the same in that it has more flavour...'

'And texture.' Butted in Karon, helpfully.

'And texture,' I continued, 'than we were used to at home. It is difficult to explain.' The others nodded. The Inspector shrugged and could not come up with a reason. There was a pause.

'May I ask a question?' I asked.

'Surely.'

'This does not seem much like a police station nor you a policeman.' The inspector then threw back his head and laughed loudly and freely until tears were beginning to trickle down his cheeks. Finally, he managed to calm down enough to speak.

'Pardon my laughter. You are right of course this is no ordinary police station, and I am no ordinary policeman. In that you are quite correct. I am sorry to have laughed at your question when you were so correct in your assumption. None of us here are your ordinary planetary police. We have a very distinct role out here. Later this evening when it is dark.' He stopped and was obviously deep in thought for a few moments. 'Pardon me, I was thinking if tonight would show what

I wanted and fortunately it does. Later this evening when it is dark, we will come out and star gaze for a while.' He stopped again. 'I shall explain then I think. Until now enjoy your meal and tell me more of your story.' He sat back and crossed his arms as if to emphasise that he had finished. There were a few moments awkward silence as we thought what to say. The Inspector filled it with another question.

'This business of not going outside without a dustsuit did you say?' Relieved to have something to say I spoke up quickly.

'Yes, that is correct. On our Planet, Enceladus 421 the air is full of dust – almost all of the time. You never go outside without a dustsuit otherwise it gets into everything, eyes, ears, nose, mouth, underclothes. It is very itchy I can tell you.'

'All windows and doors have dust seals.' Added Djon. 'To keep the dust out of the living and working units.'

'So, you never go outside without a dustsuit?'

'No.'

'This then must seem very odd to you?'

'Yes, it does.'

'That is also something I have never heard of. Your planet gets more and more intriguing by the minute. Now tell me more of your reason for being here.' There was another pause then the Inspector asked us what date it was. So much had happened that I had to think back for a moment or two.

'It is, I think, about the 15th May And gave him the year as well just for luck.' I finally said, not sure of his response or the reason for his question. His eyebrows rose in surprise.

'Well.' He said. 'That is just about right. It is actually the 18th. That means you must come from this galaxy somewhere. There are still huge areas that we thought were not inhabited but we could be wrong there. I suggest you look at your V20 in detail to find the part of the galaxy you call home.'

'We will indeed.' Said Djon and leaned over to me conspiratorially and whispered in my ear.

'Shall we tell him what we were really looking for?' I looked back into his kind grey eyes. I nodded. He turned back to the inspector and coughed slightly before speaking.

'We have one thing that we have not yet spoken about.' He began nervously.

'Yes?'

'We were looking for something that it appeared others did not want us to look for or find.'

'And that was?'

'Ultima Thule.'

The inspector looked blankly at Djon. 'And what may I ask is Ultima Thule?' This time it was Djon who looked askance.

'You don't know?'

'I have never heard of this thing.'

'It is not a thing it is a planet, our original planet.'

'I thought you said you came from Enceladus?'

'We do. No, what we mean is that we were looking for the original planet that mankind originated from.'

'You mean Earth?'

There was another stunned silence as we took in the fact that this man was not in the slightest taken aback by our quest. Then the stunned silence went on longer as the realisation sank in that he had said a completely different planet name.

'What planet did you say?' I finally managed to ask.

'Earth. The home planet of man.' I looked across at Djon, who was for once in his life at a loss for words. He sat there open mouthed in a comical way. The others were similarly shocked into silence.

'Are you sure?' I managed to ask again. The inspector had a broad grin on his face by this time.

'Of course I am sure; it is the well documented history of mankind. Why do you query this?'

'I, er.' I began, not quite sure what to say. 'We only know the original planet as Ultima Thule.' Was all I could manage.

'Interesting.' He said. 'And who told you all this incorrect fact?'

'No one in particular.' Said Terens. 'It is just common knowledge. Well, it is common knowledge where we come from but I have to admit that I am not surprised now that you have a different answer.'

Djon could contain himself no longer. 'Please sir, can you tell me where this planet Earth is and how far away it is and can we visit?'

'I'm sorry that will have to be dealt with later, now we need to find out where you have come from. Because at the moment your story does not hold much water and will not stand up in a court of law. Talking of water. You say you had to import your water for the whole planet. Is this correct?' He stopped Djon in his tracks by raising his hand and giving Djon a long hard look. Djon sunk back in his seat but I knew he was seething inside.

'Yes, it is.' Said Ruuth. 'The water on Enceladus was not drinkable so we had to import all drinking water.' She placed a hand gently on his arm.

'We had to.' Added Karon.

'Really?' Asked Djon. 'Your planet too?'

'Yes.'

'I have never heard of this.' Said the inspector. 'There is no inhabited planet that I know of that has to import water.' He stopped and looked at a small screen on the table. 'And now we know why.' He added enigmatically. 'We have taken a sample of the water on your vessel as you allowed us to and I have now the result.' He looked round at us. 'You will not be surprised to know that the water contains the same drug that is found in your bodies! So, some person or persons unknown have been drugging you for some time by contaminating your water.' There was an even more shocked silence than before. Ruuth's and Karon's faces had drained of all colour. We looked at each other for support but found only the same incomprehension.

'Who would do such a thing, and why?' Stuttered Ruuth.

'What does this drug do?' Asked Terens quietly.

'As I said before we do not know exactly. It is not something we know of. This outpost is very limited in its resources, the only guess that our guys could make was that it would be like a truth drug.'

'What does that do?' Asked Karon.

'A truth drug means that when asked a question you answer the truth because unable not to.'

'That doesn't make much sense.' I said. No one ever asked us questions.

'Exactly. So, it must be doing something else. We are not talking of one or two people either. This looks to be complete planetary drugging for some reason!'

'I still cannot imagine who would do such a thing.' Said Ruuth again, her voice full of pain and anguish. I had to agree. Who would do such a thing?

'This is not a backstreet affair.' He said. 'This is empire scale. There are people in charge of your area, and they must be stopped. It is important therefore that we find where you come from so we can stop them. It will not be easy judging by the scale of the operation. Tell me more of what you know. Who supplies your water for instance?' We all faltered again and were unable to answer. We must look like complete idiots, not knowing anything about our own homes. I tried to think who supplied our water or where it came from but could not. This was madness; I transported the stuff down to the planet! He finally got fed up waiting.

'Just tell me what you do know then.' He finally said.

Relieved, we proceeded to tell him all we knew of our old galaxy or the part of it that we came from. He asked questions every now and again but on the whole just listened intently. When we began to slow down he called for a halt. It had not taken long as we knew very little. It was rather embarrassing to know so little. How could this be?

'I suggest we have a break now.' He said. 'Do not try and leave the complex as you are still technically under arrest until we can substantiate your claims. We cannot do that until we can find out where you have come from. At twenty-two hundred hours tonight, we will meet again on the terrace just up there.' He pointed back to the paved area that we came out onto originally. 'Your vessel is impounded also until further notice. Within those constraints please relax and enjoy yourselves until then. The sergeant here will look after you until then.' He got up and bowed stiffly before leaving us smartly. The sergeant, who was a large strapping young man, left us a device to call him when we were ready. We decided just to sit under the trees and chat for a while. We needed time just to take in what we had heard. I had to laugh at the Inspector – leave? We had no idea where we were, and our V20 did not work! How could we go anywhere? We knew nothing of this planet so even leaving this station was too risky to contemplate. Terens was the only one of us capable of such an adventure.

After a very short while we used the device to call the sergeant. Fortunately, as Djon was desperate to learn more of Earth, he came out very quickly. He was a clean shaven, tall strapping young man who looked as though he could easily handle himself if confronted by criminals.

'We have some questions to ask if that is alright?' I asked, looking up at him from my seated position on the soft grass under the trees. Even though it was evening it was still hot and the cool shade of the trees was a welcome relief.

'Certainly.' He replied stiffly. 'I will answer any questions if I can.' He remained standing.

'Please, do sit with us. I feel awkward with you standing there. I can assure you that we mean you no harm or anyone else here for that matter. Our story is the truth I can assure you.' He looked at me for a moment and then sat down on the grass in front of us.

'OK, so what are your questions?' He looked at us all in turn expectantly. Djon jumped in before any of us could speak.

'We want to know more about Earth, where…'

'Please, I am sorry, but the inspector wants to show you all something first. I cannot say anything until he has spoken to you first. Is that all?'

'Surely..' Began Djon again.

'I am sorry, but I will not say any more until the inspector has spoken to you.' I could see the frustration in Djon's face. I decided to change the subject quickly.

'Well, the second one is what this God that the inspector mentioned is?' I asked.

'Wow, a difficult one.' He adjusted himself as he thought how to answer. We all sat expectantly. 'God or to give him another name, Allah as the inspector mentioned, is the supreme being, the creator of the universe and all things.'

'And where does this being live?' I asked after a longish pause as we all took in what he had said.

'God is not a corporeal being like us. He is the supreme and infinite creator which we reflect.'

'We reflect?' I said.

'Yes, we are God being expressed. That is our role in life, to express God. We are all the children of God.' He paused. As there was no immediate reply he went on. 'Have you really never heard of this before?'

'No, never' Said Djon. This is all very new to us.'

'It will take some time to grasp this if you have never even heard of this before. We have all grown up with the belief, so it is second nature.'

'You are correct.' Mused Djon. 'This is extraordinary news indeed. This is something that has never even been mentioned before that we know of.' He looked at us for confirmation. We all nodded. A supreme creator of the universe was a totally novel concept but somehow looking around at the trees and the stunning view it began to make some sense but as if I was trying to make sense of it through a thick fog. I could just about make out a vague fuzzy outline but no detail.

'OK, let us move on to another one.' Said Djon as we obviously were not going to understand this immediately. 'We have a saying about falling at the last fence? Do you know of anything like this?'

'Yes, that is or was I should say a horseracing term. It means to fail just before the end, just before you reach your goal. Much like you appear to have done. Some horse racing was over fences or jumps.'

'What's a horse?' Asked Ruuth.

'Oh, my goodness you do not know?'

'No.'

'A horse is a large four-footed animal that man, including

women, can ride on. This will be better if we go indoors and use the encyclopaedia, it will show you everything.' He stood up at that. We all dutifully rose as well and followed him indoors. He took us into a part of the complex that we had not been to before. It was along the same unusual corridors and through a very unassuming door at the end of a short side corridor. The room was large and bright lit by tall windows facing over the sunlit valley. The walls were covered with shelves that were covered with objects that I had never seen before.

'The library.' Said the sergeant.

'What are all these things?' Asked Terens stroking the variously coloured objects that filled the shelves. The Sergeant sighed perceptibly.

'These are books really old-fashioned books and not computers. As a result, they are priceless. They cannot now be replaced. Some of them are really very old. I prefer them to computers and often come in here to relax. Reading books is much more relaxing than using computers.' As he spoke, he went over to one of the shelves and with both hands drew one of the books from the shelf and laid it reverently on the large table that stood in the middle of the room. Sunlight streamed in from the windows onto the beautiful rich tabletop and the book.

'What is the table made from?' I asked running my hand over the smooth surface.

'Wood' He replied, no longer surprised by our absurd questions. 'Well, to be more exact it is a type of managa hardwood found on the planet.' He stopped. 'Sorry, I forget which planet. Wood comes from trees much like the ones you have been sitting under.' He added, knowing that we would undoubtedly ask where wood came from. He turned the pages of the book on the table as he spoke. 'Here were are' He said finally, smoothing down the page reverently and turning it towards us. 'A horse. Well one type of horse actually. This one pictured here is an Arab thoroughbred. But most horses look very similar. We all realised at the same time where we had seen a similar picture before.

'One of the pictures on that vessel that captured us!' Said Djon. 'Had an animal just like this. So, it is a horse. Why did they have a picture like that?' None of us knew the answer to that.

Djon continued to turn the pages with the same care that the sergeant had done. He stood and watched very carefully. Then Djon stopped.

'A dog.' He said. 'So, this is what a dog looks like.' The sergeant leant over.

'Yes, that is a Golden Labrador. A good-natured type of dog and gentle.'

'Why have we never seen things like this before?' Asked Terens, more to himself than anyone else in particular.

'This does explain a lot.' Went on Djon. 'We seem to have been kept in the dark about a lot of the galaxy. But why?'

'That is want we intend to find out.' Said the sergeant.

We spent a long time in that library going through that encyclopaedia and absorbing all the information that we could. After a while though we became exhausted from the amount of information that we were taking in. It was too much to retain all at once.

'I think we are going to have to return here again some other time. This is just too much in one go.' I finally said.

*

Hours later we were again out on the paved area. It was a warm dark night with a light breeze fanning our faces. We were all standing in a line along the wall edging the area looking at the night sky. The lights on the station were all switched off, so the darkness was deep. But it was the night sky that was the most dramatic. It was split almost neatly in half! One half was the normal expected night sky ablaze with twinkling stars that grew in number and brightness as the eye travelled from overhead to the horizon on the left. On the right the night sky was the darkest black with only a few lonely pinpricks of starlight. The contrast was most dramatic and something I had never seen. I found it difficult to look to the empty sky to the right as it reminded me too much of the time we spent outside the galaxy. The awesome loneliness of that time was too much to bear. I looked across at the others and noticed that they too were concentrating on the left-hand view.

The stars to the left of the sky seemed to get so close together they formed a huge swath of gossamer like band of light across the sky. It was then that a beautiful lilting sound drifted across the evening air. Sonorous sounds the like I had never heard. Judging by the surprise of the others neither had they.

'What is that sound?' I asked of the Inspector.

'That is Holst's Planet suite, which is quite apt don't you think?'

'I'm sorry, the name means nothing. I have never heard such sounds before. Is that the name of all sounds like that?' The Inspector looked puzzled. 'Or is that the name of these particular sounds?' I continued.

'Are you trying to tell me that you have never heard music before?' Asked the Inspector with incredulity.

'If that is the name for such beautiful sounds then, yes.' The others nodded agreement to this. The Inspector sat down on the wall with his mouth open. He gathered himself quickly though.

'You have never heard music?' He asked again, as if I might give a different answer.

'No.' I replied. 'Is this music, what is music?' The Inspector was at a loss for words for a moment. We all just stood and listened to the sounds washing over me, bringing up emotions from inside. I felt odd, how could these sounds affect me so. Was everyone who heard this 'music' so affected? I looked at the others and could see them also struggling with thoughts alien to them. Only the Inspector seemed unaffected by the sounds. 'Why are you not affected by these sounds?' I finally asked of him. He turned to me and stood up.

'I see that you are indeed affected by the music. Yes, everyone is affected but we have been used to music for many centuries so it is not so alien to us and we do not show it. Unless on rare occasions when the music affects us deeply. Well, what is music? It is the art form of arranging different notes or sounds of different instruments in a sequence that the human mind finds appealing.'

'Instruments?' Asked Ruuth.

'Of course, if you have not heard of music you would not have heard of instruments. Well, instruments are the means of making music. There are various ways of making sounds.' He slapped the top of the wall and clapped his hands. 'I have made sounds, but you would not call that music would you? Instruments make sounds of a particular tone and resonance in tune either by banging or plucking or bowing or blowing. The sounds you hear are made by violins, horns.' He stopped. 'We do not have time here to go through the history of music. I suggest that this is done at another time. I will cancel the music now; we can listen at another time. Perhaps now it will be too distracting. This is most extraordinary.' The music suddenly stopped. I felt empty all of a sudden and wanted it to continue.

'Is this what you brought us out to see?' Asked Terens in his usual dour way, pointing up at the sky. Perhaps he was not affected by music.

'Yes, it is.' Replied the inspector, who was now, I noticed for the first time, in civilian clothes, I noticed for the first time, a long white robe with no belt or adornment other than a rich border around the neck which appeared to be made of finely stitched thread with some golden threads intertwined. It was a very elegant robe and I had never seen a man wear anything like it before.

'The milky way.' He said and swept his hand across the starry night sky in a grand gesture. 'You will note that over there the sky does not contain many stars. That is because we are right on the edge of the galaxy! I had to check that tonight would show all this before bringing you all out here. You see that most nights we get either one or the other, either all stars or no stars. It is very rare that you get this view, and you are fortunate that tonight is the night. It helps explain where we are. The main inhabited part of the galaxy lies in the other direction heading towards the centre of the galaxy. There are approximately twenty-one thousand inhabited planets although many of those are not much more than isolated settlements of like minded individuals.'

'Twenty-one thousand inhabited planets?' I asked suddenly aware of what he had said.

'Yes, that is correct. Why?'

'We only know of four thousand two hundred and nine planets.'

'This is even more interesting. We were discussing this earlier and came to the conclusion that you must be from a previously unknown inhabited part of the galaxy. We will look at that again when we go inside; but before we do look over to that group of stars there.' He pointed to a part of the sky. 'Do you see that small group of stars?' We nodded in agreement. 'Well one of that group contains the planet Earth from which mankind came! It is approximately six thousand light years away.' He dropped his arm to his side again and I thought I noticed a wistful look in his eyes. 'Come inside and I will show you on the. What did you call it?'

'A V20.' Said Djon.

'Yes, the V20. I will show you where we are on the V20. Follow me.' He turned and strode purposefully back towards the door in the rockface. The lights came on again gently as he did so. We were soon back inside seated around the table again. Both V20's were on and again showing the same galactic image.

'Just a minute.' Said Ruuth out of the blue as she pulled up a seat. She stayed comically half standing and half sitting. 'Our V20 is reactive is yours?'

'Yes of course, they all are.'

'Can you then transfer the key to the portals to ours?' His eyes lit up as he understood what she was doing.

'Yes of course we can.' He looked again at his screen and then back at us. 'We will continue while that is done.' Almost as soon as he had looked back at us one of the doors opened and a young policeman entered carrying a short cable. He came over to the table and plugged one end into a socket in the tabletop and then tried to plug the other end into our V20. He frowned and then nodded to the inspector and left. The inspector in the meantime had been entering data into the large V20. Some details appeared beside a tiny dot near the edge of the stars.

'This is Gonfalon Royal.' He began and as he did so the young policeman returned with a tiny plug. I took it for an adaptor. He plugged it into the cable and then into our V20 and then typed in a command on the keypad. Almost immediately data began appearing, star names, planets, portals; but none of them I knew. They were all from the Milky Way. Was that our galaxy after all? If it was then which part did we come from? I hoped we were about to find out. I then noticed that our V20 was showing exactly the same model as the large one. Unfortunately, I suddenly realised that as the V20 was reactive then all the details of our portals and planets would be lost! We could not prove to this man where we came from. If only we had kept a copy. Hindsight is a wonderful thing.

'You will notice that we are right on the edge of the galaxy here as you saw outside in the night sky.' He pressed another key and nearby another star was identified. 'That star there is called the Sun and it is the star around which the Earth orbits. You can just make out that it resides in a spiral arm of the galaxy. That arm is called the Orion Arm and just behind it is the Sagittarius Arm which spreads almost right around the galaxy. The arms are not as clearly defined in reality as the machine must reduce the actual number and complexity as there are two hundred billion stars. Mankind so far has only inhabited part of the Orion arm, the Sagittarius arm and the Perseus arm where we are now. What we suspect is that you have come from a part of the galaxy that we did not think had been colonised. This outpost as you have already noticed is a police outpost. The reason why we are here is because many years ago the criminal gang that was being hunted was traced to this part of the galaxy. We caught some of them but a year later the rest disappeared. What we are hoping is that you hold the key to where they went!'

'You think the people who were drugging us and or were the ones chasing us are still part of this gang? That is amazing, after all you said they disappeared what...almost two hundred and forty years ago!' Said Djon. 'Surely it cannot be the same people?'

'Of course not. But their followers certainly. There are similarities to what you have described and what we know of them. Thirty-five years after they disappeared there was a spate of kidnappings of babies in this part of the galaxy.'

'Babies?' Cried Ruuth. 'Why babies?'

'We were hoping that you might also hold the clue to that as well. We hold the DNA codes of all the babies kidnapped and would like you to give us samples to see if we can find any match, or at least a family match.'

'Of course we'll help.' Said Karon this time. 'But how many babies were kidnapped?'

'One thousand eight hundred and two.' Said the inspector levelly. There was a shocked silence for a while.

'How many did you manage to get back?' Karon asked quietly.

'None.' The inspector looked at her with sadness in his eyes. There was another shocked silence as the inspector put five small clear containers on the table and pushed them towards us. I took mine absent mindedly as the horror of so many families being deprived of their dear children sank into my thinking. How could people act so badly towards others to kidnap babies!?

'Please swab the inside of your mouth and put the swab back in the container and close the lid. Thank you.' The containers were labelled with our names. We did as he had asked us and when complete we handed the containers back to him. The young policeman returned and took them away.

'It will not be long before we have the results. In the meantime, we need to try and find where you came from. We have come to the conclusion that perhaps it is a part of the galaxy that the rest of mankind has not yet reached. If there was anything in your V20 as you call it that perhaps would give us some clue? A star grouping for example would be a guide.'

'Our V20.' Said Djon is reactive as is yours so it does not contain anything, which is why it now shows the galaxy the same as yours.'

'I realise that, but did you record any of the information from your V20?' We looked at each other to see if anyone could remember if we had. I could not recall saving any information as we thought it was too dangerous. Then Ruuth spoke up.

'What about our search for the hidden portal?' She asked. 'That required saving information so we could...'

'Of course.' Said Djon excitedly, cutting off Ruuth before she could finish. 'The hidden portal information must still be in it! May I ....sorry Ruuth... you should do it. May Ruuth look through our V20 to see if the data is still stored there?'

'Of course, as long as I can trust you.' He looked at Ruuth.

'I most certainly want to help.' She said. 'I will do anything to help you find the people who would kidnap babies. May I?' She stood up and pointed at our V20.

'Be my guest.' He said and waved his hand for her to come and sit down beside him. Ruuth went over and sat down at the controls.

'Is there anymore that you can tell us about Earth?' Djon asked finally unable to contain himself any longer. I was glad he did as it took attention from Ruuth as she worked.

'Of course.' He tapped out a command on his V20 control panel. The galaxy disappeared and a single planet appeared in the bluish orb, spinning slowly. It was a blue-brown planet with mostly water. 'Earth.' He said and tapped out another command. This time words appeared hovering near the planet's surface. 'What you see there are the names of the continents.'

'Continents?' I asked.

'You do not even know of continents?'

'No, we have never heard of them before.' He looked surprised at that.

'The continents are the major land masses. Here you have North America and South America, over there is Europe and

Africa and then Asia and Australasia. The countries will appear now.' As he spoke the surface of the land masses was suddenly divided up into smaller units each with its own name. I could read USA, Canada, Russia, China, and Australia as the planet rotated round in front of us.

'Have you been there?' Asked Terens.

'No.' He replied curtly and again with some sadness. 'Some time ago the Earth portal failed and the planet has been cut off from the rest of the galaxy since then'

'So, you don't have vessel based portals then?' Said Djon.

'No, we do not. I was led to believe that it was not possible. Something to do with the dynamics of the operation. The portal had to stay still and distorted space around it. So, you have one?'

'We have just the one on our vessel outside. We do not know of any others except that my father managed to find the instructions to build one from somewhere.'

'That is indeed extraordinary news and could revolutionise travel in the galaxy. Are the pods surrounding your vessel anything to do with this portal?'

'Yes, they are the portal. We do not know quite how it works or how to direct travel that is the main problem.'

'For us, and I mean the galactic police, vessel-based portals would be invaluable for being able to follow criminal gangs and even out manoeuvring them. I would respectfully ask that you allow us to copy your portal for our vessels and even for the galaxy at large.'

'We have no objection to that; after all we came by it by chance more or less. It was not our design.'

'Except how do you prevent it falling into the hands of the selfsame criminals once it is out in the galaxy?' Asked Terens.

'Good point. We will just have to take that chance though, without them we will not be as flexible in our response as we would like, and certainly as we have been up to now. This is indeed a major improvement in our fight against these criminal gangs. Nothing ventured, nothing gained as I believe the saying was.'

'Some people have said that we could not have come from one planet because there are so many different types of people, white, black etc. What do you have to say about that argument?'

The inspector laughed out loud.

'We all have come from one planet. All the different types of people have come from that one planet, Earth. Diversity my friends, diversity on a grand scale unequalled in the galaxy that we have found so far.'

'I would agree with that.' Said Terens. 'After all, that DNA evidence that we were given did indicate that there was one source for all people.'

'Right.' Said Ruuth suddenly. 'I have found something at last. This should be the data for the lost portal.' She tapped out a command on our V20 and the galaxy disappeared to be replaced by the fuzzy blob that we knew to be the location of the hidden portal. Fortunately, there were also a few of the nearby stars.

'Good.' He said. 'Are there any more of the stars?'

'No.' Said Ruuth shortly. 'That is all that is in the V20.'

'That is not good news, even with the computing power we have it will take quite a time to find where this is considering the limited number of stars we have here to compare with the rest of the known galaxy. However, we will give this to our boffins and see if they can come up with something. If there is anything else that you remember about where you come from it will help us locate your homes.' He looked around at us.

'We will indeed let you know if we think of anything that will help you.' I said.

I stopped as Karon let out a long groan.

'I don't feel very well.' She said.

'Come to mention it.' Added Ruuth, who I noticed had beads of sweat glistening on her brow. 'I don't feel very well either.' She had stopped work on the V20 which was unusual for her. Then Karon slumped down onto the table. The inspector acted quickly and called for support and then came round the table. He ordered Djon away from her and ran a check himself on her as two young policemen and a young policewoman ran into the room.

'Get this woman to the infirmary please and can you take the other woman with you and run a check on her too. Thank you.' The policemen and woman sprang into action and carefully picked up Karon and carried her out of the room. Ruuth followed, assisted by the young policewoman.

'It is late gentlemen. I suggest we retire for the night and see how they are in the morning. They will be well looked after within our limited capabilities. Please follow me.' He turned and led us to another door in the far end of the room. It was a lift and as he pressed a button the doors slid open to reveal a shiny lift car inside. He stepped inside and we followed.

'There is nothing that you can do for the young woman. She is in good hands. Rest well tonight and we will see how you feel in the morning.'

'Does this mean that you are not sending us back to the cells tonight?' I asked hopefully.

'Correct, I am not sending you back to the cells tonight.'

'Why are...' Began Terens.

'Just be grateful that we are not sending you back to the cells.' Terens nodded and kept quiet.

We all then stood in silence as the lift travelled upwards. It finally came to a gentle stop and the doors slid open to reveal a long corridor. This was a normal domestic looking corridor with a drugget type soft floor covering in a deep russet, white walls interrupted regularly by doorways in a light coloured xyloid material. The white ceiling was also regularly interrupted by lights hanging down with shades of white globes. At the end of the corridor was a long window showing the night sky outside. The inspector stopped at the first door and pushed it open.

'Djim Stone, if you would be my guest and have the use of this room for the night. The others will be next door over here and here.' He pointed to two other doors. 'Good night and sleep well.' He went on and did the same to the others as I stood rooted to the spot unable to move. When all the others had been shown their rooms, he returned and stopped in front of me.

'What are those?' I asked, pointing to the picture plaques that were fixed to the walls between the bedroom doors.

'Those are the inspectors that have been in charge of Gonfalon Royal since it was first founded.'

'May I have a look?'

'Of course, be my guest. It is all right Mr. Stone, and afterwards you may relax and go to bed. I will get you up in the morning. Good night.' He bowed slightly and returned to the lift.

I went and looked closely at the first plaque, Djon and Terens joined me.

'What are they?' Asked Djon.

'They record the names of all the inspectors who have been in charge here since the planet was founded. Or so the inspector said.' I looked at the first picture that had the name Mikhail Schott and gave the dates of his time in charge.

'Look here.' Said Terens. 'It's our current inspector with the current dates.'

'So, he has been here six years. Let us find the first one.' I suggested. We walked down the corridor looking at each one. They were in date order. At last, we reached one that did not seem to have any earlier dates before it.

'This must be the first one then.' I said. 'We have not found any earlier. It reads Uleitha Charn.'

'Good.' Said Terens. 'Now what do we do?'

'We go to bed.' Said Djon. 'Goodnight.' He turned and went into his room.

I finally went into my room. It was small as most rooms seemed to be but neat and clean. The walls were white, there was a bed against one wall with clean white sheets, and the floor had the same covering and the ceiling the same light fitting. There was a window containing a glass door that led out onto a tiny balcony. There was also a small shower room containing a toilet and basin. It was covered in a white hard glossy finish divided up into small squares. I had to admit that I too was not feeling at all well. I went and lay on the bed to look out of the window onto the half starry sky and ponder on the last few days events.

It was the last thing I remember.

*

I awoke feeling very sore and with an ache all over my body. I could hardly move, and my mouth was dry and I could hardly swallow. I tried to speak but only a hoarse grunt escaped my dry and parched lips. I could not focus on where I was. I tried to move but only succeeded in creating another hoarse grunt. Then someone helped me into a sitting position.

'Here take this.' Said a woman's voice that I did not recognise. Something cold and hard was pressed against my lips. 'Its cold water; please drink as much as you can.' I tried to drink. The water was deliciously cold in my mouth, but the drinking part seemed to elude me. Slowly and patiently the person persisted and finally I managed to drink. Everything was a colourful blur and a grating jumble of confusing sounds some of which I could understand such as the gentle voice of the woman beside me. I did not know how long I had been there or even why. I tried to remember what had happened but although the thoughts were on the tip of my tongue, I could not form them into cogent ideas. Gradually though some memories surfaced just long enough to form image in my thought. I recalled a waking moment of struggling to get up but hardly able to move. The exertion of it all making me sweat profusely. Then I recalled waking to a cold sweaty shivering bout. Colours swimming in and out of view, then gentle voices.

The next thing I was aware of was waking up again. It was dark both in the room and outside. The door was open and the curtains beside the window were blowing gently in the warm wind entering the room. I gazed up at the ceiling just gathering my thoughts and strength. I felt much better and could see and hear normally although every joint in my body felt as though it had been pulled well beyond its elastic limit and then twisted into the bargain. I heard a deep rumble which I knew to be a space vessel taking off. I was not able to identify the type from the sound and felt very inadequate until I realised that I was in unknown territory. I tried to sit up.

'Oh, hello.' Said the same gentle female voice. 'Here let me help you up.' Warm soft hands helped me into a sitting position. I was panting from even that effort.

'I feel hungry and thirsty.' I said.

'Good.' Said the female voice again. 'I will get you some food.' As she left the room, I saw that it was one of the young female policemen that helped Ruuth and Karon. Ruuth and Karon! She had gone before I could speak but fortunately returned very shortly.

'Food and drink coming shortly.'

'Thank you. How are my two friends Ruuth and Karon?'

'They are much better and well on the way to recovery. They too have been asking after you.'

'Thank you. By the way what is your name?'

'Jhudithe.' She said with a big smile. Just then the inspector entered the room this time wearing his smart and crisply ironed uniform. The woman got up but he waved her to sit back down.

'Good evening Djim, it is good to see you up again.'

'Thank you. What on Erebus happened to me?'

'Well, as I have said before we are not well equipped here but as far as we can ascertain you have been experiencing withdrawal symptoms from the drug in your body. There must be some element of an addictive chemical interwoven into the matrix of the drug. It is obviously a very cleverly produced drug which will take our chemists some time to untangle. How it was invented and produced is a mystery. We do not know of anything equal to it in the galaxy. You will recover steadily now I am assured. Take your rest and make a full recovery. We will be waiting for you.'

'Thank you.' He bowed slightly and left and as he did so the food that Jhudithe had ordered was brought into the room by another of the policemen. I wondered what other work they had to do rather than just look after us.

As I ate, I talked with Jhudithe and asked her about her

life. She in turn asked me about mine and was surprised at many of the answers. When I finished in walked Djon looking bright and cheerful while I still felt weak and drained.

'Good.' He said, sitting on the end of the bed. 'Glad to see you up at last.'

'How come you are so well and cheerful?' I asked thickly. 'Didn't the effect of the drug get to you at all?'

'Oh yes it did, but it appears there was less of it in me than you or the others apparently. I used to distil my own water as much as possible. It was probably that which not only meant it did not affect me as much but also allowed me to question what was going on; particularly in looking for Ultima Thule. Funny that.' He paused. 'How come we thought the original planet was called Ultima Thule when in fact it was the Earth?'

'And not only that, but where is our own planet Enceladus 421?'

'Yes, that as well.' His face dropped from the big cheerful grin that he had when he entered. 'But enough of that. Let us get you up and about again and we can look to the future not the past.' He got up. 'Just get well soon Djim. I will see you in a bit. I must go and see the others.' He turned and with a wave left the room.

Jhudithe then helped me to eat the meal and drink the drink. I had to admit afterwards that I had no idea what the meal or drink was, but I do remember it was delicious and instantly I began to feel better.

'I think I need to rest now.' I said to Jhudithe, after I had finished and listened to something of what had been going on. She took the tray and settled me back down in the bed.

When I awoke again it was light and I felt much better. So much better that I could get up. I looked around but the room was empty. The door to the small balcony was still open and the curtain still blowing gently in the warm breeze. I struggled out of bed until I was standing unsteadily on my feet. My clothes were spread out on a seat. I staggered over and with great effort managed to dress myself. I then went to the door and stepped out on the small balcony. The view was the same as from the terrace area where we viewed the starry sky the other night but from much higher up. I could see the broad sweep of the valley way over to the distant blue mountains. Down below, way below the terrace were green fields and in those fields were small white animals moving slowly about and apparently eating the green shoots. I had no idea what these animals were.

I looked up into a bright blue sky with clean white clouds slowly and silently floating across and changing shape as they went. I felt the soft warm breeze on my face and began to feel my old self again. In fact, I felt much better than my old self. Cleaner, fresher and more positive. I breathed the fresh clean air deeply and knew it was not just the different planet that made me feel so much more alive. Something had left me, and I knew the poison was gone. I just stood and let the warmth of the sunlight soak into me. I had never felt so good before and now I knew why. We had been poisoned. Was everyone poisoned? We must have been. Hoping it was morning I turned and went to look for breakfast.

Once out of my room I turned and headed for the door at the end of the corridor. Although it was glazed it was big and very heavy to open. I had to lean on it with all my weight to get it open. It led to the outside. There was a huge wall in front of it. I turned and walked round the end of the wall to be met by an astonishing sight. I was standing at the edge of a vast level landing pad. To one side, almost hanging over the edge was our vessel, our faithful Jergan, gleaming dully in the bright sunlight. It seemed very odd to see it on planet in the sunshine in an atmosphere. It looked like I had never seen it before. The ring of pods still attached to the hull but now not extended but hung loosely and raggedly around the middle. The police had carefully made a cradle to support the vessel.

Further away were two police vessels shimmering in the heat haze rising up from the vast flat landing pad. There was no edge; or rather the pad just seemed to end abruptly with no wall or guarding at all. It was marked out though in a very familiar pattern which reminded me of the ground station at home where I worked. The landing surface was a smooth glassy finish from the power of the drives melting a thin layer of the rock surface. Although it was glassy smooth it was not slippery.

Perhaps it was the fact that the drug had now left me that now everything looked brighter somehow, and the sunshine seemed fuller of colour as did everything else. The colours of everything seemed to be richer, clearer and denser. The world seemed more solid and less transparent. Even though the landing pad was so familiar it was as though I was seeing it for the first time. It was the same for everything else as well, it was as though I had never seen walls, windows, clouds, and the sounds. Sounds like I had never heard before, full and meaningful. I felt alive and as if I had been in a dream before. Then I heard sounds I had never heard before, drifting up from the valley below. I tried to make some meaning of the sound but could not. Then I became aware of things flying in the air, drifting on the breeze or soaring upwards with flapping motions. I had never seen such things as these before either.

Then far distant memories began coming back. Suddenly it began to make sense. Was this what they meant about this 'god'? Joy, light, richness, vitality, life like I had never known before. The bright sunlight, the views, the flying things in the air. Birds, the word returned from the book in the library but to see them in reality soaring majestically in the clear air transformed the word from just a word to something more meaningful. There had to be a supreme creator, and this was the result. Nothing else could create such beauty. But why had we never heard of this before I could not fathom. But now the world, even this one which was clearer and brighter than my old home planet began to make some sense. There was a deep welling up inside of me of some great feeling that I had no words for. Now I knew that the people here would have a word for it. I felt as if my life was just starting and there was so much to learn. A huge smile spread across my face, but I could not see it but only feel it. I felt the warmth of the sun on my face and the soft breeze as though I had never felt them before or had I just done so. Everything seemed so new and fresh I could hardly tell if I had known something before or not. It was both fantastic and confusing at the same time. But I felt alive like never before. I then found myself whooping a great loud shout and then stopped, feeling foolish and hoping that no one had heard me.

I looked round and found myself still alone thankfully and then saw the building behind me and noticed, with a wry smile that it also was marked in the giant letters that every landing pad had that I knew of. The wall was primarily a very dark smooth stone with tiny slit windows. The door that I had come out of was protected by the big blast screen. I turned and went back into the building. As I did so I ran my hand along the smooth stone façade just feeling the texture as it seemed so new and different.

Leaving the bright sunlight and entering the building it became suddenly dark, or so my eyes thought. Gradually I became accustomed again to the interior light levels and could see normally again. As I walked down the corridor, past all the portraits of the previous inspectors, the lift doors at the other end opened and a policeman came out.

'Ah, Mr. Stone. We hoped you would be up. Do you require some breakfast?'

'Naturally.'

'Then please follow me.' He turned and went back into the lift. I followed him in. He took me back to the small, grassed area where we ate before. The table was there set out as before and surrounding it were my dear friends and the inspector. He stood up as I arrived.

'Welcome my friend.' He said and directed me to an empty seat. Although the sun was not yet shining into the area it was pleasantly warm already. I sat down. 'Now eat my friend while we discuss your predicament and our problem'.

'Thank you.' I said. 'How is everyone?' I asked of my dear friends. I was met with a brief but warm reply that all were now well. Now I could relax. But before we started there was something else I wanted to ask. 'Inspector, before you start can you explain something?' He nodded so I continued. 'I have been hearing sounds that I could not identify.' As I spoke, one of the sounds did indeed drift up on the breeze. 'Like that one for instance.' He smiled.

'That noise you hear is a sheep. We have birds here too, all brought from Earth. There are a number of different varieties of each of course.'

'Of course.' I confirmed, not really understanding varieties of animals but trusted that we would find out later. 'Thank you, now please continue inspector.'

'Thank you. Now as it seems you know little of this part of the galaxy, I will start by going through a little history. Do stop me if you know of what I speak.' He sat down again and also joined us in breakfast. 'Firstly, you know what year it is?' He looked across as me.

'Of course, we all agree on that. As we said before.'

'And why is it that year?' That stumped me. I looked at the others for support but could see that they too were unable to answer. 'Ah, I see that you do not know that. Well, we are counting the years since the birth of one Jesus Christ of Nazareth on Earth. His birth restarted the calendar even though many people tried to pretend that this was not the case. But of course, human history goes back many thousands of years before that event. But let us look at more recent history. For instance, who invented the portal?' Again, he looked at me, but as I did not answer he looked across at Djon. He also looked blank.

'Well, so you do not know who invented the portal. Very interesting.'

'You know who invented the portal?' I said. This was extraordinary. No one knew who or how the portals were first made.

'Yes, it is common knowledge, and one of the great achievements of mankind. Well, it was one Raichel Bluff who many years ago managed to send and get back a space flight through a portal. This was built to orbit the moon.'

'Which moon?' Asked Ruuth.

'Sorry, the moon is the moon that orbits Earth.'

'Excuse me.' Butted in Karon, raising her hand like a schoolgirl in class, her brows furrowed.

'Yes?' Asked the inspector.

'Why did they start the calendar from the birth of that particular man?' She slowly lowered her arm; suddenly realising she had it up in the air.

'Because many people considered him to be the son of God.' He paused, Karon looked blank. 'Now…'

'Excuse me.' It was Ruuth this time. When he stopped and looked her way she continued. 'But is this the same god?' The inspector had a most amazed look on his face. I was glad she asked the question because although I had no idea either I did not want to ask another question of him. He sighed.

'Do you people know nothing of the galaxy at all?' He looked round at us, searching the expressions on our faces for some clue as to our thoughts. All he saw was mystification. He continued. 'Jesus was considered the son of God. God or to give him another name Allah or Jahweh, is considered to be the creative force of the universe and yes, it is the same God – there is only one. I am not the best person to go into any depth in this matter. I suggest we leave that for others.'

'We have already spoken with your sergeant about this, and he has tried to explain it all to us. It is so difficult to grasp. We have not come across such ideas before so please accept our apologies for being so slow and asking the same questions over and over again.'

'Certainly, now, the first planet to be settled other than Earth was named New Earth but that name did not stick and the common name of Bluff's Planet took over, so called after Raichel Bluff who made it all possible by inventing the portals.' He stopped to take a drink.

'One thing that puzzles me.' Interjected Terens into the quiet pause. 'Is what sort of policemen you are.' The inspector burst into laughter again.

'And what do you mean by that?' He asked.

'You seem to be able to spend a lot of time with us and no

time at all chasing criminals.' The inspector laughed again.

'I see your point. Well, we are not your normal police. Let me put this into context. Prior to mankind leaving Earth for the first time crime became a great worry for many people and governments. This was a misconception, as crime was actually falling but the other problems and fears of fossil fuels finally running out and the subsequent unrest made it seem as though civilisation was falling apart. To many people this did indeed seem the case. For years there had also been considerable experiments to improve the human body by implants or chimeric adaptation or even memory downloading. Early successes prompted further experiments and there was a rush to be adapted and improved to become a 'super human'. Then came the backlash.

'What, did people rebel?'

'Oh, no, it was the natural human body rejection of the experiments and resulted either in the original people or their children being deformed or scarred for life. They became distorted and almost inhuman. This obviously resulted in revulsion from so called normal people. The Experimentals, as they had become known, became outcasts and were lumped in with the remaining criminals. Not being accepted they began to try and demonstrate for equality at least if they could not be made normal again. It appeared to most people that this was yet more crime.

This resulted in a fearful blitz on crime and perceived crime. When the portals allowed travel throughout the galaxy one of the first planets to be settled was a penal planet. The other was a planet where many of the experimentals went to settle.

The penal planet was set up in two thousand one hundred and fifty-five. A mere ten years later the first planet was settled. Such was the fear on Earth. Actually, what had been happening over the previous years was that crime was more visible but much less than before. Good people far outnumbered the bad but that was not how it was perceived. All that was happening was that the unrest that was pushing the thought for exodus was being confused with crime. The purge against crime did clean up the Earth and the criminals were safely put away on the penal planet. Earth then became rather a backwater, lax and lazy. A lot of the bright go-ahead people had decided to leave. The trouble was the gangs took over the penal planet and the following year escaped into the galaxy.' He paused again to take another drink. This time we were so absorbed by this extraordinary view of the galaxy that we did not interrupt.

'It then became obvious a new type of police force was required so the galactic police were formed as all the inhabited planets felt insecure knowing that the criminal gangs were loose in the galaxy. We here are members of the galactic police. We have a specific role to play and have no jurisdiction in planet law enforcement I might add. Much later on my predecessors corned the criminals in this part of the galaxy. The following year the criminals disappeared. This planet was set up as a galactic police base for this part of the galaxy as we knew the criminals could not be far away. This has therefore been a police base for the last two hundred and thirty-nine years. It was only in two thousand two hundred and eighty-two when the babies were kidnapped from various planets that we knew the gangs were still about. At least it was thought that the gangs had perpetrated the crime and I for one am inclined to agree. The only problem was that we did not know where they were hiding. We searched and used long range sensors but to no avail. We are still here and alert.' He stopped again. This time to take a bite of food. Terens took the opportunity to jump in.

'It has been a long time since the gangs disappeared, surely in all that time the police should have discovered where they were. There are huge numbers of planets that these gangs appear to control. And then there is all the portal traffic, which must surely show up?' The inspector looked somewhat taken aback but recovered himself.

'You are correct of course. But the galaxy is a vast place. Very very big.'

'Surely though.' I added. 'With all that portal activity it would soon show up on some sensors. The portals were not hidden or disguised as far as I know.'

'Yes, you have a point. That has indeed worried me since meeting you people. It just does not seem to add up. We will have to look at that point again in more detail. That makes it even more imperative that we find out where you came from. Now if I may continue with the history of Galactic expansion?' We nodded our agreement.

'Now, where was I? As yes, then in two thousand three hundred and seventy, that is a mere one hundred and sixteen years ago the Earth portal finally failed. This meant that the old planet was cut off from the rest of the galaxy. We could not communicate and could not return. This was not such a bad thing as it might seem. There were after all no more resources left. Apart from the mere emotional ties that mankind has with the planet it had grown old and tired. There were newer and more exciting planets. We had to look outward instead of backward.' He did have a slight wistful look in his eyes as he spoke, but it soon passed.

'Why did the Earth portal fail?' Asked Terens grimly. 'Was it the gangs?'

'I think not.' Replied the inspector quietly. 'It wa,s after all the very first portal and when most people left the Earth it no longer had the resources or the scientists to maintain or progress portal technology. It was inevitable I suppose.'

I knew that look in Terens' face that he thought otherwise for some reason. Even though I had not known him long I had got to know his dark moods and his thought patterns very well. He was brooding on something. I would have to dig it out of him later, now was not the time.

'Thank you.' I said. 'That was most informative and as for me completely unknown information about the galaxy. It seems where we come from there is a distinct lack of knowledge. It makes me think that perhaps there is something to hide, otherwise why such secrecy. Now the effect of the drug has worn off I can see that.'

'You see how that I think you hold the key.' He said. I gulped. He meant that it was the criminal gangs that had drugged us and controlled our part of the galaxy.

'Was the information I found in our V20 about the hidden portal of any use?' Asked Ruuth, diverting attention from me.

'Unfortunately not. There were not enough stars to be able to make a match. We need something else about where you come from to be able to locate it. Have any of you been able to think of anything? I know that you have not been well, but I hope that you have not forgotten what we were talking about before all this blew up.'

'I am very sorry inspector, but I had completely forgotten about it.' I said. I looked around at the others to see if they had remembered anything but all I saw was embarrassed glances. We continued eating breakfast in silence. Then I remembered the white animals on the hillside below us.

'Inspector.' I asked.

'Yes?'

'From my room I saw a number of white animals on the slopes below. What are they?'

'I saw them too!' Added Karon.

'My friends, they are the sheep.'

'No.' I said. 'So those are the animals that make the sound I heard earlier. I see.'

'Do you not eat meat where you come from?'

'Our food arrives on Enceladus prepacked. The planet is not developed enough to provide its own food. We have meat dishes such as lamb and beef, but we never knew where it came from.'

'Well well. Lamb is young sheep.'

'We eat those animals?' Gasped Karon.

'Do you have a beef animal here?' Asked Djon.

'No, we do not.' Replied the inspector with a broad smile. 'Beef comes from an animal called a cow. We do not have those on Gonfalon Royal. Not yet anyway.'

'What about the Arachnid Nebula?' Asked Karon innocently and completely out of the sky.

'Ah.' Said the inspector. 'That is just the sort of thing we are looking for. Something with a name will help us enormously. The Arachnid Nebula you say? It is near where you live?'

'Yes.' I was really annoyed with myself. It was so obvious that I wished that I had thought of it and not Karon. I was the pilot after all!

'Let me just enter that into the galaxy encyclopaedia and see where it is.' He entered the name into the keypad resting on the table beside him and then frowned. 'It does not appear in the galaxy.' He said looking up at us. 'Yet again your information on your home appears to leave you stranded.'

– CHAPTER 15 –

I could not believe it. Djon looked over to me and then at Terens. 'You have been throughout most of the galaxy Terens.' He said tremulously. 'Surely there must be some mistake. The V20 clearly shows the Arachnid Looped Nebula and we have been close enough to see it!'

Terens sat impassively for a few moments before speaking in his laconic style. 'You are right Djon. But there is something not quite right here.'

'You are right about that!' Exclaimed the Inspector, getting quite agitated. 'In fact, I am getting a bit sick of this silly game of yours!' He banged the table as he stood up.

'Sir.' Came a voice over the communication speaker. 'I think I might have the answer.' Even out here other people were listening to our conversation. Then I remembered that we were still being interrogated, even if at a superb breakfast table such as this. The Inspector seemed to relax a little.

'OK, Rhobin come on out.'

'I just need some time to try something first, sir.'

'OK Rhobin'. He turned back to us. 'Finish you breakfast and then we will continue this later.' He then got up and began to walk off but stopped and turned back. 'I expect you to come up with the truth and stop playing the fool. I am a patient man, but you are trying my patience.' He walked off purposefully. We just sat and stared at our plates in despair.

'What is going on?' Asked Ruuth quietly.

'I wish I knew, Ruuth.' Said Djon.

'Same here.' I added unnecessarily it seemed.

'We are telling the truth.' Said Karon also very quietly. 'We are!'

'I know.' Said Djon. 'But how do we convince them that when everything we tell them they do not believe. How can they say the Nebula does not exist? All we have to do is show them the V20.'

'Djon!' I interrupted. 'The V20 no longer seems to have our galaxy information in it any more!'

'Ghas! I had forgotten that!' He put his head in his hands and rubbed his face vigorously.

We spent the next hour or so in the deepest melancholic mood. There was nothing we could think of to back up our story. It looked bleak. Then a young policeman came around the end of the cliff and stopped. He looked around and then disappeared again. Half an hour later the Inspector returned and sat down in front of us.

My young colleague here it appears is an amateur astronomer.' He said.

'Pardon me.' I asked. 'What is an astronomer?'

'Really, you people seem to know nothing of the galaxy. But then that is not surprising considering just what I have heard. An astronomer is someone who investigates the universe, and my young colleague knows where the Arachnid Nebula is.' He paused and the wait was almost unbearable.

'Well?' Said Djon.

'My colleague is a very impetuous and young policeman fortunately for you and for some reason wanted to help you Normally I would not have allowed such foolish behaviour, but he convinced me to give him some time to try and prove an idea that he had. Being an astronomer, he knew immediately that the Arachnid Nebula does not exist in this galaxy.' The Inspector leaned forward. 'But the name made him think of something and after some research he came up with a most extraordinary answer.' He reached into his jacket and took out a picture and placed it on the table in front of us.

'The Arachnid Looped Nebula!' I said. 'I thought you said it did not....' I stopped as the Inspector put up his hand. He looked around at all of us and appeared satisfied with the expressions on our faces.

'Well, my friends it appears there may be at last something to back up your claims, but it is almost too absurd to believe.

This picture is a picture of the Tarantula Looped Nebula and is not in the Milky Way Galaxy!' I had yet another sinking feeling, but the Inspector seemed to be happy with this. At least he was smiling which may mean he thought that he finally had us rather than he was happy. 'My young astronomer colleague found this picture and convinced me to show it to you to gauge your reaction. But this nebula unfortunately as I say is not in this galaxy at all.'

The tension was unbearable.

'It appears that your Nebula is in fact in the Large Magellanic Cloud.' Said the inspector finally.

'The what?' Said Djon, putting down his drink and leaning forward. We all sat up.

'The Arachnid Nebula is in the Large Magellanic Cloud and not in the Milky Way galaxy at all and is not even called the Arachnid Nebula but the Tarantula Nebula! Are you sure that this nebula is near where you live?'

'Yes.' Confirmed Terens.

'It dominates part of the galaxy.' I added.

'Then that is even more extraordinary.' Said the inspector, sitting down heavily and placing his hands on the table in front of him. By this time, the young policeman whom we had met earlier had joined us unnoticed at the table. He looked up at the young policeman standing stiffly beside him. 'Are you sure of this?' He asked him.

'Yes, sir.' Was the formal reply.

'And how far is this Cloud?'

'Approximately one hundred and fifty thousand light year's away sir.' I could not believe what I was hearing. What was he talking about? Was he suggesting that we had come from another galaxy? That seemed such a preposterous idea I could not even consider believing it. Then with a sinking feeling I remembered our time in the space of total blackness of deep space that we took for space outside our galaxy. Had it been outside the galaxy after all? Had we then gone to the wrong galaxy? That seemed even more preposterous. But had we? I tried to remember what had happened during that time, but it was very fuzzy. I seemed to remember that we did not return in one go. Was that what had gone wrong? Was it possible for us to travel so far? I was brought back by another question.

He looked sternly at us. 'Do you seriously expect me to believe that you have travelled one hundred and fifty thousand light years without a portal?' This was not a rhetorical question and he was looking at us for an answer. Before we could reply Karon finally broke down and started crying.

'What is the matter?' Asked a concerned Ruuth as she went over and put her arms around her. The poor girl was sobbing so much she could not reply for a while. We all sat awkwardly as Ruuth tried to calm her down enough to be able to talk. While Ruuth was comforting her, I took the opportunity to gather my thoughts.

'May I say something?' I asked the Inspector.

'Of course'

'May I thank this young policeman for his impetuosity and ingenuity?'

'Of course, thank him yourself.' I looked across at the young man still standing stiffly by the Inspector.

'Thank you. I am sorry but that does not seem enough. We are innocent and we are what we say we are.' He nodded almost imperceptibly. 'How did you come up with this amazing solution?' The young man looked at the Inspector.

'Go ahead Rhobin.'

'Thank you, sir.' He said and turned to me. 'Arachnid is the family name for spiders. A Tarantula is a type of spider, so I made an assumption that somehow the name had become changed by time or by isolation. It did not take long to find it once I had made that connection.'

'Thank you.' Said Djon and the others nodded but kept silent.

'I'm sorry.' Karon finally said. 'Are you sure that we have come from one galaxy to another?' She looked imploringly at the inspector. He sat impassively for a moment.

'From the information that you have given us it appears that you have indeed come from another galaxy.'

'Will I be able to go home?' She asked. The inspector again sat quietly for a moment.

'My dear lady.' He replied. 'At the moment we cannot allow you to leave until we have discovered more about your story and more about this other galaxy from which you have come. As far as this galaxy is concerned there have not been any human settlements outside the Milky Way. To hear your story that you do not originate from here means we must make every effort to find out the background to your lives and satisfy ourselves that you are not something other than what you say. This news is very disturbing indeed.' He stopped as obviously another thought occurred to him. 'Well, this may explain why we have not been able to locate the criminal gangs. They are just too far away for the portal signals to register on our sensors. It does begin to make some sense. Now how did you manage to travel from one galaxy to another?'

'We have the vessel-based portal.' I answered. 'Those pods that ring our vessel are the external components of the portal. I can assure you it got us here although we had no idea that we had come so far or even left one galaxy for another. You must excuse us if we seem a little shocked, but this news is very disturbing for us.'

'It is disturbing for me too if correct. But it would explain why you appear to know nothing of the Milky Way.' Said the inspector sternly. 'Rhobin, can you verify their statement with the information gleaned from their V20?'

'I can try sir. If I had some idea where to look in the LMC. There are not enough stars to look at the whole thing.' The inspector looked back at me.

'You are the pilot. Can you give my colleague more information?'

'I can try sir.'

'Then go with him, now.' There was an authority in his voice that meant I should do as he said right now. I got up and left the table, making my apologies to the others. I followed the young officer back to the room where we originally were interrogated. He started up the large V20 and fed in the data that Ruuth had found in our own V20. He pulled out a seat and I sat down. The fuzzy blob and few stars appeared in the bluish orb, looking very lost in the centre. There was a big book on the table. He pulled it over in front of us and opened it at a marked page. It was a chapter entitled 'Large Magellanic Cloud' and both pages had a detailed picture of the Arachnid Nebula. I reached out and instinctively touched the page as if I could make myself become back home by so doing. The young officer had enough sense to sit quietly as I lost myself in the picture. I felt tears welling up in my eyes as I thought of my mother at home, my brother and sister and my friends. The picture brought back all my memories of childhood and then my father's disappearance. There in the picture as red and clear as if it were next door was the Arachnid Nebula. Surprisingly though it looked completely different in this picture than I had seen it before. When we were at Fyrest Prime the shape had been reversed and it was nothing like as beautiful or as richly coloured. From Fyrest the nebula had appeared as a very faint wispy slightly ruddy gossamer haze. Here in the picture the shape and colours were so much more rich and clear. Then I collected myself.

'I'm sorry.' I said. 'It has been a while since I have seen my home. I am not used to seeing the galaxy..' I stopped again. My home was not even given the dignity of being called a galaxy but merely a cloud. I felt cheated. My home was a galaxy and that is what I would call it, even if this lot here only think it differently. 'I am not used to seeing my galaxy from this angle. I normally see it from inside. Enceladus is about here.' I pointed to the picture.

'The hidden portal I would estimate to be about here.' I pointed to another part of the picture. 'I think.'

'There is more.' He said and turned the page. There were more pages of pictures of my home galaxy. I just sat in stunned silence overawed by the majesty and clarity of the pictures taken from one hundred and fifty thousand light years distance.

'Could you create some of your cl.. sorry, galaxy in the V20?'

'I will try.' I said. 'But how..?'

'We can open a creative matrix. Allow me.' He closed the hidden portal and after tapping in some commands on the keypad a grid of faint blue squares appeared in the orb. I had no idea the V20 could do this sort of thing. This machine constantly amazed me by the sheer complexity and brilliant design. Then he made a single red dot appear in one of the cubes. 'Right if we assume that each cube is ten light years per side can you mark any other stars, planets or portals, particularly the hidden portal?'

I blew out my cheeks as I considered the task.

'While you think.' He said and again tapped out commands. The word Enceladus 421 appeared by the red dot and then he looked at me expectantly.

An hour later and we had a few more portals and planets in the orb. I looked at them.

'Move that one five light years on the A coordinate.' He did so. It looked much better. 'That looks about right. The hidden portal looks to be in about the right place.'

'OK.' He tapped out more commands and the fuzzy blob appeared in the matrix.

'Rotate it through ninety degrees on the Z axis.' He did so. 'That's it.'

'Thank you. I will save that.' He tapped again. 'Right, tonight I will have to use the telescope and the long-range sensors and try and locate this in actuality in the night sky. We get a good view of the LMC from here. You may return to your friends and enjoy your day here. You are not yet free to leave though.' Although I did not like being imprisoned, I had to smile inside. Where on Erebus did he think we were going to go? We were one hundred and fifty thousand light years from home! I got up and went back outside.

It was later that evening that we found ourselves back out on the terrace looking up at the dark sky. This time there was not the dramatic division between the starry part and the empty part. Tonight, it was just the empty part. We were standing there all looking at a small smudge of light in the sky.

Home!

The young policeman had pointed it out to us before he left us to go to the observatory and check up on our story. I just hoped he could find something to prove us correct.

'Is that really home?' Asked Karon.

'It would appear so.' Said Djon, placing a hand gently on her shoulder. She was shivering slightly even though it was another warm night. I knew it was not the shiver of cold but of agitation, the agitation of being so far from home and having nowhere to go or call your own. It was also the agitation of not only being so far from home but not being able to go back either! Terens just stood staring up at the blackness of the night sky looking at that smudge of light. It was hard to believe that it was actually home. That smudge was a galaxy with millions of stars and our home planets.

'I find it hard to believe that we have actually come that far in our vessel.' Said Terens finally, without looking round. He had a point. It was an incredible distance to come in our small vessel. Perhaps we did not after all. But then any other answer does not seem to make any sense either. The facts as I saw them all indicated that we had indeed come from somewhere else.

'I saw pictures of the Arachnid Nebula and they call it the same name here too.' I said. 'It was the nebula as I recognised the shape.' I added as I saw Terens about to ask the question. 'It is in the galaxy they call the Large Magellanic Cloud. I was horrified that they did not even think our galaxy was deemed a proper galaxy at all. How dare they!' I stopped as I realised that I was beginning to ramble, and the others just wanted to be with their own thoughts as they stared at home. There were a few moments reflective silence. It seemed unbelievable that we had come all that way from our home galaxy in our small vessel. The portal was more powerful than I ever dreamed of. Unless of course we had not come all that way! But the Arachnid Nebula? They had pictures of it! It was the nebula; it was near our home. Could they have made up a fake book to keep us in mental turmoil? That also seemed too far fetched. Why should they, what had they to gain from that? Were they really policemen? I could not answer the last one, so I determined to ask Djon or Terens if they knew. But then I was jerked out of my reverie.

'At least we now know where we are going.' Said Djon out of the blue.

'What!' I replied in shock.

'At least we now know it is Earth and not Ultima Thule where we are going.'

'You cannot be serious Djon.' Added Ruuth, dragging her gaze away from the night sky.

'Why not?' He asked with an injured voice.

'We are no longer in our own galaxy.'

'So? We started off in search of the original planet. Well now we have found it, or at least we now know what it is and where it is.'

'We don't know exactly where it is.'

'We know approximately, and we can easily find out the location from the historical data before the portal went offline.'

'But that will be out of date now, we are drifting apart at ten kilometres per second at least, so that astronomer policeman said, and the portal went offline at least one hundred and sixteen years ago. That would mean we are.' I paused as I tried to work out how far Earth would have drifted away from us, or nearer us, I was not quite sure what was happening.

'That would mean we are at least six hundred million kilometres adrift from the original portal coordinates. That is a lot of space to try and search in.' Added Ruuth helpfully. Djon's shoulders sank in dejection. He sat heavily on the wall that ran around the edge of the terraced area. We all joined him and sat on the wall in a silent line looking again at the night sky. In the quiet I began to find myself feeling sorry for Djon again. I looked back up at the small smudge of light which was home. It was about one hundred and fifty thousand light years away. In the opposite direction was Earth, the original planet which was approximately ten thousand light years away. We had come so far, I found myself thinking the unthinkable and agreeing with Djon again. The purpose was to find the original planet whatever it was called and to come so far seemed absurd to then turn back. But also, we could not turn back. Home seemed to be a criminal haven full of people who did not know what was going on. Or did they?

'Djon?' I asked tentatively.

'Yes?'

'What do you think is going on at home?'

'What do you mean?'

'Well, these police here think that the criminals that they chased here left and set up home in our galaxy.'

'They didn't set up home in our galaxy Djim, they settled our galaxy, which I am sure was not inhabited before, and stole babies to make a source of slaves to maintain their lifestyles.' He replied grimly. I felt shocked, it was worse than I could have contemplated. I had known it deep down but had not allowed myself to think it. We had been slaves without knowing it. Then it sank in what the police had said earlier about us being descendants of the kidnapped babies. We had originally come from here after all, or at least our forebears had. Perhaps we had come home after all. But then I remembered my family back on Enceladus. But were they my real family? This news had put everything into doubt. Who was my mother? Was she my mother? How would I ever be able to find out? I thought before that we were encountering more questions than answers, but this now made even more questions!

'Are you thinking what I am thinking?' Asked Terens of Djon.

'I might be Terens, it depends on what you are thinking.'

'It occurs to me that those criminal gangs are stripping our galaxy of anything valuable and bringing it to Earth, which is why the portal has appeared to have ceased working.'

'Appeared to?' I queried.

'Yes, I think they have just hidden it like they did with the hidden portal at home. They must be living a wonderful wealthy lifestyle on Earth. Thy have probably enslaved the original population that was left there, the poor souls. We never knew anything else, but they did.' It was another of those very unusually long speeches of Terens.

'That thought had indeed occurred to me.'

Things began to start making sense. No wonder that there was no concern over the state of the planets because the people in charge, the criminals, only wanted the precious metals and minerals. This meant that as soon as a planet became sterile it would be left for another. No wonder that the poor people that had to get the precious commodities were treated so badly. I had thought it was because of being an outpost in the galaxy, in the forefront of new exploration, when in fact we were just being used. I felt cheated and I also felt very angry. We had to stop these criminals and the sooner the better.

'We must tell the police that the criminals are enslaving a whole galaxy.' I said at last.

'In good time Djim.' Drawled Djon slowly. 'In good time. In the meantime, they may be thinking that we are part of the criminal gangs.'

'Why would they think that? We're descended from the kidnapped babies, they said so.'

'Yes, we are, but we also come from a galaxy of criminals. How do they know who are guilty and who are not? How do we know?'

'But we are innocent.' I said innocently.

'We know that, at least we think we are but are we for sure?'

'From the outside who is and who isn't guilty? Would you know for sure?' Put in Ruuth.

'So, what do we do?' I asked.

'We can use the V20 to locate the Earth portal like we did for the hidden one.' Suggested Terens from the end of the line.

'We can.' Said Djon, and I could tell even in the dark that his spirits had risen a bit. 'We can then go to Earth.'

'What do we do then?' Asked Karon. There was a pause. I was not sure that Djon had thought any further than just getting there. What did we do when we got there? We did not know if they even used the galactic dollar so could we buy anything?

What part of the planet would we go to? It sounded from what the inspector had been saying that much of the planet was inhabited with a great deal of diversity and cultures. I thought back to the planets we had visited on our journey here and how out of place I felt. Enceladus was still home to me after all that had happened. But could I even go back there anymore? I had perhaps become a planetless person. Even though it was a warm night a cold shiver ran involuntarily down my spine at the thought of having nowhere to call my own. I felt lost and alone in a huge uncaring universe. Would I ever be able to get back and see my mother and family again? To do so, the police would have to wrest the planets free from the grasp of the intergalactic criminals, and that would not be easy. After such a long time in control the criminals grip would be so strong and fibrous, like the roots of a tree that spread deep down into the very fabric of the ground. Like a weed that is pulled up leaving the roots behind to keep growing, the very same thing could happen in our galaxy. The gangs could rise again unless completely destroyed. Djon finally answered.

'I had not thought about what happened after we got there.' He said, with a big grin on his face. Even though it was dark I could sense the grin without seeing it. 'We will see what happens when we get there.'

'You mean we will have travelled over one hundred and fifty-six thousand light years and we don't even know what we are going to do when we get there!' Spluttered Ruuth, almost apoplectic with an anger that I had never seen her express before. I think it was probably because of what had happened in the last few days.

We were interrupted by a strange noise in the sky which made us all look up and dispelled Ruuth's anger instantly. It was a noise I knew well. It was barely audible but in the quiet stillness of the night sky it did not bode well. It was a sizzling of the air that went rapidly across the sky followed by the distant rumble of the sound barrier being broken. Before we could speak there was the sound of an alarm ringing somewhere in the complex. The lights came on illuminating the sheer cliff face and the dull black bulbous shape of our vessel that loomed over the crest.

'What is going on now?' Asked Karon her voice tremulous with anxiety.

'An asteroid.' I said. 'Has just passed through the atmosphere. Did you hear it?'

'That funny noise you mean?'

'Yes, that was it, just before the alarm went off. I am not sure at this stage if there is a connection.'

'A connection?' She asked.

'Yes, if there is one asteroid there may be another, although..' I was cut off by a shout from the doorway in the cliff, now hidden in the darkness by the lighting that had just come on. Someone was calling our names. Djon called back. Out of the darkness came the inspector. He was a little agitated.

'You do not know how irritating it is that you do not have personal communicators. We were trying to contact you. We need to leave the surface. Did you hear the asteroid?'

'Yes.' I said. 'I was very surprised to hear one being so near the edge of the galaxy.'

'You and us both.' He replied, still grim faced in the gloom. 'But our young colleague, who was looking for your home planets in The Magellanic Cloud, came across these asteroids heading this way. It was very fortuitous. But the trouble is unless we get off planet and hide in the lee of the planet our vessels and us may be smashed into nothing.'

'Are you sure?'

'Yes, these are the coordinates. Now get your vessel spaceborne as soon as possible and we will rendezvous there and ride out the shower. Do not get your belongings there is not time, and besides, we will not be there for long, we should be back in a few hours. Now follow me.' He turned and led us back into the complex at a run.

'I need my bag.' I gasped as I ran behind him. He was very quick on his feet and I had trouble keeping up with him.

'Why? There is not much time now.'

'It contains our V20, we cannot go anywhere without it.'

'You must be quick though. Your friends must get the vessel spaceworthy in the meantime or you may not make it. Go now and get it quickly!' We were at the lift by this time and the wait for the car seemed an agonisingly long time. Then the door opened onto the bright shiny interior and we all squeezed into the car. We stood there for what seemed another agonisingly long time as the floor numbers silently counted up. Then the door opened onto the corridor and immediately I could hear the very low dull almost inaudible roar of the anti gravity gyros of the police vessels. There was the dull red light filtering in through the door at the end of the corridor. The others ran along the corridor as I dived into my room. I grabbed my bag and looked inside to see if the V20 was there. It was not! I knew we could not find any coordinate if we did not have it. I looked feverishly around the room in the drawers and cupboards, but it was nowhere to be found. Then I remembered where I had seen it last. It was on the table in the room where we were first questioned. I could not let anyone else know as they had by now left the building. The only thing to do was go and get it. I left a note on my bed saying where I had gone just in case someone came to find me. I ran back out of the room carrying my bag and pressed the lift button. The door opened immediately, and I dived in and pressed the floor button. The door slid shut and again I stood waiting impatiently. After what seemed an age the door opened, and I ran out but could not remember which way to go. I wasted valuable seconds trying to remember. Then I just had to go, and I ran down a corridor and tried every door I could see but none were the right room. Then I found myself back outside on the terrace area and cursed loudly before turning round and heading back into the complex. This time I remembered which way to go and soon found myself back in the room. There on the table still connected up was our V20 control panel. I grabbed it and put it into my bag and headed out of the room to the lift. Then I could not find the lift and stood helplessly in a corridor sweating from the exertion and worry. Which way to go? I tried to calm myself so I could think straight again. It seemed so long as I desperately tried to get my breathing under control and calm myself. It finally worked and I clearly recalled where the lift was and ran gratefully down the corridor. It still seemed to take forever for the lift to rise through the complex to the right floor and the door to open again onto the corridor.

As I ran out of the lift Terens came running out of my room a desperate look on his face. He finally saw me and stopped dead.

'Where on Erebus have you been?' He snarled.

'The V20 was still downstairs, and I had to go and get it.' I growled back. 'Now let us go!'

'Right, come on.' He turned and ran quickly in front of me with a surprising turn of speed. Then I remembered that he was an explorer of worlds and so must be very fit. It was not long before he left me behind.

As I ran around the end of the blast wall onto the landing pad, he was well in front of me. There was only the dull red glow coming from our vessel's anti gravity gyros as they warmed up. There were no other vessels to be seen but up in the night sky I could see the brilliant white pinpoints of light from the police vessel drives.

Then I was running panting up the makeshift ramp up into our vessel. Terens began the hatch closing procedure as I entered.

'Keep going. Get up to the control room as soon as you can!' He ordered. I needed no second order and kept running. I suddenly realised how much I had missed our dear vessel. It had seen us through some bad times and had kept us safe. Every little detail of the corridor I passed was like a long-lost friend being found again. I saw things that I had not noticed for many years, ever since pilot training in fact.

I burst into a tense control room which erupted into angry shouts as I entered.

'Where have you been Djim, the proximity sensor has been going berserk!' Shouted Djon as he leapt up out of the pilot's seat.

'Looking for the V20!' I shouted back, now angry myself

as I threw myself in the recently vacated seat which was still warm. I reached into the bag and drew out the V20 control and quickly set it into its housing in the control panel. When the tiny green light came on that indicated it was seated properly, I switched on the V20. As it was warming up, I checked the pre-flight readouts on the forward vision enhancer. All was well. Djon had done a good job getting the vessel warmed up and ready to leave. My only problem was the portal hanging limply outside the hull. I had no idea how it would react when we took off or how it would affect the trim of the vessel. If I thought taking off from that little shed on Enceladus was tricky then this was a real test of my pilot skills. It was an easy job, more or less, when it was in a weightless environment, but this was a different matter in the grip of the planet's gravity.

'Djon!' I said finally.

'Yes.'

'I am very concerned about the portal hanging off our vessel here.'

'What do you mean?' There was annoyance in his voice with a tinge of worry.

'Well, out in space it is not so much of a problem but down here the weight is all one side. I do not know what is going to happen when we take off and the weight distribution starts moving around. It could cause me real problems.'

'Can we not just use the portal to leave here?' Asked Terens. There was a stunned silence for a moment as I took in what he had said.

'Apart from the fact that it has never been done before we do not know what the affect will be if we try it on a planet's surface and with the portal not deployed. The theory..' Terens cut me off.

'How soon can we deploy the portal?'

'I don't know Djon, I really don't know. I have no experience of this and certainly do not know what will happen in gravity.'

'Can we take off then and deploy once spaceborne?'

'That is just what I was saying Djon, I do not know what

effect this portal will have hanging off the hull. It could destabilize the vessel and cause us to crash!'

'We'll just have to take a chance on it.' Said Djon. 'If we don't, we will be smashed to bits anyway.'

'That sounds familiar.' Grunted Terens.

'OK. I'll take us up. Djon can you be ready to deploy the portal when I say. I have no idea what effect that will have either. It could cause us to crash as well. I'm ready to go.'

'Then get us up. This proximity meter is going mad here.'

With great trepidation I took the controls and looked across at Djon. I could see the anxiety in his face too even though he was pretending he was not worried. The anti gravity gyros began to take the weight of the vessel in that dull rumble, almost inaudible. I could feel the point at which we were airborne and could also feel the additional load of the portal. Even though it was not very heavy in comparison to the vessel it was enough to cause an imbalance as the pods moved about. Like water slopping about in a barrel. Warning slights flashed as the imbalance began to grow wilder. I was finding it difficult to keep the vessel in trim. The best thing would have been to accelerate and make the pods fall back into a stable position. The trouble was that it could also pull the pods out of their mountings or damage the hull or the pods as they crashed against the hull. In the end I had to go with the latter. I fired the main drive much earlier than normally. So, near the surface the blast from the drive would not only damage anything in its way but the blowback could also damage the vessel or worse cause us to crash. It seemed that every option was more or less as bad as each other. As the drive fired up with minimum power the instability began slowly to dissipate. That at least was one improvement. I just hoped that there would be no effect from any blowback from the drive. The longer we continued the less chance there was of that happening. So far so good. I typed in the coordinates that the inspector had given us and zoomed the V20 into the right view. The planet became a dark inverted bowl shape taken out of the bottom of the V20 orb. The flight vectors showed up as a dotted green line arcing round to the coordinate position. I could see the other vessels in the orb as a series of small red dots. The proximity alarm and the impact alarm were also flashing silently on the control panel. I had switched off the audible alarms as they were distracting. Once the vessel became more stable and the flight path more reliable I turned the flight over to the clique computer and sat back. I was sweating and shaking from the effort.

There was a sudden movement in the vessels flight path which nearly unseated me as I just begun to release the restraint straps.

'That must be an asteroid coming in.' I said helpfully but probably unnecessarily.

'Right.' Said Djon. 'Where are we going?'

'To the coordinates that the inspector gave us and asked us to go to, that's where.' I replied somewhat annoyed. Djon knew where we had been asked to go to avoid being smashed by the asteroid shower.

'What I mean is.' He added with a sigh. 'Is that now is our chance to go to Earth.' I half stood half sat in the pilot's seat hanging onto the arms as I took in just what Djon had said. As I thought about his comment, I saw the asteroid pass through the V20 orb as a fast moving yellow dot. Its trajectory a fine dotted yellow line stretching out in front of it. It seemed an odd time to be thinking just how much calculations must be required to show all this information in the V20. Ruuth spoke first.

'We cannot just run away from the police. We will then become outlaws and have to keep looking over our shoulders expecting arrest at any moment.' She looked as worried as I felt.

'Oh, Ruuth, there is no need to worry about that. All I am suggesting is that we just go and visit Earth and finally reach our goal. We can have a good look round and then come back! We needn't be gone for too long.' He was getting excited again, which usually meant trouble. 'We can easily claim that something went wrong and we took a while to find our way back. They won't mind if we return.' How daft could I be? I actually found myself finding his argument so plausible. There was a few moments silence as the others also considered this argument. That was also bad news as it meant we were all considering a flight to Earth. Ever since the drugs had left our bodies we had all become much more independent in our thinking and actions but now back in our vessel that seemed to be vanishing like mist in the morning sunshine. We were back in the old mindset of following Djon and his crazy scheme. But there again, we had come so far it seemed a good idea to try and complete our journey. But there was still the problem that we would be running away from the police.

'Why don't we just wait a bit and leave with the agreement of the police?' Asked Karon.

'Haven't you heard what they have said?' Replied Djon. 'They think that because we have come from the region where the criminals are that we also may be criminals. They have nothing to confirm our story. They cannot allow us to go until they can confirm that we have nothing to do with the criminals.'

'If we run won't it make them think we are criminals?' Asked Karon, surprisingly calmly. In fact, I was surprised at just how calmly we were all discussing this crazy idea.

'If we just stay here.' Replied Djon trying to stay calm. 'It is possible they may never be able to prove who we are or us prove our story. We come from a long long way away and it will not be easy to find any evidence to clear us.' This made me feel cold deep down my spine. He was right. It could take a very long time for the police to prove us innocent. It may never happen; in which case we would never get to Earth at all. After initially thinking that Djon's idea was one more in a long line of daft ideas I was thinking that perhaps it made some sense after all. How did he do it I asked myself? I noted that Terens had not taken any part of the conversation at all. This was typical of him, very quiet but thinking deeply all the same. It was infuriating sometimes but I was glad he was on our side.

'Well?' Asked Djon, looking round at us all in turn with his palms spread outwards. 'What do you think we should do? Do we go?' He had a knack of making us do what he wanted.

Perhaps it was not just a drug in the water. Perhaps Djon had some way of influencing us as like the drugs. I hoped that that was just a stupid idea without foundation. 'This may be our only chance.' He added as no one answered straight away.

'I don't like the idea of running away like this.' I said, still concerned that leaving the police without authority to do so could cause us real problems even if we do come back. 'What if we cannot get back for some reason? It will not look so good then and we will have become outlaws for nothing.'

'You do have a point Djim.' He said, somewhat crestfallen. 'But I still cannot see us getting another chance. I am sure we can get back. What could stop us from returning?' How did he do it? He knew that none of us could answer that as we had no idea what we were heading for, but he had a knack of putting us on the spot and making us look stupid if we disagreed with him.

'After all.' He added again as there was still a reluctance on our part to answer. 'We have got this far so we could easily get back. We have the information in the V20.' I felt the resistance ebbing away.

'It sounds plausible to me.' Said Karon innocently. I cringed inwardly as I knew that once one of us had even considered the idea then we had lost the argument.

'Of course it is.' Confirmed Djon. 'We are not guilty and have nothing to worry about. No one can find any evidence that we are connected with any criminals or with any wrong doing. Besides when we return, we can say that something went wrong with our vessel which sent us off...I know, we had to avoid an asteroid which caused us to skip onto another part of the galaxy. We don't need to tell them we went to Earth.' He gave Karon in particular, his innocent look which I knew would work on her as she had not been long enough with us yet to be able to spot his little ways of making us agree with him. I had to try and think of something quickly to avert a disaster. But before I could speak Karon replied.

'That is a good idea Djon. I recon we should go ahead and do it. We have come this far as you say and although I did not join you to go to Earth as you call it I still think that you should finish your journey. All I wanted to do was get away from the horrible change at home. I am sure that nice policeman will not mind if you go for a few days and then come back. He has not needed us to be here really.' Unfortunately, I knew that once one of us buckled under then Terens would also want to go. He hated being cooped up in one place for long. I was surprised that he had remained calm for so long. The only reason he managed to keep his cool in the Jergan for so long was the fact that we were going somewhere and there was the worry of who was behind us. I checked the controls as I waited for the next step. It was not long in coming.

'We have been sitting around here for far too long.' Muttered Terens at last. 'We have done nothing and got nowhere. I am all for going to Ult...Earth. We can always come back and blame some piece of equipment.'

'What about our families and friends back home?' Asked Ruuth.

'What do you mean?' Asked Djon, showing just a little concern at this turn of events.

'I mean, Djon, shouldn't we be looking to help the police get our friends and families away from the grip of those criminals?'

'How?'

'How!' She cried. 'We have the vessel-based portal, that's how. With this the police can send vessels to our galaxy and take control.'

'It's not as easy as that Ruuth.' Replied Terens, remarkably calmly for him. 'A whole galaxy. Who are the criminals and who are the innocents? It will take some time to organise enough portals and also decide on a strategy. You cannot just go in there with insufficient police or with an incomplete plan. Do not forget the criminals have control of the portals and many could easily just slip away as soon as they know the police are in our galaxy. It could be a very messy business.' I stood open mouthed as I not considered that before. He was right though. In fact, until he had just given us his ideas of the problems involved, I had thought like Ruuth, that we just went there and rescued everybody. Now I was seriously worried that we might never be able to either get back or save our families. It set me thinking just how we could help the police to catch the criminals. The enormity of the task began to dawn on my thought. Over four thousand planets and millions of people! How on Erebus do you manage to undertake such a task? I was beginning to understand the dilemma that the inspector found himself and why nothing appeared to have been done. Still, it meant that a few days away would not be a problem. I could see now why Djon wanted to go now, if we waited then there is almost certainly no chance to go to Earth once the mission was underway. Then another thought struck me. How on Erebus is the mission to be kept a secret? This will require an army to be arranged and once word got out the criminals would just melt away. Or would they? Perhaps they would stage a pre-emptive attack or disrupt the mission in some way. The whole thing began to get just too impossible to even consider. What if the police think the same way? All those people still trapped in the criminal system in our galaxy and no one able to do anything about it. That thought was too awful to bear. Something had to be done!

'Djim!' Said someone and snapped me out of my reverie.

'Sorry, What?' I replied looking round.

'You were miles away Djim, what were you thinking?'

'I was just thinking about what Terens had said. The enormity of the problem has just hit me.'

'Me too.' Said Djon. 'But we have come to the conclusion that because the problem is so big that we might as well go to Earth have a look and then come back and see how we can help rescue our galaxy.'

'I was coming to the same conclusion myself. Except that I also have suddenly remembered that those criminals we thought were taking all the precious minerals from our galaxy to Earth. If we turn up on their doorstep won't they be a little annoyed?' I paused for breath. 'Not only that but we have been captured once by them and I do not wish to go through that again.'

'You have a point.' Said Ruuth and she turned to Djon and gave him a withering stare.

'I know what you are saying Djim, but we don't know for sure that those criminals are taking the stuff to Earth and if they are we don't know how much of Earth they may control. They cannot have taken hold of a whole planet.'

'They have taken control of a whole galaxy Djon!' I spluttered.

'That is true but that is not in this galaxy where the police exist.'

'We don't know if the police still exist on Earth either.'

We had come to an impasse. It looked as though there was no way Djon's idea could work.

'Oh, for sky's sake just get on and go!' Exploded Karon. 'I cannot stand this vacillation anymore. I know we will look guilty if we go and it could mean we get into trouble, but it may be your only chance. As you say, they may not be able to prove we are innocent and we will never be allowed to go. We may even end up in prison! Besides, they do not have vessel-based portals so cannot go. Even if they manage to replicate them, they still may not let us go. Just take the chance!' She stopped suddenly and there was a stunned silence broken only by Karon's heavy breathing.

I was amazed at her outburst. It seemed out of character for her to explode like that. I was surprised to see Ruuth smiling broadly and Terens nodding. I turned to Djon.

'OK.' Said Djon finally. 'We are agreed that we go then. Djim, can you work out how to get there?'

'I think so. We have the information from their V20 so we can work out approximately where it is. The problem is that I do not know exactly how to direct this portal. I assume it is a straight-line phenomenon and just plotting the length of travel. I do not know for sure though. It is a bit of a chance as to where we end up. All we need to do is work out how far away the planet Earth is.'

'We can check the start and finish co-ordinates to see where we have gone.' Said Terens.

'Good, I'll go and work out where Earth should be.' Said Ruuth. 'I can remember the distances from before.' Before she could move the police called us on the vessel to vessel communications.

'Just go Ruuth.' Said Djon. 'Djim, call them back and tell them we will be there shortly, but we are having a problem.'

'OK.' I turned and returned the call to the police as Djon had said. They accepted that and said they would await our arrival. I then checked that the portal was properly deployed and that the V20 still had the controls for it in place. All was ready and seemed to be OK. I turned on the camera to see if I could see the portal, but the view did not allow me to view it.

'Djon.' I called. 'Can you go and find a porthole that will give a view of the portal for me. I want to know that it is properly deployed and looks to be in one piece.'

'Will do.' He turned and left the control room, dragging a complaining Terens with him. A short while later they returned.

'It appears to be deployed correctly Djim.' He said breathlessly.

'I also have a distance.' Said Ruuth. 'And a direction, but it is based on old information so we could be a bit out.'

'Near enough is good enough until we know a bit more about it.' I said. 'Can you enter the coordin..'

'Already done it Djim.' Said Ruuth. 'just set the automatic pilot to follow the direction and we can skip when we are ready.'

'Thank you. Does anyone know how far away from this planet we need to be before we can operate this portal?'

'I didn't know you had to be away from a planet.' Said Karon innocently.

'Oh yes.' I replied. 'If a portal operates too close to anything it can suck part of it into the zone of influence which can cause all sorts of terrible problems. Well, that is the theory anyway and I have no intention of trying to find out if the theory is accurate!'

'Oh.' She said as I turned to set the automatic pilot to

follow Ruuth's coordinates. But almost immediately the proximity alarm light flashed rapidly in the corner of my eye. I zoomed the V20 view further out to see what the problem was and saw that there was an asteroid heading straight for us! There was going to be no time to take avoiding action. There was only one choice and that was to skip now.

'What's wrong?' Asked Djon.

'Asteroid heading straight for us.' I replied. 'I think we are going to have to use the portal now.'

'Are we far enough away from the planet yet?' Asked a worried Ruuth.

'I have no idea, but we have no other chance to get out of the way.'

'Do it then.' Said Djon getting back into his seat. The others followed and in seconds we were all seated and ready. 'OK, Djim let us go.'

'Right, we are going then.' I called up the portal controls in the V20 and as the asteroid ripped through the atmosphere towards us fired it up. Again, we all felt the feeling of falling and the screen went blank.

– CHAPTER 16 –

The forward vision enhancer blinked back into life and with great relief I saw that the view it presented was full of stars. We were still in the galaxy. But which galaxy? Having travelled from one galaxy to another I was not sure where we would end up. It took me a while to recover from the skip and I just sat and looked at the starry sky in the vision enhancer and wondered which one was the star which illuminated the solar system of Earth. The others gradually returned to normal beside me and the silence began to be eroded by the rising murmur of consciousness and the vessel came back to life. I was aware again of the general hum of onboard operations working to maintain the systems.

'Where are we?' Asked Karon. Her speech still slurred like her mouth had been numbed.

'Don't know yet.' I replied. I waited as the V20 orb began to grow again into a wobbly sphere before snapping into its perfect shape. Then the stars began to fill in the interior of the orb. Finally, the star and portal details began appearing.

'I made a note of The Sun as the Earth's star is called.' Said Djon. 'As I knew we might need the information later on.' He reached into a pocket and produced a crumpled piece of paper which he opened out and vainly tried to flatten out on the control panel. He then handed it to me. I took it and read the details.

'The Sun.' I said.

'Yes.' Said Djon. 'It stands to reason. If that is the place where mankind began then they would call their star 'The Sun' as they had not yet gone to any other sun. Every other sun to them would be a star. So, the stars all have numbers or names as we would expect.' I knew then that we had finally found the home planet of mankind. It seemed odd that it was not called

Ultima Thule as we had been led to believe but at least we were now on the right track. How Ultima Thule came about was still a mystery though except that I was beginning to suspect that it was intended to put us off the right course. There was no Ultima Thule so we could never find it and would give up. Very clever.

I checked the details on Djon's scrap of paper and inputted the information into the V20's database.

'We must remember people that this information is very out of date and will not have been updated so it will not be accurate.' I pressed enter and a new dot appeared with the details that Djon had given me hovering beside it. As I expected it did not line up with any star. It was also a long way away from us, at about eight hundred light years at a guess.

'Ruuth.' I asked. 'Do you have the old data from the old Earth portal?'

'Yes.' She replied. 'It is already in the V20 if you look under the miscellaneous file. I have not had the opportunity to refine it though, so I need to do that.'

'Well, when you are ready.' I said. 'We do not have anyone chasing us so we have plenty of time to decide where to go.'

'Oh, no we don't.' Came Karon's voice from behind me. I spun round; she had spoken with some authority which was unusual for her. She was looking straight at me. 'Djim, we didn't bring anything with us for a long trip. We have very few supplies and very little in the way of other equipment or clothes! I recon we only have a couple of day's worth of food! If we are very careful, we may make the water last three days.' I stood looking at her with my mouth open as the import of her words sunk into my slow witted consciousness.

'Oh, ghas!' said Djon finally. 'I had forgotten that. We need to find a planet very soon then.'

'We don't know the protocol for portal use or planet landings.' Said Ruuth. 'What if the police on Gonfalon Royal have notified other planets that we have left them without authority? We could find ourselves in prison! Again!' She was obviously agitated, and I had to sympathise with her. Yet again Djon's impetuosity had sent us into an absurd situation unprepared. I should have known better though. Preparation is everything on a space flight! I felt like a rank amateur and in fact could remember telling off a junior pilot for just this sort of thing.

'How long will you need?' I asked Ruuth.

'Fortunately, Djim, not long. Having done the last one I know what to do. Just give me a couple of hours.' She immediately sat down in front of the V20 and without further ado she set to work. 'I could do with a drink though.' She said without looking round.

'Don't worry Ruuth.' Said Karon. 'I will get you one. Any others?' She looked around at us. We all nodded. She left the control room. I let her do it as I knew she felt much better having something to do. She could not help at all with the running of the vessel so this was her way of feeling useful. I vowed that I must teach her something of spaceflight so she could feel a fuller member of the crew as well as increasing our safety margin should anything happen to us. As Ruuth worked I checked out what was around us to ensure there were no approaching vessels or space debris. All was clear. In fact, this part of the galaxy seemed very empty. There was nothing much else to do until Ruuth located Earth, so I took my drink from Karon and went and lay down for a while to gather my strength. I was still weak from the effects of the drug leaving my body.

I awoke later and apart from the general hum of the vessel's systems all was quiet. I struggled out of bed as the sleep had set me back for some reason and I felt really tired and had difficulty moving easily. I pulled myself upright and tried to stretch but could not do it fully. I staggered out of my room and headed for the control room. It was empty when I got there, and I panicked as the proximity alarm and the other defensive mechanisms were not turned on. I slowly sat myself in the pilot's seat and immediately turned on the systems. Fortunately, all was clear so I then turned my attention to where everyone was. I was just about to drag myself out of the seat when Djon breezed into the control room. He had not been affected by the drug as much as the rest of us and was irritatingly cheerful.

'Hello.' He said. 'Good to see you up.'

'Where are the others?' I asked.

'They have all had to go back to bed too, just like you.' He sat down beside me.

'Did Ruuth manage to locate Earth before she went to bed?'

'No idea.' He stretched and yawned.

'Hi' Ruuth came, and with a bright smile that dispersed my worries immediately, sat down on the other side of me. 'I have managed to find a location for Earth and inputted it into the V20 so we are ready to go when you are.'

'Wow.' I replied, impressed with her staying power. The girl managed to get enormous amounts of work done even when obviously very tired. 'Shall we go then?' I turned to Djon.

'Yes.' He said. 'Get a move on, we have wasted enough time already and we do not have much food or water, so get going.' Being reminded of the shortages made me galvanise into action and my aches and pains just seemed to vanish as I switched on the V20 and got back into pilot mode. The bluish orb sprang into life and the stars appeared inside it. I called up Ruuth's data and the grey blob appeared in the orb also.

'How far away is that?' Asked Djon.

'Hold on.' I ran the diagnostic check and the distance check and it came up with answer of about seven hundred and twenty light years. 'Well, there you go, it is about seven hundred and twenty light years and the blob is about half a light year across so there is an enormous amount of space to search through. Perhaps when we get closer there will be some other clues as to the location of Earth so we don't have to waste too much time looking through all that empty space.'

'Let us hope so, Djim, so get going.'

'OK. Warn the others that we are going to operate the portal please.'

'I'm on it.' He said and nimbly left his seat and left the room. Ruuth just sat impassively watching the forward vision enhancer. For all her bravado she still found using any portal a bit of a strain but always put a brave face on it. I left it just long enough for Djon to notify Karon and Terens that we were about to go into ND space before initiating the portal start-up programme.

Again, there was the feeling of falling and the screen went blank.

My blurred vision cleared very slowly this time which I put down to still being tired from the drug. The V20 orb stopped wobbling and snapped back into its hard shape. Stars quickly filled the orb but were dull and misty and the orb was filled with a dull grey.

'What has gone wrong with the V20?' I asked, more of myself than anyone else.

'I think, Djim, we are within the zone of the Earth portal. If you zoom out you might find out if I am right or not.'

'OK.' I did as she suggested and zoomed the view of the V20 to a larger area. As she had predicted the grey became a sphere within the sphere. The red dot which was our vessel showed up within the greyness.

'Right.' She said with some finality. 'Give me a while and I will see if I can locate the Earth portal more accurately. Can you turn on all the external sensors we have got please.'

'Most certainly.' I leant forward and turned on the external sensors and sat back as the data began to appear down the side of the forward vision enhancer. I studied the information carefully to see if there was anything out of the ordinary. There was not so I turned on the other defence mechanisms, but nothing showed up on them either. I relaxed and watched Ruuth at work.

I could hear the others moving about in some other part of the vessel. I then began to worry about what we would find when we got to Earth. If Djon and Terens were right then we would face the criminals again when we got there and if they were going to be aggressive then we could find ourselves stranded out in space with no food or water. Yet again we might be staring death in the face either from starvation or from the criminals! Why did we do this?

'Try this.' Said Ruuth and put the new data up on the forward vision enhancer. I drew myself upright and entered the information into the V20. The grey sphere shrank to a much smaller dot and our red dot was right on the edge of it.

'How big is it now?' She asked.

'Give me a minute.' I said as I ran the calculation. 'Well, it seems to be about two billion kilometres in diameter.'

'That is still a bit big, I will have another look. Keep your ears open for anything that the sensors pick up that could direct us to Earth.'

'Already doing that.' Then something did catch my ear. 'In fact Ruuth I have just heard something.' I isolated the signal and used another programme to get the angle and distance. Between us we managed to reduce the grey blob to a very small dot no more than a billion kilometres across.

'That is more like it.' She said. 'Well, do we go there?'

'We have no where else to go and Djon is determined to go there so I think that is where we go. I will let the others know we are going into ND space again.' I used the vessel's internal communicator to notify them before resetting the V20.

Yet again the feeling of falling and the screen went blank.

Yet again things swam back into normality.

There was a very bright star about half a billion kilometres away and some smaller bright objects which were planets. Radio traffic suddenly increased. I opened the poor telescope that our vessel carried and focused on the direction of the radio traffic. On the screen a reasonable picture of a planet appeared.

'Is that Earth?' Asked Ruuth.

'I don't know. I'll call up the image that we have in the V20.' Moments later an identical image appeared.

'It is!' she said. I called the others over the internal communicator and within seconds the control room was full of their presence and excited chatter.

'Come on Djim.' Said Djon. 'Let us get over there and get a closer look.'

We made one last trip into ND space to get us within a few million kilometres of Earth. We could see it clearly in the forward vision enhancer once the screen returned to normal. There was a silence in the control room as we finally gazed out on the planet from which all mankind had originated.

Then the defence mechanism screamed into action. Something was heading right for us at colossal speed. There was nothing for it but to go into ND space again to avoid it. I just had time to check the incoming data. The object was heading for us directly in line from the planet. It could not have been space debris or an asteroid and the speed at which it was travelling was colossal!

'Go go go!' Yelled Terens.

*

The forward vision enhancer came back online and a starlit view appeared.

'Stars. At least we are still in the galaxy.' I said as I ran a quick check on the sensors. There was nothing in the vicinity of our vessel. Then the recharge lights came on.

Oh dear.' Said Djon. 'We need a recharge.'

'Can we recharge this far from a sun?' Asked Ruuth.

'Hold on.' I said and checked the recharge systems. 'Yes, we are OK, but it will take hours though at this range.'

'How far are we from Earth now?' Asked Djon.

'Just give me a minute.'

'Why would anyone fire at us like that without warning?' Asked Karon.

'I think.' Replied Terens thoughtfully. 'They do not want any visitors at all. I can only presume it is an automatic defence system that is activated by any vessel not broadcasting the right signal.'

'Does that mean we cannot go back there?'

'It does look that way unless we can find the right signal to broadcast.'

'What do we do then?' Asked Ruuth. I looked across at Djon. He was slumped disconsolately in his seat staring at the starry view in the vision enhancer.

'Well?' I said. Djon slowly looked away from the view

and let his tired gaze rest upon my face, hardly seeing me at all.

'To have come all this way and to fall at the very last is just too much to bear. Is there no way we can go back?' He looked across to Terens.

'Not that I can think of.' Replied Terens after a few moments thought without looking at Djon.

'What do you think Djim?'

'I have to agree with Terens. If it is an automatic system and requires a particular signal, then we will just activate it again. We also do not know what other systems they have should we manage to avoid that first strike.'

'If we cannot go to Ultim....Earth then were do we go?' Asked Karon.

'We could go to any planet in the galaxy?' Suggested Terens. I was not sure if he was joking or not.

'I thought that on Gonfalon Royal they said that you needed identification to land on a planet.' Said Ruuth.

'Are you sure?' Asked Djon.

'Yes. I asked him about travel in the galaxy just in case we needed it.'

'That is very proactive of you Ruuth.'

'Well, you never know when you are going to need something.'

'In that case.' Said Karon, interrupting us. 'Where do we go then?'

'It looks as though we have no alternative but to return to Gonfalon Royal.' I said quietly. There was silence for a while as everyone pondered this.

'I think you might be right there.' Said Djon dejectedly. 'It looks as though travel in this galaxy is a lot more restrictive. We will have to get some form of identity to be able to live and move in this galaxy. The only place we know of is where we came from unfortunately. This means we will have to return.'

'OK.' Said Ruuth finally as if all discussion was over and the final decision made. 'Where are we Djim, have you found out yet?'

'Oh, sorry.' I said. 'I was still thinking about where we could go. I had forgotten that Djon had asked me where we were.' I turned to the control panel with a cold chill running down my spine. Had we been careless in not watching out for any further external threat? There was nothing showing on any of the sensors so I relaxed again. I then finished off the calculation to find out our position. The others sat quietly as I worked. I knew they were all thinking how we could avoid going back.

'OK.' I said finally. 'I have our position. We are almost exactly half a light year the other side of Earth as we were before.'

'Did we travel through it then?' Asked Karon innocently.

'No.' I replied. 'In ND space you do not travel in the normal sense of the word so we have not passed through the planet.'

'Oh.' She said. I had the feeling she did not understand. It was not surprising. 'Can you get us back?'

'Yes, that is no problem. Well, everyone do we go back?' There was a general subdued agreement. 'Go back it is then.' I turned back to the controls. 'We need to recharge for a bit though. We cannot go for at least six of hours. We might as well get some rest. Two on watch and three off. I'll just recalculate where we need to go, ready for the return.'

*

Six hours later and the portal again squeezed infinity to infinitesimally small and back again. Gonfalon Royal hung in the blackness of space in front of us shining brightly from the reflected light of its sun. The radio crackled into life. 'Welcome back! Now shut down your vessel and put it into hibernation mode and be prepared to disembark. Our shuttle is already approaching. Do not attempt to leave.'

I sent an affirmative reply and prepared the vessel for hibernation in a stationary orbit. I wondered why they did not want us to land. I looked across at Djon and could see that he too was thinking the same thing.

'Right then we had better get our bags packed and be ready

to disembark. The shuttle will be here in half an hour according to the sensors.'

'We have no bags to pack.' Said Ruuth.

With quiet efficiency we got ourselves prepared to leave and were by the hatch when the shuttled docked with a slight bump. The securing clamps snapped shut and the link pressurised. When all the lights were green, we opened the hatch and left the Jergan. The hatch closed automatically behind us and we found ourselves in the rows of seats of a standard shuttle. There was no one visible as the control room was separate from the passenger compartment. A voice over the intercom requested that we be seated and fasten our seatbelts. We did so and secured the luggage in the lockers. The screen blinked into life showing the outside view and attitude indicators as the shuttle manoeuvred away from the Jergan. I was eternally grateful for the view screen as I was not a good passenger in a space vessel particularly when changing direction. I watched the planet slide into view and then grow larger as we descended back down to the surface.

We all sat in silence, not sure of the welcome we would receive back on the planet's surface.

I followed the flight down by listening to every little noise and direction change and felt frustrated that I was not in control. Very soon I felt the landing gear deploy. Shortly after that we were then on the ground and were told to disembark.

As we left the vessel I then realised why we had been asked to remain in orbit and not attempt to land. The huge landing deck that our vessel had been parked on before had been mostly destroyed by an impact. We had landed on the only remaining level part. The rest had vanished, the huge blast wall was leaning outward at a crazy angle but it had done its job. Its face was peppered with shrapnel holes and was blackened and dirty. The wall of the building was in a similar state. The landing deck ended with a crater edge a mere fifty or so meters away from us. We stood and looked open mouthed at the damage wrought by the recent barrage. I knew the size of the asteroid would have been tiny but the result was devastating. The sky above still bore the scars of the recent asteroid storm as dark clouds roiled high up in the atmosphere and was continuous right across to the horizon. The day was dark and gloomy as were our thoughts as we knew we had to face the inspector. Lightning flashed in the distance and thunder rolled around the valley. The cold wind whipped at our clothes and the dust in the air stung our faces. I suddenly felt as though I was back home!

The inspector came out of the doorway behind the screen and stood beside it. He did not beckon us over or make any sign or movement. He just stood by the door. We all knew what he meant though and picked up our bags and went over.

We were shown into the original room where the inspector first interrogated us and we sat down in silence. Our bags were dumped in one corner of the room. I did not look behind me at the cages which I knew lined the wall but stared straight ahead. Again, I thought how stupid of me to listen to Djon's ridiculous schemes.

The inspector entered the room and stood looking at us. He did not sit down but stood hard faced with his arms crossed across his chest. He finally grabbed a chair and sat down.

'You people are unbelievable.' He said at last, and I was glad the silence had been broken.

'It was..' Began Djon.

'Be quiet!' He ordered. 'For many years we have been compiling bit by bit enough evidence to try and get the criminal gangs. What we did not know was where they were and when you turned up you seemed to have that last piece of the jigsaw however ludicrous it appeared.' He stopped for a moment. 'We told you not to leave this place and thought you were decent enough people to not require locking up until we were certain about your background and beliefs. You may have been sent here to find out what we knew. Unfortunately, the storm meant that we had to all leave and trust you not to take the opportunity to disappear. We were obviously wrong to trust you. Because as soon as you were off the planet you did indeed leave immediately.'

'We...' I began.

'Quiet.' He turned to me with eyes blazing darkly. 'We know exactly what happened and using the anti-crash mechanism you could easily have avoided the approaching asteroid.' I felt rather humbled because I had no idea that the anti-crash mechanism could be used in that way. I vowed to ask him later what he meant. He continued.

'You used your vessel-based portal to finish your quest and travelled to Earth. So, the question must be why did you return?' He again looked at us darkly. There was an embarrassed silence as we sat stone faced. Djon finally began to speak in a very awkward and halting way.

'I am most very sorry, but it was all my fault, the others are ent…'

'Do not take me for a fool. There is no way you could have left unless you all agreed. Now continue.'

'Yes, sir. We had to use the portal to escape from the approaching asteroid. We do not know of using the anti-crash mechanism to such an end. Once we had used the portal it seemed logical to at least try and finish our quest having come so far. Unfortunately, when we got to Earth we were met by what appeared to be an automatic defence mechanism that targeted us.'

'What did you say?' Said the inspector suddenly looking very agitated.

'There was an automatic defence mechanism surrounding Earth.' The inspector sat back and visibly relaxed a little.

'Do you know why that is or what it means?' He asked us.

'My guess is.' Said Terens quietly. 'Is that the criminal gangs that you seek have taken over the Earth and have hidden the portal as they had hidden the portal in our own galaxy.' The inspector put his head in his hands. He looked up at us again, his face now ashen.

'This is indeed terrible news. These people are now mocking us by capturing mankind's home planet for their own ends. At last things finally slot into place. But we need to be able to get to them. With the Earth portal down, we now need your vessel based portal to be copied for our police vessels. We need then to raise an army to retake Earth and also your own galaxy. This will not be an easy operation and has been made much worse by your little trip. Why did you come back here? You knew we would be angry.'

'We did not consider it safe to return so reluctantly we decided to come back here and try and help you find these people and free our galaxy from their evil grip.' Said Djon.

'That is indeed very noble of you and we must be grateful for such small mercies. But do you know what you have done?' There was yet another awkward silence.

'No we do not.' Said Ruuth quietly.

'I thought not. Well, you know that every portal has a unique signal that can be traced and located every time it is used?'

'Yes.' I said.

'Then, you stupid, stupid people, now the criminal gangs know that you have been to Earth and where you have returned. In short you have in one unthinking move undone a hundred years of painstaking research. Now they know that someone has been to Earth. You probably have jeopardised the whole operation. In fact, we may well be in very great danger!' I hung my head.

'I am most desperately sorry.' Said Djon. 'But…'

'There is no need to go on.' Interrupted the inspector. 'What is done is done. We cannot take that back. You almost certainly have alerted the criminal gangs that we now know where they are. And not only that but they now know where we are and where you came from.'

'Sir.' Came the sergeant's voice again. 'Just had a call from one of our vessels.'

'Yes.' Said the inspector.

'They have just discovered that the prisoner's vessel did not leave a portal signal when they used it. We could not tell that the portal had been used nor where they went!'

'Thank you.' The inspector turned back to us. 'This news means that perhaps your little venture has not been such a disaster as we had first thought.'

'You mean that no one knows when our portal has been used, unlike a normal portal?' I asked.

'That is how it would seem. We will of course have to await a full report from our vessels but initially this is some good news for a change. But.' He leant forward. 'It does not absolve you people from the consequences of your stupid actions. You did not know that your portal did not leave a trace. We cannot allow you to leave. We gave you certain freedom on the understanding that you remained here. You ignored that and without a thought for others left the planet. You could in fact have either been killed and blown the whole operation or lead the criminal gangs back here. We cannot here defend ourselves against a sustained attack. Most of the Galactic Police have left here for other part of the galaxy to search for these people. It will take time to get them back here and even longer to plan our response. We will need to notify the inhabited planets and get further money to pay for such an operation. We also need time to copy your vessel-based portal and build copies for our vessels. We must start that now. I am therefore commandeering your vessel.'

I slumped in my seat. This was bad news for a pilot to have his vessel commandeered. It was humiliating. He went on.

'How do we know that you are telling the truth?' He did not stop for an answer. 'You could have taken this trip to go and warn your 'friends' about what you have learnt here hoping that by returning you will put us off the scent.'

'My I interrupt?' I asked.

'Go on.'

'All you have to do is check the communicators on our vessel and the flight recorders. You will see that we have told the truth. We did not send any message to Earth; we did not land or tell anyone there anything. I assure you we are not part of the gangs you seek.'

'We shall see, we shall see.' Said the inspector enigmatically. 'But you do not tell me what to do.' Karon broke down and burst into tears. Between her sobs she managed to get out that she was not criminal. Ruuth went over and comforted her.

'You must believe us inspector.' She said. 'We are what we say we say we are and nothing else.'

'I sincerely hope that you are correct.' He replied. 'Your apparent honesty in your answers does stand you in good stead but we must be absolutely certain that you are not connected with these gangs before we let you have more freedom!'

'How can we prove to you that we are not part of the criminal gangs that you seek?' I asked. The inspector sat back.

'That is indeed a difficult question and not one I can answer immediately.' He stroked his small black beard as he thought.

'We will do everything in our power to help you find these people and free our galaxy from their grip.' Said Ruuth. 'Surely that should persuade you that we are what we say?'

'Had you not just disobeyed us and left for Earth then I would agree with you but now I cannot trust you anymore. It will take more than that.'

'Then we will go back to our galaxy and go undercover for you' Said Djon.

'You're going to do what!? I said.

THE END